HER SISTER'S DEATH

HER SISTER'S DEATH

K.L. MURPHY

CamCat
Books

Content Warning: This novel touches upon suicide and domestic violence and may be disturbing to some readers.

FOR DAVID, ALWAYS

CHAPTER

1

VAL
Monday, 9:17 a.m.

Once, when I was nine or maybe ten, I spent weeks researching a three-paragraph paper on polar bears. I don't remember much about the report or polar bears, but that assignment marked the beginning of my lifelong love affair with research. As I got older, I came to believe that if I did the research, I could solve any problem. It didn't matter what it was. School. Work. Relationships. In college, when I suspected a boyfriend was about to give me the brush-off, I researched what to say before he could break up with me. Surprisingly, there are dozens of pages about this stuff. Even more surprising, some of it actually works. We stayed together another couple of months, until I realized I was better off without him. He never saw it coming.

When I got married, I researched everything from whether or not we were compatible (we were) to our average life expectancy based on our medical histories (only two years different). Some couples swear they're soul mates or some other crap, but I considered myself a little more practical than that. I wanted the facts before I walked down the aisle. The thing is, research doesn't tell you that your perfect-on-paper husband is going to prefer the ditzy receptionist on the third floor before you've hit your five-year anniversary. It also doesn't tell you that your initial anger will turn into something close to relief, or that all that perfection was too much work and maybe the whole soul mate thing isn't as crazy as it sounds. If you doubt me, look it up.

My love of research isn't as odd as one might think. My father is a retired history professor, and my mother is a bibliophile. It doesn't matter the genre. She usually has three or more books going at once. She also gets two major newspapers every day and a half dozen magazines each month. Some people collect cute little china creatures or rare coins or something. My mother collects words. When I decided to become a journalist, both my parents were overjoyed.

"It's perfect," my father said. "We need more people to record what's going on in the world. How can we expect to learn if we don't recognize that everything that happens impacts our future?" I fought the urge to roll my eyes. I knew what was coming, but how many times can a person hear about the rise and fall of Caesar? The man was stabbed to death, and it isn't as though anyone learned their lesson. Ask Napoleon. Or Hitler. My dad was right about one thing though. History can't help but repeat itself.

"Honey," my mother interrupted. "Val will only write about important topics. You know very well she is a young lady of principle." Again, I wanted to roll my eyes.

Of course, for all their worldliness, neither of my parents understands how the world of journalism works. You don't walk into a newsroom as an inexperienced reporter and declare you will be writing about the environment, or the European financial market, or the latest domestic policy. The newspaper business is not so different from any other—even right down to the way technology is forcing it to go digital. Either way, the newbies are given the jobs no one else wants.

Naturally, I was assigned to obituaries.

After a year, I got moved to covering the local city council meetings, but the truth was, I missed the death notices. I couldn't stop myself from wondering how each of the people died. Some were obvious. When the obituary asks you to donate to the cancer society or the heart association, you don't have to think too hard to figure it out. Also, people like to add that the deceased "fought a brave battle with (fill in the blank)." I've no doubt those people were brave, but they weren't the ones that interested me. It was the ones that seemed to die unexpectedly and under unusual circumstances. I started looking them up for more information. The murder victims held particular fascination for me. From there, it was only a short hop to my true interest: crime reporting.

The job isn't for everyone. Crime scenes are not pretty. Have you ever rushed out at three in the morning to a nightclub shooting? Or sat through a murder trial, forced to view photo after photo of a brutally beaten young mother plastered across a giant screen?

My sister once told me I must have a twisted soul to do what I do. Maybe. I find myself wondering about the killer, curious about what makes them do it. That sniper—the one that picked off the poor folks as they came out of the state fair—that was my story. Even now, I still can't get my head around that guy's motives.

So, I research and research, trying to get things right as well as find some measure of understanding. It doesn't always work, but knowing as much as I can is its own kind of answer.

Asking questions has always worked for me. It's the way I do my job. It's the way I've solved every problem in my life. Until now. Not that I'm not trying. I'm at the library. I'm in my favorite corner in the cushy chair with the view of the pond. I don't know how long I've been here.

How many hours.

My laptop is on, the screen filled with text and pictures. Flicking through the tabs, I swallow the bile that reminds me I have no answer. I've asked the question in every way I can think of, but for the first time in my life, Google is no help.

Why did my sister—my gorgeous sister with her two beautiful children and everything to live for—kill herself? Why?

Sylvia has been dead for four days now. Actually, I don't know how long she's been dead. I've been told there's a backlog at the ME's office. Apparently, suicides are not high priority when you live in a city with one of the country's highest murder rates. I don't care what the cause of death is. I want the truth.

While we wait for the official autopsy, I find myself reevaluating what I do know.

Her body was discovered on Thursday at the Franklin, a Do Not Disturb sign hanging from the door of her room. The hotel claims my sister called the front desk after only one day and asked not to be disturbed unless the sign was removed. This little detail could not have been more surprising. My sister doesn't have trouble sleeping. Sylvia went to bed at ten every night and was up like clockwork by six sharp. I have hundreds of texts to prove it. Even when her children were babies with sleep schedules that would kill most people, she somehow managed to stick to her routine. Vacations with her were pure torture.

"Val, get up. The sun is shining. Let's go for a walk on the beach."

I'd open one eye to find her standing in the doorway. She'd be dressed in black nylon shorts and neon sneakers, bouncing up and down on her toes.

"We can walk. I promise I won't run."

Tossing my pillow at her, I'd groan and pull the covers over my head.

"You can't sleep the day away, Val."

She'd cross the room in two strides and rip back the sheets.

"Get up."

In spite of my night-owl tendencies, I'd crawl out of bed. Sylvia had a way of making me feel like if I didn't join her, I'd be missing out on something extraordinary. The thing is, she was usually right. Sure, a sunrise is a sunrise, but a sunrise with Sylvia was color and laughter and tenderness and love. She had that way about her. She loved mornings.

I tried to explain Sylvia to the police officer, to tell him that hanging a sleeping sign past six in the morning, much less all day, was not only odd behavior but also downright suspicious. He did his best not to dismiss me outright, but I knew he didn't get it.

"Sleeping too much can be a sign of depression," he said.

"She wasn't depressed."

"She hung a sign, ma'am. It's been verified by the manager." He stopped short of telling me that putting out that stupid sign wasn't atypical of someone planning to do what she did.

Whatever that's supposed to mean.

The screen in front of me blurs, and I rub my burning eyes. There are suicide statistics for women of a certain age, women with children, women in general. My fingers slap the keys. I change the question, desperate for an answer, any answer.

A shadow falls across the screen when a man takes the chair across from me, a newspaper under his arm. My throat tightens, and I press my lips together. He settles in, stretching his legs. The paper crackles as he opens it and snaps when he straightens the pages.

"Do you mind?"

He lowers the paper, his brows drawn together. "Mind what?"

"This is a library. It's supposed to be quiet in here."

He angles his head. "Are you always this touchy or is it just me?"

"It's you." I don't know why I say that. I don't even know why I'm acting like a brat, but I can't help myself.

Silence fills the space between us as he appears to digest what I've said. "Perhaps you'd like me to leave?"

"That would be nice."

He blinks, the paper falling from his hand. I'm not sure which of us is more surprised by my answer. I seem to have no control over my thoughts or my mouth. The man has done nothing but crinkle a newspaper, but I have an overwhelming need to lash out. He looks around, and for a moment, I feel bad.

The man gets to his feet, the paper jammed under his arm. "Look, lady, I'll move to another spot, but that's because I don't want to sit here and have my morning ruined by some kook who thinks the public library is her own personal living room." He points a finger at me. "You've got a problem."

I feel the sting, the well of tears before he's even turned his back. They flood my eyes and pour down over my cheeks. Worse, my mouth opens, and I sob, great, loud, obnoxious sobs.

I cover my face with my hands and sink lower into the chair, my body folding in on itself.

My laptop slips to the floor, and I somehow cry harder.

"Is she all right?" a woman asks, her voice high and tight.

The annoying man answers. "She'll be fine in a minute."

"Are you sure?" Her gaze darts between us, and her hands flutter over me like wings, nearing but never touching. I recognize her from the reference desk. "People are staring. This is a library, you know."

I want to laugh, but it gets caught in my throat, and comes out like a bark. Her little kitten heels skitter back. I don't blame her.

Who wouldn't want to get away from the woman making strange animal noises?

"Do you have a private conference room?" the man asks. The woman points the way, and large hands lift me to my feet. "Can you get her laptop and her bag, please?"

The hands turn into an arm around my shoulders. He steers me toward a small room at the rear of the library. My sobs morph into hiccups.

The woman places my bag and computer on a small round table. "I'll make sure no one bothers you here." She slinks out, pulling the door shut.

The man sets his paper down and pulls out a chair for me. I don't know how many minutes pass before I'm able to stop crying, before I'm able to speak.

"Are you okay now?" I can't look at him. His voice is kind, far kinder than I deserve. He pushes something across the table. "Here's my handkerchief." He gets to his feet. "I'm going to see if I can find you some water."

The door clicks behind him, and I'm alone. My sister, my best friend, is gone, and I'm alone.

"Do you want to talk about it?" the man asks, setting a bottle of water and a package of crackers on the table.

Sniffling, I twist the damp, wadded up handkerchief into a ball. I want to tell him that no, I don't want to talk about it, that I don't even know him, but the words slip out anyway. "My sister died," I say.

"Oh." He folds his hands together. "I'm sorry. Recently?"

"Four days."

He pushes the crackers he's brought across the table. "You should try to eat something."

I try to remember when I last ate. Yesterday? The day before? One of my neighbors did bring me a casserole with some kind of brown meat and orangey red sauce. It may have had noodles, but I can't be sure. I do remember watching the glob of whatever it was slide out of the aluminum pan and down the disposal. I think I ate half a bagel at some point. My stomach churns, then rumbles. The man doesn't wait for me to decide. He opens the packet and pushes it closer. For some reason I can't explain, I want to prove I'm more polite than I seemed earlier. I take the crackers and eat.

He gestures at the bottle. "Drink."

I do. The truth is, I'm too numb to do anything else. It's been four days since my parents phoned me. Up to now, I've taken the news like any other story I've been assigned. I've filed it away, stored it at the back of my mind as something I need to analyze and figure out before it can be processed. I've buried myself in articles and anecdotes and medical pages, reading anything and everything to try and understand. On some level, I recognize my behavior isn't entirely normal. My parents broke down, huddled together on the sofa, as though conjoined in their grief. I couldn't have slipped between them even if I wanted to. Sylvia's husband—I guess that's what we're still calling him—appeared equally stricken. Not even the sight of her children, their faces pale and blank, cracked the shell I erected, the wall I built to deny the reality of her death.

"Aunt Val," Merry asked. "Mommy's coming back, right? She's just passed, right? That's what Daddy said." She paused, a single tear trailing over her pink cheek. "What's 'passed'?"

Merry is the youngest, only five. Miles is ten—going on twenty if you ask me—which turned out to be a good thing in that moment. Miles took his sister by the hand. "Come on, Merry. Dad wants us in the back." I let out a breath. Crisis averted.

My sister has been gone four days, and I haven't shed a tear. Until today.

The man across the table clears his throat. "Are you feeling any better?"

"No, I'm not feeling better. My sister is still dead." God, I'm a bitch. I expect him to stand up and leave or at least point out what an ass I'm being when he's gone out of his way to be nice, but he does neither.

"Yes, I suppose she is. Death is kind of permanent."

I jerk back in my chair. "Is that supposed to be funny?"

Unlike me, he does apologize. "I'm sorry. That didn't come out right. I never did have the best bedside manner for the job."

I take a closer look at the man. "Are you a doctor?"

He half laughs. "Hardly. Detective. Former, I mean. I never quite got the hang of talking to the victims' families without putting my foot in my mouth. Seems I've done it again."

My curiosity gets the best of me. He's not much older than I am. Mid-forties. Maybe younger. Definitely too young for retirement. "Former detective? What do you do now?"

"I run a security firm." He lifts his shoulders. "It's different, has its advantages."

The way he says it, I know he misses the job. I understand.

"I write for the *Baltimorean*. Mostly homicides," I say.

"That's a good paper. I've probably read your work then."

Crumpling the empty cracker wrapper, I say, "I'm sorry I dumped on you out there."

He shrugs again. "It's okay. You had a good reason."

I can't think of anything to say to that.

"How did she die, if you don't mind my asking?"

The question hits me hard. What I mind is that my sister is gone. My hands ball into fists. The heater in the room hums, but otherwise, it's quiet. "They say she died by suicide."

The man doesn't miss a beat. "But you don't believe it." He watches me, his body still.

My heart pounds in my chest and I reach into my mind, searching for any information I've found that contradicts what I've been told. I've learned that almost fifty thousand people a year die by suicide in the United States. Strangely, a number of those people choose to do it in hotels. Maybe it's the anonymity. Maybe it's to spare the families. There are plenty of theories, but unfortunately, one can't really ask the departed about that. Still, the reasoning is sound enough. For four days, I've read until I can't see, and my head has dropped from exhaustion. I know that suicide can be triggered by traumatic events or chronic depression. It can be triggered by life upheaval or can be drug induced, or it can happen for any number of reasons that even close family and friends don't know about until after—if ever. I know all this, and yet, I can't accept it.

Sylvia was found in a hotel room she had no reason to be in. An empty pill bottle was found on the nightstand next to her. She checked in alone. Nothing in the room had been disturbed. Nothing appeared to have been taken. For all these reasons, the police made a preliminary determination that the cause of death was suicide, the final ruling to be made after the ME's report. I know all this. My parents and Sylvia's husband took every word of this at face value. But I can't. Sylvia is not a statistic, and I know something they don't.

"No. I don't believe it," I say, meeting his steady gaze with my own.

He doesn't react. He doesn't tell me I'm crazy. He doesn't say "I'm sorry" again. Nothing. I'm disappointed, though I can't imagine why. He's a stranger to me. Still, I press my shoulder blades against the back of the chair, waiting. I figure it out then. Former detective. I've been around enough cops to know how it works. It's like a tribe with them. You don't criticize another officer. You don't question anyone's toughness or loyalty to the job. You don't question a ruling that a case doesn't warrant an investigation, much less that it isn't even a case. So, I sit and wait. I will not be the first to argue. It doesn't matter that he's retired and left the job. He's still one of them. In fact, the more I think about it, I can't understand why he's still sitting there. I've been rude to the man. I've completely broken down in front of him like some helpless idiot. And now, I've suggested the cause of death that everyone—and I mean everyone—says is true is not the truth at all.

He gets up, shoves his hands in his pockets.

This is it. He's done with me now. In less than one minute he'll be gone and, suddenly, I don't want him to leave. I break the silence.

"I'm Val Ritter."

"Terry Martin."

I turn the name over in my brain. It's familiar in a vague way. "Terry the former detective."

"Uh-huh." He shifts his weight from one foot to the other. "Look, I'm sorry about your sister. You've lost someone you love, and the idea that she might have taken her own life is doubly distressing."

"I'm way past distressed. I'm angry."

"Is it possible that you're directing that anger toward the ones that ruled her death a suicide instead of at your . . ." His words fall away.

"My sister?"

"Yes."

"I might be if I thought she did this." I cross my arms over my chest. "But I don't. This idea, this thing they're saying makes no sense at all."

Terry the former detective's voice is low, soothing. "Why?"

My arms drop again. I'm tempted to tell him everything I know, which admittedly isn't much, but I hold back. This man is a stranger. Sure, he's been nice, and every time I've expected him to walk out the door, he's done the opposite. But that doesn't mean I can trust him.

"I'm sorry if my question seems insensitive," he says. His voice is soft, comforting in a neutral way, and I can picture him in an interrogation. He would be the good cop. "No matter how shocking the, uh, idea might be, I have a feeling you have your reasons. You were close—you and your sister?"

"We were." I sit there, twisting the handkerchief in my fingers. The heater makes a revving noise, drops back to a steady hum. "We talked all the time, and I can tell you she wasn't depressed. That's what they kept saying. 'She must have been depressed.' I know people hide things, but she was never good at hiding her emotions from me. If anything, she'd been happier than ever." I give a slow shake of my head. "They tried to tell me about the other suicide and about the pills and the sign on the door and—" I stop. I hear myself rambling and force myself to take a breath. "If something had been wrong, I would have known."

Terry the former detective doesn't react, doesn't move. He keeps his mouth shut, but I know. He doesn't believe me, same as all the others. I can tell. There is no head bob or leading question. He thinks I'm in denial and that I will eventually accept the truth. He doesn't know me at all.

The minutes pass, and I drink the water. I realize I feel better. It's time to leave. "I should be going." I hold up the crumpled rag in my hand. "Sorry I did such a number on your handkerchief. I can clean it, send it to you later."

He waves off the suggestion. "Keep it."

I gather my items and apologize again. "Sorry you had to witness my meltdown out there."

"It happens."

I'm headed out the door, my hand on the knob, when he breaks protocol.

"What did you mean by 'the other suicide'?"

CHAPTER

2

TERRY
Monday, 10:02 a.m.

The woman—Val, I remind myself—hesitates. I can see she's wary, worried I don't believe her. I don't know that I do, but I am curious. "What did you mean? There was another suicide?"

"A month ago, maybe a little longer, a woman killed herself in the same hotel. She jumped off the roof, which apparently was no easy task since there were all kinds of doors to go through to get up there. Of course, what happened to her was horrible, but it has nothing to do with my sister. I don't know why they're acting like it does."

My jaw tightens. "Which hotel?"

"The Franklin."

I look past her and think maybe I should be surprised, but nothing about that hotel surprises me. "The Franklin," I say, echoing her words.

The Franklin is one of Baltimore's oldest hotels. Built in 1918, it's fifteen stories high with marble columns and archways at the entrance. Along with the Belvedere, before it became condos, and the Lord Baltimore, the Franklin was a destination, a swanky place that attracted film stars and politicians for decades. Somewhere along the line, it fell into disrepair and the famous guests went elsewhere. For a brief time, the management offered rooms for short-term rentals, desperate to keep the hotel from plunging further into the red. Twenty years ago, the hotel was sold to an investment group. They declared the hotel historic, sunk tens of millions of dollars into it, and reopened it in grand style. The governor and the mayor cut the big red ribbon. Baseball stars from the Orioles and a well-known director were photographed at the official gala. It was a big to-do for the city at the time. Since then, it's remained popular—one of the five-star hotels downtown, which, of course, means that a night there doesn't come cheap. That's the press release version.

But there's another one. Lesser known.

Val is calm now, watching me, and I catch a glimpse of the reporter. "Do you know it?" she asks.

"Yeah, I know it." Stories have circulated about the hotel through the years. Some are decades old while others have been encouraged by the hotel itself. Ghost tours are popular these days, and the Franklin tour is no exception. "It has a history. For a while, it was called the Mad Motel."

She flinches. "What?"

"According to my grandfather, people seemed to die there. Most deaths occurred right after the Depression, victims of the stock market crash, but not all. There was one guy that killed his whole family right before he killed himself. They said he lost his mind. That was the first time it was called the Mad Motel, though there were other stories."

"What are you saying?"

I see the flush on her cheeks and know my words have upset her in a way I didn't intend. I do my best to smooth it over. "Nothing. I didn't mean anything. I've never been a fan of the name myself, but there were some guys around the department that used it."

The anger that colored her cheeks a moment earlier fades, eclipsed by something else I recognize. Curiosity. "Why would they use such a terrible name?"

It's a valid question, and I give the only explanation I can. "The first time I heard it on the job was about fifteen years ago. An assault at the Franklin. I didn't catch the case, but I remember a man almost beat his wife to death. He would have, if someone in the next room hadn't called the police."

She doesn't blink, doesn't raise a hand to her mouth. Just waits.

"Before that day, the guy was a typical accountant. Kind of nerdy. Mild-mannered. Went to work. Went home to his family. Nothing out of the ordinary. Then they fly into Baltimore for their nephew's wedding, stay at the Franklin. As they were dressing, he loses it. He hits her with the lamp, punches her, throws her up against the wall. When the police arrived, they had to pry him off of her. They rushed her to the hospital. She ended up with broken ribs, a concussion, a whole bunch of other stuff."

"And the husband?"

"That's what was so strange. According to the officers on the scene, as soon as they pulled him off, he stopped all of it. He cried, begged to be allowed to go with her to the hospital. When they took him downtown, he swore he didn't know what had come over him. That he'd never hit anyone in his life, and he couldn't even recall being angry with her. They kept him in jail until she woke up. Oddly, she corroborated his story. She said he didn't have a violent bone in his body before that day."

Val's forehead wrinkles. "I don't remember ever reading about that case. What happened?"

"He was charged in spite of his wife's insistence that she didn't want that. When he went to trial, his lawyer put him on the stand. That's when I heard his story." I pause and run my hand over my face, scratching at my chin. "He told the jury that while he was putting on his tux jacket, a cold breeze blew in. He said he checked the room, but the windows were closed, and it was winter, so the heat was on. Then according to him, this cold air got into his body, in his hands and his feet and then his mind. He said when his wife came out of the bathroom, he didn't recognize her, that she was someone else, something else."

"Something else? What does that mean?"

"He described a monster with sharp teeth and claws. His attorney even had a drawing done by a sketch artist. She held it up for the jury, but the man wouldn't look at it. Refused. He claimed he panicked, grabbed the lamp, and swung, but the monster kept coming. He said the monster howled—that was probably his wife screaming—and came at him again. That must have been when the guest in the other room called the police." I pause again. Even as I say it, I know how it sounds. "So, he tells this story at trial, and everyone looks around at each other thinking this guy is crazy. But his wife is in the audience and nodding like it's true. The prosecutor goes after him, but he doesn't back down. He admits he attacked someone, but he swears he didn't knowingly hurt his wife. He breaks down on the stand, and it's basically bedlam in the courtroom."

Memories of that day flood my mind. I sat in the back of the packed courtroom, watching the melee. It was hard to know what to think. Was the man delusional? A sociopath? Or was he telling the truth? Fortunately, Val doesn't ask my opinion, and I tell her the rest.

"The prosecutor decided to cut his losses," I say. "He let the man plead to a lesser charge and get some mental help."

"That's all?"

"Yep. The man did three months in a mental health facility, then went back to Omaha and his wife. End of story."

"So that's why the Franklin is called the Mad Motel?"

"It's one of the reasons. But like I said, the place has a history." Newspaper articles and pictures and evidence files flit through my mind. Many of the images are gruesome. Others just sad. Although the library is warm, I'm cold under my jacket. My voice drops to a whisper, the memories too close for comfort. "A history of death."

1 9 2 1

CHAPTER

3

BRIDGET

B ridget Wallace touched the slippery silk of her wedding dress, her fingers trembling as they trailed over the length of the gown. The white dress hung before her, draped over the three-sided panel. She admired the plunging back, though she'd been careful to choose a gown with an appropriately reserved neckline. Even so, Lawrence was likely to disapprove.

"Trousers on women?" he'd asked one day as he caught her perusing the latest issue of *Harper's Bazaar*. "What's next? Skirts above the knees?"

She stepped back, studying the white gown. Loose chiffon sleeves ended just past the shoulder, and the tiny waist was cinched by a wide band of satin. But it was the long train that had drawn her to the dress. It was made of the same chiffon, so light and sheer that she worried she would snag it before the ceremony. Dozens and dozens of white flowers had been embroidered onto the train. She loved that dress so much.

Her mother came into the room, her arms full of gifts and packages. "Look at this," Catherine said. "I don't know how we're going to get all of these out to the country."

Bridget's teeth closed down on her lower lip. After the wedding, she would live in the country. She was a city girl with friends and a job. What would happen to her?

Her mother sorted through a handful of envelopes, raising one in the air. "Why, this one is from your uncle Ezra up in New York. You know who he is, don't you, dear? I'm sure this will be most generous." She held it up to the light, as though she could see through the thick paper without her spectacles. "Oh, I'd love to open it now, but that would be bad luck, wouldn't it?" She let out a long sigh. "Unless you wanted to see what's inside. Well, then I would be obliged to open it right away."

The young bride-to-be couldn't bring herself to wonder about the envelopes. Whatever was inside wouldn't change the way she felt, but then again, no one seemed to care about that.

"Bridget?"

She shook her head and flicked her hand. "Open it if you must, Mother."

"Are you sure?" She toyed with the envelope, then set it aside. "Dear, you look a fright."

The young woman lifted a hand to her hair, smoothing the flyaways, and wondered what kind of mother says such a thing to her daughter on her wedding day. She walked to the small mirror hanging over the sink. Any amusement faded. Her mother was right. It would take all her powder skills to hide the pouches under her eyes. "I didn't sleep much last night," she said.

Catherine clucked her tongue. "Of course, you didn't, dear. No woman sleeps the night before her wedding." She sat down and folded her hands in her lap. "I suppose I should tell you what to expect, you know, after the wedding."

Bridget sat down opposite her mother. *This should be interesting.*

"After the wedding supper, you will retire to the Franklin. I have to hand it to Lawrence. He's chosen one of the finest hotels. I've been told the bridal suite is nothing short of spectacular. Imagine it. You will be staying in the same room once slept in by Mary Pickford. Your father promised to take me to her next film, you know." Catherine's skin glowed as she talked. "I keep telling you, Bridget, this is one of the advantages of marrying a man who is established, a man who knows how to show his wife that he cares about her. You understand how important that is?"

Bridget worried she understood far more than her mother realized, but she knew better than to comment. "Yes, Mother."

"Good. Well, as I was saying, you will be spending your first evening as husband and wife at the Franklin. Lawrence will be expecting you to perform your wifely duty, as all men do. It can't be helped, but you're young, and both of you will be wanting children as soon as possible."

Would she? Bridget tried to picture herself with a baby in her lap, a toddler at her feet, and Lawrence at her side, smoking a cigar. But no matter how many times she tried to imagine it, the image wouldn't come into focus. Was something wrong with her?

She wished her sister would arrive.

Her mother snapped her fingers. "Oh, I almost forgot." She jumped up and rushed to the mahogany chest. From the top drawer, she pulled out a garment wrapped in tissue. "I got this for your wedding night." She unwrapped the package and held up a nightgown. The pale pink satin cascaded to the floor, the sound of it unfolding like a whisper. "Isn't it lovely? It's exactly your color, dear. Surely, no man could object to this."

Bridget stared at the gown. Like her wedding dress, it was beautiful and elegant and a reminder of what was about to happen. Her mouth went dry, and she clamped her knees together to keep them from knocking. Lawrence objected to a great many things.

Her mother set the nightgown aside. "About tonight, no doubt you may be shocked by what is to happen, but you'll get used to it."

Bridget's heart skipped. *Get used to it.* She understood most of what happened between a man and a woman, but her mother's words were nevertheless unsettling. Lawrence never stopped reminding her that a woman should be held in high regard. He'd touched her less than a half dozen times, and though he'd brushed his lips across her cheek and hand, he'd not yet kissed her on the mouth. "What do you mean, I'll get used to it?"

Catherine's features softened, and she took her daughter's hands in hers. "A lady doesn't discuss these things, my dear, but you're my daughter, so just this once." She stroked Bridget's hand with the curve of her nail. "The first time you lay with your new husband may be difficult or even painful, but that won't last."

"I don't know. I don't want . . ." She blinked. Was this the supportive talk she'd been expecting? There was so much she wanted to say, but she didn't know how. "I'm afraid. Lawrence is not—"

"There's nothing to be afraid of," her mother interrupted, patting Bridget's hand. "No one dies from marital duties, you know." Bridget opened her mouth to say that wasn't what she was afraid of, but she didn't get the chance. Catherine got to her feet. "I'm quite sure you will be fine, dear. After all, Lawrence is a wonderful man. He's promised your father and I that he will take care of you until his dying day. His devotion to you is absolute. We are so happy to know that you will have a husband who adores you so."

Bridget stared at the floor. It was true that Lawrence had promised her parents all of these things. And he'd promised her sister. And her. But he'd made other promises too. Promises Bridget had never shared.

"You are a lucky woman, Bridget. Truly lucky."

CHAPTER
4

BRIDGET

"I'm so sorry I'm late." Margaret rushed into the bedroom, her hair flying behind her. "The trains were running late again. I got here as quick as I could." She bent over at the waist, a hand to her side. "Charles and I had to practically run here." She wiped beads of sweat from her hairline. "Goodness, it's warm in here, isn't it?"

Catherine crossed the room, embracing her eldest daughter. "Thank heavens you made it, Margaret." The lines around her mouth deepened and she wagged a finger. "You and Charles should have made the trip yesterday as I told you."

"You're right, Mother. You always are," Margaret said as she sat down, winking at Bridget over her shoulder.

"I saw that," Catherine said, swooping about the room, rearranging the hairbrushes, and tidying the stockings. While she worked, she prattled on about the small wedding party and the lunch and the weather until Margaret stood up again.

She kissed her mother on the cheek and said, "It's lovely to see you, Mother, but I'm the matron of honor, and I do believe it's time to start getting the bride ready." She placed her hand on the small of her mother's back. "Out with you now."

"How did I raise such a bossy child?" Catherine asked, even as she allowed herself to be pushed from the room.

"Some would say I take after my mother," Margaret shot back and closed the door after her. "Well," she said with a flounce, "I never thought she'd leave."

Bridget burst out laughing. She hugged her sister then. "I'm so glad you're here."

"Me too." She dabbed at her forehead again. "It is hot, isn't it? Shall I open a window?" Without waiting for an answer, Margaret wrenched the small window open. The chilly December air swept through the room. Bridget shivered. Margaret, though, turned her flushed face toward the cold. "That's better."

"Margaret, it's freezing outside," Bridget said, no longer laughing. "Are you ill?"

Her sister lowered the window again. "No, not at all. I'm—" she paused and glanced toward the door. She came closer to her sister and lowered her voice. "I'm with child."

Bridget raised a hand to her mouth.

Margaret had been married nearly three years, and up to now, there'd been no sign of a baby. She wrapped her sister in a warm hug. "I'm so happy for you."

"Shhh. I don't want Mother to know until after the wedding."

"Oh, Margaret, I don't mind. This is such wonderful news."

"Thank you, dear sister, but I do mind." She sat down on the edge of the bed. "Charles and I agreed that before the wedding, I would share this news with you alone. Like old times." Margaret patted the bed, and Bridget sat down beside her. "Do you remember how it would drive Mother crazy when we had our secret language?"

"Oh, yes," Bridget said with a laugh. How old had she been then? Six? Seven? "And remember how she forbade us to use it outside the house, but we did anyway?"

Margaret giggled and unpinned her hat. "And when we got older, we would whisper so she couldn't hear?"

"And the coded messages we would tap out under the table. Do you remember the one about Uncle Carlton and his eyebrows?"

"Old Spiderbrows? The way they looked like they were creeping across his giant forehead?" Her sister laughed louder. "Mother nearly went apoplectic when she found out about that one."

The sisters exchanged grins. "I don't know if I've seen her so angry as that night. She barely spoke to us for days."

"Hallelujah!" Margaret said and the pair giggled again.

"When will you tell her?" Bridget asked.

Her sister tossed her head. "Oh, I don't know. Tonight maybe, although I might wait until we have to leave. She won't be able to pester me with everything I'm already doing wrong when I'm boarding a train. Can't you hear her now?" Margaret launched into an imitation of their mother, then shook her head. "Thank goodness we don't live here in Baltimore."

"Is that why you and Charles moved to Washington? To be farther away from Mother?"

"Yes, I suppose."

"I miss you."

"I miss you too." Margaret raised a hand and pushed a lock of Bridget's hair behind her ear. "But you won't be alone, Bridget. You'll be married. You'll move to Lawrence's farm. And it won't be long before you have children too."

Bridget shifted on the bed. "Mother was talking to me about wifely duties. It sounded terrible."

Margaret waved her hand. "Don't listen to her. She said the same thing to me, and I was petrified. But she's wrong. It's not terrible at all. It's the opposite of terrible."

"The opposite?"

"Yes. Don't let Mother get in your head," Margaret insisted. "She's probably pacing right now, sure you will be late to your own wedding. She's the queen of spreading doom and gloom, remember?"

Bridget did remember. But lately, Mother had been different, and Bridget had never clashed with her in quite the same way her older sister had. Catherine had been more positive of late, particularly when it came to Lawrence and the wedding. Had she been the same with Margaret and Charles?

"You and Lawrence will be very happy at the farm. It will be just the two of you, away from everyone and everything," Margaret said. "Away from Mother. Don't worry so much."

A hardness formed in the pit of Bridget's stomach. *Just the two of you.* Margaret thought she was easing her younger sister's fears, calming her in the final hours before her wedding, but Bridget's heartbeat drummed, echoing in her ears. *Away from everyone and everything.*

Margaret stood up. "If we don't start getting you ready, we really will be late."

Bridget heard her sister's words, but they were muffled as though spoken from far away. She wanted to move, but she couldn't, frozen where she sat. *Don't worry so much.* The room in front of her spun around and around. Her arms and legs went limp. Her head fell forward in the second before her body slipped from the edge of the bed, and she sank to the floor, unconscious.

PRESENT DAY

CHAPTER
5

VAL
Monday, 11:24 a.m.

I leave the library with Terry Martin's card in my pocket. He asked for mine too, although I don't know why he bothered. Polite, I suppose. And nice. I steer the car toward home, remember the wadded-up handkerchief in my bag, and think, *Terry the former detective is a dinosaur, a relic from another time.* I consider whether or not that's a good thing, but I can't decide.

My phone chirps. "Val Ritter."

"Val, it's Wyatt."

I suck in my breath. I don't want to talk to Wyatt. I don't want to see Wyatt. He gets to be the grieving husband in spite of all he did to my sister. It makes my skin crawl.

"What do you want?"

He stumbles over his words. "They're done. I mean she's done. The medical examiner."

My fingers tighten around the phone. "What did she say?"

"A detective called. He asked me to come down to the station to talk. I'd like you to be there."

This takes me by surprise. "When?"

"An hour." His voice is thick, almost garbled, as though each word is an effort. "Can you make it?"

"I'll be there." I pause. "Did the detective say anything else? Give you any idea about the report?"

"Nothing different than what they said before. He says there's a question. Val, I feel like—"

I hang up. Wyatt's feelings don't concern me. They might have once, back when I thought he was devoted to my sister, but those days are gone. I turn the car around and head for the station. Passing the Baltimore campus of the University of Maryland, I force myself to calm down. If I go in with guns blazing—which is exactly what I want to do—I'm liable to be run out the door again. I've already been down there a half dozen times and called twice that many times.

The last time I showed up unannounced, the receptionist came around the desk and held up her hand.

"I'm sorry, Ms. Ritter, but you don't have an appointment."

"Do I need one? This is still a public building, isn't it? And you know me." How many times had I met with detectives or their PR rep when I was working a story?

"I'm sorry," she said again, in a way that made me think she wasn't sorry at all. "You can't go upstairs." The scowl she wore reminded me of every teacher I had in middle school. "I've been told to tell you that there is no new information at this time, and the family will be notified as soon as there is."

I had no choice when the security guard took notice. I wonder now if the detective knows I'm coming. After all, he didn't call me. He called Wyatt, the simpering would-be ex. I continue along West Fayette Street until I see the sign for the headquarters. I'm early, but I'm hoping to use that to my advantage.

When I push through the doors, the receptionist rises and greets me with one hand glued to her ample hip. "Ms. Ritter, I thought we had an understanding."

"We do," I say. "But there's new information now." She stares at me, unimpressed. "I was called." I conveniently leave out that no one from the police department phoned me. "I know I'm early, but I thought maybe I could have a word with the detective before any other family arrives."

Like the other times, she's a battle-ax. "I can't let you upstairs until I get permission."

"Can you call him? The detective, I mean?"

A security guard approaches but halts after one look from the receptionist. "Fine." She inclines her head toward a wooden bench. "Sit over there."

As the minutes tick by, all I can think about is talking to the detective before Wyatt can get to him. Not that it's done any good so far, but I have a feeling it might be different now. This time, there's news. And a question. That has to mean something.

Otherwise, why have Wyatt come all the way down here when a simple phone call would have sufficed?

The receptionist is back. "Detective Barnes is waiting for you upstairs."

"I thought I'd be talking to Detective Newman."

She doesn't have time for me. "Detective Barnes is who you get. Take it or leave it. Third floor."

I take the stairs. When I walk through the door, a young man is there to greet me.

"Valerie Ritter?" He holds out his hand. "Detective Barnes."

I freeze. He's a child. Or at least he is from my perspective. He's sporting a pimple on his chin and one of those haircuts that are long on top and short on the sides. I wonder how many years it's been since he graduated from high school. His handshake is firm though, and I follow when he leads me to a tiny, windowless room.

"Take a seat," he says. The boy-man lays a thin file folder on the table. "I'm Detective Newman's new partner. I'm trying to get up to speed on our cases, so I'm glad you came in early." He opens the file, and I catch a glimpse of an official-looking report before he shuffles it to the back. "I've been reading over his notes." He pauses as he flips through two pages, and I feel my anger swell. *That's it? Two measly pages?* "According to this, you've already spoken to Detective Newman."

"A few times."

"Uh, yes, I see that." He gives me that look, the one that tells me he's already heard about me. "I get the impression you don't think your sister died by suicide."

"No, I don't."

"Can you tell me why you think that?"

"Isn't it in the report?" I snap. He blinks, and I'm quick to backtrack. It won't do to alienate the kid before I've had a chance to tell him about my sister and about Wyatt. "Maybe your partner didn't write everything down."

Detective Barnes lifts one eyebrow. "I'm not as interested in what the file says as I am in what you have to tell me," he says.

It's my turn to stare open-mouthed. "What do you want to know?"

He takes out a notebook and pen. "Start at the beginning."

"For one thing, there was no reason for her to be in that hotel. Or in Baltimore. She told me she was going to North Dakota. She does that a few times a year for work."

He reads from his notes. "Marketing consultant with Banford."

"Right. She helps companies identify and refine their target markets. It's mostly data-driven stuff, but sometimes she works with whatever ad agency has been hired to beef up the company image or brand." Barnes's glazed expression tells me he either doesn't understand or isn't interested. I move on. "Her client in North Dakota is a snack company. They've been expanding, and she's part of the marketing team. Whenever she goes out there, my parents help out with the kids. Except she didn't have business in North Dakota this time. I called and checked."

"We have that." His pen hovers over the page, but he doesn't write. "So, your sister lied to you about going out of town?"

"And to my parents." I tap my finger on the table when I say that. It's the most important part.

"She lied to everyone." He speaks slowly, and I want to shake him. Haven't I just said that? "Instead, she stayed in Baltimore, in a hotel."

"Right."

"I'm not following."

I stifle a groan. Either I'm not explaining this very well, or this is going to be harder than I think. "She was hiding."

"From who?"

"Her husband."

He sits back. "Why would she be hiding from her husband?"

"They were separated. For the last year. He was having an affair. The usual. He met her at a conference. She understands him. Blah blah blah. My sister found out about it and kicked him to the curb." The words pour out of me, and I see he's writing everything down. Finally. I keep talking. "For all Sylvia knew, it wasn't his first either." His dark brows rise higher. "Detective Newman asked me if she'd been depressed, but she wasn't. She was upset at first—that's normal—but not the way he means. The affair took her by surprise, is all. But she got over it after a few months, and she did her best to keep things positive around the kids. Never said a bad word about Wyatt in front of them. She was that kind of mother." I pause, trying to read the boy-man's face. Nothing. "I know she wasn't sad anymore. She was dating someone, someone she really liked. Wyatt must have found out about it. Maybe he saw her with the guy or something and flipped out." I sit back. "You need to follow up on that."

He looks up from his notebook. "Your sister had a boyfriend that her ex-husband may or may not have known about?"

"Well, yes, and he's not her ex. Technically, they're still—or were—still married."

"Is that all?"

For the first time, I'm flustered. What does he mean, *Is that all?* Isn't that enough?

Barnes spreads his hands. "I don't understand why you think your sister was hiding from Mr. Spencer."

It occurs to me now that I should have started with this part. I hold up my phone. "You don't know him. Listen, Wyatt called me a bunch of times last week. He knows I hate him, but he kept calling me asking me if I knew where she was, that she wasn't answering her phone. I saved some of them." I scroll through my messages and hit play.

The sound of Wyatt's voice, near screeching, pierces the air.

"Val, answer the fucking phone. I know you don't want to talk to me, but I don't care."

I steal a look at the detective. Does he hear the anger, the venom in Wyatt's voice?

"Stop being a bitch and tell me where your sister is!" There's a slapping noise as though he's banging on a table. *"Shit,"* he says, and the phone goes dead.

"When was that?" the boy detective asks.

After checking my phone, I tell him. "Tuesday afternoon. Four sixteen."

He turns to a fresh page in his notebook and writes something. I try to make out the words, but I can't see clearly. "Any other messages?"

"There are four or five like that," I tell him. "A couple others not so bad."

"Can I hear the last one?"

I find it and hit play.

"Val, please pick up." There are a few seconds of dead air before he speaks again. *"I need to speak to Syl. It's about the kids."* His voice drops. There's no more venom. He sounds like a robot, as though he's reading the words. *"Please."*

When it's over, he asks when I got this last message.

"Thursday morning, about an hour before she was found."

He writes that down.

"And did you try to call your sister during this time?"

"It went to voice mail, but I wasn't worried."

His forehead creases. "Why not?"

"Right before she left to go out of town, she reminded me she'd have limited service for a few days." His brow creases, and I explain. "The town where she goes has like fifteen hundred people, tops. Maybe less. That's why there aren't many cell towers there. Service is spotty. I told Detective Newman this already."

"So, this was Sunday? When she told you that?"

"Yes."

"And you weren't concerned?"

"Have you ever been to North Dakota? Cell service can be a luxury there. I did get one text from her. I tried to text her too, but I don't know if it went through."

The boy detective looks down at his notes, then at his file. "Right. The text. She checked into the Franklin on Sunday evening. The next night, Monday, she texted you." He pauses. "About her husband."

I sit up straighter, glad we're getting to the reason I rushed over to the station. "Yes. When I saw it, I was glad she was in North Dakota and far away from Wyatt. At least I thought she was." Goose bumps erupt on my arms, and I shudder. "They had a fight. A big one, she said." I show him the text then. He reads, and I see him draw back at the words on the screen.

He scares me, Val.

"Do we have a screenshot of this?"

"I gave it to Detective Newman." He asks for another, and I send it. "They were fighting about the divorce, I think. It was the first time she'd confided in me about it. Lately, whenever his name would come up, she'd shut down, not say anything. I thought she was doing what she always did and taking the high road, but now I know the truth, the real reason she didn't want to talk about him. She was afraid of him. All this time, she was afraid of him." A tear slides down my cheek, and I swipe at it. Now is not the time to weep. "That's why she was hiding, why she made up this whole work-trip thing. She didn't want him to know where she was. She needed time to think." I press my palms against the table. "Somehow, he must have figured it out. When he couldn't find her, that's when he started calling me."

"And what did you say to him when he called?"

"I didn't answer. I had nothing to say to him."

He takes that in. "Did you call anyone when your brother-in-law left you those messages?"

"I called my parents after the last one. I wanted to make sure the kids were okay, but everything was fine. The kids went to school like normal. No problems at all."

"Had Wyatt been in touch with your parents?"

"Yes, but I didn't know that then. I didn't find out until after . . ." my words falter.

"Would you like some water?" he asks.

"No." Heat rises from my belly to my chest and to my face. "What I want is for someone to say it isn't true, that she didn't kill herself. I want you to talk to Wyatt."

Detective Barnes rakes his hand through the mop of hair on the top of his head and stares down at his notebook. I inhale, waiting for him to speak.

"We've talked to your brother-in-law about his relationship with your sister, but he didn't mention anything about harassing her."

"Of course he didn't."

"He gave us a different version of the story than the one you've given us."

"All sunshine and roses, I'll bet." He says nothing, and I hold up my phone. "You've heard the messages and seen the text for yourself. Syl was terrified. I know he did something."

"Maybe." He hesitates again. "It's true that there are a few holes in his story, and it's possible your sister was upset, but either way, she was alone in that room and—"

A knock on the door makes us both look around.

A detective pokes his head in the room. "Barnes, there's a Wyatt Spencer here to see you."

The boy detective gets to his feet. "Is Newman back?"

"Haven't seen him."

"Okay. Tell him we're in here when you see him." The other detective nods, and Barnes glances at me briefly. "You can show Mr. Spencer in."

I say nothing while we wait. Barnes fiddles with his pen, watching the door.

Wyatt looks like hell. His shirt is wrinkled and bunched up around his waist as though he couldn't tuck it in properly. There's a faint coffee stain on his pants. Based on his uncombed hair, I'm not sure he's showered. I have to hand it to him. He's playing the bereaved husband to the hilt.

"Val, I'm so glad you're here," he says.

"It's about my sister. Where else would I be?" Although I don't try to hide my irritation, he doesn't notice.

He shakes hands with Detective Barnes and sits down. "Are you the detective that called me this morning?"

"One and the same. Detective Newman is taking care of a personal matter. He should be here soon."

I doubt that—Newman has been avoiding my calls and siccing the receptionist on me—but I keep my opinion to myself.

"As I told you on the phone, we've received the medical examiner's report." His long fingers drum a dull beat on the table. "There are a few things I need to go over with you."

My mouth goes dry at his words, the way it does whenever I know the news I'm going to hear isn't good.

He opens the file folder and pulls out an official-looking report. "The immediate cause of death has been cited as the toxic effect of eszopiclone."

"What's that?" Wyatt asks.

"Sleeping pills." He gives us the brand name. I recognize it from TV ads. "Your wife—Mrs. Spencer—had a prescription."

"Oh."

My worthless brother-in-law seems shocked by this, although I don't know why. Does he think Sylvia was as heartless as he is? It's true she sometimes had trouble falling asleep in those early weeks after they separated, but that was normal enough. Struggling to reconcile the upheaval in her life and still take care of her children, she got a prescription. I didn't like it, and I told her so.

"Val, I'm not addicted. I promise. I cut the pills in half when I do take them. Otherwise, I'm too groggy in the morning, and you know that's my favorite time of day." Oh, I knew that all right. "If it makes you feel any better, I have an appointment with Emily later today." It helped—a little. Emily was my therapist, a woman we'd known most of our lives. I recommended Sylvia see her. "And I have a checkup with my regular doctor next week." Dr. Hart and Emily shared an office building. He wrote the prescription at her request.

In spite of what Sylvia said, I wasn't satisfied. "It's not only because they're addictive," I told her. "You could start hallucinating or get dizzy in the middle of driving or start forgetting things."

She set the pan she'd been drying on the counter and stared at me. "Where are you getting all this?" Before I could answer, she held up her hand. "Never mind. Don't tell me. You looked it up." She tossed the wet towel next to the dishes. "Are you seriously thinking I'm going to turn into a junkie and smash up my car or forget how to brew coffee or whatever? Come on, Val. You know me better than that."

I did, but that didn't stop me from being a big sister. "Are you taking them every night?"

"No, Val." I flinched. It wasn't like Sylvia to get angry. "I'm sorry. I didn't mean to snap. I only take them when I'm having trouble. I promise."

"What kind of trouble?"

She stood there for a moment. "Sometimes I lie there and go over it again and again in my mind. How did we get here? Why did things go wrong?"

"Sylvia, you didn't—"

"Don't worry. I'm not about to give him a pass. Wyatt . . ." Sylvia's voice dropped to a whisper. "Wyatt threw everything away. He threw us away."

I took her hand in mine and squeezed. "He's an idiot."

She tried to laugh, but it came out more like a snort. "Sometimes I don't know about that. Maybe we got married too young. We rushed into it, so sure we'd never end up a statistic, and look at us now. Didn't you give me all those articles about waiting?" Her tone had a bitter edge to it. "You told me we should live together first. I wouldn't listen, would I?" She shook her head. "Now, who's the idiot?"

I wanted to hug her, but I knew she was tired of my sympathy. She wanted to be past the sadness and the feelings of abandonment and loneliness. These were things I couldn't do for her, and it broke my heart.

"You are the most amazing mother and sister there ever was," I said. "And I was wrong. If you'd waited, you wouldn't have Miles and Merry."

She pulled her hand away and blinked back tears. "They're pretty awesome, aren't they?"

"They are."

"I'm worried about how all this is affecting them though." She talked about the children and the idea of divorce many times before, and I'd never stopped her. I didn't then either. I understood her need to speak about her worries, her anxieties. And they lessened as the weeks and months passed. She found her new routine, her new normal. Things were good. Or at least that's what I thought.

Detective Barnes is talking again, his focus on the sleeping pills. "We've been in touch with her doctor, the one who prescribed the medication—we had a few questions for him, but he wasn't as much help as we'd hoped."

I sit up straighter. "What kind of questions?"

He clears his throat. "The prescription bottle was from about a year ago, dated January eighteenth. According to both the doctor and the local pharmacist, one prescription was written and filled. No refills or other scripts. I'm wondering if either of you know if she switched doctors or filled her prescription at a different pharmacy."

Wyatt doesn't speak, so I jump in. "Did you speak to Emily? She might know."

"If you mean Ms. Rodgers, yes. I take it you know her?"

"I do. Dr. Hart is Sylvia's primary, but Emily is her therapist. Mine too. We've known her since we were kids."

"Did your sister ever mention switching doctors or therapists?"

"No. She would have told me. Why?"

Barnes fingers the pages in front of him as though deciding how to answer. "The level of toxicity in Mrs. Spencer's system, even after three days, was four point six." He looks from Wyatt to me. "This would be considered extremely high under any circumstance, but in this case . . ."

I lean across the table, hanging on his every word.

"I don't understand," Wyatt says.

Barnes clears his throat. "The level of eszopiclone found by the ME doesn't match the prescription."

His words take a minute to sink in, but even after they do, it's not clear to me why this matters. Somehow, I manage to keep my voice steady. "What does that mean?"

"Well, like I said, the prescription is from last January." He pulls a picture from the file. The photo shows a bottle lying on its side on a bedside table, the label visible. I know in an instant that it must have been taken in the hotel room, the one where they found my sister, and I shiver. He taps on the image of the bottle. "As you can see, the prescription is for one pill to be taken in the evening as needed." He looks up again. "According to Ms. Rodgers and Dr. Hart, there would have been fourteen pills in this bottle. Enough for two weeks. Both said Mrs. Spencer was worried about taking pills, and they agreed on a low dosage on a trial basis. And when Mrs. Spencer returned for her follow up visit, she said she was sleeping better and didn't need a refill."

This is consistent with what Syl told me, and I say so. "She was cutting them in half when she did take them because she didn't like the way they made her feel in the morning."

Barnes accepts this. "Let's say that's true. If she took them for a week— even if it was only half a pill—she'd have no more than nine or ten pills left in the bottle." He spreads his hands on the table. "Do you see my point?"

I don't at first. His words tumble over one another in my brain. Syl's prescription was for two weeks. She didn't refill the prescription, but the levels of the drug in her system were high. I grip the edge of the table. "That's not enough pills, right? She couldn't have done that even if she wanted to. So, that means—"

Barnes cuts me off. "It means that the amount of medication believed to be in this bottle doesn't match the level of medication that was in her system. Nothing more and nothing less."

I sink back down. The boy detective is turning out to be like his partner after all.

Wyatt rubs the whiskers on his chin. "How much did she . . ." he pauses. "How much was in her system?"

"The ME couldn't put an exact number on it, but the range was twenty-four to thirty."

Wyatt, bless his hateful heart, says what I'm thinking. "But if she never had that many, how is that possible?"

"We don't know how many she had. Even though this prescription was for fourteen, she could have other prescriptions. That's why I asked you if she switched doctors or pharmacies. Maybe she got a refill somewhere else and combined the contents of the bottles."

I'm quick to knock that idea down. "No. I told you, if she wanted a refill, Dr. Hart would have been the one to write it. And I know she was still seeing Emily once a month. There would be no reason to go to someone else."

"There would be if she wanted to hide an addiction."

Gritting my teeth, I say, "She wasn't addicted."

Wyatt jumps in again. "I agree with Val. Syl hated taking anything stronger than headache medicine. She wouldn't have done that."

"And yet, she had this prescription."

Wyatt winces, and I want to smack him again. He was the reason she needed the prescription in the first place. He drove her to it. The detective flips to a page in his notebook and writes something down. I have no idea whether he believes us or not, but I'm more convinced than ever that none of this makes sense.

The door opens and Detective Newman steps in. "Barnes, can I see you outside for a minute?" The young detective gathers his folder and his notebook, leaving us to wait. I'm alone. With Wyatt. Hives erupt on my skin, and I scratch at them.

"Val, I'm glad we have a few minutes."

"I have nothing to say to you." I start to get up and swing back around to face him. "Wait. I do have something to say." I jab my finger into his chest. "Just because Sylvia isn't here to stop you, don't think this means Dani is going to step in and replace her. She can't be around the kids. Especially right now."

"Dani isn't a demon, Val. You don't know anything about her."

It's all I can do not to scratch his eyes out. "Oh, well," I say, my lip curling. "If you say so, then it must be true."

Wyatt ignores me. "Val, listen, there are some things I need to tell you. About Dani and me." He runs a hand through his hair. Nervousness, or maybe guilt, makes his eyes jump back and forth.

A wave of nausea almost knocks me over. Could he actually be choosing this moment to tell me he's engaged? Is there no end to this man's lack of sensitivity?

He licks his lips. "And about Sylvia. Something you're not going to like."

I'm on my feet now. I have no intention of giving him the chance to make his announcement or whitewash the latest ways he was making my sister's life a living hell. I don't want to hear another one of his apologies or another weak excuse for why he was a total bastard to Sylvia.

"Not going to like?" My fingers tighten over my phone, over the evidence I've shared with Barnes. "There's nothing you have to say to me that I don't already know. Sylvia texted me from the hotel, Wyatt. Did you know that?"

His mouth drops open. "She told you?"

"Yes, she told me," I say. "Did you think she wouldn't? Christ, why couldn't you leave her alone? God knows I don't know why Sylvia gave you a pass for so long, but to be clear, I'm not my sister. I won't make the same mistake she did." I take a breath, my outstretched finger swinging between us. "You and me. Unless it's about Merry or Miles, we have nothing to say to each other."

Without waiting for him to respond, I leave, the door slamming behind me. Outside in the hall, I flex my hands to stop them from shaking. The buzz of voices drifts over the sounds of clacking keyboards and ringing telephones. Newman is talking to Barnes.

I slide down the hall and turn my ear in their direction, catching snatches of conversation.

"Shut it down."

"Still questions."

"Waste of time."

I tiptoe closer, sticking to the wall, and peek around the corner. Newman and Barnes are ten feet away, huddled near a coffee machine. Detective Newman's mouth is turned down, his hands jammed in his pockets. Barnes is sipping from a Styrofoam cup.

"These people have families," Newman says. "We already know the woman killed herself. You're making it worse, encouraging them."

"I don't think so. And what about that text? The one from the deceased to her sister?"

Newman hesitates. "The husband said they weren't fighting, didn't know what I was talking about."

"And you believe him?"

"It doesn't matter whether I believe him or not. We've got the ME's report. And it was the deceased's fingerprints on the bottle. What more do you need?"

"His story though. There's no proof that any of what he said is true."

It's all I can do not to whoop out loud. The kid was listening to me after all.

Newman, though, sighs heavily. "Barry, it doesn't matter. Whether they were fighting or doing the dirty doesn't change what went down in that hotel room. We followed procedure. We talked to the family. The staff. You saw the pills. No sign of foul play. We're not in the business of trying to figure out why she offed herself, only if it's the cause of death. If so, that's that. Are we clear?"

"Yeah, we're clear," Barnes says and takes another sip of coffee. "But I'd still like another day or two to track down the source of the pills."

The older detective lifts his shoulders in a shrug. "Whatever makes you feel better, Barry. But if we catch an actual case, I'm gonna need you to shut this down. You understand?"

"Sure. I'd better get back."

I scurry down the hall and position myself outside the door. I can't let them shut down the investigation. A day or two isn't much time, but it will have to be enough.

CHAPTER
6

TERRY

Monday, 2:20 p.m.

I sit at my desk, untwisting one paper clip after another. I keep thinking about Val, the woman from the library, and her sister. And the Franklin. It's none of my business, but that doesn't stop me. I place a call to the department, where I still have a few contacts.

"Sure. I'll wait," I say. Two more paper clips turn into crumpled metal sticks.

My old friend Woodward comes back on the line. "Suicide. OD on a bottle of sleeping pills. ME report came in a couple hours ago."

I thank Woodward and sit back. If Val persists in believing her sister didn't swallow those pills, she'll be swimming upstream. A part of me feels bad for her. She's lost her sister in a heartbreaking manner. Not that there's a manner that's not heartbreaking, but in my experience, suicide has a strange way of making the people left behind feel some measure of guilt. I don't really know Val, so I can't say if that's what's going on with her, but it doesn't take much to recognize when someone is hurting. Val is a woman hurting.

Sweeping the pile of twisted paper clips to one side, I pull open my top drawer and dig in the back until I find the blue file. The cover is faded, and the corners are folding in on themselves. It's thicker than I remember, filled with clippings, printed pages, and old photos. I flip through the newspaper articles one by one. Each story is different. Murders. Suicides. Men. Women. There are years and sometimes decades between the stories. One thing ties them together.

"It's none of my business." Saying it out loud doesn't work the way I hoped, and another paper clip joins the pile. I look at the mangled clips and hear the voice of my former partner, Chet Holden.

"I know you're thinkin' hard when you got a box of those paper clips, Martin. What is it this time?" He'd laugh then, the sound rolling over the squad room. I miss Holden. And the job.

Reaching in my pocket now, I take out the card Val gave me. The *Baltimorean Daily*. It's one of the oldest papers in the city. Many of the articles in my blue file were printed in that paper, although none were written by Val Ritter.

I type her name into my computer. There's an archive of her stories on the paper's website. She's listed on a couple of other journalism websites, but I can't find any social media accounts. Either she doesn't have any, or she uses a different name.

Scrolling through the papers for the last several weeks, I find the coverage on the two suicides at the Franklin. The jumper was more than a month ago. Karen Hill, twenty-six, with a history of mental illness. Karen traveled to Baltimore from New York by train the previous day. According to medical reports, she skipped her meds. In one article, the woman's parents claimed that without her meds, Karen tended toward psychosis and debilitating depression.

That, combined with the note left on the woman's bed, led the authorities to determine her death was suicide. I search the articles for any other details but find nothing of significance. A more recent article mentions the foundation the young woman's mother established in Karen's name.

K. L. Murphy

The article about Val's sister is brief, and I read the words twice.

Police were called to the scene of a death at the Franklin early Thursday morning. Although the victim has not been named, the woman is reported to be a resident of Baltimore County and the victim of alleged suicide. This is the second suicide at the Franklin and the 601st in the state of Maryland this year. Nationally, close to 50,000 lives were lost last year to suicide, an increase of nearly 25 percent since 1999. According to the CDC, the suicide rate among males is three to four times higher than the rate among females. Both suicides at the Franklin this year were female.

The victim was discovered in her hotel room shortly after nine a.m. by hotel staff. The Franklin declined to comment.

Doing a search on each of their names, I discover that Karen, the younger woman, had multiple social media accounts. Her activity was sporadic and appeared to be tied to her state of mind.

A flurry of bright, sunny posts in good times and more somber and alarming ones during darker moments. Maybe if she'd stayed in New York, things might have been different. I find a link to the mother's foundation and make a small donation.

Val's sister's name turns up a business profile and a Facebook account. Her lone social media account is private. I take out a notebook and jot down what I've learned. Names. Sex. Age. Background. Exact cause of death. There's nothing similar about the deaths of these women other than their gender and the location. Is that enough? I can't say, but I don't think I can let it go. I pick up the phone again.

"Billy? How's it going?" I listen, ask about his family. "Yep. I'm good. Look, I was wondering if you could do me a favor." I explain what I want. Billy doesn't answer right away. When he does agree, he warns me that his help will be limited. I tell him I understand, and I'll call back later.

After hanging up, I finger Val's business card.

Her sister's death was a suicide. I can't change that.

And yet, Val's insistence that it's not nags at me. I want to help her, although if I'm honest with myself, her doggedness is not the sole reason. *It's none of my business.* And what can I possibly learn that will make any difference? I tap the business card against my desk, and in spite of my doubts, make a decision. I hope it's not the wrong one.

1921

CHAPTER

7

BRIDGET

Margaret knelt on the floor, cradling her younger sister's head in her arms. "Bridget. Bridget. Please wake up."

Bridget's eyelids fluttered. Margaret's face hovered over her, features blurred. Bridget blinked and struggled to sit up.

"You fainted," Margaret said, worry lines visible under her dark bangs. "Do you want me to call Mother?"

"No."

Her sister arched one penciled brow.

"Please," Bridget begged. "I'm fine."

"You're not fine, Bridget."

"I'm just hungry." She got to her feet, stumbled, and reached out to grab the bed post. Margaret kept a grip on her elbow. "I don't need Mother."

"Fine. I won't call her." Margaret frowned. "But you don't look hungry. You look scared."

Was she? Bridget couldn't be sure anymore, couldn't trust her own feelings. Both women sat down again.

"What are you not telling me?"

Bridget dropped her chin to her chest. Would speaking be a betrayal? And what if she was wrong about Lawrence?

"Is it because Lawrence was married before? Is it about what Mother said?" Bridget sat silent. Margaret wrapped an arm around her. "You're my sister. If you're afraid of something, you can tell me. In fact, you must."

Bridget opened her mouth, but the words wouldn't come.

Margaret took her by the shoulders. "Why did you faint? What are you afraid of?" She searched her younger sister's face. "Surely not Lawrence."

Bridget bit her lip. Maybe Margaret couldn't understand either. Louella had taken her seriously, but then of course, she would. She'd been married to Lawrence for eight years.

But no one knew she'd spoken to Louella, and no one would believe what his former wife had said. Certainly not her mother and father, nor Margaret. Bridget wasn't even sure if *she* did.

She stared at the floor, silent.

"You're not, are you? Afraid of Lawrence?"

She gazed down at the soft swell of Margaret's belly. Bridget couldn't begin to think about burdening her sister with her worries now. It wouldn't be right.

"No, of course not." The lie tasted like rancid oil on her tongue. "Getting married is a bit frightening though, isn't it?"

Margaret's hands pressed into Bridget's skin. "You're sure that's all?"

Worried she'd alarmed her sister, Bridget forced her lips to stretch wider into something approaching a smile. "I guess I'm a bit nervous."

"Oh. Well, goodness, Bridget. That's normal," Margaret said, loosening her grip. "Why, the day Charles and I got married, I couldn't even choke down a bit of egg that morning. Do you remember? Mother swore I wouldn't eat because I refused to wear that corset, but it wasn't that at all. I was so terrified."

Bridget sat forward. She didn't remember anything other than excitement and happiness. "You were?"

"Oh, yes. What if I tripped or said the words wrong? What if I couldn't have babies? So many things went through my mind that day."

"Did you ever worry you'd made a bad choice?"

"You mean, married someone else?"

"Yes."

"No. Never," Margaret said, fresh concern etched into the contours of her face "Are you sure this isn't about Lawrence?" A few seconds passed. "Is it, Bridget?"

Her mind screamed yes, but if she admitted the truth, how could she explain her fear when she didn't understand it herself? Aloud, she managed a whisper. "He's so much older."

"Is it twelve years?"

"Thirteen."

"That's not so much. Although he was married." Her expression grew pensive. "Mother told me his first wife had to be sent to a mental institution for a while. The poor man. Can you imagine?"

Bridget hid her shaking hands in the folds of her dress. "No. Terrible."

"Exactly." Her voice brightened. "Come on, little sister. Let's get you in your dress." She rose. "And I promise you, after Lawrence takes one look at you in that gown, you'll be fine. You will be the most beautiful bride anyone has ever seen."

The silky fabric of the white dress cooled her skin and racing pulse. She slid her feet into satin slippers, powdered her pale skin, and stained her lips. Margaret brushed Bridget's hair until it shone, pinned it in the new style, and fixed the comb of the veil.

"There," her sister said. "Beautiful."

Bridget gaped at her reflection in the glass, transfixed. The gown shone in the morning light. The lace train floated behind her like a cloud. Margaret wasn't wrong. She did feel better. But even as she thought maybe she'd been overreacting, Louella's words echoed in her mind.

"*Run away. Run away as fast as you can.*"

CHAPTER

8

BRIDGET
Three Days Earlier

B ridget walked the four blocks from the trolley stop, the wind whistling in her ears. With each step, she feared her legs would give out. She looked behind her, but there was no one there. She needed to get control of herself. Lawrence had traveled to New York on some kind of business. Her parents thought she was at the store, though she'd taken the afternoon off. There was nothing to worry about.

Standing on the brick stoop, Bridget raised her hand to knock, dropped it again. What if this was a mistake? What if she was making something out of nothing? Her mother had remarked more than once that it was one of her specialties. Why, just the other day, Catherine had brought up the time Bridget insisted their neighbor had tried to burn his house down only to find out it was nothing more mysterious than a fireplace cinder sparking and catching on the heavy drapes. And then there was her mother's personal favorite: the time Bridget insisted a friend had stolen her treasured bracelet.

"You merely dropped it, Bridget," her mother had said after it turned up in the parlor. "And now you've made such a fuss, accusing poor Hannah.

I sincerely wonder if the Atkins family will ever forgive us. Lord knows, I wouldn't blame them if they didn't."

"I didn't drop it."

"Don't argue with me." Her tone was harsh, but no harsher than any other time her mother had decided she'd misbehaved. "You're getting to be more and more like your sister every day."

Her father had flashed her a warm smile and patted his wife's hand. "Now, Catherine. Bridget didn't mean to falsely accuse Hannah. I'm sure she had a perfectly good reason to do so."

And she had. More than once, she'd spotted Hannah wearing something that didn't belong to her or seen her brag about her "new" hat or lipstick or another item she'd lifted from a friend. Only the year before, she'd stolen Margaret's favorite parasol—the one with the painted horses—and claimed Margaret had thrown it away. This wasn't true, but Bridget's mother and father weren't prepared to call Hannah a liar after Margaret admitted she had left it outside. Bridget's sister was scolded for carelessness and Hannah got to keep the parasol.

"I haven't stepped foot in the parlor in two weeks," Bridget had insisted. "And I was wearing the bracelet on Saturday." It was Hannah's brother who'd tipped her off, confessing he'd seen his sister flaunting it to her new friends. When Bridget had gone to her parents, Hannah had feigned innocence, and the bracelet had shown up a few days later. "It couldn't have been me who put it there."

It hadn't mattered though. Her mother had chalked it up to Bridget's fanciful imagination. Bridget suspected the Atkinses knew better. They'd moved to another neighborhood soon after the bracelet incident.

Bridget shook away the unpleasant memory, drew herself up to her full height, and knocked on the heavy door. When no one answered, she knocked again. The door creaked open a few inches. Spectacled eyes looked out at her.

"Can I help you?"

"I was hoping to speak with Louella."

"Are you a friend?"

She considered lying but decided against it. "I don't know."

Frown lines creased the elderly woman's forehead. "You don't know?"

"Well, we've never met, but I think I might know her."

"You think you might know her?"

Bridget cringed at the way the woman kept repeating her words. "I've come all the way across town hoping I could talk to her. Just for a few minutes."

"From across town, eh? Must be important."

"It is to me."

The woman came out onto the stoop, her head on a swivel. "Are you alone? No one followed you?"

Confused, Bridget tried to see who or what the woman was searching for. The street was quiet, far from the busy downtown where she worked and several blocks from the fancy apartment buildings close to her own home. The houses here were short and squat. There were no arched doorways or porches or pillars. A single automobile was parked at the end of the road, but she saw no one else. She shivered at the chill in the air. "I'm by myself."

"How'd you get here?"

"I took the trolley and walked."

The woman seemed to consider this before saying, "Come in."

Bridget blinked, her eyes slow to adjust to the dimly lit entry.

"You can wait in here." The woman led her to a small living room. This room, too, was dark, the heavy drapes drawn against the afternoon sun. A single lamp burned in the corner. "I'll get her."

Bridget sat on the sofa. After several minutes, Louella appeared in the doorway, a slip of a woman with ashy hair and hollowed-out cheeks. Bridget got to her feet. "Louella?"

"Yes. Do I know you?" There was no animosity or anger in her voice, only a kind of mild curiosity. She perched on the other end of the sofa, her hands folded in her lap. "Have we met?"

"I don't think so," Bridget said, sitting down again. "I hope I'm not bothering you."

"It's no bother. I don't get many visitors. I spend most of my days in the garden or with my paints."

"You must be feeling better then."

The woman cocked her head to one side. "Who told you I was ill?"

"Oh, well, uh," Bridget stammered. "I heard that you'd been in the hospital for a while, but you're out now. I'm glad you're better."

Louella blanched. "I haven't been in the hospital. Who told you such a thing?"

Bridget's thoughts tumbled over each other. *Had she somehow heard wrong? Or was Louella lying?* She glanced at the doorway. "This was a mistake. I shouldn't have bothered you."

Louella's outrage turned to accusation. "Who told you I'd been in the hospital?" Her hand clutched at her throat, and she ran to the window, pulling aside the drapes to peer out the window. "Is he here? Is he watching me right now?" She whirled around toward Bridget. "Is he?"

Bridget shook her head. "No one's watching you."

"Are you sure?" she asked, her bony fingers locked together.

"I promise."

"You're alone?"

"Yes."

"Did he send you here?"

"No one sent me here. I came on my own."

Louella sank back down on the sofa, her narrow chest rising and falling. Her head dropped into her hands.

Bridget glanced at the doorway again. "Are you okay?"

"Fine." She sniffled without looking up. "I'm sorry. For a minute, I thought he was back."

"Who?"

"Lawrence," she said, the word a whisper.

Bridget blinked at the woman, unable to speak.

Louella shuddered. "Did he tell you I was in the hospital?" She gave a single shake of her head, not waiting for an answer. "I know it was, but it's not true, you know. Not that he didn't try. He wanted to have me put in a mental institution. He even took me there once, but the doctor was a friend of my father's, and he sent me home. Heaven knows he couldn't have his name mentioned in connection with the Altoona Sanitarium. Not that going home to Father was much better." Her words were tinged with bitterness. "He sent me back to Lawrence. Back to my husband, he said, where I belonged. The sanitarium might have been better."

Bridget shivered.

She'd made a mistake. Beneath Louella's mild manner was an angry woman, a woman scorned.

"In the end, it didn't matter though. Lawrence had our marriage annulled." Louella looked up, and the features of her face contorted into something that reminded Bridget of a wild animal—hunted, dangerous. When she spoke again, her small voice had grown larger. "Did you know that? No? We were married for eight years. I was with child twice. Both times, I lost the babies after a few weeks. He became convinced that I must be full of sin, that the sin was making me incapable of bearing him a son. There were . . . punishments," she said, spitting out the word.

Bridget's hands flew to her mouth as she drew back. "Wh-why are you telling me this?"

If Louella heard Bridget, she gave no indication, but continued: "In the last two years, I was unable to become pregnant at all and he became angrier and angrier. And then, it happened. I was with child." The words caught in her throat. "I wanted to have a baby—more than anything—but I was afraid. Bringing a child into that house? I—" her voice faltered. "I didn't tell him about the baby. He found out later. Maybe if I had . . ."

Bridget wanted to cover her ears, didn't want to hear any more, but she couldn't move.

"I—I lost the baby after a bad night. He blamed me for keeping it a secret, for forcing him to punish me. I didn't care anymore. I wanted to die with my baby." She dropped her head into her hands, her shoulders shaking. After a moment, she wiped away her tears with the backs of her hands and lifted her chin. "That's when he decided to get our marriage annulled." She gave a harsh laugh. "Having me committed didn't work, so I was labeled barren."

"I'm sorry," Bridget said, voice shaking.

All of Louella's body seemed to sink into itself as though swallowed up in some kind of invisible pain. "Don't be. I was lucky to get away."

Bridget peered around the dark room. There were shadows on the walls and on the woman's face. She didn't get many visitors, spent most of her time alone. There was nothing about her life that appeared lucky. "Are—are you happy?"

Louella's colorless eyes narrowed. "You didn't say why you were here." She angled her head as though considering Bridget for the first time. "Do you know Lawrence?"

Not trusting herself to speak, Bridget nodded. She shifted under the woman's scrutiny, her skin flaming.

"How do you know him? What reason do you have for coming here?"

Unsure how to answer, Bridget opened and closed her mouth. Everyone said Lawrence was devoted to her, and she knew this to be true. So, what was it that bothered her so much she'd trekked across town to find out more? Was it because he put her up on a pedestal that she knew she didn't deserve? Was it the sharp look he gave her once or twice or the cross words that followed when she'd said the wrong thing? Of course, there'd been gifts and praise and apologies after. Even Margaret had commented she'd never seen such devotion. Suddenly, she was embarrassed she'd come. "I'm engaged to be married," she said, her voice soft.

"I see." Louella's small hands curled over the fabric of her dress. "You're very young."

Bridget didn't say anything.

"I was young once." She stared down at her hands, twisting them in her lap. "But that was a long time ago."

Bridget hesitated. "The man you've described . . . it doesn't sound like Lawrence."

"Doesn't it?" she asked, her voice brittle. "You're not married yet. He wasn't like that when I first met him, you know." Her words softened. "I thought he was the most wonderful man in the world. He used to call me his angel back then."

Bridget gasped. It was the same name Lawrence used for her.

"I am but a poor sinner who is fortunate to be in the company of an angel, my golden angel," he'd said the other evening. Then he'd raised his glass in a toast. "To Bridget, kind in spirit, gentle as the wind, and the angel of my dreams."

She'd blushed and laughed. "You would not have thought me so angelic had you seen me with one of my customers today."

Bridget had started to launch into the story of a demanding customer at the store, but he cut her off before she could even get a few words out. "You could never be anything but perfect, angel. And that is why I can't wait for us to be married." As he talked of their wedding and the life he was planning for them, her mind had wandered.

"Did you mind?" Bridget asked Louella now. "Being his angel, I mean?"

"Oh, no. Not then." Her thin lips rose in a half smile. "I was flattered. More than flattered. I did everything to live up to that name. I spent all my time try-ing to please him. And for a while, we were happy." Her words fell away, and she raised a shaky hand to her temple. She watched Bridget as she spoke. "After I lost the baby the first time, he started calling me something else."

Bridget tried to reconcile Louella's story with the man she knew, but even at his worst, he was nothing like the man Louella depicted. Punish-ments? How could that be true?

Louella stood, the corners of her mouth turned down. Her face hard-ened. "You don't believe me."

"It sounds . . ." She couldn't finish, unwilling to offend the woman.

"You're a fool," Louella said, her pale skin coloring. "You don't know what you're doing." Wild-eyed, she stared hard at Bridget.

Bridget shrank back, unable to meet Louella's feverish gaze. She didn't want to offend her, but the woman didn't make sense. Yes, there were things that sounded the same, but not most of it. And there was something strange about Louella, something that made Bridget afraid. It wasn't hard to picture this woman in a hospital, in an institution. "I came to hear what you had to say, and I've done that now."

"You don't believe me," she said again. "But you have doubts, or you wouldn't be here."

"I didn't say that."

"You didn't have to."

Bridget rose, every muscle in her body tensed. "I'm sorry to have bothered you."

"I'm sorry too, but not for me." Louella reached out and wrapped one bony hand around Bridget's arm. "Please don't tell him you found me."

Bridget jumped and her heart clutched. Even if she didn't believe Louella, there was no mistaking the woman's fear. "I won't. I promise."

"Thank you." Even as the lines around her mouth smoothed, her hand tightened, her fingers pinching Bridget's skin. "Run away. Run away as fast as you can."

CHAPTER
9

VAL
Monday, 2:45 p.m.

My phone vibrates on the passenger seat. I don't recognize the number, but I haven't recognized much of anything these last few days. I certainly don't recognize a world without Sylvia, much less one where everyone believes she could have taken her own life. Willing the caller to be the bearer of better news, I answer, swerving to pass a slow-moving clunker from another century.

"I hope I'm not bothering you." A man's voice comes over the line. "But I thought maybe we could meet for a cup of coffee."

"Who is this?" I ask, regretting my decision to answer.

"It's Terry. Terry Martin. We met at the library this morning."

"Oh." I fall back against the leather seat of my car. *Was the library only this morning?* "Sorry," I say. "I didn't recognize your voice."

"No need to apologize. How about that coffee?"

I can't speak at first. I don't know why I would want to have coffee with the man who was a front-row witness to my breakdown. I would think he'd be happy to be rid of me. I know I would be. My surprise shifts to suspicion.

Whatever he wants, I don't have time for it. I'm headed to see my sister's therapist—our therapist. After what I learned from the police about Sylvia's prescription, I've decided it's time to take my research from passive to active.

"It's not a good time," I say. "I'm on my way to see someone."

"Not a problem. I'm at the office taking care of a few things. We could meet after your appointment." There's a pause. "There's something I'd like to discuss with you."

I take the exit ramp that leads out of the city. "Why can't we discuss it now?"

"I'd rather do it in person."

"I have plans." Turning onto a four-lane road, I pass strip malls with high-priced grocery stores, boutique shops, and nail salons. I'm in the suburbs now. My sister's house isn't far, but I turn the car in the opposite direction. That stop will have to wait. "I need to go," I tell him.

"It's about your sister's death."

My breath catches. I'm irritated again, but I'm curious too. "Where's your building?" I ask. He tells me. It's not far from the medical suites where Emily has an office. "There's a coffee shop on the corner. Java Beanery," I say. "Do you know it?"

"Yes. Four o'clock?"

"I'll be there." I click off, pushing Terry the former detective from my mind. I have other things to think about.

Emily rises when I walk in and wraps me in a hug so brief, I can't be sure it happened. "Val, I was so sorry to hear about Sylvia," she says. "I can't imagine how difficult this must be for you and your family."

"Thank you. I know you were a big help to her after the separation."

She retreats to the safety of her desk and waves a hand toward the patient chair. "How are you, Val?"

I have no interest in talking about myself, so I don't. "Sylvia had been coming to you for almost a year."

"Yes." She presses the pads of her fingers together but says nothing more. I know she'll let the silence stretch, let it percolate until it bubbles over and the quiet is louder than any words. It's an old trick, one I've used often as a reporter. Even the most resistant sources will fill the silence given enough time.

"Emily, I'm going to be blunt. I don't believe Sylvia took her own life."

If I thought this pronouncement would earn me some kind of reaction, I'm sorely disappointed. I press on. "You've known Sylvia and me almost our whole lives."

Emily says nothing.

"Syl was still seeing you, wasn't she?"

"Not as often as before. Only twice in the past few months. The last time was"—she pauses and scrolls through her phone—"six weeks ago. She was supposed to come in the Tuesday before last, but she didn't show up."

I can't hide my surprise. "That's not like Sylvia."

Emily shrugs. "She called me later to apologize, offering to pay for my time. Of course, I told her not to worry about it."

Emily and her family lived in our neighborhood when we were girls. We played in the same park, went to the same neighborhood schools. Emily had always been nice, never ignored us like many of the older teenagers did.

"Did my sister say why she didn't show up?"

"No, and I didn't ask."

I file this information away. "I need to ask you some questions about Sylvia's medication. Whether she said she was still taking it and how often."

Emily sighs. "Val, I can't talk to you about what Sylvia and I discussed. That's privileged. Even from you." Her hands drop to her lap. "You know this is why I was reluctant to see Sylvia in the first place. I don't normally see patients from the same family unless it's a group therapy situation."

"I understand, but this is different. She's gone now."

"It's not different to me." Her facial expression remains neutral. "Val, if you'd like to talk about your grief, I'm here for you."

Again, I ignore her concern, and take a different approach, sharing what the police have told me.

She wears her doctor mask, the one that can't be shocked or shaken. When I'm finished, she nods once. "The police were here earlier."

I keep my mouth closed.

Two can play at this game.

"I can't tell you anything specific, but I can tell you what I told them. At my recommendation, Dr. Hart wrote one script for Sylvia. No refills. I've spoken to Edward. If she got more, it wasn't through us."

"Did you and Sylvia discuss how the medication was working?"

"Yes."

"Did she indicate she wanted to continue using it?"

"These are areas I can't talk about."

"The last time you saw her, how did she seem? Did she seem depressed to you? Unhappy?"

"Val." She draws out my name.

"Okay. How about this? I tell you what she told me, what I thought about how she was doing, and you can tell me if I'm wrong." When she doesn't say anything, I take her silence as permission to continue. "I thought Syl was doing great. That's why none of this makes sense. I mean, right after she found out about Wyatt, she was devastated. That's why I sent her to you. I was worried. The first few weeks were difficult. She barely got out of bed on the weekends when the kids stayed with Wyatt. She lost weight. Wasn't seeing her friends. But after a couple of months, things started to get better. Merry and Miles needed her, and she needed them. She rallied. She forced herself to start running again, to start participating. Even when her heart wasn't in it. She told me that was your suggestion."

"True."

"She was coming up on the anniversary of the separation, and I was worried, but when I talked to her about it, she told me I was overreacting. It seemed like she was right. I mean, she seemed happy. She was laughing all the time, even dating." I pause, watching Emily's face closely. "She was involved with someone." I almost miss the flicker of her eyes. Sylvia confided in Emily. I'm sure of it. "Do you know who it was?"

She evades my question with one of her own. "If she told you she was seeing someone, why do you think she didn't tell you more about him?"

I open my mouth to answer, but I can't. I've asked myself the same question. It wasn't that her dating was a secret. She showed me the new dress she bought for a recent date, mentioned he brought her flowers, but nothing more. Not that I hadn't tried.

"What does he do? How old is he? Is he tall, dark, and handsome?" I asked as we walked along the Inner Harbor. The sun shone down on us, the day unseasonably warm. Sweating under my turtleneck, I shed my jacket. Syl, though, looked as cool and beautiful as ever. The sun caught the lights in her hair and her cheeks glowed. Her scarf fluttered around her neck, the deep greens of the silk matching her eyes.

"He's a businessman," she said finally. "And he has brown hair. Dark brown."

It was like pulling teeth. "Is he tall?"

"Taller than me."

"So tall then."

"I guess."

"Is he divorced? Widowed? Does he have kids?"

She threw her head back, laughing. "Val, please. No more questions. Just let me enjoy it for a little while."

I was so glad to see Sylvia happy that I didn't push. Now I wish I had. Eyeing Emily, I ask, "Do you know who he was? Do you know his name?"

"Is it important?"

Her question takes me by surprise. "I don't know. Probably."

"I'm sorry, Val, but I can't help you." She's lying. I know it and she knows I know it, but there's nothing I can do. Emily would never betray Sylvia or any patient. "I've got to cut this short," she says. "My four o'clock will be here soon."

I stand up. My legs are shaking, and I have to steady my nerves.

I haven't asked the one question I need to ask, the one I'm most afraid to hear the answer to.

"Emily, do you think Syl did this? Do you think she killed herself?"

Her lips part. "I'm not a perfect therapist, Val. I see patients with all kinds of problems, big ones, small ones. Sylvia is not the first patient I've lost." For a moment, Emily's smooth expression cracks, and I catch a brief glimpse of the pain and emotional toll of her job.

My entire body is trembling, but I don't let up. "But Sylvia wasn't like your other patients. She wasn't sad or depressed. And she wouldn't have left Merry and Miles. I know that in my heart."

Emily is silent.

"Please. Do you think she would do that? Take her own life?"

Emily's shoulders sag as she considers.

After another long minute, she lifts her hand and straightens. "If I give you my opinion, it shouldn't be taken as fact. You understand, don't you, Val? It's only my opinion. The same as I gave the detective who was here earlier."

A new terror races through my mind and rips at my heart. Still, I need to know. "I understand."

Emily takes so long to answer, I wonder if she's changed her mind. "Sylvia was a beautiful person, Val. I was very fond of her, you know." My heart lurches in my chest. "I've seen many patients through divorce, other losses. Some never get over it, but that wasn't your sister. She didn't look backward. And as you said, being a mother was everything to her."

I bite down on my lower lip.

"So, no, I don't think she would be capable of any type of self-harm."

I exhale. I want to run around the desk and hug her, but her next words stop me.

"But that's my opinion and one not shared by the police. They have their reasons, and nothing I say will change their minds, as far as I can tell." There's sadness and pity in her voice. "I'm sorry, Val." She pauses. "None of this speculation will bring her back, you know. I'm worried you're not dealing with your grief, with losing her." If she notices my physical withdrawal, she doesn't say. "I can make you an appointment if you'd like to talk more."

"I don't." I know she means well, but she should know me better. I can't deal with anything until I know the truth. "The police are wrong," I say. "She didn't do it. She wouldn't." I grab my bag and fling it over my shoulder. "I have to go."

"Take care of yourself, Val."

The door closes behind me before I remember to tell her about the last text from Sylvia and my worry that Wyatt has grown angry, maybe violent. I could go back, but I don't. Emily may have couched her words carefully, but she's already told me what I wanted to hear. Sylvia didn't kill herself.

I stand outside the Java Beanery, peering through the large glass storefront. Terry is sipping from a paper cup of steaming coffee and watching the door. A cold wind blows, and I pull my coat around me. I don't know why I'm here, wasting time, but I would like some coffee.

A bell rings over my head when I enter, and he gets to his feet. He's taller than I remember and broad-shouldered in a way that suggests he's not just a former detective but also a former athlete. I notice there are gray flecks woven through his curly brown hair. The same gray peppers the light stubble covering his strong jaw. I don't remember any of this about him although I can't imagine why I should have.

"Thanks for coming," he says and gestures at a second cup on the table. "I ordered you a black coffee. I can get you something else if you'd like."

I touch a hand to my hair, wondering when I combed it last. I'm sure I look a mess, but I figure that makes sense. I am a mess. Exhaustion washes over me, and I take the coffee, grateful for the caffeine.

"You called, and I'm here," I say, lifting the cup to my lips. "What do you want?"

"Are you always so friendly?"

I open my mouth, but whatever words I might have snapped die on my tongue. His lips are turned up at the corners in a half smile. He takes another sip of his coffee. *Damn. Why does he have to be so nice? And easy on the eyes to boot?*

I set my cup on the table. "I checked you out."

He doesn't flinch. A positive. "I would expect nothing less."

"You were in homicide for fifteen years. Impressive closure rate. No infractions. Two citations. Why haven't I heard of you before?"

Although there's no outward reaction, his skin colors a fraction. This I find interesting.

"I'm not big on the spotlight, I guess."

"You worked some high-profile cases, although none I covered."

"I wouldn't know who did the stories for the paper. That's for the press department to handle."

His answer fits what I learned about him. Solid. Smart. It makes me wonder again why he quit.

"Do I pass?" he asks.

"For now," I say. "You said you wanted to talk to me about my sister."

"I do. I'm curious as to why you think your sister didn't take her own life."

"Because she wouldn't."

He holds my gaze, unwavering, silent. *Damn him.*

He leans back and finishes his coffee. The barista at the counter calls out names, setting fresh cups on the counter. The bell rings every time the door opens. It makes me want to scream.

His voice is soft now. "This feeling—that she wouldn't take her own life—does your family share it? And her friends? Do they believe as you do?"

I sit up straighter. Before I can open my mouth, he holds up his hand.

"If I were the detective assigned, you wouldn't be the only person I would talk to. Presumably, your sister had friends. There would be other family, co-workers. I'd question more than one source. No detective would rely on one person's word here. It's been my experience that there are times when people are too close to see what's right in front of them. And even in the case of an obvious suicide, a full report would have to be written.

Medical Examiner's report. Description of the scene. Interviews with the family of the deceased."

I pull my arms in tight to my chest. I don't give a crap about police reports, and I'm questioning this whole role-playing thing. Terry the former detective—no matter how attractive or well-meaning—is wasting the limited time I have to convince the police to keep this investigation open. But he's relentless, a trait I can't help but recognize. And like.

"Was your sister married?"

I give him the shorthand version about Wyatt and the affair and the separation.

"That must have been hard for her." The way he says it makes me steal a glance at his ringless hand. He switches back to the case. "I'm guessing the police have been talking to him about what's happened then?"

What's happened? The phrase strikes me as wrong, as trivial and fixable as spilled milk or tracked mud or a flat tire and wholly inadequate to describe the loss of Sylvia. Death is not a "what's happened." It's gut-wrenching. It's mind-numbing. It's a searing pain no medicine can dull. Believe me, I've tried. A tear slips over my cheek, and I no longer care that he's trying to help. I reach for my bag, but he catches my hand.

"Please. I'm not trying to upset you."

I don't move. I tell myself it's not because of the warmth of his palm on my skin. It's everything, all of it. I'm so tired I can't muster the strength or the energy to pull away. The bell at the door rings then, and I take back my hand.

"Yes, the police have talked to him."

"And do you know what he's told them about your sister's state of mind?"

Thoughts fly through my brain—none of them kind. "I know what he claims he told them."

"Which is?"

"He said it doesn't sound like her."

If he hears the scorn in my voice, he doesn't let on. I find myself wondering about all the suspects he must have interviewed when he was a detective. For one moment, I envision Terry having a go at Wyatt, staring him down, getting him to confess. How would it start? Would he admit he was a failure as a husband? That he dumped a wonderful woman for a childish copy? That when she was finally happy again, he tormented her, scared her? That he lost control and went too far?

The stupid bell rings again, and my imaginary *Law and Order* scene evaporates.

Terry is staring at me. "What?"

"I asked you how their relationship was after the separation."

"Oh." It's a loaded question. How can I explain the arc of their marriage and separation in a way that will make him understand? Aloud, I say, "It's complicated." I glance at my watch and stand up. "Look, I know you're trying to help, but I have to go."

He pushes up from the table. "I'll come with you."

"You don't even know where I'm going."

"I don't have to. Something tells me wherever you're going has to do with your sister's death, and I'd like to help—or try to."

The man is persistent. I have to give him that. "Don't you have a job?"

"I took the rest of the day off. Besides, I haven't explained what I wanted to talk to you about. The idea I have."

I can't help myself. In spite of everything, I'm still curious. "Tell me now. If I'm interested, you can come."

"Fair enough," he says. "The Franklin. It has cameras. Most hotels do."

I think about this, and I know he's right. Even so, I don't understand how it matters. "So? They don't have them in the rooms."

"But they have them in the lobbies, hallways. Some even use them in the elevators." He shifts, leaning toward me. "Like I told you earlier today, I'm in security. We're a pretty tight community. I know the guy who runs security at the Franklin. I wrote his recommendation for the job."

"And?"

"I might be able to get us a look at the video from the days your sister stayed there."

My hand closes over the back of the chair. I'm playing catch-up, but the wheels are grinding now. Maybe the cameras wouldn't be able to catch what happened in my sister's room, but they would show who walked through the lobby in the hours leading up to Sylvia's death. I already know Wyatt was threatening my sister. That's motive. But if he's on the video, that's opportunity.

I hold up my keys. "I'll drive."

CHAPTER

10

TERRY

Monday, 4:51 p.m.

Val pulls off the two-lane highway into a neighborhood fronted by a white fence and evergreen trees. She drives past a community pool, tennis courts, and a playground. I don't miss the way her lip quivers as we pass a half dozen young mothers sitting on benches, each smiling brightly as they watch their children swing and slide. She jerks her head forward and locks her fingers over the steering wheel.

I'm holding my phone to my ear, waiting for Billy. He comes back on the line. "Yes," I say. "Those are the dates. Thanks, Billy, I appreciate your help."

Val glances over at me. "Well?"

"He's pulling the video, said to give him until tomorrow morning."

"Is this . . ." I hear the hesitation in her voice. "Is this legal? I mean, the video is private, right?"

"Technically, it's the property of the hotel, so yes, it's private. But there's nothing illegal about watching it so long as we have permission."

"What about the police? Wouldn't they already have watched it?"

"Depends, although I doubt it if they don't suspect foul play."

She accepts that. We pass two-story colonials and brick mini-mansions with manicured lawns and sweeping drives.

"Nice place," I say as she comes to a stop in front of a large house the color of butter.

"Yep." She jumps out of the car in a flash, her coat flying behind her. Before I can get up the sidewalk, she's turning the key in the lock. She walks inside a few feet and freezes, her body rigid. She covers her nose with her hand. Following her, I stop too. The smell is overpowering. The house is filled with the bitter, musty odor of dead flowers. As a former homicide detective, I've smelled much worse, but it's pretty bad.

"Are you okay?" I ask.

She leans against the wall, her skin the color of wax. "My sister loved flowers." The words are half mumbled, half sobbed. I wait. "She put them everywhere. They made her happy, she said."

I don't doubt her. On the hall table are three short vases with what was once hydrangea and feathery greens, the petals dried brown now. The bottom of each vase is dark with mildew. There's another large vase in the living room. Dead roses droop over the rim. "Val?"

Her chest heaves once and then she lifts her chin. With outstretched arms, she sweeps the dead arrangements from the table. "I'm fine. Can you help me get all the vases, please?"

We fill two trash bags with dried-out blooms and slimy stems. We wash vases of all sizes and colors. She says little as we work. There are more than a dozen containers lined up along the counter when we're finished. I step back and dry my hands. The cloying odor of dying flowers has faded, and she looks better, stronger.

"Is this the house your sister shared with her husband? Before they separated?"

She gives a single nod. "They thought it would be better not to uproot the kids. Sylvia didn't want to take them away from their school and their friends."

"Makes sense," I say. "Tell me about the husband. What's he like?"

I listen to the words, but I get a better idea of how she feels from the way her mouth pulls downward at the corners and the way her body seems to stiffen. When she's finished, I ask another question, a harder one.

"Do you think the affair—the one your sister knew about—was the only one?"

Her lips purse as though she's tasted something sour. "Sylvia thought so, although now that you mention it, I'm not so sure. I don't know why, but women seem to like him."

"Any particular reason?"

"What do you mean?"

"Is he good-looking? Does he have a lot of money? I don't know."

She chuckles, but not in a way that makes me think she's amused. "I couldn't say how good-looking he is. He's okay, I guess, but I'm probably not the right person to ask. He was my sister's husband. I didn't think about how he looked." She pauses, thinking. "He makes good money, has a good job, but nothing amazing. They were comfortable."

I let my gaze wander over the gourmet kitchen and large family room, but I don't say anything. "So, what makes you think women like him?"

"He's funny. Quick with a joke. He's good with people and kids. When he talks to you—or at least he used to be this way—he always has some-thing nice to say. I remember Sylvia said it was his special talent. To make you feel like you mattered." Her frown deepens. "If you ask me, his special talent is being a fake. It's all about his ego. About making himself out to be the good guy when he's anything but."

"A gigolo type?"

"No. He's not that smooth." I sense reluctance in her admission. "Not polished or rehearsed. Maybe that's why women are drawn to him. He's like the male version of the girl next door. Or we all thought he was." She hesi-tates, her head angled to her shoulder. "Why does it matter?"

"I don't know that it does," I say. "But it might help me get a handle on the guy. You said women like him. Anyone stand out?"

"His girlfriend, of course. Dani."

I know it's a loaded question even as I ask it. "And what's she like?"

"You don't really want to know what I think."

"Is she younger?"

"Ding ding ding. Give the man a prize." She smiles a little, but she doesn't laugh. "Twenty-five maybe. Looks like a younger version of Syl except bottle blond, not natural like my sister. Same build. Works with computers or something. A little dependent maybe. I remember Sylvia telling me once that Wyatt said Dani needed him. Something about her parents dying young and her being alone." She looked up at the ceiling. "Like that explained everything. Dani needed him."

"I guess it's safe to say the relationship between Sylvia and the girlfriend wasn't good."

"What relationship?" Val says with a snort. "Who would want a relationship with the woman who stole your husband?"

"Good point."

She draws in a breath. "But Sylvia wasn't the vengeful type, if that's what you're thinking. She hated Dani—sure—but she didn't talk bad about her or anything to their friends." I must look surprised because she offers an expanded explanation. "Sylvia realized that no one made Wyatt have an affair. I think that's what hurt her the most. He chose to cheat on her instead of going to counseling or trying harder. Of course she blamed Dani, but she blamed Wyatt more." She pauses, and her voice softens. "It was hard on Sylvia. You know how it is when couples split up. People take sides. They stop spending time with the husband or the wife, then eventually both of them."

I consider her words and wonder briefly if she's still talking about Sylvia. Steering the conversation back to Wyatt, I ask, "What about at his job? Friends there?"

She takes her time answering. "I don't know who he spends time with anymore. When he and Sylvia were together, they had a tight group of friends, some of them from his office. There's his assistant, Angela. Sylvia and I used to talk about her sometimes. She's young too." She starts to say something more but changes her mind. She straightens and surveys the room. "Enough about Wyatt. That's not why we're here. Let's look around."

"Sure." I repeat what I said in the car on our ride to the house. "Our focus is looking for anything that strikes you as unusual or out of character for your sister, something that might imply things weren't the status quo."

"Such as?"

I can't tell if she's deliberately being obtuse or not. Val's agenda appears singular, but I don't know her well enough to assume anything about her.

"I don't know. A major purchase. Rescheduling or skipping appointments." Again, she hesitates. Although I wonder if she's holding something back, I decide not to press. "And anything that seems weird or threatening," I finish.

"Fine." Her gaze sweeps past me to the stairs. "You take the kitchen and the den," she says. "I'll start in the bedrooms."

I'm opening drawers before she makes it up the first step. Although better organized and three times the size of my own, it's a typical kitchen. Silverware, plates, and glasses. There's a junk drawer filled with playing cards, matches, pens, and a few screwdrivers. Nothing out of the ordinary. I move on to the den. Photos in black frames cover the mantel. Most are of the children, but in the corner, tucked behind the others, is another, smaller one. It's a man and a woman on a sailboat, the cloudless sky behind them a brilliant blue. I pick it up, squinting. The man's face is hard to see; the woman the focus. She's smiling, not the polite kind or the there's-a-camera-on-me kind, but the kind that comes from the inside, radiant and joyous. I feel my own lips turn up looking at her. I slide it back behind the others, careful to leave the pictures and the happy images of Sylvia's life exactly as I found them.

After looking through the shelves loaded with books and knickknacks, I turn my attention to the desk in the corner. The files are filled with bank statements and bills and school grade reports. It's in the middle drawer where I find the calendar. I turn to the current month. The Franklin is written in large letters across several blocks. I stare at the words for a long time before I flip the pages. The initials make me turn back.

I take the steps two at a time. There are three bedrooms on the right. The doors are open, and the rooms are empty. The first two are children's rooms, one pink, the other as blue-green as the sea. A closet door and a few drawers are open, as though someone packed in a hurry. The third bedroom looks unlived in. A guest room. Down the hall, another door is half open. As I get closer, I hear Val's sobs.

It's different from her meltdown at the library: quieter, sadder somehow. I push open the door. She's sitting on the bed, a notebook of some kind in her lap. She doesn't see me or hear me. I don't want to startle her, so I wait. When the cries stop, I step into the room.

"Val?"

Her cheeks are stained with tears. She holds up the book, and her body sags. "Sylvia's diary." I walk in a few more feet. She wipes her eyes. "She's been keeping a diary since she was in third grade." Pointing at the walk-in closet, she says, "All the old ones are there. In boxes." She holds up the one in her hands. "This is the most recent I could find."

I don't keep a diary, but I know they are different things to different people. Some are hardly more than exaggerated calendars, listing the day's activities. Others are long monologues of emotion. Most are something in between. "What does it say?"

She runs her fingers over the cover. "Not much, really." She skips through the pages. "There's this one thing. It's so Sylvia."

"Read it to me."

Val doesn't speak for a minute. "This was right before Christmas a year ago." Her voice wobbles as she reads, and I move closer to hear.

Merry has inherited my voice, I'm afraid. Earlier tonight, I thought it would be fun to make hot chocolate and take the children to sing carols with the neighbors. Miles rolled his eyes, but he went. Merry, though, was overjoyed and belted out "Jingle Bells" with more enthusiasm than any four-year old I've ever seen. Unfortunately, most of us would have preferred a little less enthusiasm when she opened her mouth. Miles

covered his ears once or twice until I told him to stop. After the first
house, I had her stand next to Mr. Moxley. He's deafer than a lamppost.
We should all be so lucky.

"You get her, right?" She looks up at me. "So funny."

"Yes," I say and mean it. I've gotten a sense of the woman in a short period of time. Sylvia was organized, but her refrigerator is crowded with pictures of her children and their artwork. She loved flowers and had a sparkling wit. And based on the pile of sneakers in the mudroom, I can guess she was a runner. Her house is tastefully decorated but comfortable, a home. This was a family. This is how it is during a homicide investigation. The victim becomes a person. Living and breathing.

Tears fall again. "I don't know what's wrong with me," she says. "I didn't even cry for days, and now I'm a leaky faucet."

I sit on the edge of the bed, at the corner, careful to keep some distance between us. "I'm sorry you're having to go through this, Val."

She wipes her cheeks with her fingers and closes the diary. "Here's the thing. This diary isn't the last one."

The words she spoke earlier come back to me. "You said it was the most recent one you found."

"Right. It goes to mid-summer. Which means the latest is missing."

If her sister was as consistent with her diary as Val seems to think, six months is too long. "Perhaps she took it with her to the hotel."

"I doubt it. She didn't like the idea of losing them or having them where a stranger could find them. Besides, Newman and Barnes didn't say anything about a diary. It must be missing."

Her quick assumption is a leap, but I understand. She's eager to find an answer to the unanswerable. "You should ask the detectives. To be sure."

Val stares down at the book in her hand. "I will." Her gaze slides over to me. "Why did you come up here?"

"Oh, right." I hold up the calendar I discovered in the desk. "I found something."

1921

CHAPTER
11

BRIDGET

Bridget couldn't take her eyes off her reflection. She stared at the veil, which floated over her head and cascaded down her back. The cool silk of her gown rippled and shimmered with her every movement. Her fingers fluttered to her throat. She'd never felt so beautiful—certainly never imagined she could.

"Oh, Bridget," Margaret breathed. "You are the loveliest bride I've ever seen." She reached out and squeezed Bridget's hand. She brushed at a tear, her lower lip trembling "Oh, don't mind me. I know it doesn't seem like it. I've just been so happy these days."

Bridget's heart swelled, and she handed Margaret a handkerchief from the dressing table. "You're the one who's lovely. I'm so lucky to have you."

Margaret sniffled and laid a hand on her belly. "Enough of this sappiness. I can't be weeping, or I'll look a mess."

"Never."

Smiling, Margaret dragged a comb through her hair and pinched her cheeks for color.

"As ready as I'll ever be, I guess." She stood in front of Bridget, holding out her arms. "Let me look at you again."

Bridget held still, as though if she moved, it would surely break the spell.

Margaret's red mouth widened. "Wait until Lawrence sees you. He'll be speechless. I know it."

The words hit Bridget like a bucket of cold water, and she staggered, catching herself on her sister's outstretched arm. She caught sight of her reflection again. The dress she loved so much served merely as a prop in a show, a costume for a performance Bridget was no longer sure she wanted to be part of. In less than two hours, she would become Lawrence's wife. She would stand in front of her parents and her friends and take a vow to be loyal and true.

She should be happy.

"Bridget? What's wrong? You look as though you've seen a ghost."

"I'm fine."

Margaret's mouth was no longer smiling. "You're not fine. The minute I mentioned Lawrence's name, you . . . you changed. You looked scared. That isn't nervousness, Bridget. I know what you look like when you're nervous. You crack your knuckles and drive Mother crazy." She studied Bridget's hands, holding them in hers. "You've been biting the skin around your nails again." She pulled Bridget closer. "You're scared. Of something. You can tell me, Bridget. We're sisters, remember? Through thick and thin?"

She almost told Margaret everything then, but she couldn't. Instead, she settled for half-truths. "I am a little scared."

"More than a little. This isn't wedding jitters, is it? Has Lawrence done something?"

"No." This, at least, was not a lie. He hadn't done anything she could point to or complain about. "Sometimes he's, um, very strong-willed in his opinions. I don't know if what I think or feel matters. Perhaps I'm being a child. I don't know."

It was clear from the set of Margaret's jaw her explanation was not satisfactory. "Go on."

Bridget's mouth went dry. Her story had to be true enough even if it wasn't the truth. "Well, I can't tell him about Joseph."

"Joseph? The boy you worked with at the store?"

"Yes." She stared at the floor as she spoke. "We started working at the same time. He was stocking the floor, and I would tell him what we needed, and sometimes he would carry packages for customers. And he was doing the window displays."

"You became friends?"

Bridget nodded.

"More than friends?"

She looked past her sister. Had they? She couldn't be sure anymore. "I don't know. After he quit the store, I never saw him again."

Lines appeared between Margaret's perfectly rounded brows. "But you liked this boy?"

Bridget's skin flushed. It was bad enough Joseph forgot her so easily, but admitting it out loud made her heart hurt in a way she didn't want to think about.

"Did something happen between the two of you?" Margaret stepped closer, her voice a whisper. "I won't tell anyone, Bridget."

There had been a few walks through the park. An exchange of jokes and stories. There was the time he'd taken her hand in his and stood close, his warm breath caressing her cheek. He'd touched his lips to hers. Her skin tingled at the memory. And he'd kissed her a second time, longer. She hadn't been able to forget the rush of blood through her veins or the urge to wrap her arms around his neck. But the next day, he was too busy for a walk and the next day and the next. Before the week was out, he was gone, as though he'd never been there at all.

Worse, there was no one to tell. Lawrence had been coming around the store by then. For weeks, he treated her like a princess before declaring his intentions to her father. Lawrence was a successful businessman, while Joseph was a store clerk who'd run away after snatching a couple of kisses.

"Bridget?"

Startled, it took Bridget several seconds to remember the question. "Nothing happened. Not really. He left the store, and I never saw him again."

Margaret's eyes searched hers. "But you liked him."

Bridget shrugged. Yes, she liked him, more than liked him if she were honest, but that was something she wasn't ready to confess. Not to Margaret and never to Lawrence. He'd asked her once if she'd ever kissed another man. Something about the way he'd looked at her when he'd asked had made her hesitate.

"Why would you ask me that?"

"If I were to make you my wife, I would want to know your loyalty was to me and no other, Bridget. I'd want to know that when you kissed me, it wasn't another man you were wanting to kiss."

"Are you planning to kiss me?" she'd asked, tilting her head.

"Don't play the coquette, Bridget," he'd said, voice snapping. "It doesn't become you."

He'd dropped the question, and she hadn't been forced to lie, but now she wondered what would have happened if she'd told him the truth then. Would she still be standing in a dress the color of fresh snow, her stomach in knots? Would there be a wedding at all?

As she'd done with Lawrence, Bridget evaded Margaret's question, asking one of her own instead. "Did you kiss Charles before you were married?"

Margaret wagged her finger. "You're changing the subject."

"I still want to know."

"Ha. Well." Pink spots appeared on her sister's cheeks. "Y-yes, a few times. Not that Charles didn't do the proper things, you know. But we were to be married, so . . ." With a single finger, she lifted Bridget's chin. "What does this have to do with Joseph or Lawrence?"

"Lawrence thinks it's important to wait." This, too, was the truth though incomplete. "Sometimes I worry he isn't interested in me at all."

Margaret half laughed. "Well, I know that's not true." She paused. "Bridget, I've seen the way he looks at you. He adores you. It's as though you're so perfect he's afraid you'll break."

"But I'm not perfect, and I won't break." She knew how she must sound—a woman complaining that her betrothed adored her too much. But she couldn't help it. All that adoration, the expectations—they were more than she could fulfill. And the conversation with Louella had fanned the flames of fear that were already keeping her up at night. "I have kissed a boy," she whispered. "Once."

Margaret stepped back. "Ah. Joseph."

"Yes."

"And you're worried Lawrence wouldn't understand?"

"I know he wouldn't."

"Bridget, I'm sure you're mistaken. Lawrence was married once before. He's shared many kisses with another woman. You kissed a young man you were fond of one time. One time, Bridget."

Bridget heard the fear in her voice, but she couldn't hold back now. "He thinks I'm pure."

"Oh, Bridget. One kiss doesn't make you a temptress, you know. You're still the same wonderful and kind girl you were before you met Joseph. You're still the woman Lawrence fell in love with. Please don't worry about this for one more minute."

"If he found out, he wouldn't forgive me. He would be angry. Maybe more than angry."

"You're exaggerating now." She pulled her closer. "Aren't you, Bridget?"

CHAPTER
12

BRIDGET

Bridget stared unseeing out the window, the streets and the buildings they passed a blur. Margaret sat close with Bridget's veil stretched across her lap. In the front of the automobile, their mother and father chattered on. Margaret's husband followed in Uncle Anthony's new Ford. It was to be a small and intimate wedding, limited to close family and a handful of friends. Lawrence had asked if she minded.

"I know it's our special day, my dear, and I do want to make you happy in any way I can, but I would feel a bit awkward having one of those lavish affairs—especially what with my having been briefly married before. I don't have much family, as you know, so the few people I will gladly receive at the celebration can be of your choosing. You do understand, don't you, dear?"

"Oh, yes. Absolutely," Bridget had assured him. Since agreeing to marry Lawrence, she'd felt strangely disconnected from the planning.

"You are my angel." In an unusual gesture of intimacy, he'd touched an icy hand to her cheek. "All that matters is we are wed and can begin our lives together."

She'd smiled up at him in what she hoped was an angelic manner. "Well, thank you for lunch, Lawrence. I have to get back to work now."

"Do you have to? Why don't we go for a walk down by the river?"

"You know I can't."

"I know I'm going to be happy when you don't have this job anymore."

"I like my job."

"Be that as it may, you won't be working as a shopgirl much longer. You'll be my wife," he'd said.

Bridget had looked away, but not before he'd caught the dismay on her face. "Bridget," he'd said, voice stern. "That's what you want, right? To be my wife?"

They'd arrived in front of the store. She'd let her gaze wander over the window display Joseph had set up. The last one before he'd disappeared. "Of course," she'd told him. If there was no feeling in her answer, he didn't seem to notice.

"That's my girl." He'd straightened the bowler hat he wore. "I'll be gone for two days, but I'll be back before the weekend. Try not to be working the next time I'm in the city, hmmm?"

She'd promised to do her best before hurrying into the store. She'd breathed in the perfumed air as she made her way to the second floor. She liked her job, loved it even, but maybe it was for the best. Lately, being there reminded her of Joseph.

Bridget felt the touch of a hand on her shoulder, and her head jerked, banging against the glass.

"Are you okay?" Margaret asked, sliding closer on the bench seat. "We're almost there."

Bridget leaned forward. The chapel was up ahead, the gold of the steeple shining under the bright midday sun. Her hands clenched and unclenched in her lap, damp with perspiration. Margaret reached for her.

"You don't have to do this." She kept her voice low, her mouth close to Bridget's ear.

"Mother and Father."

"They'll get over it. You're the person I'm worried about."

But Bridget knew her parents wouldn't forgive her, wouldn't under-stand how she could take the word of a woman rumored to be insane over that of her betrothed, potentially sullying her reputation enough to repel other suitors. They'd been in favor of her courtship with Lawrence imme-diately, pushing her to match his swift and steady interest. It was true she'd never matched his level of affection, but for them, she'd tried. And Louella's story might be a reason for her reluctance, but it sounded far-fetched even to her own ears. Why would her parents believe it when she didn't know if she believed it herself? "I'm fine."

The automobile rolled to a stop. Her father jumped out, opened the door, and extended his hand. "Let's hurry. It's freezing out here."

The group slipped through the back door of the church, congregating in the small room that doubled as an office. Reverend Michaels greeted them there, shaking hands with Bridget's father.

"Just in time, George. I was beginning to get a little worried," he said. The three women followed him inside. Bridget, her steps slow and hes-itant, found an empty space near the window. Margaret stayed close, her hand finding Bridget's. The pastor glanced over at the young women. "Your groom is very eager, Miss. He's been here more than a half hour already. And your guests. Shall we get started?"

CHAPTER
13

VAL
Monday, 5:38 p.m.

Terry pushes the calendar across the countertop and taps one of the blocks on the page, a Saturday two weeks before Sylvia died.

"Do you see what I mean?" He reads the entry out loud. "S. M. Seven o'clock." He points out another date, this time a Monday. "S. M. Noon."

I barely listen, entranced instead by the smiley face my sister has drawn next to the initials. My hand trembles as I reach out to take the calendar. S. M. could be anyone. He could be a business appointment. He could be a friend. He could be a she. But I know it isn't. I scan the days of the month and find more dates with the same initials. One is marked drinks, the others dinner. I flip the pages back to the previous month and count the number of times the initials S. M. appear. Eight times. Lunches and dinners. I turn to the month before that, and I find the same initials again, although fewer this time. I go back further, but there are no more entries referring to the mysterious S. M.

There are other appointments with other initials. Hairdresser is H. D. and our parents are M & D. V. G. is me. Syl loved nicknames and when we were young, she dubbed me "Valley Girl," but it had more to do with my name being Valerie than the traits ascribed to California girls that I possessed. As a teen, I was more bookworm than ditzy or fashionable. Still am. Either way, it stuck. And once, after Wyatt brought his girlfriend Dani to a school event, she began calling her B. D., for Barbie Doll. Every time she used the nickname, she made me giggle. These are the initials I know. Others I don't. There's a K. D. next to Merry's name and an S. G. I don't recognize, but they only appear once each. I return to the first S. M. notation. Next to the letters is the word "drinks." There is no happy face. Instead, the S. M. is followed by two question marks.

"What are you thinking?"

I hold my finger up to my lips, and I flip through the calendar again. The first time the initials appeared were in the fall, more than two months before the last entry. I rack my brain trying to recall when Sylvia first mentioned she was dating someone.

We sat together on the back porch, a blanket over our legs. Pumpkins of assorted sizes lined the wooden railing. Yellow, red, and orange leaves floated down from the trees onto the grass. We were discussing a new TV series before Sylvia changed the subject.

"So, what would you say if . . ." She rubbed her hand back and forth across the soft blanket in her lap. "I mean, I don't know if you'll approve, but what if I—"

I knew my sister and the words jumped out of my mouth. "If you started dating again? Of course, I approve. Are you kidding?" I elbowed her in the ribs. "How did you meet? FindMeASexyMan.com?"

Her cheeks flushed pink, and she blew on her cocoa. "Don't be ridiculous. Besides, I don't know if you'd call it dating."

"Wait," I said. "You've already gone out with someone? On an actual date?"

"Well, I don't know what to call it really. I haven't dated in so long, and I don't know if it even counts as that. Dating, I mean." Her fingers flicked the blanket aside. "It's kind of weird. Doing this again."

"Oh, please. It can't be any weirder than a man who leaves his wife and children for a Barbie doll."

Sylvia jerked as though I'd hit her. "Wyatt didn't leave me. I kicked him out."

"I know you did. I'm sorry." I moved closer to her, until our shoulders touched. "It's just you know how much I can't stand him for what he did to you."

"Val . . ." she started. It was an old argument between us. She refused to speak ill of the father of her children in spite of what he'd done. I admired her for it, though I couldn't do it myself. She shifted toward me. "I want to ask you something."

I knew by her tone that I wasn't going to like the question, but I also realized she'd ask anyway.

"Do you think one of the reasons you're so angry with Wyatt is because of William?"

"William?" I hadn't thought about my ex-husband in years. "No. That was a long time ago."

"Are you sure?"

I looked past her then, my focus drifting. William Trenton Harper. The fourth William Trenton, to be exact. Part of Harper Communications. What the Harper family didn't own, they bought. That used to be a running joke around town. Probably still is, although I admit I never found it particularly funny. It was one of the reasons I didn't change my name. Of course, it's also possible I knew deep down how things would end up. William was sweet when we first met. Quiet. Romantic. Things I'm not. Maybe that was part of the problem. Along with his affair. Still, his fling was one thing. His parting words were another:

"Val, isn't it you who's always telling me to be my own man? Stop being my father's puppet? But it's not him that's always telling me what to do. It's you, Val. You."

If I learned anything from my marriage, it's that blame is easy to parcel out, not so easy to shoulder. William's jab hurt, but he wasn't wrong. Back when I was in the third grade, my teacher wrote, "Valerie is bossy," in the comments section of my report card. My parents were delighted. My mother even clapped her hands as though I'd been awarded a prize. On some days, my take-charge attitude is the reason I've built a career as an investigative reporter. On other days, I don't know how it's received. In hindsight, I guess William didn't appreciate it so much.

Either way, none of this has anything to do with Wyatt and what he did to my sister. Sylvia is not me any more than Wyatt is William.

Aloud, I said none of this.

"You're changing the subject, Syl. We were talking about you, not me."

"It's getting late." She let the blanket slip to the ground when she rose. "I have an early day at the office tomorrow."

"Oh, no, you don't," I said. "You can't tell me you've been on a date and leave me hanging. Who is he? How'd you meet him? How many times have you been out?" I grinned and winked. "Are you crazy in love?"

Sylvia burst out laughing. "How many questions can one person ask? I'm so glad I'm not one of the people you interview every day. They must want to kill you."

"They do." I tried to stay on topic. "One more question."

"No. Please, stop," she said, holding up her hands, still smiling. "There's not much to tell. He's someone I," she paused. "He's just a guy I met."

"Oooh. Interesting. What else?"

She shrugged. "We've been out twice. Drinks once and dinner once."

"And?"

"And there's nothing more to tell."

While it was short on details, it was long on promise. I decided not to press. "You don't know how happy it makes me to see you moving on, Syl. You deserve to be happy."

She touched a hand to my shoulder. "And what about you, Val? Don't you deserve the same?"

"I am happy." I trotted out the same song and dance I always did. Work didn't leave me much time for a personal life, and when I did have time, I wanted to be with her and the kids.

"It's not enough," she told me. "Ever since Wyatt moved out, you've been here for me, for Merry and Miles, and I love you for it. I do. But I don't need you to babysit me anymore. The kids and I are doing fine. I promise. We're a family."

I ducked my head. This was what I wanted, wasn't it? Sylvia back on her feet. Happy again. They'd found their new normal. *We're a family.*

She squeezed my hands. "You need to do more than spend every weekend with us."

I feigned outrage, burying any hurt I might have felt. "You make it sound like I'm a spinster spending every night sitting in a rocking chair."

She rewarded me with a playful slap on the arm. "Don't be ridiculous."

"And you know I went out to dinner with Britt and Gayle the other night."

"That was two weeks ago."

Was it? "Well, I had happy hour after work a few days ago." Her expression didn't change. "And I have book club."

"That's once a month."

"I go to the gym."

"Not much. And when you do, you have headphones on the whole time and talk to no one. I know you, Val. It's been months since you've been on a date."

"Well," I drew out the word, "that might be true." I spun around. "I promise I'll date when I have more time." I paused and elbowed her lightly in the ribs. "Maybe we can double."

Her smile widened even as she shook her head at me. "Fine. You win." She leaned over and picked up the blanket from the ground. "By the way, did I tell you Miles is taking guitar lessons? He started last week."

Remembering how proud she was of those music lessons, I pick up the calendar now, paging through the weeks and months. Miles's first lesson and the initials S. M. followed by question marks appear in the same week. I drop the calendar on the counter. It feels like a lifetime. "S. M. must be the man she was dating for the past couple of months."

"Must be? She didn't tell you about him?"

"She did."

"Did you meet him?"

"No, but they hadn't been dating long."

"Fair enough, but according to this," he says, pointing at the calendar again, "they were starting to see each other more often. I think we should ask her new boyfriend a few questions. How do we get in touch with him?"

"I don't know. She never mentioned his name."

He looks at me then, his eyebrows raised. Heat rises from my chest. I know what he's thinking. My sister didn't trust me enough to confide in me, or we weren't as close as I thought we were. It's a fair assumption but dead wrong. At least, I think it is. *I don't need you to babysit me anymore.* At the time, I accepted that she would tell me when she was ready. Besides, not giving her mystery man an identity was a way of protecting herself. If no one knew who he was and things didn't work out, then he never really existed in the first place.

I explain my thinking, but Terry's not prepared to let it go.

"He may have some insight into your sister's state of mind."

"State of mind?" I ask, my face flushed now. "As in, did he think she was depressed?"

"As in, why would she lie about going on a business trip and then check into a hotel a few miles from her house? Maybe she told him about it."

I want to tell him to mind his own business, but the words die on my tongue. I've let him make it his business, something I'm starting to regret. But the truth is, the question of why Sylvia lied keeps me up at night. If she'd confided in me about Wyatt's threats before, would she be alive now? Detective Newman is convinced the lie was part of her plan to take her own life, but I know better. Wyatt is the reason. He has to be. I tell Terry the same thing I told Detective Barnes. I show him the text from Sylvia and play the voice mails from Wyatt. I watch him as he listens. When Wyatt's tone changes from pleading to threatening, I stare hard, but there's nothing. Not so much as a blink. I don't know why, but I'm disappointed.

"The detectives heard these voice mails?"

"One did. Both saw the text."

"You suspect her husband?"

"Wouldn't you?" He's not ruffled by my outburst, nor is he convinced. "It's the most logical explanation."

"And yet, all the evidence in the hotel room seems to contradict that explanation."

Anger burns again. "Whose side are you on?"

"Whoa," he says, drawing back. "There are no sides, Val. There's only finding out what happened."

"Tell that to the police," I say.

He holds up the calendar again. "Do you suppose it's possible she wasn't planning to be alone at the hotel? Maybe she didn't go there to hide but to meet someone." I don't follow at first. Then he says, "Maybe she was meeting the new boyfriend, S. M. After all, we don't know anything about him. Maybe he doesn't even live in Baltimore. Maybe he travels here for business."

Wyatt is momentarily forgotten, and my mind races. I try hard to remember how Sylvia talked about her "business trip." "I suppose it's possible," I say.

Surprising me again, Terry drops the idea as quickly as he suggested it. "But as far as we know, she checked in alone, and no one has come forward saying anything otherwise." He taps the calendar again. "Though I still think we should talk to the boyfriend. If your sister was afraid of her husband, she may have confided in him."

That Sylvia would share her fears with a man she knew for less than three months rather than me doesn't make sense, but then again, none of this does. I push my own feelings aside. "How do you suggest we go about finding him?"

"The usual way. We talk to her friends, her co-workers, her neighbors."

"I'll make a list." I grab a pen and notepad from a drawer. "I think it's possible Wyatt knew she was dating someone," I say as I write. "What if it made him mad?"

Doubt creeps into his voice. "Look, I don't know the guy, but if he wanted out of the marriage like you say he did, why would he care if your sister was dating someone else? Wouldn't that be a good thing?"

Newman, the first detective, asked the same question. "In a normal situation, I would agree. But Wyatt is a grade-A narcissist who thinks the world revolves around him. Just because he didn't want to be married to Sylvia anymore doesn't mean he didn't want her under his thumb. I used to think he was a good guy, but the man has an ego the size of an aircraft carrier. Even after she kicked him out, he kept coming around, and there was nothing she could do about it. She didn't want to deprive the kids of their father. I couldn't understand it." My voice cracks and I avert my face. "If I'd known about the way he was scaring Val, I would have told her to get a restraining order, or we could have called the neighborhood watch or—"

"Whoa, whoa, whoa." He places his hands on my shoulders. "Whatever did or didn't happen between your sister and her husband is not your fault. None of this is your fault."

The tears flow again, sliding down my face. I hang my head and mumble agreement, but I know better. It is my fault.

"Val, if Wyatt walked through the lobby of the Franklin for any reason at all, he'll be on the video."

I sniffle and lift my head. His words can't erase my guilt, but they do make me feel better. "And then I'll know."

He gives me an odd look. "You need to get some rest, Val." Taking the list from my hand, he says, "This can wait."

There is a weariness in my bones, but I force myself to sit up straighter. There isn't much time before the police shut down the investigation—if it can even be called an investigation. "I'm fine."

"An hour. Two at the most. You need to sleep to think clearly."

I want to protest, but he says it so softly, with no accusation in his tone, that I can't muster the energy.

He gathers up the calendar and my bag and leads me out to the car. I walk like a zombie, feet shuffling, arms dragging. I hand him my keys and slide into the passenger seat. As he backs out of the driveway, my gaze is locked on my sister's house. Terry had the forethought to switch on a light in the living room and check and double-check all the windows and doors. With the cul-de-sac behind us, my head rolls toward the window. I watch the house in the mirror. It gets smaller and smaller, shrinking like a waning moon, until it's gone.

CHAPTER
14

TERRY

Monday, 8:16 p.m.

Val sits bolt upright on the sofa, flinging the blanket from her body in one motion. I see the moment she spots me in the dim light.

"You're awake," I say.

She inhales, the sound sharp in the quiet of the small house. "What are you doing here?"

"You let me in."

"But . . . why are you still here? What time is it?"

"A little after eight. You were upset, delirious with exhaustion, but you refused to go to bed. The best I could get you to do was lie down on the sofa."

Her hands close over the blanket. "Did you put this on me?"

"I hope you don't mind. I found it in the closet."

She seems to consider this. "And you've been sitting here the whole time."

"Well, not the whole time," I say. "I ducked out to the store and picked up some food. I checked your fridge. Didn't look like there was much to eat."

Her belly growls in response. "I have no idea what was in there."

"You don't want to know." I get up and move into the kitchen. "Are you hungry?"

"No." A second rumble makes her lay a hand on her stomach. "Well, maybe a little."

She follows me. I open the fridge and pull out my purchases. A pair of chicken breasts, a stick of butter, and two lemons. Next to that, I place a container of mixed greens and a bottle of wine. I gesture toward the bottle. "I figured you could use this." Her eyes widen before they narrow. "I'm trying to help. To be a friend." Her expression is closed, wary. I don't blame her. "If I wanted to hurt you in some way, I've had plenty of time already."

I watch her as the realization I'm right sinks in. "Be a friend, huh?"

"If you'll allow it."

Val appraises me another minute. "We'll see," she says.

"Good enough for now. In the meantime, there's food and wine. Corkscrew?"

She pulls one from a drawer. I pour two glasses and set one in front of her.

"Look," I say. "You need food. I need food. And if we're going to go over what we know, we might as well do it while we eat, right?"

She cocks her head. "Go over what we know?"

"Yes. And eat. Unlike you, some of us can't survive without food. You don't mind if I make dinner, do you?"

"Do I mind if you make dinner?" Her finger trails the rim of her glass. She takes a sip. "That's a new one." I wonder what she means, but her shoulders relax.

I sauté the chicken in butter and wine, then add freshly squeezed lemon juice. Enticing smells fill her tiny kitchen, and she stretches forward, watching the chicken sizzle.

"I still don't understand why you're helping me," Val says. "To be honest, you don't seem convinced I'm right. You said yourself Barnes and Newman have the ME's report. It's a formality now."

I can't disagree with her. My buddy in the department said as much.

But there are those pills. And then there are the other suicides. I open a small jar of capers and add a spoonful to the sauce. "Maybe it's the ex-cop in me."

She sets her glass down with a clank. "I'm not helpless, you know. I can do this on my own."

"I would never call you helpless." Her jaw drops for one brief second, long enough for me to know I've taken her by surprise. "A little rude maybe, but I'm chalking that up to your tough exterior." The corners of her mouth twitch.

I'm not lying when I say nothing about Val makes me think she's helpless. Hell, she could be the mother in that football movie, *The Blind Side,* a bulldozer ready to take down anyone who threatens her loved ones. She's not afraid to say what she thinks or force her way in. Even if she hadn't told me, I'd know she was a native Baltimorean. That toughness is bred into you here. Her walk and the tilt of her head says, "Don't mess with me." But I sense there's more to Val Ritter than toughness. The way she startles when I stand too close or offer comfort. The way she can't hide her suspicious nature. The way she believes in her sister in spite of the medical examiner's report. Her pain is like an open wound, visible to anyone who can stand to look past the prickly personality and stubbornness.

I say none of this, though.

"I don't know you that well, but I don't think I'm wrong. Definitely not helpless."

I turn the stove off to allow the chicken to rest. While we wait, I prepare and dress the salad. Taking two plates, I dish up the greens, add the chicken, and drizzle the sauce. "Shall we?" I ask.

Val dives into her plate, eating so fast I'm not sure she isn't inhaling the food. "So, you're not just a retired detective and security chief, you're also an accomplished chef? What else should I know about you?" she asks between bites.

"Accomplished is a stretch," I say with a laugh. "I can make about three things that aren't cold cereal. This is one of them."

"Thank goodness. I was feeling pretty bad about myself there." She takes another bite. "So, what are the other two things?"

"I can make a mean burger." I raise my glass to her. "And a decent omelet."

"Breakfast, lunch, and dinner," she says, clinking her glass with mine. "Three square meals."

This makes me chuckle. "I never thought of it that way, but I guess you're right."

"Well, if your other things are this good, you're all set."

We finish the rest of our meal in an easy silence.

"I'll clean up," she says when we're done.

I hand her the plates and wipe up the counter. She rinses and loads the dishwasher. The discomfort from earlier is gone. She feels it too.

"This is weird. The way we met." She picks up the nearly empty bottle. "It must be the wine."

"Maybe." I smile. "Maybe not."

"Coffee?"

"Sure."

She takes out two mugs and pops a pod into the coffeemaker. After the second pod is finished, she hands me a cup and taking hers, pads over to the sofa. She curls her legs under her and sinks down lower. Dark blond hair falls across her cheek, hiding the hollows of her face. She seems smaller, less sure than she did earlier.

I wonder again if this is a mistake. Talking my way into another case that involves the Franklin is one of the last things I wanted to do. And I don't want to hurt Val. I could still walk away. I should walk away. But I know I won't.

I take the seat on the opposite side of the room and pull my notebook from my pocket. Interest flickers across her face. "Should we do the 'what we know' part now?"

She sets her mug aside and gestures toward my pen and paper. "I'm the reporter. It's usually me who takes notes."

"I'm sorry. Do you mind?"

"I don't know if I do or not." She chews at her thumbnail. "It still feels a little strange. My sister being gone. The police. You being here, taking notes. All of it."

"I'm sorry about your sister," I say again. "But I can live with strange if you can."

Her smile is strained this time, but she sits up straighter. "Okay. You're taking notes." She looks around then, her fingers tapping on the arm of the sofa. "Where's that list I made? I should start calling some of Sylvia's friends, people she worked with. See if they noticed anything. Or anyone."

"About your list," I say. "While you were sleeping, I made a few calls."

Val's fingers stop moving. "You did what?"

I hold up one hand. "Only a few. Three or four." With each word I say, her face gets redder. "That's all. I promise."

Val is on her feet now, seething. I can't say I blame her, but I had my reasons. "I apologize. I should have waited for you."

"You're damn right you should have. I don't understand why you would do that."

"I thought they might be more willing to tell me things they wouldn't tell you." In my former profession, I learned friends don't always like to be the ones to pile on the bad news. If Sylvia was having issues, those friends might not want to tell her grieving sister, but they might be willing to speak with an investigator or outsider. "I only talked to three or four people on the list."

"What people?" she asks through clenched teeth.

"Some of her co-workers at Banford Marketing and Consulting. I took a chance a few folks might still be at the office. I managed to get her assistant and a couple others." I flip a few pages in my notebook. "Her assistant's name is Lenora."

"I know that," she snaps.

I read from my notes. "Lenora said she kept your sister's calendar at work and about two weeks ago, Sylvia scheduled some time off—the same time off that coincides with her reservation at the Franklin." I keep reading. "Lenora did know Sylvia was seeing someone but not who. She also corroborated your story about Sylvia being in a good mood lately." I look over at her. "I wasn't doubting you, Val, but the more people who confirm it, the better."

She shifts in a way that tells me she's not convinced.

"Now, here's where it gets interesting. Lenora said she saw Wyatt hanging around their office building a couple of times. She couldn't remember the exact dates but once was the week before Sylvia died. The reason she noticed him is because he was wearing sunglasses, and it was drizzling outside. She thought that was odd enough, but even stranger was the way he kept watching the building. She said it made her want to stock up on pepper spray."

"Did she tell my sister?"

"She said she tried to, but your sister was so preoccupied by her newest client"—I pause to check my notes—"Headliners—which I gathered is some kind of entertainment company—that she never got the chance."

"I remember. Syl was excited about that client. She thought they could be the next touring Broadway company with the right marketing strategy. And it was so different from the straight product marketing she'd been doing."

I nod, but marketing and Broadway are not things I know much about.

"Poor Lenora. She must feel terrible." Val falls back on the sofa. "What about the others?"

"Nothing other than that Sylvia seemed fine to them. Maybe better than fine."

She thinks about this. "More corroboration, right?"

"Right. One more thing though. There was a graphic designer she worked with." He flips the page. "Wendy Polk."

She nods. "I've met Wendy a couple of times."

"Ms. Polk said she asked Sylvia if she was planning to do anything special with her time off."

"And?"

"And she said no, just a staycation to use some of the days she'd accrued." I take a breath and wait. Val's hand grips the arm of the chair now, her fingers like claws.

"Sylvia lied."

"Yes." It wasn't my intention to cast Val's sister in an unfavorable light, but she needs to understand Sylvia was intentionally deceiving everyone around her. Being in that hotel, on those days, was not random. Everything about it was planned. "The reason I bring this up is because the designer said she thought for sure Sylvia was going somewhere like the Caribbean or a cruise."

"Why did she think that?"

"Because Sylvia seemed almost giddy."

"Giddy?"

"Her word, not mine."

"Giddy might be a bit strong, but I thought things were good." Val raises a hand to her temple, rubbing absently. "So did everyone else. No one knew about Wyatt and his threats. Maybe she didn't want us to worry. Maybe she didn't think it was as bad as it was. She could have been fooling us all, acting happy."

"Maybe," I say and close my notebook. "It is interesting your sister's ex-husband was hanging around her building."

"Do you think anyone else saw him?"

I hand her the list. "There's one way to find out."

An hour later, she sags, her head in her hands. "Nothing. We don't know anything new."

I cross the room and sit next to her. "That's not true. The one neighbor"—I pause and pick up the list again—"Mrs. Harrison. She saw Wyatt's car drive by your sister's house late one night. She said he slowed down but didn't stop. She couldn't be sure if he was there another night too. Based on Lenora's observations and Mrs. Harrison's, it's more evidence Wyatt was checking up on your sister."

"Stalking sounds more like it."

"Possibly."

"But we still don't know who S. M. is. No one knew much, other than she was dating someone."

Holding up the list, I say, "There are still two of your sister's closest friends we couldn't reach. If anyone knows who the boyfriend is, it could be one of them." A glimmer of hope flickers, but I know she's not convinced.

"Can I ask you a question? I know we don't really know each other, but this being a detective thing, it seems like who you are. I don't understand why you're not still doing it."

She's right on both counts. It is who I am, and we don't know each other well enough. "It's late, and you need to get some sleep," I say instead, getting up again. "I'll pick you up at nine."

"Sure. The Franklin?" she asks.

A cold dread falls over me, settling in my bones. "Yes," I say. "The Franklin."

1921

CHAPTER
15

BRIDGET

The organist pressed the keys, and music filled the sanctuary and vestibule. Bridget's father waited nearby. Her mother and a handful of old schoolmates turned in their seats. The vibration of the organ pipes made Bridget's teeth chatter, and she shivered, swaying on her feet. Time slipped back to a day filled with light and sweet summer scents. Under a canopy of dense, green leaves, she ran through the park, her hair flying loose behind her. A soft wind caressed her cheek and the sun shone down through the trees. She ran toward the lake, toward the water. Diamonds of light rippled across the dark, inky surface.

She ran faster and faster.

"Bridget." The whisper of her name dragged her back to the present. "Bridget. It's time." Margaret reached out. "Are you sure you want to do this?"

Before she could answer, her father approached. Smelling of wool and pipe tobacco, he looked from one daughter to the other. "This is no time for you two to be prattling on." Bridget blinked. Her father stepped between them. "Lawrence is waiting. Your mother is waiting."

Bridget nodded, mute, and he moved into place beside her. He lifted a hand toward his eldest daughter. "Margaret," he said, "get going."

Bridget's father wrapped his large hand around hers in a tight grip. When Margaret reached the altar, Bridget heard the inhale of her father puffing his chest. She knew the seats held relatives and a few school friends, but the faces before her blurred along with the church itself. Her father stepped forward, pulling her along. She tripped once, her legs as heavy as lead.

"Bridgie," he whispered, using her childhood nickname, and moved his hand to her back. With a gentle push, he lifted her up as though she were no more than a feather. Her mind drifted again, and in the moment she found herself standing before Lawrence, her father already seated with her mother and Margaret holding her flowers, she couldn't have said how she'd gotten there.

From what seemed far away, words were spoken. The organist kept playing. Bridget's feet felt glued to the floor, but her mind drifted. The midday sun poured through the stained glass and colored light dotted the floor around her. Red and blue and yellow. So beautiful. A hand at her waist pushed her forward. Startled, she looked up to find Lawrence standing over her, and she shivered.

He glanced over at the pastor and back at her. "I, Lawrence, take thee, Bridget, to be my wedded wife." His booming voice was loud enough to rattle the rafters. "To have and to hold from this day forward, for better for worse, for richer for poorer, in sickness and in health, to love and to cherish, till death us do part, according to God's holy ordinance; and thereto I pledge thee my troth." He smiled wider, and Bridget's heart stopped. His wasn't a smile of joy, or even love—at least not the kind Bridget understood.

The reverend directed Bridget next, but the words stuck in her throat. She dared not look at Lawrence but stared down at the patches of colored light instead. The silence in the church grew louder. Lawrence stepped closer and took her hands in his. The reverend prompted her again. A murmur of voices reached her ears. Lawrence's hands tightened over hers, crushing her fingers until the pain nearly knocked her to her knees. "Bridget," he whispered. "Everyone's waiting." The beautiful colors on the floor turned dark and mottled.

"I, Bridget, take thee, Lawrence, to be my wedded husband." Tears dripped from her eyes. "In sickness and in health, to love, cherish, and to obey, till death us do part."

Lawrence released his grip, reached into his vest pocket, and slipped a golden ring over her third finger. Bridget stared down at the cool metal, and bile rose in her throat. A hush fell over the church and the air changed, charged with expectation. Lawrence lifted the veil and with his thumb, wiped away her tears. It occurred to her she was married now, that she should feel something—happiness, or even relief—but all she felt was empty. And afraid. Lawrence drew in a breath. "My angel." He leaned in close and pressed his cold, pale lips to hers.

CHAPTER
16

BRIDGET

B ridget's mother passed a tray of deviled eggs across the table.
"Lawrence, you've outdone yourself. Why, truly I believe the Franklin is far superior to the Belvedere. Don't you, Margaret? The food here is simply divine."

Bridget exchanged a glance with Margaret. As far as Bridget knew, her mother had never eaten at the Belvedere or even set foot in the lobby of Baltimore's other famed hotel.

"I wouldn't know, Mother," Margaret said. "You've never taken me."

Bridget's father ducked his chin, but Catherine didn't blush. "Well, then you'll have to trust me on this. The Franklin is the best in the city."

"It's my pleasure, Catherine," Lawrence said. "It wouldn't be the same without my dear wife's family."

He snapped his fingers, and a waiter placed a fresh round of teacups on the table. A second waiter poured champagne from the teapot, and Bridget wondered how much Lawrence paid for the contraband. It wasn't that she was naïve enough to think Prohibition had eliminated the consumption of spirits. No. The truth was something closer to the opposite. But the subterfuge, the teapot, would not have come cheap.

Lawrence raised his cup. His eyes glittered under the glass chandelier. "I hope you don't mind. I've taken the liberty as I want to make a toast to my beautiful bride." They raised their cups, one by one. "To Bridget, my angel in white."

A tap on Bridget's foot made her look around at her sister. Although both Margaret and Bridget had found Louella's chilling tale hard to believe, neither could discount the coincidence of the endearment he favored. Margaret seemed particularly unsettled when Bridget had finished telling her about her visit to Lawrence's first wife.

"Have you spoken to him about Louella?" she'd asked.

"I didn't tell him I went to see her, if that's what you mean."

"No. About what happened between them."

Bridget had nodded. "One time. He told me she tried to harm herself. More than once. That he had to have her committed. He said it was the hardest thing he'd ever had to do, but it was for her own good."

Margaret had considered what she'd said. "Did you believe him?"

"It made sense. And the marriage was annulled. So . . ."

"And yet you went to see her." She'd held Bridget's hands in hers. "Why?"

Having no answer, she'd felt foolish and changed the subject again. "We should be going."

"Lawrence can wait, Bridget. Tell me. Why did you go see this woman?"

Bridget had tried to pull away, but Margaret wouldn't let her. It was a question she'd asked herself. Was it because Lawrence was a man who spoke too often of himself? Or was it because she'd heard harsh judgment in his words whenever he complained of a business deal or some other trade? Or maybe because she'd seen the way his face colored in anger when he didn't get his way? Aloud, she'd said, "I wanted to find out for myself."

"And did you?"

With a slow roll of her head, Bridget had told her the truth. "I don't know."

Now, Bridget sat with her new husband and her family under the glow of a twinkling chandelier. Waiters hovered nearby to attend to their every need. Lawrence stood, clutching his cup.

"To my wife. May she be forever remembered as she is on her wedding day, as pure as the driven snow, as lovely as the freshest flower, as sweet as a Lord Baltimore Cake."

Bridget's cup shook in her hand.

"To you I pledge my undying love."

"How sweet," Catherine said.

"May we never be parted in life or death." Raising his cup with a flourish, he added, "To Bridget."

Margaret held her cup without drinking. Charles bent toward his wife, but Margaret waved him away. "I'm fine." She lifted her cup higher. "To Bridget," she said. Lawrence arched his brows. "May she be forever loved for who she is, for her imperfections, for her wicked sense of humor, for her inability to hum a tune, for her stubborn ways, for her love of even the weakest of creatures." Bridget stole a glance at her new husband. Although the expression on his face remained unchanged, the fingers wrapped around the handle of his cup whitened. "And not—"

"Thank you, Margaret," Bridget interrupted. She loved her sister more in that moment than ever, but she suspected Lawrence would not tolerate much more. "I'm so lucky to have you, but now it's my turn." She shifted back toward her new husband. "To Lawrence. Thank you for believing in me always and for your devotion. May all our days be bright and happy." Bridget drank from her cup and hoped it was enough.

Catherine got to her feet. "Should we all make a toast then? To Lawrence and Bridget," she started. Her words droned on. Bridget stared at the table and the cups and the silver.

The toasts ended. New plates replaced the old. Bridget picked at her halibut with a fork.

Lawrence reached over and touched her hand.

"Do you like your ring? It's not too big, is it?"

She studied the foreign object on her finger. The thin gold band caught the light, a shiny reminder of the vows she'd made. "It's fine."

"Is anything wrong?" he asked. He kept his voice low.

Without looking, Bridget knew Margaret was watching, worrying. She did her best to assuage both their minds. "Nothing is wrong. I'm a bit tired is all. I didn't sleep much last night."

"Don't tell me. Wedding jitters?" he asked, his voice tight.

"I suppose." She forced a chuckle, fumbling for the right words. "Margaret told me she couldn't sleep the night before she married Charles, either. She was so worried she'd trip or something."

He stroked his mustache. "And what was it *you* were worried about, my little angel?"

She dropped her hands to her lap. "Oh, it's too silly to say."

A vein pulsed at his temple. "I'm your husband now. Are you going to keep it a secret from me?"

Every part of her went still. She'd been right. He was angry. She did the only thing she could. She lied. "I was worried you weren't as happy as I was."

Lawrence stilled. "Why would you be afraid of that?"

"You could have had your pick of women. I'm so young and inexperienced compared to the others." This much she believed to be true. Despite having been married before or maybe because of it, Lawrence had suffered no shortage of potential would-be brides. His stony face was handsome enough, and he cut an impressive figure in his waistcoat and top hat. And he had money.

"I didn't want the others. I wanted you."

Why? The question was on the tip of her tongue, but she bit back the word. Bridget wasn't sure she wanted to know. Aloud, she said, "Well, now you know what kept me up half the night."

"And at the church today?"

She rubbed at her hands, remembering the way he'd pressed into the bones of her fingers. She kept her voice light. "Nerves, I'm afraid. I'm so sorry. I was so nervous I couldn't talk at all."

He sat back and pulled his pipe from his vest pocket. Around them, she heard the clink of silver and low hum of conversation. Under the table, her legs trembled, and she thought how much she would like to slide under the canopy of tablecloth and disappear.

"You embarrassed me today," he said. "Standing up there. Everyone watching."

In an instant, she was back at the altar, afraid to speak her vows, afraid not to. "I'm sorry. That was not my intention. I hope you can forgive me."

Lawrence tapped his pipe against his palm. "Well, what's done is done."

She exhaled. "It's good of you to understand."

"I trust it will never happen again."

Although he hadn't shouted or couched his words in a harsh tone, it didn't matter. Bridget understood the meaning behind the declaration. "No, Lawrence."

"Good girl." He laid his hand over hers. The cool pads of his fingers slid across her skin, and a chill crawled up her spine. "No more reason to be worried or nervous. As my wife, you belong to me now. Nothing—and no one—will ever tear us apart." Lawrence lifted her chin with his finger and brought his face close to hers. "I promise you that."

CHAPTER
17

VAL
Tuesday, 8:38 a.m.

I avoid the mirror in the hall and suck down my fourth cup of coffee, savoring the bitter tang. I've been up since four, making notes and writing down everything I can remember. I push aside the half-eaten piece of toast, gather my notebooks and a handful of photos, and move to the front window to wait. Unsurprisingly, Terry arrives on time. Sliding into the passenger seat, I see Terry's mouth set in a hard line, his hands locked over the steering wheel. Silent, he pulls out into the last of the morning traffic.

The blanket of clouds in the sky matches my mood, and I'm glad I grabbed a scarf on my way out. The Franklin isn't far—ten minutes by car. I considered walking, but it's chilly, and I didn't want to waste the time. And Terry offered. The sooner I see those recordings, the better. As we get closer, I lean forward, craning my neck to see. The hotel is built from brick and white stone with tall windows and arched lines. An elaborate crown sits atop the fourteenth floor. The name, the Franklin, is etched in stone above the covered entrance. Oversized lanterns hang over the Roman-style letters. A man in a red and black uniform stands on the carpet near the smoked glass doors. For some reason, the forced smile on his face reminds me of an old Eagles song, the one that says you can check in anytime you want but never leave. I take deep breaths and tell myself it's only a hotel—a nice one, sure— but still just a brick building like any other on the block. It's not the reason my sister is gone. I've walked by this hotel countless times. I've had drinks in its famous Juniper Bar, though it's more of a tourist destination now than a local favorite. It's a hotel, nothing more. The car comes to a stop, and I feel better.

"You okay?" Terry asks.

"Fine."

The man in the uniform takes Terry's keys and hands him a ticket. I don't wait. Another uniformed employee opens the heavy door for me. Inside, I tilt my head upward, taking in the lobby ceiling. Three stories high, it's painted in black, gold, and red, the dark colors reflected in the heavy chandeliers. The lobby itself is a swirl of deep couches and shiny marble offset by a massive stone fireplace where orange flames dance and crackle. I have to give it to the decorators. They've created an atmosphere that's both rich with history and modern and inviting at the same time. But standing there, all I know is this hotel is the last place my sister ever saw.

Terry appears at my side. "I always forget how fancy this place is."

"You don't like it?"

He jerks his thumb toward the sculptures carved into the walls. "I don't like those." I glance back at him. His expression is grim—not admiring or even approving.

"It's art."

"If you say so."

"Seems like you don't appreciate the Franklin all that much."

"It's not really my style," he says, but there's a steely set to his jaw and a hardness in his voice I haven't heard before. For a moment, I wonder what I'm doing here, why I'm standing with a man I've known for less than twenty-four hours in the last place my sister was alive. When he mentions the video, I remember. If I want to find the truth, I need him.

"Billy texted he's in a meeting," he says, waving his phone at me. "He'll be out in about twenty minutes. Sorry about that." He points at a golden couch. "We can wait over there."

My gaze sweeps past the couch and the marble to the elevators. The doors slide open, and guests spill out. "There's something else I want to do instead."

"What's that?"

"I want to see the room. Sylvia's room."

"It's still sealed."

"I want to see it."

He sighs. "I thought you might. Billy got us cleared. There should be a key waiting for us at the front desk."

I stare at him. "How did you—"

"I'm getting to know you." At the desk, the clerk hands Terry an envelope. Inside is a note and card key. Terry reads the note, then stuffs it in his pocket.

"What's it say?"

"Room number."

In the elevator, he pushes the button. Fourteen. I step closer. The numbers skip from twelve to fourteen. I know this trick, one that's common during renovations of old buildings and hotels like this one. Sometimes they use 12A and 12B or some other nonsense, but I'm not fooled. It doesn't matter what you call the floor. It's still number thirteen.

The doors slide open, and I follow him down the hall.

"Is this it?" I ask. There's no crime scene tape or extra lock, nothing to keep someone from entering other than a single Do Not Enter sign hanging from the door.

He holds up the key. "Yep."

"I thought you said it was sealed."

"Figure of speech."

"Bullshit. If they were treating this like a potential homicide, there would be tape. It would be sealed."

"Not necessarily. It's locked to guests. Staff have been instructed to stay out. There's no reason for tape."

I notice the way he stands a few feet back from the door. "What's wrong?"

"Nothing. Are you sure you want to do this?"

"Why wouldn't I?"

He searches my face as he speaks. "She's not in that room, Val."

"I know that." I force a laugh. "I'm not crazy. It's not like I believe in ghosts or something." The way he flinches, I think my words make me sound exactly that. Crazy. "I have to see it," I say. "Please."

With a nod, he waves the key in front of the door and pushes it open.

I step inside and gag, slapping my hand over my mouth. Even though it's been five days since Sylvia was found, the sickly, sharp odor of decomposing flesh still lingers under the scent of bleach and Pine-Sol. "Oh, Syl," I whisper.

He lays a hand on my shoulder. "You don't have to do this."

I breathe through my mouth and tell myself this is no time to be a wimp. "Yes, I do. For Sylvia."

I leave him at the door and pull open the curtains, bathing the room in warm light. I take my notebook from my bag. The room is large, a suite. A sitting area is outfitted with a sofa, two chairs, and a flat-screen TV. There's a bar area and a half bath. I write in my book. Expensive room. This is another reason I can't understand my sister being there. Tight as a tick doesn't even scratch the surface when it comes to Sylvia and money. Terry's question from the night before echoes in my head. Why would Sylvia book a suite for herself?

The bedroom has another flat screen and a king-sized bed. The bedding and mattress are gone now. I walk closer and try to imagine Sylvia here, watching a movie, reading, working. I can't get my mind around it, can't reconcile her being here at all. I make my way to the bathroom. There's a massive shower, a soaker tub, and double sinks with brass fixtures that wink under the lights. It's a bathroom for two. The thought makes me push aside the towels and peer under the sink, but there's nothing to find. Whatever personal effects were there are gone now.

"Is it cold in here to you?" Terry calls out from the suite's doorway when I come out of the bathroom.

I want to ask him how he would know, since he's barely stepped inside the room, but I don't. Reaching out with my hand, I touch the headboard and close my eyes. This is where she was found. I can feel him watching me from the other room, sense his discomfort. He thinks I'm crazy, but I'm not. I'm not trying to channel her spirit. I know she's gone, and yet, I want to feel her presence, be where she was, to trace her footsteps, to find out the truth.

Terry's phone buzzes. "He's ready for us."

I turn away from the bed, the last place my sister was alive. The suite is cold—Terry is right about that. And empty.

"You didn't look around," I say, catching up to him in the hall.

"The police already cleared the room." His answer is quick, though I don't consider it satisfactory. He was a cop once. Surely, he should have wanted to see something. The elevator starts its descent, and his shoulders loosen with each floor. I start to ask why but change my mind. He's all business now, and whatever his problems are, I have enough of my own.

The security office is on the mezzanine that overlooks the lobby. Screens line a long wall. On the first row of monitors, I see a view of the front entrance, another facing the elevators, another of the laundry facility, and yet another that looks to be outside the restaurant downstairs. Three men sit in front of the computers and control panels. The largest of the men gets up to greet us.

"Terry, my man. It's been too long."

I watch them shake hands, exchange a few words. Terry asks about the man's family and the job. I'm forced to wait, and I drum my fingers against my bag until Terry introduces me.

Billy leads us to a corner of the large office where a single monitor sits on a desk. He taps on the keyboard as he talks. "I went back to the day you said the deceased checked into the hotel. That would be Sunday. Check-ins don't begin until after three, so that's where it starts." A frozen image of the lobby appears on the monitor. He points at some buttons. "Fast forward. Pause. Zoom. You can rewind to where the recordings begin."

"Where do they end?" Terry asked.

"When she was found." His eyes cut to me, then back to Terry. "Just like you asked."

CHAPTER
18

TERRY
Tuesday, 9:42 a.m.

Billy toggles another key, and I do a quick mental calculation. There are almost one hundred hours of recorded video in the time Val's sister checked in until her body was found. Per camera. We could be here for days.

"This is the camera for the main elevators," Billy says. "You can go back and forth between these two recordings."

I gesture at a series of screens on the other side of the room. "You have more than these two cameras. Is there anything on the fourteenth floor?"

"Can't give you that, Terry. The lobby is a public place. But upstairs gets into privacy stuff. We don't turn that over without a warrant. You understand."

"I figured. I appreciate your help, Billy."

"Sure. I'll leave you to it."

We sit down, and Val slips out of her coat. Her feet tap, bouncing up and down off the floor. I hesitate, suddenly worried this is a mistake. It's not too late. The coroner's report said overdose. Suicide. Val is convinced Sylvia was driven to do what she did, maybe even helped along. Am I getting her hopes up? Probably, and yet, I know she'll keep going until she's exhausted every avenue to find the answer with or without me. She's relentless that way. And I've come this far. "Ready?"

"More than ready."

I push play, and Val slides closer to the monitor, squinting at the screen. The lobby isn't particularly busy, which makes sense. It was a Sunday. Not a high travel day. Business travelers would be checking in for Monday meetings, but most of the leisure travelers would be gone. We watch as two men in suits enjoy drinks near the fireplace. A few other guests pass through and leave the hotel. After about fifteen minutes, someone comes in rolling a suitcase and heads straight for the main desk. Another ten minutes pass before there's another guest.

"Do you know what time your sister might have checked in?" I ask.

Val slaps the table. "God, I'm an idiot. I was at Sylvia's when she was packing. She scheduled a ride to pick her up at five thirty."

"Okay. Allowing drive time to get to the hotel, she couldn't have checked in until close to six."

"Go to five forty-five," she says.

I hit the button and the action on the screen speeds up. She taps her feet faster and with my free hand, I fiddle with a pencil. At the five forty-five mark, I stop the recording, restarting it at normal speed. At five minutes before six, a woman walks through the doors. I recognize her from the photo on Sylvia's mantel. She's older now, but it's her. Val inhales, and her foot goes still. There's a softness to her face as she watches the action on the monitor. Onscreen, Sylvia walks toward the desk, pausing halfway to look up at the painted ceiling.

The camera catches a clear shot of Sylvia's face.

"Stop the tape." She presses her body as close as she can. "Zoom in."

With the mouse hovering over Sylvia, I enlarge the picture. Val reaches out and touches the screen with her fingers. The banter between the guards behind us fades into the background. She stares, unblinking, at her sister's upturned face. Her fingers fall away, landing on the desk.

"I can't believe that was one week ago. One week." The words are spoken so quietly, I have to tilt my ear toward her. She's crying again, but it's softer, more heartbreaking somehow. I find another handkerchief in my pocket. If she thinks it's old-fashioned, she doesn't say. She takes it and wipes her eyes.

"Do you want to keep going?" I ask.

Her foot bounces again. From across the room, I hear the crackle of a chip bag and the slurp of a soda. She focuses on the screen and sits up taller.

"Back up the tape to when she walks in and goes to the front desk," she says.

"Okay."

"Can you do it in slow motion?"

We watch her come into the hotel again, dragging her bag behind her. She stops to admire the ceiling, then spins around, presumably taking in the beauty and charm of the historic hotel. She heads to the front desk, passing directly in front of the camera. When she reaches the clerk, only her profile is visible. We watch her hand over her credit card and check in. Signing, she takes her key and grabs her bag, moving in the direction of the elevators. After a few steps, she stops and looks back at the desk clerk, who is waving a white envelope. Sylvia takes it.

"What's that?" Val asks.

"Something about the room?"

She shakes her head. "She didn't give an envelope to the other guests when they checked in."

Val is right. Sylvia is the first guest to receive an envelope. I watch as Sylvia steps to the side, opens the envelope, and pulls out a slip of paper. I watch her eyes brighten and see her face break into a lopsided grin, exactly like Val's. Whatever was in that note made her happy.

"Can you zoom in again?"

I do my best, but the angle of the camera makes it impossible to see what was on the slip of paper. Still, there's no denying that whatever the message said, it was welcomed.

Her foot smacks the floor. "Damn it."

"She's heading for the elevator," I say. "Let's switch over." I change the recording and fast forward, stopping it again as Sylvia comes onto the screen. She drags her suitcase to the doors and pushes the button. As she's about to step on, a tall man with dark brown hair runs over. She turns and smiles again. I hear the catch in Val's breath. The man leans in for a hug.

"Do you know him?" I ask.

"No. At least I don't think so. It's hard to see."

I slow the tape, but the man doesn't turn around enough for us to get a clear view. For one brief second, there's a partial profile. He lays an arm over her shoulder, and they step into the open elevator together. The doors slide closed.

She doesn't need to ask me to rewind again. I play the scene twice more, but there's no clear view of the man. We switch recordings again. He's not on the tape that captures the lobby and front desk.

"Where did he come from?" she asks.

"Isn't the restaurant down the hall from the elevators?"

She looks over at me. "So, you're thinking he was having dinner?"

"Or drinks at the bar. I don't know where else he could have come from."

"She knew him." Her voice is tinged with wonder and sadness, and I understand. Whoever the man was, Sylvia was happy to see him, yet he was a stranger to Val.

"Seemed like it."

"Do you think that's the boyfriend? S. M.?"

"It would make some sense." I spin around in my chair to face her. "But let's not make assumptions too soon. If they're together, they might come back down in the elevator for dinner, and we can get a better view."

Her hands tap along with her foot. "Good idea. Let's focus on the elevators for now."

We watch the recordings at a faster speed to save time. The elevators are busy with new guests arriving and others going up and down to the restaurant or the lobby. In spite of the monotony, I can't look away any more than Val. Time passes, and I make notes. I want to know about the envelope and the man on the elevator. More time passes, and still, Sylvia doesn't come down.

"She might have ordered room service," Val says.

"We can check." I stand up, stretching my legs. "Do you want some coffee?"

Val tells me yes, her gaze never leaving the screen.

"Let me know if I miss anything." I'm joking, but she doesn't laugh.

It feels good to get out of the security room, even for a few minutes. I've seen my share of homicide victims, beatings, weird stuff. But there's something unnerving about watching the last hours of someone's life play out on a screen. As I walk down the hall, I remember the Juniper, the hotel's bar and nightclub. It's on the mezzanine too, the same floor as the security office. It hits me that Sylvia may not have gone to the restaurant after all. She could have come here, to the second floor and the Juniper. Grabbing a couple of coffees, I make a mental note to tell Val about my idea.

The security doors slide closed behind me and I cross over to our corner. "Val," I say, touching her lightly on the arm.

She reaches back to take the cup, half turning, one eye still on the monitor. The cup nearly slips from her hand as she jerks forward. "Oh, my God."

"What?" I ask as I sit down.

"Stop the tape. Now." I press the button. "Back it up," she says, and I rewind. "There. Hit play."

I scan the screen, but I don't know what Val is seeing. I check the time stamp on the recording. Eight thirty-nine. It's been almost three hours since Sylvia checked in and took the elevator up in the company of a man with dark hair. The time clicks over to eight forty. A man enters the screen, his face in profile.

"I knew it," Val says, her voice a half growl.

Pointing at the man, I ask, "Him?"

"Yes."

The man has a black computer bag hanging over his shoulder. He pushes the elevator button and glances behind him, surveying the lobby.

"Freeze it."

I stop the recording again. Val's skin has gone white. It dawns on me then. "Is that the husband?"

"Yes," she says, choking out the words. "That's him. Wyatt."

1921

CHAPTER
19

BRIDGET

Bridget clung to her sister, hot tears slipping over her cheeks. Margaret's husband looked on and clucked his tongue. "Supposed to be a happy day, right? Women," he said with a measure of wonder. "I'll never understand 'em."

Bridget heard Lawrence's displeasure in his silence, and still, she didn't let go. It was her mother who forced them to separate.

"Bridget, darling, give your mother a hug," Catherine said, tapping her on the shoulder. She spoke in the kind of singsong voice that made Bridget wonder if her mother had drunk too much champagne at lunch. "Your father and I want to wish you our very best."

Margaret pulled her tighter, shifting her out of Catherine's reach. She whispered in Bridget's ear. "If you need me, I'll come. I promise. No matter what."

Bridget swallowed the lump in her throat. Her mother swooped in for a brief hug followed by an even briefer one from her father. Margaret's husband shifted from one foot to the other. Finally, he reached out and shook Lawrence's hand.

"Welcome to the family then. Guess we'll be seeing you 'round at the holidays."

"The holidays?" Lines appeared between Lawrence's brows. "Well, I usually spend the holidays at my farm."

Catherine clasped her hands together. "Did you hear, dear? The holidays at the farm. Wouldn't that be nice and cozy?"

Bridget's father frowned, the ends of his mustache twitching. "Why would I want to travel thirty miles for the holidays when my home is right here?" He looked over at his new son-in-law. "No offense there, my boy."

"None taken, sir." Lawrence's forehead cleared.

"The country would be a lovely place to spend Christmas," Margaret said.

"I agree, dear," Catherine trilled. "And clearly Lawrence is the most thoughtful of husbands, inviting us so Bridget won't miss us too much." Lawrence cleared his throat, but Bridget's mother didn't notice. "Don't you see, dear? We absolutely have to go to the country this year for Christmas. For Bridget." The sisters exchanged a glance, and Margaret winked.

"Darling," her father said, taking his wife's arm. "I think it's high time we left these newlyweds on their own."

Catherine pushed out her lower lip. "Not until you say you'll think about it."

"Think about what?"

Bridget stole another glance at her sister. Both knew their father was deliberately being obtuse.

"Going to the farm for the holidays." Catherine turned her attention to Lawrence. "Tell him you insist, dear."

All eyes shifted to Lawrence. Every muscle on his face appeared frozen, even as he gave a short nod. "I insist, George. It would mean a lot to me and to my wife, I know. I'd enjoy showing you around."

For the first time, their father seemed to consider the idea. "Well, with an invitation like that, I will certainly think about it. Might be a nice change of scenery."

"Glad to hear it," Lawrence said and shook his new father-in-law's hand.

"We'll be there too," Margaret said, her voice overly loud. "That is, if we're invited."

Catherine cut in, oblivious to Lawrence's growing irritation. Bridget fidgeted where she stood. "Of course you're invited."

"I may even come early for some sister time," Margaret said, her words directed toward her new brother-in-law. "If it's all right with you?"

Lawrence's jaw tightened. "Sister time?"

Margaret's husband touched a hand to the small of his wife's back. "Well, darling, that depends on—"

"The holidays are only a few weeks away," Margaret said, cutting him off. "It will be the perfect time for travel."

"It's settled then," Catherine said and clapped her hands like a child.

Bridget kept her head down, hiding her joy at this welcome development. She whispered a silent thank-you to her drunken mother and her clever sister.

"All together for the holidays," Catherine sang, grabbing at her husband's arm. "Isn't it wonderful?"

"Wonderful," her father said. "And with that, we'll be going." Margaret lingered long enough to squeeze Bridget's hands before catching up to her husband.

Bridget followed them to the door and stepped over to the large window, watching them through the glass. Margaret lifted one gloved hand. Bridget pressed her palm to the window, her throat tight with unshed tears. She watched the automobile pull away and motor up the road, out of sight. She stood unmoving for several minutes, her breath fogging the glass.

From behind, Lawrence placed his hands on her shoulders. She jumped, and he pressed his mouth to her ear. "Nothing to be nervous about, my angel."

She forced herself to relax, keep her tone light. "I'm not. At least no more than any other bride, I suppose."

"Be that as it may, there's no hurry to get to our rooms." He spun her around. "I thought you might enjoy a tour of the hotel first. The truth is, I've stayed here so often it's become something of a second home to me." He held out his arm to her. "Let me show you around, my love."

He led Bridget through the lobby, talking all the while. "As I recall, the artist who painted the ceiling is European. They brought him over from France just for that purpose."

She gazed up at the intricate design. It was very pretty but too dark for her taste. She liked the chandeliers better. Their glass pendants glowed orange and red and yellow, reflecting the flames crackling in the large fireplace.

"And the sculptures in the stonework," he said, walking on. "Aren't they magnificent?"

"Who are they supposed to be?"

He laughed. "All in good time. The man who built the hotel was Albert Franklin. He built his fortune in shipping and traveled all over the world. Certainly, you can see he's been influenced by European design."

"Yes," Bridget said, although she knew little of architecture.

"Well, the story is that the man who built the hotel was enamored of all things Roman. So, each of these statues is one of the gods of Rome. There are twelve in all." His hand hovered over the sculpture closest to them. "Here is Vulcan, the god of fire. And there's Pluto and Jupiter." He steered her around the lobby. "And here is Cupid, the god of love."

She peered at the cherubic figure with its bow and arrow and frowned. "It's a bit silly when you think about it, isn't it? A child as the god of love?"

Lawrence gave her an indulgent smile. "I suppose you're right." He showed her the remaining sculptures, naming them as he walked. Then he pointed at the floor. "The marble is Italian and was brought over by ship."

She whirled around on her toes. In spite of herself, he'd brought the hotel to life. "How do you know all this?"

"I know a great many things, my angel. A great many things." They climbed the staircase to the second floor and passed by a ladies' parlor. "Perhaps you might take tea in there before we leave tomorrow."

She peeked into the sunny room. Tall windows lined the far wall, the heavy glass glittering in the light. Cloths with delicate flowers covered the round tables, and soft pastels adorned the walls and rugs. "Oh, I would like that," Bridget said and meant it.

"Then you shall." He sauntered further down the hall. "Over here is the famous Juniper."

"Juniper wasn't a god, was he?"

He laughed. "No, but the juniper tree is believed to have a strength of its own as a protector against evil."

She stepped closer. Tall juniper trees laden with berries were carved into the dark wooden doors. "What kind of room is it?"

"A gentlemen's club of sorts."

"Oh." Bridget knew what her new husband was alluding to—a place for men and their cigars and pipes and, in spite of Prohibition, alcoholic drinks. "What's it famous for?"

"Debauchery, of course." He stroked his mustache with his long, thin fingers. "But that's not what made it famous." He paused, lowering his voice. "There was a murder. Or so they say. So much for protecting against evil."

Bridget's hand rose to her throat. "A murder?"

"Two years ago, now. Over a woman, is the story." She cringed at the scorn in his voice. "Men with weak temperaments given too much whiskey, if you ask me." He sucked in his cheeks as he spoke, giving him the pinched look of a much older man. "Prohibition couldn't have come soon enough."

She knew better than to remind him they'd both indulged in champagne at their wedding lunch. Instead, she asked, "What happened?"

He guided her away from the doors. "No need for you to trouble yourself about it, my angel. Much too sordid a tale for your ears." Bridget started to object, but he cut her off, his voice hard. "I wouldn't want to think my new wife was fascinated by wanton ways and murder. I would be a terrible husband indeed to fill your pretty head with thoughts of evil men. Best if I say no more." His hand tightened over her arm, and she shivered in spite of the warmth of her wrap. "Unless you're not the woman I think you are."

CHAPTER
20

BRIDGET

"Please have the bellhop bring the bags to our suite," Lawrence said to the clerk. He slid two coins across the counter. "Exactly as I asked earlier."

The young man's response was quick. "Of course, sir. I have your instructions."

Bridget followed Lawrence to the small elevator. As the car rose, she watched the arrow on the dial tick higher, one floor after another. The elevator operator sat quietly in the corner.

"Are you nervous still, my angel?"

Could he see her doubts, her fear? Aloud, she said, "Not too much."

"But you're happy, aren't you?"

The elevator saved her from answering, ringing as they landed on the thirteenth floor. The operator cranked the door open, and Lawrence took her by the arm. Stopping in front of a tall wooden door, he slid a large, golden key into the lock. "Shall I carry you over the threshold, Mrs. Hartwood?"

Even as her knees threatened to give out, she squeaked out the answer she knew he expected to hear. "Yes, please."

Lawrence scooped her up in his arms in one quick motion. Her feet dangled over the floor, swinging with every step. Marching straight to the center of the suite, he set her down on a white tufted chaise longue.

He straightened and with outstretched arms, asked, "How do you like the room?"

Running a hand over the soft fabric and gilded trim of the chair, she let her gaze wander to the golden drapes hanging over the windows and the soft rugs adorning the floor. A chandelier, a smaller version of the ones in the lobby, lit up the room. "It's very beautiful."

He shrugged off his coat and vest, rolled up his sleeves, and gestured toward a small table set with silver plates, small sandwiches, and a bottle of champagne. "Shall I pour you a celebratory drink?" A knock on the door made him look around. "Our bags."

Bridget lay back against the soft cushion as he went to the door. There were voices, then silence, then voices again.

"This way," Lawrence said. The bellhop backed into the room, pulling a cart with several bags. "Sorry about the abundance of baggage. I've just been married, you see."

"Yes, sir," the boy mumbled. Struggling to maneuver the bags, he shuffled sideways, his profile coming into view. Bridget sat bolt upright. The boy's hair flopped over his eyes, escaping from the bellman's cap he wore. It couldn't be. She hadn't seen Joseph in weeks, not since he'd left the shop. Her skin burned hot at the memory.

What was he doing here?

"You can put the bags right here."

"Yes, sir."

"How are you liking this job, young man?"

"Fine, sir."

She winced at the smallness of Joseph's voice, and she was ashamed for him. Where was the laughing, bold boy she'd met?

"I suppose it's much better working here than working as a stock boy, now isn't it?"

Bridget gasped, and Joseph spun around. She looked from him to Lawrence and back again, and she knew. It wasn't smallness in Joseph's voice she'd heard. It was fear.

Lawrence shoved his hands into his pockets. "Well, isn't it? Better than being a stock boy?"

"Y-yes, sir."

"Precisely." He pulled out a single coin and laid it in Joseph's hand. "Wouldn't you like to congratulate my wife on our wedding? I believe the two of you know each other."

"Congratulations," Joseph repeated without another glance in her direction. "Will that be all, sir?"

"You may leave."

The door slammed shut. Bridget's skin burned again. Dizzy, she couldn't make sense of it. Lawrence knew Joseph. Lawrence knew they'd worked together. Joseph was afraid of Lawrence.

Lawrence popped open the champagne and poured himself a glass. He drained it and poured himself another. "How did you enjoy seeing your old friend, my dear?"

"How? What? I don't understand." She spoke in fits and starts, unable to put her questions into words.

He sipped from his glass. "How do I know Joseph? Well, do you remember when I first started coming by the shop to see you? It was no secret I was smitten the first time I saw you. On one of those days, I'd thought to surprise you with a walk, but it was I who was surprised. For you did go for a walk that day. With Joseph."

Her fingers curled over the edges of the gold-painted wood.

"Being as I had already made up my mind to make you my wife, naturally I followed you."

He'd followed her? She was light-headed, and her nails dug into the wood. "Why?"

Draining the rest of his champagne, he set his glass aside. "I asked you a question once before. You didn't give me an answer then, but make no mistake, you're my wife now." He crossed the room. His eyes, boring into hers, were the color of ink. "When I ask a question, you will answer me." Lawrence's fingers traced the bones of her cheek. "I'm asking you again. Have you ever kissed another man?"

Bridget pulled away, recoiling from his touch. The last time he'd asked, she hadn't known he'd followed her. Had he followed her beyond the entrance to the park? Down the paths they'd walked? To the pond? Had he seen Joseph holding Bridget's hand?

"I'm waiting for my answer," he said, seizing her by the wrist. She cried out, but he held tight. "Now, Bridget."

She shrank back against the cushions, looking wildly around the suite. There was nowhere to go and no way to escape. Worse, she knew he wouldn't let her even if she tried. There was nothing to do but answer. "Yes. Once. In the park the day you followed me."

His nostrils flared, and spit flew from his mouth. "Another man has touched you."

"Yes," she said, the word a whisper.

"Stand up."

Bridget clutched the cushion, her fingers digging into the upholstery.

"I expect you to do as I say when I say it, Bridget," he told her. She wondered if she'd imagined the playfulness in his voice in the lobby. Now, she heard nothing but ice, as hard-edged as stone. "Get up."

Her body trembling, Bridget pushed herself up.

"Not one kiss, Bridget. Two kisses."

She swayed on her feet, her knees knocking. In a blur of motion, his fist hit her in the stomach. She fell backward onto the chaise longue.

"That's for kissing another man." He raised his fist again. "This is for lying."

She covered her head with her arms and rolled away, but not before she heard the crack of a rib, then another. Struggling to breathe, she slid off the cushion, landing in a heap on the floor. Blackness descended.

PRESENT DAY

CHAPTER
21

VAL

Tuesday, 11:12 a.m.

Wyatt's face fills the screen. My hands shake as I watch Terry zoom in and replay the video. I've watched this scene five times now, and each time, I grow angrier and, to my surprise, a little sadder. "He's the father of my children, Val," Sylvia would say, even after everything that happened. "That will never change." It breaks my heart.

I think about one of the last times I saw Wyatt. He was with Dani, of course, standing in a line outside a movie theater. The minute I saw them, I slipped behind one of the trees that dotted the walkways of the outdoor mall. Her arm wrapped around his, her body pressed up close, no space between them.

If he minded the way she clung to him, he didn't show it. She tipped her blond head back to look up at him, red lips turned up in a smile. Her hair was longer than the other times I'd seen her, and she'd let her roots grow out in that way that was popular these days. She still looked like a blond Barbie doll, but a slightly edgier version.

I try now to remember when that was. Months ago, or only weeks?

Terry pauses the recording, plays it again, and I sit forward, drawn to the screen once more. Wyatt is dressed in khaki slacks and a golf shirt. He's carrying a black computer bag over his left shoulder. At the elevators, Wyatt pushes the button. While he waits, he glances over his shoulder. Once, twice, three times. I press my palms against the desk. "It's like he's looking for someone."

"Or something. It's hard to tell." Terry rubs his hand over his chin. "Let's start over from the beginning and watch it in slow motion."

Wyatt enters the picture from the direction of the lobby, his back to the screen. When he reaches the elevator doors, he looks around, his face visible. He's not quite scowling, and he's tapping his hand against his side.

"He's nervous," I say.

Wyatt presses the button. In slow motion, his actions are clear. His gaze sweeps over the lobby. It's quick, maybe a millisecond each time, but it's enough. His hand bangs against his leg. When the doors slide open, he checks behind him again. The lines between his brows smooth. He gets on the elevator. The doors close, and he's gone.

"He's definitely looking around," Terry says.

"For Sylvia? Or her boyfriend?"

"Maybe." He switches recordings. "Let's watch from the lobby camera. We should be able to see where he came from or if he was with anyone."

The idea makes so much sense, I almost kick myself. "Good idea."

Terry starts the lobby video fifteen minutes before we see Wyatt at the elevators. I stare so hard while we wait, the dry air stings my eyes. After several minutes, we see him come through the glass doors. Alone.

"He doesn't have any luggage," I say.

"You're right. Just the computer bag."

"Do you think he's checking in?" I ask.

Wyatt passes by the front desk, pausing once to cast another quick look around the lobby. Then he heads straight for the elevators. He's on this recording for less than sixty seconds.

"Not checking in," Terry says. He stops the tape. "So, that leaves a couple of possibilities. Either he already checked in or—"

I shake my head. "His apartment is a mile from the hotel. Why would he do that?"

"Why did your sister?" He doesn't wait for me to answer. "He's taking the elevator. Could be to a room, but it's possible he could be going somewhere else in the hotel."

"Like where?"

He doesn't think about it long. "I don't know, Val. The Juniper. Conference rooms. The gym?"

"He could take the stairs to the Juniper."

"True, but the elevator is closer."

Across the room, voices rise. A pair of security men change shifts.

"Why is he carrying a computer bag?" Terry asks. "Don't you think that's odd?"

My brain is whirling. I'm still focused on Wyatt acting nervous. "Lots of people carry computer bags."

"But why does he have it with him on a Sunday night? Does he work on the weekends?"

"How would I know?"

Terry either doesn't hear the snark in my tone or doesn't care. "What does he do for a living?"

"He's a lawyer."

Terry seems to think about this. "Is there any chance he could be at the hotel for a work meeting? I know a Sunday night would be unusual, and it's a little on the late side but not impossible."

"He's not that kind of lawyer. Estate law. Boring." I don't even try to hide my irritation now. "Are you defending him?"

"Val, we have to consider every possibility."

I don't care why Wyatt has his computer.

I care about why he showed up in the same hotel as my sister a few short hours after she checked in.

"We know he was following her, and here's proof he was doing it again. That's the only possibility I care about right now." I jab my finger in his direction. "And if you're trying to help me like you say you are, you would know that."

"If he was following her, why did he wait almost three hours to show up?"

It's a good question, but I know the answer to this one. "Because he took the kids to dinner like he does every Sunday night. He picks them up at six thirty and brings them back at eight. They were staying with my parents, so he would have dropped them off there." I don't like saying this, but I know Sylvia would be upset if I didn't give Wyatt his due. "He never misses time with the kids. Sunday nights are a tradition. Even when they were still married, he would take them out for special daddy time."

"So, he drops them off at eight, right?"

I nod.

"And where do your parents live?"

I give him the address.

"Oak Hills? That's about twenty minutes from here. Assuming no traffic, that would put him back at his apartment at approximately eight twenty. Maybe he changes. Maybe he picks up his computer bag. Then he drives over to the hotel."

"He would walk."

Terry takes that into consideration. "Allow fifteen minutes to walk then. That fits the timeline of when he showed up at the hotel."

I follow his logic, but I don't know why it matters. "Fine. He did all that."

"We need to establish he knew your sister was here. How did he know when she'd told everyone she was going out of town, and he was out to dinner with the kids?"

I rack my brain. It's a good question, and then I have it. I snap my fingers. "Easy. He followed her when she left her house."

"Why?"

"To see if she was meeting her boyfriend before she supposedly went out of town, or maybe to find out if the boyfriend was going with her. Either or both."

He picks up a paper clip and twists it into something unrecognizable. "The timing is possible. Your sister checked in before six, giving him plenty of time to get back and pick up the kids by six thirty."

"Exactly."

Terry, though, isn't satisfied. "He follows her and sees her enter the hotel with her suitcase. He would have known she was alone when she checked in. Why come back?"

A new realization hits me. "He knows she's lied about her business trip."

"He's angry?"

I open my mouth, but no words come. Verbalizing what I'm thinking is too horrible, too sad. Once upon a time, Wyatt and Sylvia loved each other. They had children together. Sure, he strayed, and the marriage ended, but that happened to couples every day. And Sylvia had moved on. She was dating. She was happy again. The old Wyatt would have understood. This Wyatt though, the one who followed his ex-wife at all hours and left hateful voice messages, wasn't the man my sister married. In his mind, she belonged to him. Still, was he really capable of what I was thinking? I shake off my doubts, remembering Sylvia's final text.

"It's possible he wanted to confront her boyfriend, or talk about the divorce, or something. Maybe he caught her before she came inside, and they argued . . ." My voice lets me down. Saying it is more difficult than I expected. I lift my chin. "Maybe I should call Detective Barnes."

Terry shoots me down. "There's nothing that suggests his presence in the hotel is anything more than a coincidence."

"But the way he was acting. Looking around like that. It's"—I pause, searching for the right word—"it's suspicious."

"But we can't prove he ever saw Sylvia." He gestures at the screen. "And the timing is wrong. The estimated time of death is Monday night or early Tuesday."

This detail has been confirmed in the ME's report. Unfortunately, the heat in my sister's room had been turned up to the highest temperature, making it difficult to give a more exact time of death.

"That's the next night," Terry is saying. "Not Sunday."

I slump down in my chair. "But if he isn't in the hotel because of Sylvia, then why is he there?"

"We could ask him."

"He'll lie. I know he will." The more I think about it, the more I realize Terry is right. What we have is next to nothing, but it is enough to convince me we need to keep digging. "Besides, asking him will tip him off that we're investigating."

"I agree. We wait."

I want to hug him in that moment. Maybe he's on my side after all. I've had my doubts more than once. "Thank you."

Terry pivots toward me. "Do you have a picture of Sylvia with you?"

"Yes."

"Good." Terry reaches for the keyboard and switches the recording to the elevator view. He rewinds the tape until Sylvia appears on the screen. He lets it play until the dark-haired man appears. Although there isn't a clear view of the man, he stops the tape, holds up his phone, and snaps a picture. He hits fast forward. When Wyatt's face pops up, he takes another picture. Terry pushes back and stands up. "Let's go."

I stare up at him. "But we haven't finished watching."

"It will take days to get through these recordings."

Although I know this, I don't move. "It's all we have right now. We need to keep watching."

"I disagree." He holds up his phone. "I've got another idea."

Terry and I stand outside the Juniper. The doors have been pushed open and the early lunch crowd has started to file in. "Why here?"

"It stays open later than the restaurant, and it's not on our camera feed. Maybe someone in here will recognize the man with your sister or saw them together at some point."

Too tired to argue, I shrug and follow him inside. We take two seats at the far end of the bar. A woman appears in front of us, the image of a juniper stitched on the breast pocket of her white shirt. "Here for lunch?"

I start to say no, but Terry interrupts me. "Yes. We'll take two menus."

She lays them on the bar in front of us. "What can I get you?"

"Iced tea," he says. Numb, I order the same. A minute later, she's back with the drinks and a basket of sugar. "How long have you worked here?" he asks.

"A couple of years."

He gives her a smile. "Gets pretty crowded, I bet."

She smiles back. I feel like a piece of furniture and shift on my barstool.

"Yeah. Especially the weekends. Tourists are always coming in, but we have a lot of regulars too."

Terry sips from his tea. "Do you mind if I ask you a few questions?"

The woman's face changes. "You a cop?"

"Retired," he says. "I run a security firm now."

"So, nothing official?" She looks past him to the hostess stand. A man in a blue suit stands next to a woman checking a list.

"No, but it is kind of important."

"Yeah? To you maybe." She tips her head toward two men who've taken seats at the other end of the bar. "I've got customers."

"We can wait."

With an eye on the man in the blue suit, she tells Terry she can't help him. "Sorry. I don't want to get in any trouble." Her hand lands on her belly and for the first time, I notice the slight swelling there. Behind her is a picture tucked into the corner of the glass. A little girl with blond curls and saucer-sized eyes. She dips her head. "I need this job."

"It will only take a minute of your time," he says. "I promise."

"Please," I say. She looks back at me now. The open, friendly expression she wore earlier is closed now. I lean forward, my hands clasped around the edge of the bar. "My sister died a week ago. She was staying here. I need to know what happened." My voice drops to a whisper. "I need to know why."

A range of emotions crosses her face in a fraction of a second. Surprise. Horror. Sympathy. "The suicide?"

Terry answers for me. "Yes. Room 1401."

She gives one shake of her head. "I don't know anything about that."

The man in the blue suit leaves, and her shoulders relax. One of the men at the end of the bar raises a hand to get her attention.

"Please," I say again before she gets more than a couple of steps away. "She has two children. A boy and a girl."

She slows and stops, muttering something I can't make out before swinging back around. "Look, I've gotta take care of these customers, but I'll come back." Her hand is back on her belly, her gaze softer. "Give me a few minutes, okay?"

Terry nods for me, lays his phone on the bar, and picks up the menu. I can't understand how he can think about food, but then I remember. It's not his sister who's gone.

The bartender is back. "I'm sorry about your sister," she says and wipes her hands on a towel.

I say what I'm supposed to, although I can't for the life of me figure out how it's supposed to help. "Thank you."

"I've only got a couple of minutes. That's all."

"That's all we need," Terry says, pulling up the picture of my sister with the dark-haired man. He holds it high enough for her to see.

"Is that her?" she asks.

He tells her it is. "I was wondering if you saw them together. At the bar maybe, or one of the tables."

"Sorry. Not on my shifts. I usually work lunch though. Someone could have seen her if she came in for dinner or drinks."

"Okay. Who works nights?"

"Benny and Marsha most nights. They'll be in at four thirty, when we change over."

"Okay." He taps the picture again, zooming in on the dark-haired man. "What about the guy?"

"Hard to tell. It's a side picture, and it's a little blurry."

"I don't have a better shot." He pulls the phone back.

"Wait."

My heart thumps. She's leaning closer to the phone. "It could be Steven."

"Who's Steven?"

"He stays here every other week. Some kind of salesman."

"What's his last name?"

She frowns. "Morgan or Morris or something like that."

My mouth goes dry, and the thump turns to a fast drum. S. M., the initials written on my sister's calendar.

Terry glances at his phone. "What makes you think it might be him?"

"The way his hair is parted. And the curl at the back of his neck. He wears his hair longer than most of the other businessmen that come in here, you know." She stands up straighter. "I'm not saying it is him. I'm saying it could be."

"Understood," Terry says. "Do you remember if he was here last week?"

"I think so, but I can't be sure of the exact days. Benny could tell you. Steven usually has a nightcap when he comes in after a date."

The hair on the back of my neck stands up. "He was dating someone in town?" I ask.

"That's what he said."

Terry scrolls back to the picture of Sylvia. "But you never saw him with this woman?"

"Nope."

Terry changes the picture. "What about this guy? Ever seen him?"

She studies the picture. "There's something familiar about him, but I don't think so."

"Can you look again?" Terry pushes the picture at her. "Same time frame. Last week."

"Sure. Why not?" After a few seconds, she taps the photo with her finger. "I remember now. He was the guy making a scene out in the lobby. I couldn't hear what he was saying, but it might have had something to do with his room and key or something. I don't know. They might have called security, but I'm not sure."

"Security?" I ask, the word sticking in my mouth.

"What day?" Terry asks.

"Last week. Monday or Tuesday maybe. During the day."

Terry and I exchange a glance. Sylvia checked in on Sunday evening, and Wyatt showed up a few hours later. "Not Sunday?" he asks.

"Definitely not," she says, no uncertainty this time. "Had to be Monday or Tuesday. I don't work Sundays."

CHAPTER
22

TERRY
Tuesday, 12:05 p.m.

Val hurries to catch up with me, her skin pink with the effort. "I agreed about not going to Barnes before, but after what we heard," she says, raising her palms. "I think this could change things."

"Maybe. But I thought you didn't want to tip your hand."

"That was before Wyatt was acting like a lunatic. The police should know that. This with the voice mails and text might make them take me more seriously."

"Possibly, but not necessarily." I slow but don't break stride. Val is right on my heel.

"It's not your decision to make." I stop and glance back at her. "She's my sister. Do you understand? Mine." Her hands are on her hips now. "And Wyatt is my good-for-nothing brother-in-law. He was stalking her. If I don't go to the police soon, they'll close the books on this case. I can't risk it. It's too important."

"Cases can be reopened."

"It won't be. You didn't hear Detective Newman. He doesn't even want to hear the possibility it's not suicide." Val's voice rises and her hands fly through the air, punctuating each word. "You don't know what he's like. He doesn't care about what happened. He'd have closed the case from day one if he could. I can't let that happen. Not yet. If Syl did," she pauses, choking out the words. "If she did what they say she did, I'll accept it. I will. But there are too many questions right now. And Wyatt being here at the Franklin—not once but twice—is a big one." She looks away from me then. "I can't give up until I know the truth."

A handful of hotel guests hovering nearby head toward us and the Juniper. I take her by the shoulders and steer her to a corner. "I understand, Val. But we need more than one minute of video and a bartender's word. You wouldn't go to press without more, would you?"

"Of course not. But I'm not asking Barnes to publish a story. I'm asking him to look into where Wyatt was and find out what he was doing in the hotel."

She's not wrong. On the other hand, there's still no evidence Wyatt was at the Franklin the day Sylvia died. The days don't line up.

"If Wyatt was stalking her the way it looks," she continues, "and he got up into Syl's room, if he forced her to take those pills . . ." She struggles to keep her voice from breaking. Val pauses before looking back at me. "It's a plausible theory based on his recent behavior, one the police might be interested in. Do you agree with that?"

"Yes, that's one theory."

"You have another?"

"S. M. Was he there? Did he leave her in the room? What's his role here?" Val is listening now, no longer glaring at me.

"I'll give you that. Theory two."

"Yes, and as much as you don't like it, there is still theory three. You said it yourself." Unassisted suicide, or theory three, is currently the only theory believed by the police and most everyone else. The sour look on her face tells me she doesn't appreciate the reminder.

"Is that all? Theories one, two, and three?"

It's not, but the fourth theory is one she would like even less, and I have no intention of sharing it right now. Instead, I say, "It's enough."

She stares at me for a moment before waving a hand back in the direction of the Juniper. "I'd like to see if we can find out more about Wyatt's movements and what the hell he was doing here."

"Back to theory one?" When she says yes, I offer a plan of action. "We go back to Billy then. If security was called, Billy should be able to tell us what the problem was. The bartender said something about a lost key. It's possible he had a hotel room of his own."

"To keep an eye on Sylvia." Val's face clouds. "God, this is so sick. Was he really following her, threatening her? He wasn't always like that, but ever since the divorce . . . I don't know anymore." Her voice drops. "She was his wife."

The depth of her disappointment touches me, but in my experience, domestic violence—in all its forms—has been around for a long time. "You'd be surprised what a husband can do to his wife." She visibly shudders, and I switch gears. "Theory one is not as farfetched as you would think, but neither is theory two." I don't wait for her to respond. I take her arm and lead her back to the security offices. "When we talk to Billy, we'll ask about Wyatt. But let's see if we can find out more about this guy Steven too. Maybe confirm the last name. If he was her boyfriend and they were together Sunday, where was he Monday night?"

"Fair enough." She counters with her own line of questioning. "We still haven't checked to see if she ordered room service. According to the detective, there was no activity on her credit card after she checked in. She had to eat. How much she ordered might tell us something."

I grin. She returns my smile, and a small measure of the anxiety she's worn is replaced by something else—something that suits her better—a driving curiosity.

We find Billy in the break room wiping chip crumbs from his mouth. I take the lead, starting with Wyatt and the reported outburst in the lobby.

"Yeah," the security chief says. "There was an incident at the front desk. It was Tuesday. I remember 'cause my son had a soccer game at four, and I was trying to get out of here early."

I hold up the picture of Wyatt from my phone. "Was this the man?"

"Yep. That's him."

"Can you tell us what happened?"

Billy shrugs. "Don't see why not. The guy goes to the front desk and tells the desk clerk he's lost his key. She asks him what room he's in."

Val takes notes.

"What room did he say?" I ask.

"The suite—1401." Billy shifts toward Val. "Sorry about your sister."

"Thanks." She nods, all business now. "Go on."

Billy clears his throat. "So, the guy gives her the room number, but as you know, that room was registered to your sister. He says it's his wife, but the clerk's not buying it."

"Why not?" I ask. "People do that, don't they? They don't always come in together."

"Sure. It happens, but the names didn't match."

I glance at Val.

"Sylvia had been using her maiden name," she says. "She always used it for business anyway."

"Okay. Well, he asks the desk clerk to call up to the room. She does, but there's no answer. He gets louder, says he's been trying to reach the woman, and she's not answering her cell either. He demands she make him a new copy of the key so he can check on her." Billy pauses, folds his hands together. "The clerk calls security. One of my guys takes your man aside, calms him down. While that's going on, I find out the woman checked in alone. She did get two keys, but lots of people do. Doesn't mean a thing. The thing was though, the lady asked to be left alone. She made a call to the front desk Monday night asking not to be disturbed. Said she wasn't feeling well. Didn't want maid service. Nothing."

Val presses for confirmation. "Are you sure Sylvia called Monday night?"

"Yeah, I'm sure. Eight fifteen, to be precise. The night staff put a hard hold on the room."

"What's a hard hold?"

"Don't disturb unless the hold is lifted. People do it for lots of reasons. It's not our place to ask."

"Did you tell Mr. Spencer that?" I ask.

"Sure. I told him there was a guest in that room who'd asked not to be disturbed, and since he was not a registered guest, I couldn't help him. Then we escorted him out. It was all nice and polite."

"Why didn't you mention this to the police?"

"I was going to, but they said things were pretty well wrapped up. Said it was suicide. Made sense at the time. The hold was still on the lady's room. Nobody had been in there as far as we could tell." He brushes the last of the crumbs off his fingers. "It was suicide, right?"

"One more question," I say before Val can interrupt. "You said she got two room keys when she checked in."

"That's what the system shows."

"And when they found her, how many keys did they find in the room?"

Billy blinks, his round face flushing. "One. That's all they found. One."

1921

CHAPTER

23

BRIDGET

Bridget lay on her side, her legs twisted under her body, her arms covering her face. She rolled a few inches, far enough to straighten, the effort an avalanche of hurt and shock. Her eyelids fluttered open. She took shallow breaths, each gulp of air bringing fresh pain.

She couldn't be sure how long she'd been lying there. Five minutes? An hour? She thought maybe she'd passed out, but even that was fuzzy in her brain. The room had darkened, grown colder. She heard the clink of glass and the whoosh of a bottle plunged into ice.

Footsteps sounded. She closed her eyes again. Bridget caught the scent of him—the sharp odor of tobacco and the saccharine, sweet smell of champagne—even before he reached her. There was the rustle of movement and the thud of his knees hitting the floor. Trembling inside, she willed her body to be still.

Lawrence bent forward and caught a lock of her hair in his hand, curling it over his finger. "I didn't want to hurt you, Bridget," he whispered. He spoke slowly, his voice soft, designed to soothe. It was the same voice that had proposed to her. The same voice that had promised to take care of her and cherish her. But she didn't believe that voice anymore. She knew the other voice now, the one that threatened, the one that inflicted pain. She bit the inside of her cheek to keep from crying out. He dropped the lock of hair. "I had to punish you. You understand, don't you? I couldn't abide the idea of you and that, and that . . ." His hand shot out toward the door, and he snorted. "That imbecile stock-bellboy person." His chest heaved as he spoke. "The very idea he touched you makes my blood boil. That you allowed it. Surely, no man should be expected to forgive such a thing."

Her body tensed. She waited.

A minute passed, and his mood changed again. He reached out and patted her head. "There, there. All will be well now."

How could all be well? The memory of his fists pounding into her flesh would never fade. The act could never be undone. She knew now. She should have listened to Louella. She should have believed her.

"Bridget, I know you're awake." He shifted his weight. "No wife of mine is going to lie on the floor like a common harlot," he said. He slid his arms under her and carried her across the room. His touch burned like a million tiny bee stings. He laid her out on the soft bed. "There. Isn't that better?"

She curled in on herself, a soft whimper escaping from her lips.

"Are you hurt, Bridget? Can I get you something?"

She buried her face in the pillow. She wouldn't look at him. She couldn't.

"Do I need to remind you that as my wife, you will answer me when I speak?"

Her insides twisted. She was afraid to open her mouth, but she was more afraid not to. "I would like to rest, please."

He took his watch out of his pocket and snapped it open. "Well, I suppose it has been quite a bit for one day, hasn't it? Weddings can be such tiresome affairs. It's no wonder that you might need a little rest." He trailed one finger down her arm. "And after you rest, we'll have our wedding night to enjoy."

Her tears dripped onto the pillow.

"While you rest, I'm going downstairs to have a cigar. And I'll swing by the cook to see about our wedding dinner. Pheasant would be wonderful, don't you think? And more champagne, of course." He crossed the room and slipped on his waistcoat. At the door, he paused. "Don't get any ideas about wandering around. Perhaps you've noticed the double-sided lock? One of the niceties of this grand hotel, wouldn't you say? We can't be too careful these days." She peeked out from under her hair. He pulled a room key from his pocket and unlocked the door. "One hour," he said. The door clicked shut behind him. The sound of the tumblers turning over echoed in the silence.

Sobs racked her body then, erupting from the bottom of her soul. Pain tore through her, and she wrapped her arms and elbows over her ribs. When her cries faded, an empty silence filled the room. From this, she took some comfort. She was alone.

The afternoon bled into evening. The chandelier cast a dim light over the length of the room. The empty champagne bottle had been turned over in the silver bucket. The sandwiches had been nibbled on and pushed aside. The washroom door was ajar, her bags next to it. She blinked. They'd been moved. The smallest, her overnight bag, stood open, its contents on the floor. The pale pink nightgown her mother had selected hung from a hook. Overwhelmed with the need to retch, she slapped her hand over her mouth. She had no one to blame but herself. She knew the truth of what she'd done. She'd married a monster.

CHAPTER
24

BRIDGET

With tentative hands, Bridget moved her fingers over her chest and belly, pressing down to find the source of the pain. Her stomach and ribs were tender and sore, but nothing seemed broken. She put her feet on the floor, forcing herself to stand, and took baby breaths to minimize the pain. Reaching the door, she turned the brass knob, but the lock caught and held. She looked around wildly, but there was no other key. Running back to the door, she pressed her ear to the polished wood, but the heavy door was too thick. She raised her fist, banging until the skin of her hand was red and hot. Bridget cried out, but there were no sounds other than that of her own voice.

Spent, she leaned against the door. Her gaze swept over the suite. "The window." She crossed the room slowly, her feet shuffling over the heavy rugs. She pushed the velvet drapes aside and laid her head against the glass. The streetlamps glowed in the dusky, evening light, casting miniature halos over the ground. What she guessed was a man and a woman walked south on the opposite side of the street, their heads close together. An automobile, so small from high overhead, rolled by, slowing at the corner before disappearing.

K. L. Murphy

Bridget pulled the curtains further apart. The tall window reached almost to the ceiling and was as wide as two doors. She ran her fingers up the edge until she found the latch. Her pulse quickened. She turned the lock and pushed the window open. Cold air rushed into the room. The velvet curtains rippled and settled again. Bridget lowered herself onto the marble windowsill. In the distance, she could make out the shape of the Fidelity Building on Charles and the clock tower on Lombard. She imagined she could smell the fish that arrived each day in the harbor. Ignoring the pain in her chest, she breathed in the night air.

Calmer, she took in the city. Lights twinkled from the houses and apartments, spreading out like a beaded fan. She'd never seen the city like this before. Leaning forward, she looked left toward the harbor, sure she could see the lights of the ships floating above the dark mass of water. She lifted her eyes upward, to the night sky, thick with clouds. A sliver of moon peeked out from behind gray clouds before vanishing again. She pulled her feet up onto the sill and swung her legs around. She inched forward until none of her remained inside the room. The frigid air blew back her hair and crept into her bones. Goose bumps rose on her arms and legs, and her body trembled.

She measured the lights and streets until she found her neighborhood. She told herself the brightest light shone from her house. She thought about growing up in that house, about her favorite rag doll and the garden out back and the silly secrets she shared with Margaret. She pictured Mother flitting about the house, chirping at them to quiet down and wash the dirt from under their nails. Bridget missed home, but she missed being with Margaret most of all. She remembered the way they'd walk to school together, hand in hand, giggling and skipping over stones. Bridget sighed. They were good memories to have. Her father would arrive home each evening a little after five. They would sit down to dinner at six, never a minute earlier or a minute later. After dinner, her parents would retire to the parlor, where her father would smoke his pipe and her mother would pull out her sewing. Margaret and she would lie in their beds, telling stories until they fell asleep. She leaned her head back against the glass of the window. What she wouldn't give to be that little girl again, to be home again.

Bridget's chin fell to her chest then, and she was ashamed. She should have been kinder. She should have appreciated her life more. Fresh tears fell, and she wrapped her arms over her knees. She wasn't a child anymore. She was married. What would life with Lawrence be like? Would she be isolated at the farm with only a handful of servants for company? Would she grow old and hollowed out like Louella? Fearful and skittish as a trapped animal? She shuddered at the truth of it. Lawrence wouldn't stop. What if she couldn't have a child? Or she lost it before it was born? Worse, what if another man spoke to her? She bit her lip. Life with Lawrence would be worse than dying. She was sure of that. She raised her head and looked down at the city. A handful of lights faded, went out. Her gaze shifted to the empty street. The roadway below was quiet, peaceful even. It could be over in seconds. Drawing herself up, she shifted sideways, her feet dangling high above the ground. Her fingers, stiff with cold, loosened on the ledge. Her lips moved silently in a forgotten prayer. She edged forward, the wind swirling around her, and let go.

PRESENT DAY

CHAPTER

25

VAL
Tuesday, 12:32 p.m.

Terry's brows furrow. "Has the other key turned up somewhere else? Maybe somebody found it in the bar or the restaurant?"

Billy tells us no. "But lost keys happen all the time." He rises, and a few potato chip crumbs fall from his shirt to the floor.

"Can you ask the maids if any random keys have turned up?"

"Sure," he says with a shrug and little enthusiasm.

I listen to the two of them talk about the missing key, and I'm not sure why it matters.

"My sister always requested two keys," I say. Both men look at me, and I straighten my shoulders. "It's not that weird. She was notorious for misplacing things. Sunglasses. Her phone. Keys. My father's the same way. There's a family joke that it's in the genes."

Terry wears an expression that tells me he's skeptical, but I'm inclined to agree with Billy. Keys get lost. So what? What does matter is Wyatt caused a scene trying to get up to my sister's room. A reasonable person might think I would take this as further evidence he'd been harassing my sister, but for some reason, this bothers me. A lot. Wyatt isn't that guy. And he's smart. Why would he draw attention to himself?

"Val? What are you thinking?"

My head snaps back to Terry. "I'm thinking we should move on from the missing key."

He waits a beat. I can't tell if he's offended or not, but I'm too tired to care. He jumps to the envelope Sylvia received when she checked in.

"Most likely a message someone left before she checked in," Billy tells them.

"Would you mind finding out?" Terry asks.

Billy agrees. Terry turns his attention back to me. "I want to find this Steven guy. Find out if he's S. M., what he knows. Theory two."

I want the same thing, but the ticking of the clock in my head is getting louder with each passing hour. I see the words "Closed" stamped across my sister's file.

"I've been thinking," Terry says, speaking slowly. "Why hasn't this guy she was dating come forward? Where's he been through this whole thing?"

I find myself nodding along with his questions. Have I let Wyatt and his erratic behavior distract me? I look toward Billy again, taking the lead this time.

"Can we show you a picture of a guest?"

"Don't know if it'll do much good. I don't interact much with the guests."

"He's not your typical guest. We think he's a regular."

Billy shifts his weight from one foot to the other, and the bulk at his waist sways with the motion. Even his jowls seem to move up and down. "What is it you're looking for?"

"My sister was seeing someone."

"Guess I gathered that."

"Right. The thing is, she was being secretive about it, and she might have been meeting him here."

"Secretive, huh?" Billy says.

Even though the man's expression is innocent enough, his tone has taken on a voyeuristic quality I don't like. "She was separated from her husband. The husband who showed up making a scene. She was dating again, but she didn't want him to know. That's all. He'd been following her. Threatening her. Maybe if you'd called the police when he was here before—" Terry places a hand on my arm.

"Domestic situations aren't a part of the job, Ms. Ritter," Billy says, his voice tight now. "Besides, if we called the police every time someone made a scene, management wouldn't be too happy. That's what they hired us for—to take care of it. That's what we did."

Before I can tell him what I think of how they took care of it, Terry defuses the situation. "We understand, Billy. No one is blaming you. You've already been a big help." He nods at me. "Isn't that right, Val?"

I stand silent. I know none of this is Billy's fault. Not really. I should tell him that, but I can't. He had Wyatt, and he did nothing. Nothing at all.

"Val's a little on edge," Terry says to Billy.

The security chief eyes me for a long minute, his thumbs hooked around the belt hanging low on his waist. He has the puffy skin of a man who likes to eat and drink more than he should, not necessarily in that order. Terry said he'd been a cop, like him, but I don't think I'm wrong in guessing they're cut from different cloths.

Billy strikes me as the kind of cop who struggled. His heart may have been in it, but he lacked the stamina and the stomach. For a man like him, the Franklin is a dream job. It's steady work and usually without the drama or the headaches that are a daily occurrence in the life of a Baltimore homicide detective. It wouldn't be a stretch to say he's probably already regretting letting us in—or at least me. Even so, he appears unflustered by my implied accusation.

His thick shoulders rise and fall in single motion. "Well, we all got our issues, don't we? My wife says ain't none of us who don't take a little getting used to." He gives a short laugh. "It's been twenty years, and I don't know that she's used to me yet."

There's a hint of southern twang when he talks. It's not obvious every time, coming and going, but enough that I know he didn't grow up in the city. The slow lilt of his voice now reminds me of long-ago days and warm, sunny vacations with Sylvia and my parents. Images of sandcastles and frothy waves and picnic baskets filled with homemade sandwiches and colas fill my head.

I shake away the memories before either man notices.

Terry is holding up his phone to show Billy the picture of the dark-haired man with my sister. "Do you recognize this guy? We think he might have been the boyfriend."

"Can't say I do."

"What about the front desk? Can we ask them?"

Billy's face clouds. "They can't tell you anything even if they recognize him. Invasion of privacy."

"How about a name at least?"

"Nope. Need a warrant for that."

Terry isn't ready to give up. "How about this? You go downstairs and show the picture. If they know him, you contact him. Not us. That way, you haven't told us his name."

"I don't know. What would I say to the guy?"

"Nothing. You call him and tell him we want to ask him a few questions. If he doesn't want to talk to us, he doesn't have to. You keep the information to yourself, and no one gets in trouble."

It's a reasonable request. Billy shoves his hands in his pockets. "I guess I can do that," he says slowly. "If it helps the lady find out what she needs to know."

He doesn't say it with any guile or sarcasm, and whatever wall of resentment I'd erected crumbles. A little. "Thank you," I say.

"What about the husband?" Terry asks me.

Wyatt. He hasn't picked up my calls or returned them. The things he may or may not have done eat at me in spite of my resolve to focus on the facts. I can't forget that last text or those horrible phone messages. Sylvia put a brave face on things, but she also lied to everyone. To me. For the briefest of moments, I wonder what else she was hiding.

"Maybe we should split up for a while," I say. "You and Billy see what you can find out about this guy Steven, and I'll see if I can track down Wyatt."

Terry shoots me a look of doubt. "Are you sure you don't want to wait? I can come with you."

"Nope. I got it." I scoop up my coat and sling my purse over my arm, fresh determination shooting through me like a jolt of electricity. "I'll be back in an hour."

I don't get ten steps from the hotel when I see him. He's halfway down the block, huddled under an overhang, his face shrouded in shadow. He's peering at the hotel, his head tilted back. I follow the direction of his gaze, and the coffee in my gut churns. He's looking at the suite, the one where Sylvia died.

A large group exits the restaurant where he stands, and I lose sight of him. I start walking, keeping my eyes peeled, but he's swallowed up in the small crowd. There's a flash of movement and the figure of a man in a dark coat slips around the corner. It's him.

"Wyatt," I shout, breaking into a run. I dart through traffic, barely hearing the blare of the horns. The crowd near the corner disperses into groups of two and three and I shove my way through. "Wyatt!"

I round the corner, pulse pounding, and scan the street. There he is. I shout again. He doesn't hear me, or ignores me, and turns right onto the next block without a backward glance. I run faster, my boots pounding on the pavement. My breath ragged, I slow on the next street, searching. Cars move steadily in both directions, and the sidewalks are busy with businessmen and women heading to meetings or lunches, shoulders hunched against the wind blowing in from the harbor. I dodge and weave, but I don't see him. I keep going. My skin under my sweater is sticky with sweat now. Huffing, I tell myself he can't have gotten far. I check the windows of every restaurant and store I pass, but still, I don't see him. Walking closer to the water, I catch sight of a man in a dark coat ducking into a cab. I start to run, but stop as it pulls away, too far ahead for me to catch up.

When I catch my breath, I pull out my phone and dial, but it goes right to voice mail. I click off before the greeting can get past his name. I grab the next cab and head to his office building.

"I'm sorry," his assistant says. "Mr. Spencer isn't in right now." I was so sure he'd been going back to work that I can't speak for a minute. "Is there something else I can help you with?"

Finally, my mouth works again. "Angela, I'm Val, Sylvia's sister. Maybe you remember me? We met at the Fourth of July party about a year and a half ago." I have no idea if we actually met, but I haven't forgotten the way she followed Wyatt around the party, waiting on him and bringing him food, disappearing whenever Sylvia was nearby. With dark hair that hangs to the middle of her back, high cheekbones, and red lips, she reminds me of a Hollywood actress, although I couldn't say which one. That day, she wore a sundress and heels—designer if I had to guess—that were better suited for the private dining room at a club than a family-friendly cookout. Sylvia and I talked about it after.

"It's kind of cute," Sylvia said.

"Cute? She's a grown woman."

"Young woman, Val. Don't you remember being that age? Didn't you ever have a crush on a teacher or a boss?"

"Eww. No."

Skepticism tinged her voice. "Well, you aren't normal then."

"Did you?"

"Sure. Professor Healy. Twentieth-century lit." I gaped at her then. It was the first I'd heard of it. "Don't ask," she said. "Leave Angela alone. She's just a kid." But that was before Wyatt proved himself untrustworthy—before Sylvia began to wonder.

I mention the holiday picnic again. "It was at one of those estates outside the city. There was a clown and a juggler."

Her lips part, and her hand comes up. "Oh, my goodness. I should have recognized you." The phone on her desk rings, but she ignores it. "I'm so, so sorry about your sister."

"I appreciate that. As you can imagine, this is all very difficult, and there are the children . . ." I let my voice trail off for effect. God forgive me, it's all I've got.

"Yes, Wyatt's been so upset. Devastated really."

I bet he has, I want to say, but I bite back the words.

"He talks about the kids all the time. Merry and Miles, right? I mean, most of the lawyers in this office, you'd never even know they had kids if you didn't see them once a year at that picnic."

My God, is she gushing? Is this what happens when you hire an assistant fresh out of school?

Angela is still talking. "But Wyatt isn't like that." She waves a hand toward the office behind her. Her dark hair swings like a curtain each time she moves. "There's like a thousand pictures of the kids in there. He's a great dad. Anyone can see it."

It crosses my mind that her opinion might change if I were to play Wyatt's voice mails, if I were to show her Sylvia's text. Would she be shocked? Or was she too snowed to see the truth? The way Sylvia once was.

"Everyone here feels terrible. Is there anything we can do?" Angela bites her red-stained lip. "To help or anything?"

I make noises of appreciation. "I need to speak to Wyatt."

"Have you tried him on his cell?"

"He didn't answer."

"Oh. Well, he hasn't been into the office much at all since"—her voice drops lower—"since everything happened."

"But he must call in. Get his messages."

"Ye-es." She hesitates. "I haven't heard from him at all today though. To tell you the truth, I'm a little worried."

I don't know how to respond to that, so I keep my mouth shut. Instead, I study the short stack of messages on her desk, but I can't make sense of the letters upside down.

"I canceled all his appointments for tomorrow—just in case. It's not like him to miss meetings or not check in." She's still talking, her fingernails tapping the desk. "I even tried calling Dani."

The way Angela says Dani's name makes me look up again. Her nails hit the desk harder. *Rat-a-tat. Rat-a-tat.* "She hung up on me though. Typical. One time I called, she told me to go pick up his dry cleaning after I was done washing his car." *Rat-a-tat.* "Can you believe that? I mean, who does she think she is?"

I can believe it for more reasons than one, but I mumble something that sounds like no.

Her fingers still, and she runs those nails through her dark hair. Again, she tells me she's sorry about Sylvia, but the words sound robotic to my ear, almost rehearsed.

Sylvia was only a disembodied voice on the phone to Angela. They met two, maybe three times, before Wyatt moved out. "I know Mr. Spencer was upset. He was trying to reach your sister and—"

"Wait? When?"

"Last week, you know, before . . ."

I stand there, struck dumb, although I don't know why. He called me daily looking for Sylvia, screaming and cursing. But it was news to me that his assistant witnessed this strange behavior, this borderline stalking too.

"You should tell the police. We can call Detective Barnes together."

Angela blinks at me, her glowing cheeks suddenly white. "Why would I speak to the police?" she asks, her face a mask now. "I have nothing to tell them."

"I think you do."

Again, I catch a flash of something—maybe stubbornness or maybe fear—but it's gone as quickly as it appeared. "Then you're mistaken." She laces her fingers together, her blood-red nails glowing under the office lighting, their tips filed to points. "I'll let Mr. Spencer know you came by." She slides her chair toward her computer and shows me her back.

Although I didn't find Wyatt, I leave with the knowledge that his assistant is loyal enough to lie for him. She's hiding something. I'm sure of it. Still, I have no more insight into why he made a scene at the Franklin or why he was standing outside the hotel earlier. Is it triumph? Guilt? Or maybe regret? I lean against the stone wall of the building, my head aching and heart hurting. I steady my hands and my breaths and gather my resolve. Not wanting the trip to be wasted, I push Terry's warnings from my mind and take a detour to the police station only to find myself at another impasse.

"They're out," the receptionist tells me, her weary tone matching the saddlebags under her eyes.

"Can you give Detective Barnes a message?"

She blinks once, already looking past me. Not for the first time, I'm convinced this woman must take lessons in apathy with a side of disdain thrown in as a bonus. She shoves a pad toward me. "Write it and leave it."

My spirits low, I return to the Franklin. Shedding my coat, I tell Terry about spotting Wyatt outside the hotel, my visit with Angela, and my suspicions. I leave out the wasted trip to the station.

"Do you want me to pay her a visit?" he asks and pulls out my chair for me.

I consider the idea but tell him no. Whatever Angela is hiding is probably only added evidence of stalking, and I'm not sure I want to hear more right now.

"Okay," he says, watching me. "Are you sure it was Wyatt you saw today? You said he didn't react when you called out to him."

"It was. Who else could it be?"

He doesn't comment.

"Why would he be there at all? It doesn't make sense."

"I don't know, Val. People do strange things sometimes."

A new idea occurs to me then. "I'll call my parents in case he shows up there to see the kids."

My father answers. He's confused by my request, but he goes along with it. After ending the call, I catch Terry's eye and gesture toward the monitor.

"Do you think we can fast forward to Wyatt's scene at the front desk?"

"Good idea," he says.

Terry speeds up the recordings until he gets to Tuesday afternoon. Wyatt walks across the screen, his stride longer and quicker than usual. A coldness creeps up my spine. Neither of us speak as we watch. He crosses the lobby in a hurry, practically jogging to the desk. When he gets to the desk, all I can see is his backside. He paces in place as he waits for a clerk. At first, there's nothing to see. Then his head is shaking from shoulder to shoulder, and he gestures upward. The clerk pales, but she continues speaking. I notice a second clerk watching, picking up a phone. The first clerk has been typing on her computer and appears to be trying to help Wyatt. By now, he is leaning over the desk, trying to see what's on the computer. There's no audio and I don't read lips, but it looks like she's asking him to step away. A couple has come up behind Wyatt, and the man tries to speak to him, reaching toward him. Wyatt jerks away, and the couple steps back. Wyatt pokes his finger in the clerk's direction. I don't know what he's saying, but it's clear he's yelling now. A small circle has gathered near the front desk. By the time the security guards arrive, Wyatt is out of control. His face is red and swollen with anger. That's when I see it. The thing I didn't expect.

"Oh, my God," I whisper. "He's crying."

CHAPTER
26

TERRY

Tuesday, 1:31 p.m.

Billy didn't mention anything about tears. Crying by itself doesn't mean much to me. I've seen plenty of guilty men cry. Val seems stunned though. I guess the crying doesn't fit the image she has of the guy. Before I can ask her about it, Billy comes back in.

"He'll talk to you," he says. "The man with your sister."

Val leaps out of her seat, Wyatt forgotten. "When? Can we call him now?"

Billy shakes his head. "Not yet. He said he's in meetings for the next couple of hours, but you can call him at three thirty at this number." He hands over a piece of paper with a number and a name. Steven Morris. She nudges me, and I know what she's thinking. S. M. The initials fit.

"What did you say to him?" I ask.

"I did like you suggested," Billy says. "I told him we were interviewing some of the guests that stayed here last week."

"And?"

"He asked if it had to do with the suicide. When I told him it did, he said sure, he'd be happy to answer any questions."

Val steps forward. "What do you know about him?"

Billy shakes his head. "Nothing." There's a finality to the way he answers, and I know it's time to move on. I thank him and take Val aside.

"Look, there's something I want to talk to you about." What I'm about to say next will be difficult, but she needs to know the possibilities. "I think we need to consider the guy could be married." It makes a kind of sense. A guy comes into town, meets a woman, carries on a relationship, but he keeps it under the radar.

It would explain why he hasn't shown up since her death. Hell, it could even be one of the reasons she's gone. Maybe she found out he was married. Maybe she couldn't deal with being the other woman after it had been done to her in her own marriage.

I don't say any of this though. I know better.

"Sylvia would never date a married man."

"I didn't say she knew he was married."

Her reaction doesn't surprise me. I've known Val for less than forty-eight hours, and I can say with certainty that she's more obstinate than any woman I've ever met. I swing back toward Billy.

"When you were telling us about the scene at the front desk, you didn't mention the guy started crying. How come?"

He lifts one beefy shoulder. "Didn't think it mattered. The guy was a fruitcake as far as we were concerned. We got him out of the hotel as soon as we could. My bellman saw him hanging around across the street a couple of times, but he never came back in."

Val's skin colors. "What? He was hanging around across the street? How could you not tell us?"

Billy stiffens. I can understand Val's anger. He should have mentioned that before, but now isn't the time to say so. "Do you have any video from the front of the hotel?"

"No."

"Is there any chance we can talk to the bellman working those days?"

He shoots a wary look at Val. "I don't know. There's nothing to tell."

"Five minutes," I say and shift my body, partially blocking Val. "I want to get an idea what time of day. Was he on the phone? Did he do anything unusual?"

Billy rubs his hand over his chin. "I'd need to clear it." He starts to walk away before turning back. "I asked about the envelope. No one remembers anything about it."

"Are you sure?" Val asks.

He stops then. The disappointment in her voice is like a heavy, driving rain on the last day of vacation. He apologizes, avoiding her gaze. I knew it was a long shot, but I thank him anyway. After he's gone, I call Cullen O'Connell, one of my best men, a whiz at finding information without much to go on. I give him Steven Morris's name, number, and the few details we have. When I hang up, I find Val hunched over the monitor.

"What is it?"

Her eyes are brimming with tears. There's a new melancholy in her voice, a sadness that's different from before. "All of this." She lifts her palms. "Wyatt watching my sister, following her. Making a scene. Why didn't she tell me about Wyatt's threats before last week? And this boyfriend. Why wouldn't she talk to me about him?" Her chest rises and falls with each heavy breath. "She told me not to worry about her, that she was fine." She lifts a finger, gesturing at the screen. It's the image at the elevator where Sylvia is smiling at Steven Morris. "I don't know anything about this man," Val says. Her hand drops again.

I know what's coming before she says it, but I don't stop her. She needs to get it out.

"It makes me wonder if I knew my sister at all."

1921

CHAPTER
27

BRIDGET

A rap at the door made Bridget gasp. Startled, she slid her hips forward an inch, closer to the edge. With cold, stiff fingers she caught hold of the ledge before her body could pitch forward any further. Wide-eyed, she stared down at the dark street below, her chest heaving, the icy air burning her lungs. A second knock made her gasp again.

"Message for Mrs. Hartwood." The man's voice cracked with fear, and she knew who stood in the hallway outside her suite. Joseph. From over her shoulder, she watched as a thin, white envelope was pushed under the door. She stared at it from across the room. Who would be sending her a message?

"Have a nice evening." Joseph's voice rang out again, the words stilted as though he were being forced to say them. Any wisp of remorse she thought she heard was gone.

Cocking her head, Bridget heard the muted sound of retreating footsteps. Shame made her skin burn. Joseph. Had she really thought she might love him? It seemed so long ago now. Even telling Margaret about him felt like ages earlier, not mere hours. Before the wedding. Before everything.

Why had she bothered to speak of him at all? He'd never cared about her. She knew now that she was a fool.

The wind gusted, whipping her hair across her cheeks. On the street below, the twinkling lights blurred. She couldn't be sure how much time had passed since Lawrence had left the room, but she knew it wouldn't be long before he was back. She inhaled and told herself it wasn't too late. She could still do it. She shifted forward another inch, but her hands remained locked over the concrete ledge. She sat frozen, high above the streetlamps and automobiles. She glanced over her shoulder again. The white envelope was still there, waiting. Slowly, she edged backward. Legs shaking, she climbed back inside.

A train horn blared in the distance, but inside the suite, there was only silence. She padded across the floor and picked up the envelope. Her name—her new name—was written in black ink, the lettering thick and curling. She didn't open it, sure it was nothing more than a congratulations message from the hotel. Or worse, a message from her new husband. That must be it. While downstairs, he'd written her a note. An apology? Or was it something else? Something to terrify her further? And he'd forced Joseph to deliver it. To torture her. To remind her she belonged to him, no more or less important than his horses or his new Ford automobile. She was a thing, a possession. The knowledge made her nauseous, and she held the offending thing away from her.

Her mind raced with possibilities. If he came back and she hadn't opened it, he would be angry. She bent forward and wrapped an arm around her ribs, the pain intensifying with every breath. She thought about Louella, his first wife. When had the beatings started? After she didn't get pregnant in the first few months of marriage? After she lost the first baby? The second? Bridget couldn't remember, but she wasn't sure it mattered. Lawrence didn't need a reason. The envelope burned her fingers, but the air in the room blew cold.

She walked back to the window, drawn to the darkness outside. Maybe it wasn't too late after all. The drapes fluttered and fell with the night breeze.

Goose bumps covered her arms and legs. Her hands dropped to her side, the envelope heavy in her hand. The sky, thick with clouds, beckoned. A sense of calm washed over her. She would take the message with her. Whatever it was. They would find it on her, and they would know. She pried the envelope open and pulled out a single slip of folded paper. A swirling gust of wind caught the page and sent it sailing over her head. It spun in a circle before landing on the floor. She laughed a harsh, hollow laugh that echoed in the quiet of the room. She bent over to grab the paper. The words came into focus, but it wasn't the message that made her heart race and her hand fly to her mouth. The handwriting didn't belong to Lawrence at all. The handwriting was Margaret's.

CHAPTER
28

BRIDGET

B ridget read the letter a second time, drinking in the words.

My dearest sister,

It is with great joy that I wish you the best on your wedding day. Unfortunately, I am also writing to tell you of my great sadness that you are gone. Mother and Father are no consolation, and I find myself desolate. Lawrence told Mother you will be returning to the farm late tomorrow. I explained to my dear husband that if I don't see you as soon as you arrive, I will become quite unwell. I may have fainted as I told him this. He was quite alarmed, and lovely man that he is, he has agreed to take me to the farm to meet you upon your arrival. There is no need to tell Lawrence about our impending arrival as it will be our little surprise. We will be sisters reunited. Love and hugs until we are together again.

Your sister always,
Margaret

Bridget wiped her tear-stained face and held the letter against her chest. All at once, she startled, remembering the time. The clock read nearly six. Lawrence would be back in a few minutes. She looked around, her frantic gaze landing on the bedside table. She flew across the room and shoved the note inside the drawer, between the pages of a leather-bound Bible. As quickly as she could, she closed the windows and drew the curtains, wincing at the pain in her chest. She washed her face in the sink and brushed her hair back into place. She stared at her reflection. Her skin was pale but unmarked. The bruises he'd inflicted had landed below her neck, invisible to anyone who might see her. She smoothed the folds of her dress and searched the room for a place to wait.

While she most wanted to curl up in the bed and sleep, to forget all that had happened, she couldn't be there when he came back. And she didn't want the chaise longue either. Instead, she spotted the small table still set with food and drink. The silver bucket, now slick with condensation, held Lawrence's empty champagne bottle and melted ice. The half-empty tray of sandwiches smelled of cucumber and mint. She perched on a chair to wait, her hands folded in her lap.

When the key turned in the lock, she was ready.

"There's my young wife," he said, pushing open the door. He wore the glazed expression of a man who'd drunk more than a little champagne. She sat still, silent. He placed his hat on the hook and scowled. "It's quite chilly in here, isn't it? Shall I complain?"

"Oh, no," she said. "I opened the windows to get some fresh air." His dark brows rose. "I hope you don't mind. I wasn't feeling well and thought it might help."

He removed his jacket. "And did it?"

"Yes, thank you."

"Good. I wouldn't want my wife to be unwell."

Bridget might have laughed but managed to remain straight-faced. She had the letter now.

"So, what did you do with yourself while I was gone?"

If asked by someone else, the question might have struck Bridget as caring or at the least, polite, but not when asked by her new husband. She allowed herself a quick glance at the night table before answering. "Rested mostly. I was quite tired."

"Before or after you opened the window?"

She hid her trembling fingers in the folds of her gown. "Before, I'm afraid. I got up unwell, but I'm much better now."

He shoved his hands in his pockets. "Dinner should be arriving any minute," he said finally.

As though on cue, there was a knock on the door. Lawrence watched as a waiter wheeled in a table covered in a snow-white cloth. Three silver domes had been placed in the middle of the table, and a place setting sat at each end. A fresh bottle of champagne peeked out of a shiny new bucket. The old platters and bucket were whisked away. After the waiter left, Lawrence grabbed the bottle and twisted off the cork. It flew across the room, and he threw back his head and laughed. She wondered now how she'd ever found his barking laugh amusing. The frothy drink bubbled over the rim, and he poured until his glass was full. Pouring a second glass, he handed it to her.

"To my lovely wife." He lifted his glass. "I fear we did not start out marriage as you might have hoped, but it couldn't be helped."

Bridget bit her lip but said nothing.

"I believe we have a better understanding of each other now, wouldn't you say?"

"Yes," she said. "I do believe you're right." She softened her tone, adding, "It's best that a wife understands what her husband expects."

His hard features relaxed. "Yes, just so, young Bridget. Just so."

She exhaled and steadied her breathing. She knew that had been close, that she would have to be careful about the words she chose before her sister arrived at the farm. Until then, she would be on her own.

CHAPTER
29

VAL
Tuesday, 1:45 p.m.

When Terry hands me his handkerchief, I try to make a joke. "Does it feel like we've played this scene before?" He half smiles, but he can't hide his concern. He doesn't move any closer or reach out with his hand, but I feel his worry all the same. I'm not sure I've known a man like him before. There's a persistent quality to everything he does, whether it be investigating or talking or listening. "I'm fine," I say. "Really." The lines of his face smooth a little. "What now?"

He checks the time on his watch. "We've got almost two hours before we can speak to Morris. Let's get out of here for a little while."

I'm tempted, but I remind him I've been out of the hotel. "Besides, I feel like we should watch more video."

"There are better ways to use the time while we're waiting."

"Like what?"

"First, we need to analyze what we've learned about Wyatt and this guy Morris. Let's write it down. Maybe even put together a timeline. When we do watch the recordings, we can add things to it." His idea has merit, but I don't say anything. "And second, we should write up a list of questions for Mr. Morris."

"Why do we need a list? How about, why did you leave my sister and why haven't you said a word since she died, you asshole?"

Terry's lips turn up again. "Not one to mince words, are you?"

"I'm a journalist. Every word counts. Why waste them?"

Terry slips his coat from the back of the chair. "List of questions or not, I still think it's a good idea to get out of here for an hour. Do the timeline. Come on, Val. There's a grill right around the corner. Besides, I'm starving."

I hide my smile. There's that persistence again. Food this time. I consider telling him to go without me, but the truth is, I don't want to be alone. And Terry is a bit pale, as though being trapped inside the Franklin has sapped him of strength. "Sure. One hour. That's all."

The cold air outside stings my nose and fills my lungs. I shove my hands deep in my pockets searching for gloves. Even with the sun breaking through the clouds, the temperature has dropped since morning. Winter has settled in, promising frosty days and nights.

I half-run to match Terry's long stride, and I'm grateful when he stops outside a pair of heavy wooden doors. I've never been to this restaurant, but it reminds me of every other neighborhood grill in Baltimore. There are dark wood walls, beams across the ceiling, and booths up and down each side. The scarred wooden bar is located at the far end, and the whole place smells faintly of grease and furniture polish. If I had to guess, I'd say the pair of men perched at the corner of the bar and sipping from glass mugs are regulars. It's that kind of place. I steal a look at Terry. He seems to have shed some of the tension he's been carrying around since we first got to the hotel. He's less hunched and not as jumpy. I don't know what it is, but there's something about the hotel that gets under his skin. I don't think I'm wrong about this.

As we find our way to an empty booth, I remember the story he told me about the man who almost beat his wife to death while staying at the Franklin. For the most part, the man had gotten off. Even his wife had stuck by him, but that wasn't unusual in cases of domestic abuse. I try to recall what else he'd said. Then I remember: *a history of death*. If I hadn't been such a basket case when we met, I might have had some questions. Appraising him now, I decide there's no time like the present.

"I want to ask you something."

He settles into the leather banquette. "Shoot."

"Yesterday morning, at the library, when I told you my sister had died at the Franklin, you said something odd."

"Odd?" He draws out the word, his jaw tightening. There's definitely something. "How so?"

"You said the Franklin has a history of death."

"I guess I did. I'm sorry about that. It was insensitive of me, considering what you were going through."

"Thank you," I say, watching him closely now. "But I want to know why you said it."

"I told you about the man and his wife." He squeezes a lemon into his iced tea and lifts his shoulders as though that explains everything.

"No one died though. It's horrible, but not quite as evil as the way you made it sound."

"Evil. It's a funny word, isn't it? Can be so many things." He looks pained as he says it.

"What do you mean?"

His gaze drops to the table. "I don't mean anything."

The silence stretches into minutes, but I can't let it go. "Working homicide must have been hard. Trying to understand why," I say, thinking about my own fascination with covering crime. "What makes them do it."

He looks up again. "Most of the time, it's simple. Power or money or sex or some variation on the same old theme. Sometimes a combination."

I hear what he doesn't say. I'm catching on now. "But not always. That's where evil comes in."

His mouth droops a little as he nods. "Yes. Sometimes."

"What do you think makes people evil?"

Terry doesn't answer right away. When he does, it's no answer at all. "Evil comes in many forms."

The set of his jaw tells me he'd prefer to end this conversation, but that only makes him like half the people I interview. I try another tack. "But what does that have to do with the Franklin and what you said?"

Sighing, he says, "You know about the ghost tours."

"Sure. A few people died by suicide during the Depression, and the tour companies have found a way to make money off of it. You can take those tours in New Orleans or New York or anywhere." He doesn't say anything. "I want to know why you said the Franklin has a history of death. Why you looked like"—I rack my brain trying to remember how he seemed when he uttered those words—"like you might be afraid."

"Afraid?" Terry gives a short laugh. "Are you sure you aren't imagining things?"

I start to tell him I'm not—I wasn't—but I hesitate. It's true my eyes were wet and bleary, and I could be misinterpreting what I saw. It might be that I'm projecting my own emotions on him, projecting my own fears. But I know what I heard. There was something like dread in his voice, something that under any other circumstance would make me dig in and find out what he meant. *A history of death.* Even the words have an ominous ring. I think about his demeanor when we went up to my sister's suite, the way he stood near the door the whole time, the way he didn't even come into the room. "There's nothing to see," he said. His expression was guarded, the same as it is now.

"You're right," I say. "That's probably it."

There's something like relief in his eyes, and he raises his glass in a mock toast. "Great. Let's order and then do that timeline."

I listen to the warm timbre of his voice as he talks to the waitress. I watch the way he holds his head toward her when she speaks, giving her his full attention. He's kind to her, the same way he is to Billy, and to me. He hums with the music playing on the jukebox after she's gone and sips his drink. Not for the first time, it strikes me that he's a good guy. It's the reason

I didn't press him. Maybe I have other reasons I don't want to think about just yet, but it doesn't change what I know.

Good guy or not, he lied to me. He was afraid.

"Your sister had been seeing S. M. for more than two months by the time she checked into the hotel. No one knows who he is, and no one has met him." Terry takes a sip from his iced tea. The waitress walks by, humming along with an old Fleetwood Mac tune playing on the speakers. "She tells you it's too new to talk about, which is understandable. But if we assume she was meeting him, it's serious enough to sneak away to a hotel and tell everyone she's out of town."

"You make it sound so seedy," I say.

"I'm not trying to make it sound like anything. What I'm trying to do is find out what we can learn from it."

"Which is?"

"She wasn't comfortable enough in this relationship to share details with anyone. Yet it appears the relationship may have been more than casual, or it was about to be."

I tap my fingernails on the tabletop. "She did tell one person—at least I think she did." Terry leans forward. "Her therapist. Call it an educated guess, but I went to see her—she's my therapist too—and she knew Syl was seeing someone." I see him start to ask a question, but I raise my hand and cut him off. "She didn't give me a name, but she knows. And there's something else I've been thinking about." He waits. "The diary."

"You think her diary would include stuff about her new boyfriend?"

"Definitely. And maybe stuff about Wyatt. But it's missing."

"Right." He rubs his hand over his chin. "Is it possible she stopped writing?"

"No," I say, shutting the idea down. "The diaries were a part of her. She wrote all through high school and college and when she got married. Not

every day, but most days. It was her bedtime ritual for as long as I can remember. After she had kids, she wrote even more."

"Okay. Let's assume she didn't stop."

"She didn't."

"What makes you so sure it's missing? Maybe it's misplaced."

"I don't believe that. Every other diary was there. Lined up in those
boxes in the closet. The last one I could find ended a few months before she
started dating S. M. and right before all the problems with Wyatt. That can't
be a coincidence."

"Maybe not," he says, but I can't tell whether he agrees or not. "We
could go back and check again. Maybe we missed it."

"No, it's gone." What I'm going to say next might seem far-fetched, but
I can't help myself. I've already come this far. "Someone took it. Someone
who didn't want anyone to read it."

"Have you asked the police yet if they found it in the hotel?"

"They didn't. And I was there when she packed. The diary was on her
nightstand. I remember because we joked about it."

The memory comes rushing back.

"I can't believe you still write in those old composition books, Syl. Why
don't you get something nicer? They make leather journals, you know."

"Please. That's too fancy for me. And too expensive. Besides, I'm not
the writer. You are."

"I don't keep diaries and you know it. No one would ever want to read
about my life."

She laughed. "No one wants to read about mine either. Merry choked
on her green beans again. Miles is starting to notice girls. It's time to get the
house power washed. Boring."

"Miles likes girls already? He's only ten."

"I know. Lord help me."

But I knew her diary held more than snippets about food and the kids.
When she'd met Wyatt, she'd spent hours writing about him, writing about
the way he made her feel.

She'd told me about it once. "Val, I've never felt this before."

Coming off my own disappointing marriage, I'd been wary. "Are you sure? Is this what you really want?"

"I'm sure. I've never felt more loved in my life." I'd looked at her, saw the glow that came from happiness, from love. Perhaps I'd been less surprised by her words than I'd been by the strength of her belief in them. Where I'd analyzed compatibility and life expectancy before I'd walked down the aisle, my sister had chosen to rely solely on emotion. "My poor diary. I think I've written hundreds of pages about Wyatt alone."

I was happy for her, and for a long time, Wyatt was the husband Syl deserved. Even now, I can't say what changed, why he decided being a cliché was better than the beautiful life he already had. But his feelings hadn't mattered to me since the day he admitted the affair. Sylvia was all that mattered.

I feel Terry watching me now, waiting. "She used old composition notebooks," I say. "The kind you used in school. Do you remember them?"

Terry sits back against the high-backed bench. "Yeah. I hated those. We used them for essay tests. Give me multiple choice or fill in the blank anytime. I like my odds with all of the above."

I laugh. "Not a writer?"

"Hardly. You should have seen my incident reports. Even those were pretty bad." His smile is sheepish, and he takes another sip of tea.

We watch the regulars at the bar slide off their stools and throw cash on the bar. Most of the other tables have emptied. It's quiet except for the eighties pop playing in the background. I push my plate away, my sandwich more mangled than eaten. His gaze comes back to me.

"How many people know your sister kept a diary?"

I lay awake the night before asking myself the same question. It isn't a long list. "Me. My mom. I don't even know if my dad knew about it. Her kids."

"Did you check their rooms?"

"Yes."

"What about your mom? Would she have taken it?"

"I asked. She hasn't seen it."

"Okay. Anyone else?"

"Her best friend from college, but she lives in California. Emily, her therapist. And Wyatt."

He seems to take that in. "If I'm following your thinking, you think someone deliberately took the most recent diary because it's somehow related to your sister's death. What we don't know is whether or not this man Morris—if he's our guy—knew about the diaries."

"No, I guess we don't."

His finger traces the rim of his glass. "When we were at your sister's house, I walked around the entire downstairs. I checked the windows, the doors, the garage. I didn't see anything out of the ordinary or any sign the house might have been broken into."

I stare at him. The idea hadn't even crossed my mind.

"Did Wyatt have access to the house?" he asks.

I remember then, and my mouth drops open. It had long been an argument between my sister and me. I couldn't understand why she hadn't changed the locks after the separation. "Yes," I whisper. "He had a key."

CHAPTER
30

TERRY
Tuesday, 2:51 p.m.

We walk back to the hotel in silence, each lost in our thoughts. Val keeps checking her phone, and I'm glad she's distracted. As we get closer to the Franklin, my muscles tighten into knots. It's the same as every other time. The frigid air presses in on me, making it hard to breathe, and I have to force myself to forget what I know, to pretend. Val knows something isn't right, but so far, I've been able to evade her questions. When her thoughts are less focused on the boyfriend and the ex, she'll wonder again what I'm not telling her, but if I admit the truth now, it would only add to her pain.

Rounding the corner, I glance at Val. Her mouth is set in a hard line, and she holds her phone in a vise-like grip, as though she might choke it to life. More than once, she's commented that Wyatt should have called her by now. I don't disagree, but I've refrained from making any comment. According to Val, Wyatt Spencer is a boneheaded, prize-worthy ass, which may or may not be true. There's the stalking, the scene in the hotel, the missing diary, and now the key. No matter how I look at it, these facts—such as they are— don't paint the man in a favorable light. But having worked homicide, I've learned not to accept things at face value. Too many times, I've seen cases collapse under the weight of false evidence, evidence that wasn't properly picked apart and vetted. This isn't to say some of the cases I worked weren't cut and dried, clear and straightforward. But I'm not ready to rule this time. Whether Sylvia's death was a planned suicide or something more sinister, as Val is inclined to believe, I do believe the circumstances surrounding what happened appear to be complicated.

Our steps slow as we approach the large overhang of the Franklin. The doorman beams in a robotic manner and opens the heavy doors.

"Welcome back," he says.

The words are pleasant enough, but the boredom behind the tired phrase doesn't escape me. How many times a day does he say the same thing? How many guests does he see every day? But something out of the ordinary might break up the day. Something like a man lurking across the street.

Val hurries into the hotel, probably eager to get warm, but I pause outside, swinging back toward the doorman.

"Thanks." I take a quick glance at his name tag. "Robert, is it?"

"Yes, sir."

"How are things going today?"

The man blinks. "Fine."

"Good. Chilly, isn't it?"

"A little. I don't mind though. It's better than the summers, when it's hot as blazes."

I offer some measure of understanding. "I can imagine. I guess you've worked here a long time."

"Seven years. It's a good job."

"Can I ask you a question?"

The doorman shrugs. "Why not?"

"You know how they have those ghost tours?"

"Sure. The Franklin is on a couple of those. They mostly talk about stuff from like a hundred years ago—stuff during the Depression. I don't pay attention anymore."

"Right. What I was wondering was whether or not anyone who's worked here ever takes it seriously."

Robert tips his hat back on his head. "What do you mean?"

"Well, like the lady that killed herself last week. Does anyone ever say it's because the hotel is haunted?"

Robert half laughs. "Sure. We've had a few folks who've quit 'cause of scary stories. Say they've seen a ghost or heard spooky voices or something."

My mouth is suddenly dry. "Someone quit last week?"

"Nah. At least not that I know of. But it's happened before. And once, there was a maid who tried to conduct a séance in a room on the fourteenth floor. Swore she was gonna rid the hotel of evil spirits."

The fourteenth floor. Or the thirteenth to be more accurate. "What happened?" I ask.

"Nothing that I know of. When management got wind of it, she was asked to leave. I gotta say, I don't know if I believe in ghosts, but I don't mind having an outside job. Those sculptures of all those gods they got in the lobby give me the creeps. The eyes, you know." He laughs and inclines his head toward mine. "Don't tell anyone I said that though."

"It's okay. I don't care for them much myself," I admit.

"Oh, yeah?" His grin fades, and he gives a shake of his head then. "Shame about that lady last week, though. She was real nice."

I can't keep the surprise out of my voice. "You talked to her?"

"I talk to everyone. Same as I'm talking to you now."

"How did she seem?"

Robert's thick brows shoot up under his hat. "Why're you asking?"

After a brief hesitation, I decide to tell the truth. I gesture toward Val, who's waiting and watching. "Because the lady you talked to was her sister. She's pretty upset about it."

The doorman follows the line of my hand.

I see the way he takes in the dark circles and drooping shoulders. "That's the sister?"

"Yes. She's trying to find out what happened. Why, I mean."

He's still staring at Val. "The police already came."

"That's what I've been told, but she still needs to know for herself. She would appreciate knowing how her sister spent the last days before she died." The doorman doesn't respond. "Do you remember what you talked about?"

His gaze comes back to me. "Who are you? A cop?"

"A friend." It's accurate enough, I think.

"I—I don't know if I'm supposed to be talking to you."

"It's between us. I promise. You said she was nice?"

"I didn't talk to her long, but sure, she was nice."

"When was it that you talked to her?"

Robert considers Val again as he makes up his mind. "Monday. Early. She was on her way out."

"How long was she gone?"

"Not long. She came back with a bag of bagels from Chives and Charm over on Clay." His voice sinks lower. "She seemed happy. I never would have guessed."

"Did you tell anyone what you saw?"

"Nobody asked."

"Did you see her again?"

"Nope. But I didn't work again until Wednesday."

I pull out my phone and hold up the blurry profile picture of Steven Morris. "Do you know this man?"

Robert shakes his head without looking, but I inch a half step closer. "Val . . . she didn't know her sister was staying here. She's trying to fill in the blanks, you know." I indicate the phone. "Please. If you could take a quick look."

He stares at me, his mouth twisting as he thinks. I let out a breath when he finally takes a look. "Yeah, I've seen him. He stays here sometimes. I think he's a salesman or something."

"Did you see him with the woman?"

"No. I only saw her the one time."

"Okay." I scroll to a photo of Wyatt. "What about this guy?"

"Yeah. I saw him hanging around across the street." The doorman lifts his finger and points. "He walked up and down the sidewalk in front of that building over there."

"How long?"

"An hour or two. One of the guys from security told us to let them know if he tried to come in. I kept my eye on him as much as I could, but it got kind of busy. All I know is, he was gone the next time I checked."

"What day was that? Do you remember?"

"Wednesday."

I stare at the empty spot where Wyatt, lurking like a vagrant with nowhere else to go, watched the hotel. It doesn't make sense. What did he want? Sylvia was already dead by then. Did he know? Was he returning to the scene for some reason? While strange, it wasn't unheard of. I've seen that kind of thing before. Sociopaths. Psychopaths. They all have their obsessions.

Wyatt knew about the diary. Val's words about the missing journal echo through my mind. Someone took it. Someone who didn't want anyone to read it. If she's right, the thief had to take it from the house. But the doors and windows had been shut tight. The locks had not been tampered with, and nothing appeared to have been disturbed. If it was stolen, the thief must have had a key. And something they wanted to hide.

1921

CHAPTER
31

BRIDGET

Bridget laid her napkin in her lap, smoothing the heavy cloth with her fingers. Lawrence filled his glass and waved his fork in the air.

"Isn't the duck divine?" he asked. His cheeks were flushed and his words less crisp than they'd been before his last glass of champagne.

"It's very good," she said.

"Doesn't look like it." He gestured at her plate. It was true she hadn't eaten much, but it had more to do with the pain in her ribs and her fear of him than the taste of the food. His upper lip curled. "I hope you aren't going to be skin and bones like my first wife. A man needs a little meat to hang on to." He laughed out loud then. "Oh, don't be a prude, Bridget. We both know you're not as innocent as you appear."

Tears welled and the duck meat blurred with the sauce and the delicate peas, forming a blob of color.

"Are you crying again? Good grief, I can't have a wife who goes around blubbering every time I say something. Buck up, my dear." He tipped his head back and drained the rest of his glass. "Surely, things aren't all that bad.

You're a married woman. No doubt your father is glad to have me in the family, considering the trouble he's gotten into." Her head shot up. "Oh, you didn't know about that, did you? I can't say I'm surprised. A man—even a man as careless as your father—doesn't want to fall too far off the pedestal in the eyes of his daughters."

Bridget struggled to keep up. "What are you talking about?"

"You never wondered why your father took to me so quickly?" Lawrence sat back and snickered.

She realized she'd never considered the reason before now. It was true her father—and her mother—had taken to Lawrence immediately. They'd pushed her to spend time with him. "He's older and more established," her mother had said. "You'll never have to worry. That's a comfort of its very own." And her father: "Lawrence has carried on his family name, done his family proud. You could do much worse, Bridget." His voice had cracked as he'd placed his hands on her arms. "He's promised to take care of you. That's all I want for you. To know you're taken care of." She'd heard the words, but she knew now she hadn't really listened. She'd been too preoccupied with her own sadness over the lost promise of something more with Joseph. After he'd disappeared, Lawrence had seemed to be around more and more. How had she never noticed the way he'd retired to the small parlor with her father? How her father had grown quieter, more withdrawn. How he'd begun to defer to Lawrence.

Bridget stared at her new husband now. "What did you do to my father? What did you say to him?"

His harsh laugh echoed in the suite. "Do to him? The only thing I did was save him. He was close to bankruptcy, but I suppose you wouldn't have known, would you? You were too busy flirting with a worthless shop clerk to see that your own father had made a fool of himself."

Her hands twisted the napkin in her lap into a ball. Fresh tears threatened to fall. Her father had been in financial trouble. It explained so much. Her father's sadness. Her mother's anxiousness. Until recently. Until her engagement. "You gave my father money."

He smirked in a way that reminded her of a spider spinning its web. "Yes, Bridget. I gave your father money. His little company will survive. Your parents won't be in the poorhouse. Yet."

Her skin flushed at a new realization. Her parents had pushed her into marriage for money. How could they?

"Don't blame them, my dear," Lawrence crooned. "They knew I was very fond of you, and I wanted very much to marry you. I do believe they were quite happy with the match."

Her anger burned out as quickly as it flared. Her parents must have thought they were doing what was best. And they must have thought she cared for Lawrence. After all, she'd said nothing and done nothing to disabuse them of that notion. Another thought made her sit up straighter. "Did my sister know?"

"Your sister? I sincerely doubt it."

Her arms and legs went limp with relief, and she thought of the hidden letter. Margaret would be at the farm the next day.

"Enough about that. It's our wedding night. There are other, more interesting things to occupy us."

Bridget's gaze fell to her lap, and she pulled her arms in close. Her mother's words came back to her. *No one dies from marital duties.* She wasn't so sure that was true.

Lawrence pushed his plate away and wiped his mouth with his napkin. He came around the table then, placing his hands on her shoulders. His fingers pressed into her flesh, and it took all her willpower not to pull away. He leaned down, his face over her shoulder. She could smell the champagne on his breath.

"What do you say I have this table taken out and we freshen up for the evening?"

Bridget stood up, shifting before his hands could move any lower. "If you'd like." She stepped around him. "Why don't I pour you another glass of champagne before I change?"

"Excellent idea, my dear Bridget," he said, a new glint in his eye. "Excellent idea."

CHAPTER
32

BRIDGET

B ridget stared at her reflection in the bathroom mirror. She no longer resembled the young bride-to-be of that morning, the girl Margaret had admired. The bloom on her cheeks was gone, along with her naivete. Her skin was blotchy and sagged where there should have been a smile. Her red-rimmed eyes were flat, whatever sparkle she'd once had now gone. Had she aged so much in a few short hours?

She thought about Margaret and the way she glowed when she spoke of Charles, the way she blushed when he took her hand in his. Her sister had promised their mother was wrong about the marital bed, but now Bridget knew her fears with regard to Lawrence were justified. Their wedding day had been bad enough. What new horrors would these next hours bring?

Bridget plunged her hands into tepid water and rinsed her face. With a shaking hand, she picked up her ivory-handled hairbrush and pulled it through her hair, the curls bouncing back after every stroke. She took her time, stretching out the minutes as long as she could. Through the door, she heard the plunk of the bottle in the bucket.

Had he finished it already? Should she ask him to get another?

"Bridget," he called out. She gazed again at her reflection. "Not much longer. Your new husband is not a patient man." She stiffened. He was right outside the door. He knocked, the sound a sharp reminder time was running out. "If you aren't ready soon, I'll be forced to come in there."

"I'm almost ready," she said, her voice a squeak.

She reached for the pale pink nightgown. Her trembling fingers trailed over the smooth silk of the bodice before she slipped it over her head. Wincing at the yellow-purple bruises dotting her bare arm, she pulled on the matching dressing gown. "One more day," she whispered. "Then I won't be alone." Bridget squared her shoulders and opened the door.

Lawrence had retreated to a high-backed chair, his legs crossed, foot bobbing up and down. His shirt was unbuttoned to his chest. Dark hair curled over the edges of the light fabric. She stepped into the room, her knees and legs shaking. Her ribs ached with every breath, but she knew better than to say anything.

He got to his feet and crossed the room in three strides, standing so close she could see every whisker, every pore, every tic under his skin. His nostrils flared, and he pushed her dressing gown off her shoulders in a single motion. She held herself still. He bent and kissed her neck, the stubble of his beard scratching her skin. He moaned and straightened again. His fingers trailed over the ugly bruises on her arm.

"We'll have no more of that," he said. She looked up at him then, unsure whether his words were an apology or a warning.

The wind outside rattled the windows. Behind them, the clock on the mantel struck nine. She wanted to flee, to run from the room screaming, but she knew it would be futile. Before she could reach the door, he would grab her by the hair and yank her to the floor. There would be new bruises and new hateful words. No. She would stay, and she would be patient.

With one hand, he unbuttoned the rest of his shirt. He pressed her to him and buried his face in her hair. She could feel his desire, feel the heat of his skin against her cold and rigid body. "My wife," he whispered. "My wife."

CHAPTER
33

VAL
Tuesday, 3:19 p.m.

I can't stop thinking about Sylvia's diary. Wyatt had a key. If she'd written about their fights and his threats, he would have reason to take it. "We could ask Detective Newman to get a search warrant for his apartment."

Terry shoots me down. "It doesn't work that way, and you know it."

I do, but I'm not the kind of person who gives up easily. "It's enough for probable cause though, right? The diary's missing and he has a key to the house. Also, the text from Sylvia shows things were getting ugly between them. We know he was stalking her."

"Maybe," he says. "But assuming he did take the diary, he may have thrown it away or even burned it by now. Besides, it's hard to get a warrant from a judge when the police don't seem to want to investigate."

I sit back, deflated. "Then what do we do?"

He gestures at my phone. "Right now, we're going to make a call. It's almost three thirty."

This shakes me out of my doldrums. "I want to ask the questions," I say.

"You should."

This surprises me. I might wonder about me doing the talking if I were him, but I don't have time to think about it. I place the piece of paper with the phone number on the table. "That's settled then."

"But I reserve the right to jump in."

"Fine."

He takes out his notebook and pen. I would have preferred to record the conversation, but Terry has already vetoed the idea. "It's not legal, unless you want to tell him we're recording."

Now, I tap out the numbers on my phone. The man answers on the second ring. My heart bangs under my skin.

"Hello?"

I raise my voice to keep it from shaking. "Is this Mr. Morris? Steven Morris?"

"Yes."

"My name is Val Ritter, and I'm here with Terry Martin. Billy Johnston from the Franklin gave us your number. I appreciate your willingness to talk to us today."

"Yeah, sure. He said it was about Sylvia Spencer. I heard what happened."

Somehow, I manage to keep my expression neutral and concentrate on the questions I've laid out in my mind. "Sylvia was my sister."

"Oh. I'm sorry."

"Did you know her, Mr. Morris?"

"Yeah, I did. I met her a few months ago through a friend."

I look at Terry to see if he's caught the timing. "Do you remember who introduced you?"

"Sure. Sherry Parker." I've heard my sister mention the name, but I can't place it at first. "I work with Sherry sometimes when I come into town," he says. "She had a happy hour one Friday when I was there, and I met Sylvia then."

"How did Sylvia and Sherry Parker know each other?"

"Their kids are in the same playgroup or something."

I remember then. Sherry Parker has a daughter the same age as Merry. They were in preschool together.

Terry taps on his notebook. He's written *playgroup* with a question mark, then *father* and another question mark. My heart sinks. He's right. Only another parent would use the word playgroup. I remind myself, though, that being a parent doesn't mean Steven Morris is married. He could be divorced or separated.

"How can I help you, Ms. Ritter?"

"Were you with her at the hotel?"

"Sure, I saw Sylvia. But I checked out of the hotel on Tuesday morning. I don't know what happened to her other than what I heard." I open my mouth to ask another question, but he cuts me off. "I'm sorry about Sylvia, but I have another meeting. I hope you find the answers you're looking for."

"Please. A couple more questions," I say.

The sound of his sigh echoes from the speaker. "I wish I could help you, but I don't know anything."

"She didn't kill herself," I blurt out. The dead air crackles over the line, and I rush to fill the silence. "You of all people should know that. You were with her and—"

"What are you talking about? Why would I know what happened to your sister?" He doesn't wait for an answer. "Look, I have to go. I've got another call. I wish you luck."

"Please, I—"

Terry speaks over me, cutting me off. "Mr. Morris, Terry Martin here."

"Listen, I really—"

"This will only take a couple of minutes. You said you checked out on Tuesday." Silence. "Mr. Morris?"

"Yes. Tuesday."

"Does your wife know how you spend your time when you're in town?" My head whips around. Terry's tone is soft, but his words are sharp.

"I—I don't know what you're talking about." There's no mistaking the catch in Morris's voice.

"I'm guessing your girlfriend and your wife don't know about each other. Am I right, Mr. Morris?" Terry asks.

"I don't have a girlfriend. And whatever my wife knows or doesn't know is none of your business." Any trace of friendliness or cooperation is gone. His tone is cold, hard.

"It might be," Terry says, "if you're involved in your girlfriend's death."

"Wh-what?" he sputters. "What the hell are you talking about?" Each word is louder than the one before.

"You know what we're talking about," I say. My voice and my hands are trembling.

The man on the other end of the line is nearly shouting now. "This is ridiculous. I'm hanging up now."

Terry again. "You can talk to us now or to the police later."

"What?"

"You don't want them to call your wife, do you?"

A crash echoes over the line, and I jump. "Goddammit. Goddammit." Morris is muttering and cursing. "You made me knock over my laptop. Jesus, the screen is cracked. Goddammit."

"I asked you a question, Mr. Morris."

"Christ. This is not happening." I hear papers shuffling. "You are not pinning this on me."

"No one is pinning anything on you, Mr. Morris. We're trying to find some answers. That's all."

"By threatening to tell my wife about my girlfriend, which I never—did you hear me—*never* admitted I had? Oh, no. That's not happening. Now, you listen to me. If you or anyone else wants to talk to me, call my lawyer. Until then, I have nothing to say."

"Wait—" I say, but it's already too late. The phone line's gone dead.

"Shit." My blood is boiling, and I stalk the tiny room like a caged animal. "Shit. Shit. Shit. How did that happen? He won't talk to us again, you know." I spin around, pace in the opposite direction. "It's my fault, isn't it? The suicide comment. He got scared." I stop moving. "No. It was when you asked him about being married."

"He got pretty defensive," Terry says. "The bartender was right. There's a girlfriend, and now we know there's also a wife."

I stop and stare at him. "Why aren't you more upset we lost him? We didn't find out anything." I'm pacing again. "Shit."

Terry holds up his notes and taps his fingers on the page. He's underlined two words. *Sherry Parker.* "If Morris was seeing your sister, he has too much to lose to talk. But we did get leads. We'll follow up with this Sherry Parker. She knows where he works, where he's from."

He's right, but I got tripped up on the first part of what he said. "What do you mean *if* he was seeing my sister? It seems pretty obvious he was."

"It's possible he's the guy, but we don't know that yet. All we have are leads. Not facts."

I want to argue, but I can't. I've been doing what I do for too long not to recognize the truth of what he's saying. We know Morris is married. Probably has kids. We know he met Sylvia. We're reasonably sure he had a girlfriend, and we know he rode up in an elevator with my sister. It's flimsy at best.

I sit down again. "May I see your notes?" Terry slides the notebook across the table. I read over them twice. "He claims he checked out of the hotel on Tuesday morning," I say. The timing could be significant. The Do Not Disturb tag was put on the door to her room on Monday.

"Easy enough to check," Terry says.

There's another thing that's been nagging at the back of my brain, but I've been letting my emotions cloud my vision. "I've been wondering why they would have two rooms."

Terry has an explanation. "Appearances. In case his wife calls." He knocks the pad against his leg as he talks. "And didn't you tell me Sylvia wanted to take this new relationship slow? That she didn't want to rush into anything?"

"So, you're thinking this little meeting at the Franklin was kind of like a trial? She keeps her own room, and he has his for appearances."

"Maybe," he says.

There's a strange kind of logic in it. According to the bartender, Morris has been staying at the Franklin when he's in town for a couple of years. He would keep up appearances. Shifting on the chair, I flip to a clean page in his notebook.

"Do you mind?" I ask, reaching for his pen. Scrolling through the photos of Sylvia's calendar I have stored on my phone, I write down a series of dates. I check the list twice before pushing it back across the table. "These are the all the dates she was seeing S. M. We should check to see if he was in town on those dates."

"Good idea," Terry says. "Do you know the friend Morris works with? Sherry Parker?"

"I've met her. She was at Merry's birthday party last year."

"Why don't you track her down while I dig up what I can on Morris?"

I stand up and grab my bag in one motion, already halfway out the door.

"Text me as soon as you learn anything," Terry calls out.

Lifting my hand in acknowledgment, I race out of the hotel. I try Sherry's office and find out she's working from home that day. I do a quick search for her address and give it to my taxi driver. My phone buzzes. I pull up my messages and freeze. It's an unknown number, but the name in the text is anything but.

Val, I'm so sorry to be writing you this way. I hate having to send my condolences through a text, but I know you'll hang up if I try to call you. I'm sorry for your loss, but that's not the reason I'm writing. Wyatt hasn't been himself lately. Something is wrong with him. He's angry all the time, and last week, he punched a hole in the wall of the living room. I know you would rather not hear from me, but I wouldn't be able to live with myself if I didn't tell you this.

There's a single name at the end of the text. *Dani.*
Wyatt's girlfriend.

CHAPTER
34

TERRY

Tuesday, 4:02 p.m.

Billy scowls at me from across the room, his normally placid features contorted. "I told you not to talk to the employees until I cleared it. Now I've got the manager up my ass about why you're here at all. The hotel doesn't need this kind of gossip."

"What kind of gossip are you referring to?"

"The kind that involves killing. A murderer in the hotel. It's bad for business."

I might laugh if there was anything funny about it. "But being a hotel where people die by suicide is good for business?"

Billy throws up his hands. "All right. So, neither is great, but the idea that a killer came into the hotel isn't going over well."

"I never said any of that. I said Val was upset about her sister. I asked a few questions. That's all."

"The police have been here. They searched the room, the lady's stuff. You don't trust them now? You have to do your own investigation?" Billy's tone sharpens. "I did you a favor with the videos, but I can't lose my job over this. Besides, you were a cop. How's that look—you going behind their back?"

"I'm not going behind anyone's back, Billy. I'm asking questions for a friend."

"For a friend, huh? Maybe more than a friend?"

Although I ignore Billy's insinuation—no matter how innocent—it's something I've been wondering myself. "I'm sorry if I got you in any trouble. You can understand how Val feels, right? She wants to know what happened to her sister."

"C'mon, Terry, I'm not trying to be a jackass, but you already know what happened. The lady checked herself into a swanky hotel, put up a Do Not Disturb sign, and offed herself."

"Maybe."

"What maybe?"

"The police might not be here right now, but they haven't closed the case." I pick my words carefully. Billy doesn't need to know the police have left it open merely as a courtesy to Val, or because the young detective felt sorry for her. In a few hours, even that's likely to change. "They told Val there are still questions. If it were open and shut, why would I be here?"

This much, I tell myself, is true.

Still, I understand Billy's position. I've asked a lot of the man already. Changing my approach, I tell Billy about Wyatt, his relationship with Sylvia, and the accusatory text from Sylvia.

I remind him of the bizarre scene in the lobby and the way Wyatt stalked the street outside the hotel.

"He didn't get back into the hotel on my watch. No way."

I nod, although I know there are plenty of ways to sneak into a hotel this size. Wyatt could have changed his appearance. He could have come in through the back or with a delivery service.

"Mrs. Spencer had a new boyfriend." I give Billy a brief overview of the conversation with Steven Morris and share Val's suspicion that he was dating Sylvia. "Morris was definitely hiding something."

"Well, you said you figured he's a married guy. Makes sense he'd be a little cagey."

"Morris says he checked out on Tuesday morning. Mrs. Spencer placed the Do Not Disturb sign on her room on Monday evening. Maybe they had a fight. Maybe she found out about his wife." I pause, seeing the wheels of Billy's brain begin to turn. "Maybe it got ugly."

"So, she gets upset. That's when she kills herself."

I lean in, lower my voice. "And maybe she threatened to tell his wife."

"They said she had a bottle of pills though." Billy says the words in slow motion, as though trying to convince himself. "She must have taken them."

"Or . . ."

Billy catches on. "Or she had a little help."

"Possibly. That's why I need to know how many times and the dates Morris stayed here during the last three months. I need proof he was seeing her."

Billy's heavy brows furrow. "I don't know."

I give one final push. "If Morris did something—or even if he knows something—how would management feel about him staying here in the future? Wouldn't they want to know?"

Billy draws out his words. "Yeah, I guess."

"That's what I thought. You'd be doing them a favor by making sure he's not a potential problem, a liability."

His face clears a bit. "You're right. I would."

I pull out my notebook. "Great. These are the dates we need to run down."

1921

CHAPTER
35

BRIDGET

Bridget pulled the heavy quilt up over her body, covering her nakedness. Lawrence lay next to her on his back, one arm flung over his head. The rumble of his snores, so foreign to her, rose and fell in waves, drowning out the quiet. The single lamp burning in the corner of the room cast looming shadows over the brocade walls. Her mind shuddered at the dark images and her even darker thoughts. She blinked, but she couldn't stop the tears that slipped over her cheeks. With a shaky hand, she wiped them away before they could stain the sheets. Shifting, she slid her legs over the edge of the bed. Her feet landed on the cold floor. Creeping across the room, she found her gown on the floor, the fabric crumpled and torn. Goose bumps crawled over her bare skin.

As quietly as she could, she searched through her bags for another gown and slipped it over her head. She tiptoed to the washbasin. Raising the gown again, she scrubbed until her skin was raw. Exhaustion washed over her, and she sank to the floor. Bridget brought her legs up to her chest, wincing. Across the room, Lawrence slept on, his snores as loud as a thundering train. She laid her head on her knees. When sleep finally came, she welcomed the escape.

Bridget floated alongside her sister, arms swinging, their hands filled with flowers they'd picked in the gardens. Mother would be so pleased. The sun beat down on them, bathing them in yellow-gold light. The bright green leaves of the trees fluttered in the soft breeze. Margaret giggled, the sound reminding Bridget of tinkling bells, and she laughed too. They skipped over the lawn, the daisies flopping with each step. A cloud rolled in, and the girls slowed, their dance coming to a stop.

"We're dirty," Margaret said, the bright smile she'd worn earlier gone.

Bridget looked at her sister and down at herself. It was true. Their dresses were covered in grime and grass stains. Her hands and feet were black with soil. She dropped the flowers to the ground.

"Hurry," Margaret said and took her by the hand. "We have to wash up." She pulled Bridget to the stream, but when they got there, it was nothing but rocks and dried leaves.

Bridget's lips quivered. "What will we do?"

The clouds overhead thickened and blotted out the sun. The girls grew cold and shivered.

Margaret raised her eyes to the sky. "If it rains, we can get clean again."

"But he'll still be mad we're wet."

A cold wind blew, and the tree branches groaned. Thunder crashed around them, and birds squawked and shrieked in the distance. "I'm afraid."

Margaret took Bridget's hands in hers. "You mustn't be frightened," she said. "I will be with you. Always."

The thunder came closer, and Bridget trembled. "Don't leave me."

Margaret shook her. "Be strong, Bridget," she said. The vision of her sister wobbled and faded, disappearing under the dark sky, but her voice echoed over the wind. "Be strong, Bridget. Be strong."

"What the hell are you doing?"

Bridget's eyes snapped open. Lawrence stood over her, dark with fury. "Get up before I put you on the floor for good."

CHAPTER
36

VAL
Tuesday, 4:18 p.m.

"I still can't get over it," Sherry says, waving me inside. I follow her to a sunny kitchen. "I'm so sorry for your family, Val."

"Thank you."

"Coffee?"

"No, thanks. Actually, the reason I came by is because I was wondering if I could ask you a couple of questions. About Sylvia." She sits down, and I take the chair across from her. "I was talking with someone you work with, and he said you'd introduced him to Sylvia."

"Really? Who?"

"Steven Morris."

Sherry gives a short laugh. "Ah. Yes, Steven. It was maybe a few months ago. I was having some friends over for drinks and he was in town, so I invited him. I thought my husband might appreciate having another guy around—even out the odds a little. I saw Steven and Sylvia eyeing each other, so I introduced them. Not that Steven needs my help meeting women. He's got that down."

Already, I don't think much of Steven Morris. First, the contentious conversation earlier and now this. "What do you mean?"

"Well, he's gorgeous for one thing. Fit. Tall, but not too tall. And he's fun to have around. He has a great laugh. I mean, I'm married, but if I were single, I might be interested."

"And was Sylvia? Interested?"

"Well, you know your sister. She was pretty quiet about stuff like that. I do know she gave him her number. And I remember him asking about her a couple of times. Does she have a favorite restaurant? A favorite wine? Stuff like that."

"Do you know if they went out? On any dates?"

She blinks at me. "Why are you asking, Val?"

I can't tell her what I think—that in spite of his denials, I wonder if he was with my sister in the last hours before she died. "Did you know he was married? Steven Morris?"

"What? No, I don't think that's right. He doesn't wear a ring. I mean, I know not all husbands do, but I know he dates. It's not a secret. I even met his ex-girlfriend last year." Her brow furrows, even as she shakes her head. "Besides, if Sylvia knew he was married, she would never have gone out with him."

"I agree. Which means either she never went out with him, or she didn't know he was married. That's what I'm trying to find out."

"Why?"

Sherry, like most everyone, has heard about the pills and drawn her own conclusion. "Because I miss her." As I say the words, I feel a physical ache in my soul. "So much. Maybe it won't help, but I need to know everything about every minute before she . . ." I can't finish my sentence.

"Val." Her voice is tinged with pity now.

"I'd like to know she was happy. And if she was dating this guy Steven, I'd kind of like to know that, too."

There's a soft whoosh of breath. "I think she was, but I couldn't swear to it."

I knew it. "Is there any reason? Anything she said?"

"About a month ago, I invited her to another happy hour. She said she couldn't make it because she had other plans. Something about the way she said it made me know it wasn't just dinner with the kids. When I asked, she admitted she had a date. I was so happy for her, Val. She deserved to have somebody nice, you know."

"Did she say she was going out with Steven?"

"Not exactly. I asked about Steven, but all she would cop to is that I knew the guy." She looks up at me. "She gave me a little wink when she said that."

It's not proof, but it's something. "Anything else?"

"I pressed her for details, but you know Sylvia. She doesn't like to talk about herself." Her voice catches, and she stares down at her hands. "Didn't, I mean."

I lean forward. It takes all my willpower to stay calm. "It's okay."

She gives a brief nod. "I don't know if it helps, but she did tell me she was enjoying herself more than she'd expected."

This tracks with what I already know. Sylvia wasn't eager to get back out in the dating world. She said the idea made her sad. I pushed, telling her she deserved to have someone appreciate her.

"Dating. Please, Val," she said. "It makes me feel like a high-school girl again. Who calls who? Do I like him? And where do you meet someone? A bar? No, thanks. Besides, I would need a babysitter, and I don't want to do that to Merry and Miles."

I told her I would stay with the kids and there were other ways to meet men.

"Dating sites? Nope. I'm not doing it."

But she had met someone. And she was happy.

I look back at Sherry now. "Did she ever say it wasn't Steven?"

"No."

Sylvia played coy with me too, and I wonder now if Morris wanted it that way, if he'd convinced her she should keep it quiet because of Sherry. Was he afraid Sherry would find out he was married?

Sherry raises clasped hands to her chest. "Did I do something wrong?"

Hell yes, a part of me wants to scream. She introduced my sister to a married man and put her in the position of being the other woman, made her into a Dani. But in my heart, I don't believe Sherry would knowingly do that.

"Of course not. What about Steven?" I ask. "Did you invite him to the happy hour?"

"Sure. He couldn't make it though."

"Why not?"

"He said he had other plans."

Back at the Juniper, I manage to snag a table in the corner, as far from the noise as we can get.

"The dates fit," Terry says, sliding into the booth after me. The workday crowd spills into the bar around us, perching on barstools and sipping happy-hour specials. "And with what you got from your sister's friend, it adds up to a reasonable assumption that Steven Morris was your sister's new boyfriend in spite of his denials to that effect."

Terry hands me the file his man has put together. There isn't much. Steven Morris. Salesman. Age forty-four. Married fifteen years, three kids, and a job that takes him out of town at least half of every month. Tailor-made for a man leading a double life. I realize the whole scenario sounds like the kind of thing you'd see on *Dateline* or *20/20*.

"Other than the family thing though, the man is clean," Terry says. "Not even so much as a speeding ticket."

"What's that supposed to mean?"

"It means that even knowing he was most likely the man she was seeing, as far as I can tell, cheating is the worst thing he's done."

"The worst?" I think of Sylvia and the anguish she endured when she discovered Wyatt's affair. This guy Morris is no better. The thought depresses me, reminding me why the police are sold on theory one. "You make it sound like it's no big deal."

"That's not what I meant. I'm trying to put the pieces together—same as you—make it add up to something that explains what happened to your sister."

This is what I want. More than anything. I check my phone again. No messages. Not from Wyatt or Barnes. It's been more than twenty-four hours since the detective promised to keep the case open. "A day, a day and half," he said. Time is running out. Terry picks at the cocktail napkin on the table, pinching the corners. "What are you not telling me?" I ask.

"You're not going to like it."

"Try me."

"Not one thing we have adds up to evidence. Even with all we know." He holds his hands up in the air. "Don't. I know what you're thinking. It's strong. I'll give you that. But think about it. We've got one image of them together near the elevator. They had separate reservations in the same hotel, a hotel he frequents on a regular basis, often enough that her dates coincide. Compelling? Yes, but not proof. Add to that your sister's friend, this woman Sherry, who can only say with certainty that she introduced them at a happy hour, which he freely admitted. But he denied anything more, and not one soul has been able to put them together after the initial introduction. Would this be enough for you to go to press?"

Damn Terry. He knows it's not enough.

Not without verified corroboration. Sherry's best guess is only that—a guess. I switch tactics. "I'm thinking she found out he's married, and they had a fight. But it had to be sometime after she checked in. We saw her on the tape when they went up the elevator. She was smiling, so it had to be later."

"I agree, and I'll go a step further. The doorman said she was happy on Monday morning when she went out to get bagels."

"Where's the timeline?" I ask. He pulls it out. "But on Monday night, she told the front desk she didn't feel well and didn't want to be disturbed."

"And she put the sign on the door."

"Morris was still in the hotel."

"Right. But he told us he checked out on Tuesday." He taps on his notebook. "Your sister's reservation was through Thursday."

"Yes."

"Okay. Hold on."

He picks up his phone and makes a call.

"Billy, I have one more question."

I can't hear the security man's answer, but it's clear he's not pleased. "I promise this will be the last one," Terry says. He listens, then asks his question. "Sure, I'll hold."

I sit forward, wishing I'd asked Terry to put the call on speaker. Although I stare hard, there's no sign of what he's thinking. There's no flicker of an eyelash, no tic at his temple, no tap on the table. His silence as we wait presses in on me.

"I'm here," he says, and then, "Thanks, Billy. I owe you."

"Well?" My hands are flat against the table. Terry's question was a shot in the dark, and I know it, but that doesn't mean the answer doesn't matter. It does. A lot. "What did he say?"

"Steven Morris checked in on Sunday afternoon and checked out on Tuesday morning. Early. Before eight. Told the clerk he needed to leave unexpectedly to catch a flight."

"Unexpectedly." The skin on my arm tingles, the way it does whenever I get a solid tip on a story. "Does that mean what I think?"

"Depends on what you think." Before I can throw something at him, he grins. "Steven Morris was scheduled to check out on Thursday."

I exhale. "The same as Sylvia."

"Yes."

I rub my hands over my arms, my thoughts swirling. "Sylvia died sometime Monday night or early Tuesday morning, before he checked out. Unexpectedly."

"True again."

I collapse back against the chair. I've spent days stoking a burning fire of resentment against Wyatt, casting him in a starring role. Now, I'm not so sure. Morris may have denied having a girlfriend, but every date on Sylvia's calendar coincided with him being in town. And now this.

I look back at Terry. "Do you still think it's only circumstantial?"

CHAPTER
37

TERRY

Tuesday, 5:12 p.m.

Val crosses her arms over her chest, waiting. "Well?" she asks.

I admire her determination, but I'm still a cop at heart. Nothing we've learned is the kind of proof that would hold up in a court of law. "You already know the answer, Val."

Her chin lifts a fraction. "Yeah. But hundreds of cases have been made on this same kind of evidence. I've been at enough trials to know."

I sit back. "I'm not disagreeing with you. In fact, I'd be willing to say that if you can prove Morris was seeing Sylvia, and that she found out he was married while they were staying together here at the Franklin, and that she threatened to tell his wife, you might—might—have a case for motive as well."

"That's what I've been saying." She uncrosses her arms. "I think it's time to take this to Barnes and Newman. I'll show them the calendar, tell them about Morris and his wife. How Wyatt was stalking her. All of it."

"You're handing this off?"

She seems surprised by my question.

"No. But they can ask questions we can't. We need more."

I understand her reasoning, but I'm not ready. There are other questions—ones the detectives won't ask—that need to be answered. My reasons for helping her may have expanded, but they haven't changed. She grabs her purse and slides across the bench.

"Wait." I reach out and take her arm. "I have an idea."

I drive east until the congested roads give way to a two-lane highway and eventually, to a less-traveled rural road. I'm glad to be out of that hotel, away from the ever-present chill in the air and the walls that watch my every move. Next to me, Val stares out the window. We pass through a small town populated with broken-down houses, a boarded-up grocery, and an abandoned gas station. Fields of tall grass glow in the last light of the day.

"Where are we?" she asks. "It's like the middle of nowhere out here."

"Almost there."

"Where's 'there' anyway?"

I slow the car, searching for my turn. "Edgemere. We're going to a restaurant called Bayside Eats."

"Why?"

"Your sister had takeout packages from there. I saw them in her recycling bin." Val's head comes around. "A few days before Sylvia went to the Franklin, she had a date with S. M."

"You think she went there with Morris?" she asks.

"I do." She says nothing, and five minutes later, I pull off the road to a small lot. "We're here."

She looks from the restaurant to me. "You know it's also possible she ordered takeout because she heard the food was good. Or someone brought it to her. Or they brought it into her office."

"Maybe." I glance past her. "But if you wanted to bring a woman somewhere intimate and out of the way, what could be better than this?"

"Out of the way," she repeats, her expression turning darker. "Because my sister's boyfriend is married." I don't correct her presumption that Morris is S. M. We've been over this, and it's the reason we're at Bayside Eats. She stares out the front window, her voice going quiet. "This is crazy."

I unbuckle my belt. "Look, we're here now. Let's go inside and see what we can find out." I'm halfway across the parking lot before I hear her footsteps crunch over the gravel behind me. The front of the restaurant is unremarkable, but the location is special. Bayside Eats faces the Back River. Across the water, I can see Wildwood Beach and the reflection of the setting sun.

The restaurant is one of those "seat yourself" types with a sign near the front. In spite of the season, the outdoor deck is nearly full. Space heaters are scattered across the floor and a large fire is roaring in a stone firepit. At each end, a heavy curtain of clear plastic has been drawn against the wind. It's cozy and warm enough. We take the last empty table. A waitress approaches with a pair of menus.

"Hiya, folks. First time here?"

"It is," I say and point at Val. "Her sister might have been here, though."

"Oh, yeah?" the waitress says with a knowing grin. "That's what happens. People come here once, and they wanna come back. The soft shells are kinda famous, you know. And our oysters."

"Sounds like you've worked here for a long time."

She laughs. "Yep. It's my family's place. I've been working here since the day I could carry a tray of food." She gestures at the menu. "Do you need a minute?"

"Actually," I say, "I was hoping we could ask you a couple of questions."

Her friendly smile fades. "What about?"

"Her sister." The waitress's gaze shifts to Val and back to me. "We're trying to find out if she was here one night about a week or two ago." I hold up a picture. "This is her."

Still looking at Val, the waitress asks, "Why don't you ask your sister yourself?"

"I—I can't."

The woman stares, her face softening. "Something happen to her? Your sister, I mean?"

Val pales but holds her gaze. "Please. It's . . . I need to know."

I hold up the picture again.

Sighing, the waitress relents, squinting at the photo. "I'm not sure. I don't recognize her." I see the way Val's face falls. The waitress catches it too, because she waves her hand at another waitress. "This is my Aunt Linda," she tells them. "She works most nights." The first woman explains the situation to her aunt.

Aunt Linda eyes Val a moment. "Your sister, huh?"

"Yes."

She shrugs. "Sure. I'll take a look." I hold up the picture. "I think she was here. I mean, she looks familiar, but we get a lot of people in here, you know." She leans in. "Yeah, it was her for sure."

"Was she alone?" I ask.

"Not if it's the woman I'm thinking of."

I find the headshot of Morris from his company's website that my man Cullen sent. "Is this the man she was with?"

She studies the picture. "I'm not sure. The hair seems different." Her head comes up again. "Hey, did he do something to her? Is that why you're trying to find him?"

"No, we don't know if he did anything." Although I speak the truth, I can feel Val's glare from across the table.

"Oh, good. You had me worried for a minute."

"Is there anything else you can tell us?" Val asks. There's still a small measure of hope in her voice, although I'm worried I've made things worse by dragging her out here for nothing. "Did my sister seem sad or upset?"

She shrugs. "Nah. She seemed in a good mood. They both seemed nice. Happy. I heard them laughing a couple of times." She tips her head back. "I do remember one thing. She called the Franklin—you know that hotel in Baltimore. I didn't mean to eavesdrop, but since I had their food in my hands, I couldn't walk away either. I think they were planning a trip or something. She seemed happy about it. I remember that. Excited and happy."

Tears dot Val's lashes. "Thanks for your help," I say.

"Wait. I just thought of something." The waitress taps her pen against her notepad. "Can I see that picture again?"

1 9 2 1

CHAPTER
38

BRIDGET

Bridget lay still, her knees drawn up to her chest, her back to her new husband. She clutched the heavy quilt in her hands, drawing it tighter over her shivering body. She blinked, her eyes gritty with exhaustion. The silvery light of the moon had long since faded, replaced by a darkness that reached into her heart and flowed through her veins. Even thoughts of Margaret's letter couldn't cast away the gloom.

She could picture the morning, the ride to the farm, the arrival of her sister and her husband. Her joy would be short-lived. It wasn't hard to imagine Lawrence's displeasure at the sight of her family. Perhaps he'd wait until after Margaret's departure to inflict whatever manner of punishment he felt she deserved, but Bridget knew better than to count on even an ounce of kindness. She supposed she could tell her sister everything, but she dismissed the idea almost immediately. To upset her while she was with child would be cruel. No. She would lie. She would lie to her sister, to her parents, to her husband. This was to be her life now.

A life of lies.

Lawrence snorted in his sleep, rolled over, and snored. It was better than the pompous tone of his voice or the harshness of his laugh or the crunch of his fist. Her body ached under the quilt, but she welcomed the pain. It would serve as a reminder. A reminder to play the dutiful wife. A reminder to keep up her guard. A reminder never to anger him. In the morning, she would thank him for a lovely wedding. She would sit quietly as they traveled. She would speak only when spoken to. She would wear the clothes he laid out for her. She would eat the food he put before her. She would lie with him in the night. A sob rose in her throat, and she bit down hard on the inside of her mouth. The moment passed.

The minutes stretched into hours, and still, she didn't sleep. A cool light crept across the rug toward the bed. Lawrence stirred and turned onto his side. She closed her eyes, feigning sleep. He shifted and sat up. She felt the heat of his body hovering over her motionless one. After a minute, he slid out of bed. She heard the soft pad of his footsteps and the splash of water in the basin. She exhaled and threw back the heavy quilt. Pulling her wrapper tight across her bosom, she tiptoed to the window. Bright sunlight stretched over the block, an announcement of the start of a new day. In a few hours, they would leave her beloved city behind.

"You're up."

Bridget turned around. Lawrence was dressed in a shirt, pants, and suspenders. He'd combed his hair back off his forehead. She arranged her features in what she hoped was a pleasing way. "Yes. Did you sleep well?"

"I did." He crossed the room. "I can't say you look well rested, my love. Are you ill?"

She knew better than to tell him that any woman would find it impossible to sleep lying next to a monster. Aloud, she said, "Oh, it's the excitement of being a new bride, I'm sure."

"No doubt, you're right. Shall I order breakfast then?"

Although she had no appetite, she wouldn't tell him that either. "I was wondering if we could go to the dining room for breakfast."

"Tired of my company already?"

"Not at all. But I've never stayed at the Franklin before, and well, I thought maybe I'd like to enjoy the dining room one more time." Bridget clasped her hands together. "If you'd rather breakfast here, I would understand."

A slow smile spread across his face. "No, no, the dining room is fine. In fact, you've given me an idea." He touched a hand to her cheek and stroked her flaming skin. She curled her fingers into fists and dug her nails into her palms. "We're going to have the finest breakfast the Franklin has to offer. Fruit and eggs and codfish cakes. Oh, and bacon and coffee. Only the best for my wife."

Her lips stretched wider, but inside, every fiber of her being recoiled. "That sounds wonderful. Can you arrange that so quickly?"

His barking laugh filled the room. "You have much to learn about your husband, Bridget. I'll go downstairs right now and see to it. When I get back, I'll expect to find you ready to join me in the dining room." He stepped back. "Do you think you can manage that?"

"Yes, Lawrence."

"Good girl," he said, slipping on his suit coat. "Good girl."

CHAPTER
39

BRIDGET

Lawrence sat back and wiped his mouth with his napkin. "A fine breakfast, wouldn't you say, Bridget?" He patted his waistline and slurped the last of his coffee.

She looked down at her plate and her half-eaten codfish cake. Her bacon had grown cold and limp, and her eggs had congealed into a golden clump. She couldn't remember when she'd last had an appetite. Yet, she didn't mind. The dining room was awash in light, and best of all, it was filled with other guests.

"Bridget?"

"Oh, yes." She spooned a bite of melon into her mouth.

"You haven't eaten much. We discussed this, didn't we? A little meat, yes? Although, it's best you remain trim." The stern countenance he'd taken to wearing softened. "Of course, when little Lawrence comes along, you'll be packing on enough pounds, but that won't be for long."

Bridget stopped chewing. It was as Louella had said. Lawrence wanted a child, a son, and soon.

It had taken Margaret nearly three years to be with child. She felt sure Lawrence wouldn't have that kind of patience.

The waiter rescued her from speaking. "Anything else I can get for you, sir?"

"Did I call for you?" her husband asked, his eyebrows high on his forehead.

"I don't believe so, sir."

"Then I guess there's nothing you can get for me, is there?" He made a flicking motion, waving the waiter away. The man's cheeks flushed, and Bridget lowered her lashes. Why had she never noticed this side of Lawrence when he came around all those weeks and months? Why hadn't she been paying better attention? His laughter made her look up again. "Oh, please, Bridget. Don't tell me you feel sorry for that simpering boy." Her mouth fell open, and he laughed again. "That's what I love about you. You think everyone is as innocent as you pretend to be, don't you, Bridget? Well, they're not. As a matter of fact, I can assure you nothing could be further from the truth."

Bridget watched as the young man carried a silver pot across the dining room and placed it on a table near the window. A woman in silk stockings smiled up at him. A man in a charcoal-colored suit sat down opposite her. The waiter bowed to each in turn and filled their cups. The man in the suit reached out and took the woman's hand in his. The lady angled her face toward the sunshine streaming through the glass. Her skin glowed, and Bridget was reminded of Margaret, of sweetness and goodness.

Lifting her chin, Bridget forgot her vow of earlier. "Perhaps it is misguided, but I prefer to assume the best of people rather than the worst. Life is much more pleasant that way."

"Is it? Ignorance is blindness, and there is nothing pleasant about blindness." He pulled his pipe from his suit coat, tapped it against his hand, and packed it with tobacco. He lit it and drew on the pipe, puffing until smoke drifted toward the ceiling. He glanced over at the couple near the window and took her hand in his, but there was nothing tender about his gesture. His fingers pressed into her flesh, into her bones. She dared not move. When he spoke again, his tone took on a steely edge. "But I will be your eyes now, Bridget. As your husband, I will make all the decisions. When we'll go out. Whom we shall have over for dinner. Who will come to the farm for the holidays. And don't think I didn't see through that little charade your sister put on yesterday." Her breath caught in her throat. "But don't worry, they can come. I won't make a fuss about it this time, but make no mistake, this will be the last time your family will bully me into anything. Do you hear me?"

Not trusting herself to speak, she nodded.

"Your life will be as"—he paused—"as pleasant, to use your word, as I decide it should be."

CHAPTER
40

VAL
Tuesday, 7:04 p.m.

Terry is silent as he drives back to the city. I look out the window, unsee-ing, the restaurant waitress's words playing on repeat through my mind. *She was happy. Excited and happy.* I'm doing my best to hang on to that im-age. I have to. The alternative is too depressing.

The sun has slipped below the horizon, a sliver of moon rising in its stead. Stopping the car in front of my place, Terry shifts toward me, his hands falling from the steering wheel. "Are you okay?"

I'm not, but I don't have the energy or the will to explain. I only know I don't feel as lonely as I did before. Terry's done that for me. By sticking with me and being on my side, he's given me the support I didn't know I needed, didn't know I craved.

His reasons for helping me—whatever they may be—don't matter to me as much as they should. Maybe it's because we're too close to the truth for me to risk pushing him away, even if the trip to Bayside Eats didn't turn out as we both hoped. Going over it in my head now, I wonder if it's done the opposite.

"The more I think about it," Aunt Linda said as she studied the photo, "the less I think that was him. The guy your sister was with had a different look."

"What do you mean?" I asked.

"I don't know. Less movie star." She pointed at Morris's headshot. "This guy looks a little like Bradley Cooper, right? I mean, he's hot." It would have been hard to argue the point, so I hadn't bothered. "The guy your sister was with was more like Jim from *The Office*—except with darker hair. I remember thinking that about him. Don't get me wrong. He was cute, but he was more normal-looking."

We made the drive back in silence, each lost in our own thoughts. Normal-looking. Dark hair. It isn't much to go on, and the waitress could be wrong. I can't stop my mind from turning over her words. *Excited and happy.* All that happiness is gone now. Tears prick and I blink hard.

"I'm tired," I say.

Terry reaches behind the seat and hands me the takeout bag the waitress prepared. "You've got dinner."

I'm not hungry, but I take the food.

"You need to get some rest, Val. I'll pick you up in the morning, and we can watch some more video. I cleared it with Billy. We should concentrate on Monday afternoon until Tuesday morning when Morris checked out."

The thought of watching more recordings makes me groan out load, but I know he's right. Even if Morris wasn't her boyfriend—which we don't know—I find myself wondering about his unexpected departure. The coincidence is hard to swallow.

"Sure." My phone rings, and I snatch it up without checking the number. "Val Ritter."

"Val, it's Dani."

"What do you want?" At my sharp tone, Terry glances over at me.

"Did you see my text?"

"I saw it." Talking to her is making me nauseous and my head pound. I'm about to hang up when her next words stop me.

"I left him. I thought you should know."

"When?"

"Does it matter?"

She's right. I don't even know why I asked.

Her voice is shaking now. "He's changed. He's . . . I don't know how else to say it, but he's been out of control." A muffled sob then. I wait it out. "I'm so sorry," she says finally. "About your sister. Maybe if I'd come forward sooner, none of this would have happened."

My jaw clenches. "What do you mean if you'd come forward sooner?"

"Nothing. I don't mean anything. It's just that Wyatt, well, he seemed so nice at first, but . . ." There's a long silence, then another sniffle. "But I was wrong about him. He isn't a nice guy. Not a nice guy at all. I don't know what he might have done." The hair on my arms stands up. A horn sounds in the background. "He's so angry. It's not safe for me to be with him anymore. You don't know what it's been like." Her voice drops to a whisper. "He hurt me."

In spite of myself, her words trip me up. "Jesus. What did he do?"

"My eye was swollen shut for two days."

Every nerve ending in my body comes alive.

"Where is he now?" I ask.

There's an audible sigh. "Home probably. Or working late."

"No. I went to his office. Angela says he hasn't been in."

"Angela." Dani spits out the name, her sniffles gone. "That woman would do anything for him. You know that, don't you? She can have him. I'm sure she has no idea what he's really like. I didn't. That's for sure. Last week, she lied to me. She told me—" The horns grow louder, and whatever complaints she has about Wyatt's assistant are lost in the noise. "I've gotta go. Be careful, Val. Very careful."

Her warning hits me like a jolt. "No, wait. What do you—" I start, but she's gone. I hit redial and get her voice mail. I try again, Three times. Five. She doesn't answer. I slap my hand against the car window. "Shit."

"What was that about?"

"I don't know." Dani's words play on repeat in my mind: *Angry. Not a nice guy.* Hadn't I been thinking the same things when I learned the police were suggesting my sister ended her own life? Look what he'd already done to her. He was a jerk. He was stalking her. Was I letting my obsession with finding Sylvia's mysterious boyfriend distract me from what I already knew?

"That was Dani, Wyatt's girlfriend." I tell him everything.

Terry listens without interruption. "We need to talk to Wyatt. Now."

———

We're halfway to Wyatt's apartment when I remember. "He's not there," I say. "Turn the car around." He does it without asking why. "He won't be home until nine, not until after the kids are in bed."

"The kids?"

"He's been going to my parents' house every night for dinner. To be with the kids. His apartment's too small and . . ." my words trail away. It was me who insisted they stay with my parents. The apartment was where Dani lived, and I didn't want them anywhere near her. It was one of my sister's rules about visitation and as far as I knew, Wyatt accepted it. But earlier today, my mother uttered the words I'd been dreading.

"Wyatt wants to discuss moving the kids," she said.

I held my breath—not that I hadn't known it was coming. He was their father. But that didn't mean I had to like it. "Where is he planning for them to live?"

"The house," my mother said as though it were obvious.

"What?"

"Honey, it's still his house too. They weren't divorced."

This morning, the idea that Wyatt and his girlfriend might move into my sister's house gave me a raging headache. My mother, though, is like my sister. Forgiveness flows through her veins the way cynicism flows through mine.

"Mom. That's Sylvia's house. He can't."

"It's best for the children, Val. They need to be in their own rooms. In their own beds. They need to remember their mother. Not wipe everything away."

Under any other circumstances, I might have agreed with her. This morning, my opposition centered around Wyatt *and* Dani, but that was before Dani confessed she'd left him. Now, I think maybe I have worse things to worry about.

Terry stops at a red light. "Should we go to your parents' house?"

I'm tempted. There's nothing I'd like more than to confront Wyatt, to put him in his place, but I won't do that in front of Merry and Miles. Or my parents. They've suffered enough.

"To my place, I guess," I say, holding up the takeout bag. "We can heat this up if you want."

He laughs. "If I want? Unlike you, I'm starving. And I've gotta say, those crab cakes smell amazing."

I try to match his lighthearted manner. "Yeah. Great."

Terry focuses on the road again, his thumb tapping the steering wheel. "I've been thinking," he says.

We pass a string of apartment buildings. I sit silent, watching the blur of lights.

"About the extra pills your sister had. Where did they come from? You said the doctor didn't order any refills, and as far as anyone knows, she didn't have any other prescriptions."

"They weren't hers. Someone else must have given her the pills."

"Maybe. But there's no denying it was her pill bottle on the nightstand."

"What are you getting at?"

"Didn't you tell me your sister stopped taking those pills? That she hadn't taken any in months?"

"She hadn't."

"So, how did the pill bottle get in her hotel room?" His thumb tapped faster. "If she wasn't taking those pills, why would she have packed them?"

It's a good point.

The last time I saw them was when I went through my sister's bathroom in search of a bandage and antibiotic ointment for Merry. The bottle, half full, lay on its side at the back of the medicine cabinet. But that was weeks ago, maybe longer.

"I don't think she would have."

"You don't think . . ." He lets the words lie there, shooting me a questioning glance.

"No. It's possible, I guess." I work hard to keep my tone neutral. If Sylvia packed those pills—for whatever reason—everything we'd learned could be moot. And that's a fact I'm not yet willing to accept. "But I don't think she would have." I tell him about the medicine cabinet and the dust on the cover of the cap.

"Okay. We assume she didn't pack the pills." His eyes are on the road again. "Then how did they get there?"

I turn the question over in my mind. The police—everyone—assumed Sylvia took the pills with her.

Terry is still talking, thinking out loud. "What I can't stop thinking about is the key."

My head jerks in his direction. "What key?"

"The second key for the hotel room."

I'm only half listening now. "We've been over this. She probably lost it. She always lost her keys. That's why she would get two."

Terry's thumb is still. "Okay, but whoever put that pill bottle in your sister's room had to get in somehow. Either your sister let him in, or . . ." He drags out the last word, his voice trailing away.

My stomach flutters. It's that same feeling I get when I ride a roller coaster with Miles or pedal downhill on bikes with Merry. Anticipation. Apprehension. Fear. He's right to ask how the pills got from her house to the Franklin. I think about Wyatt making a scene in the hotel and trying to con a key from the desk clerk. A key to my sister's room. A key he says he lost that is mysteriously missing. I lean my head back.

"Or he had a key."

CHAPTER

41

TERRY
Tuesday, 9:19 p.m.

Wyatt wipes his hand over his chin and rubs at two-day-old stubble. "Who are you again?"

"Terry Martin. I'm a friend of Val's." Val's brother-in-law cracks the door, only his head and chest visible. His hair is matted and his shirt rumpled. He wears the haunted look of a man who hasn't slept in days.

His gaze flicks past me to Val. "It's kind of late."

Behind me, Val huffs. I take a single step closer. "We wouldn't be here if it wasn't important."

Wyatt's hand drops lower, sliding down the hard edge of the wood. "Fine," he says.

We follow him down a short hall to one of those open living-dining-kitchen combos. A large wall of windows looks out on the Inner Harbor. Lights twinkle over the water as though suspended in the air. The expensive view is matched by an overstuffed white sofa and modern art pieces.

"Jesus, Wyatt," Val says. "It smells terrible in here."

She isn't wrong.

The apartment reeks of dirty laundry and garbage. There are dishes in the sink and on the counters. Takeout cartons and empty beer bottles litter the coffee table. A blanket sits at the end of the sofa, and I wonder how many nights the man has fallen asleep there, not making it to the bedroom. Searching the walls, I spy a large, crudely spackled hole, partially covered by a thumbtacked calendar.

Using two fingers, Val plucks a wrinkled shirt off an armchair and drops it on the floor. "Where's your girlfriend? Or should I say ex-girlfriend?"

I stand back, watching and listening. If Wyatt hears the iciness in Val's voice, he doesn't show it.

"I know she left you, Wyatt. What happened?"

He doesn't respond right away, slumping on the sofa. When he does, there's acknowledgement in his voice and something else. Something distant and without remorse. "We broke up."

"What did you do to her?"

His head jerks up again, but he remains silent, picking at the torn skin around his ragged nails.

"I'm going to have to tell my parents," Val says. "The children can't be around you like this."

"Don't." His voice quivers when he speaks. "Please. They're all I've got left."

"You should have thought of that before."

"I haven't done anything wrong."

"Sure. Cheating on your wife. Scaring her and then your girlfriend. You're a great guy to have around."

Wyatt springs to his feet. "I'm sick of you judging me, Val." His lips glisten with spit, and his arms swing wildly. "You don't know anything about what happened between Sylvia and me. Yes, I fucked up. Yes, things were awkward for a while, but since—"

"Awkward? God, if that isn't the understatement of the year."

I step between them then, my hands raised. "Why don't we all calm down?" I look over at Val. "This isn't why we came here tonight. Is it, Val?"

She bites down on whatever she was going to say, and I take advantage. "Right," I say and focus on Wyatt again. "Sit down and we'll talk."

He doesn't move, his body tightly coiled. "About what?"

"Like whether or not you still have a key to Sylvia's house," Val says.

"It's still my . . ." He withers under Val's glare, and his words drift away.

"Fine. Yes, I still have a key."

"Did you use it?"

"No."

"I don't believe you."

I watch the exchange between the two of them and clear my throat. "Why don't we talk about the hotel and Sylvia and what happened in her room?"

The lines of Wyatt's face shift and crack. "The police . . . Detective Barnes. He thinks I did something."

This is news to me, and I have to assume to Val too. I sense her moving behind me, but I wave my hand at her to stay back. It's my turn to ask the questions.

"Okay. Let's talk about that." I speak slowly, in a low, soothing tone. "Why don't you sit down?" I ask again.

Wyatt stares, unblinking, his chest rising and falling. A minute passes, but still, he doesn't move. I gesture to the sofa, take a seat at one end, and wait. After a few seconds, he sits too. From the corner of my eye, I see Val standing back.

"What does Detective Barnes think you did?" I ask.

"I don't know," Wyatt says. His words are mumbled, as though the beer he's chugged since arriving home has gone to his head. Beads of sweat dot his hairline. "But it's not good. He thinks I threatened Sylvia. But I would never, ever do that."

"When did you speak to Detective Barnes?"

"Today. This afternoon." Wyatt's hands ball up to fists and he holds them against his forehead. Val moves toward him as he speaks. "I didn't do anything." He rocks forward and backward. "I wouldn't. I swear."

I scoot closer, my voice soft. "Why do they think it then?"

The rocking slows. "How would I know? They gave me some story about how they'd seen a text Sylvia sent saying she was afraid of me." His voice cracks. "They're lying, trying to trap me into saying something."

"Sometimes, detectives use inventive tactics," I say, "but in this case, the police did have a reason." I cast a sideways glance at Val. "Maybe you should explain it to him."

Val inhales through her nose and lets out a long breath. She's a few feet from Wyatt now. "Fine," she says. Wyatt looks up at her expectantly. "The police weren't lying. Someone did show them a text. Someone who wanted them to know the truth."

His head moves slowly from side to side. "Wh-who?"

Val leans over until her face is only inches from Wyatt's. "Me."

The color drains from Wyatt's face. "But Sylvia wasn't afraid of me. You must have misunderstood."

"I don't think so." She scrolls through her texts and holds up the screen. He reaches for it, but Val draws back. She reads the words out loud. "Wyatt and I had a fight. Another one. It was bad—the worst one yet. He scares me, Val. I haven't told you about the fights before, about how he is now, because I didn't want to upset you. I know how much you worry about me. But I can't handle him by myself anymore. I'm going to tell him to stop coming to the house. To leave me alone. Sorry to drop this on you right now. It's just gotten so bad. We'll talk when I get home." Her hand drops to her side when she finishes.

He looks up at her, his brows knitted. "It doesn't make sense. Val, you've known me for fifteen years. I know I failed Sylvia, but I've never hurt her the way you're saying. You know that's not me."

Her head swivels toward the spackled hole in the wall. "Do I?" He follows her line of sight, and his face reddens. "Are you calling my sister a liar? Me a liar?"

"No, no." He sits up a fraction. "No. I mean yes." He points at her phone. "It's not true. None of it."

"Are you denying you went to the hotel."

His mouth opens and closes. "No. I was there. I told the police that."

I see Val's lips part in surprise, but she recovers quickly. "I saw you there today. Staring up at the top floors. What were you doing?" She takes a step back, as though even the idea of his voyeurism is somehow catching. "Looking at her room, Wyatt? The room where she died?"

His cheeks flush red again. "Yes."

In the brief silence that follows, I wonder what these admissions might mean.

Blinking, Val asks, "Why? Why would you do that?"

He shrugs, his eyes downcast. "I don't know."

Val stares at him another moment before drawing herself up. "I'm going to have to tell Detective Barnes about everything." If I expected to hear triumph in her voice, I'm wrong. There is no gladness, only resignation. "And about Dani."

Wyatt's eyes glisten. "What happened with Dani was my fault. Not hers."

Again, Val is momentarily at a loss for words. "It doesn't change anything, Wyatt," she says finally.

"I wish . . ." His chin falls lower, and whatever words he was going to say are lost.

Val touches me on the shoulder. "Can we go?"

I hesitate. I have more questions, but the dark hollows in Val's cheeks are enough to make me turn around. Wyatt and the struggle to reign in her warring emotions have taken a toll. We leave him there, unmoving, head in his hands.

In the car, Val sits, silent, and I think about Wyatt, the things he said and the way his anger burned hot and fizzled almost as quickly as it flamed. I think about the things he didn't say. He clammed up when Val pressed him about Dani and her accusations. He stared at the floor, picking at his fingers, unwilling or unable to return Val's angry glare. He was hiding something. On the other hand, he didn't deny being at the hotel or having a key to

Sylvia's house. In my experience, it could mean one of two things. Either he's an accomplished liar, well versed in the ways of using partial truths to create a false narrative, or he was telling the truth.

Val sighs and lays her head against the glass. "Well, that was fun."

My gaze finds her in the glow of the streetlight. A single tear rolls down her cheek, and whatever I was going to say is forgotten. I close my mouth and drive.

1 9 2 1

CHAPTER

42

BRIDGET

"Shall I show you the Juniper before we ride out to the farm?" Lawrence gripped Bridget's elbow as they left the dining room.

She walked faster to keep up, but the ache in her ribs and her bones made moving quickly difficult. Although she'd been curious about the lounge the day before, she was eager to get to the farm now, eager to see Margaret. Even so, she knew better than to say so. "I thought it was a gentlemen's lounge."

"Oh, I wouldn't say all those who've patronized that particular lounge could be called gentlemen," he said with a laugh. "Rogues and scoundrels make more than a passing appearance. But it is true ladies are not normally admitted to the Juniper."

"Then how—"

He lifted his hand. In it she saw a shiny gold key. "I've arranged a private tour," he said. The sun shone through the tall windows of the hotel, warming her skin. The light from the large chandelier danced over them, flickering across the marble floor. "Consider it a small wedding present."

Bridget didn't know how visiting a gentlemen's lounge could be called a wedding present, but she bit her tongue. "Thank you, Lawrence."

Her words seemed to please him, and his grip loosened. As they climbed the stairs, she could feel her heart hammering under her day gown. The hallway ahead was empty and stretched the length of the second floor. The click of her heels echoed, the sound reminding her of her late uncle's funeral and the nails being driven into the coffin in the moments before it was lowered into the ground.

She shook away the thought and hurried to keep up, her legs trembling under her.

"Ah, here we are," he said. "As I told you yesterday, the juniper tree has long been regarded as a symbol of protection and innocence. Ironic really. No doubt, whoever chose the name did not adequately research all the meanings." He stroked his mustache as he spoke. They stood in front of the intricately carved doors. "They're quite beautiful, don't you think?"

"Yes," she said. "May I touch them?"

"We're alone, Bridget. Be my guest."

She reached out and ran a hand over the finely honed wood, tracing the branches and berries. "It's lovely."

Lawrence slipped the key into the lock and pulled open the heavy doors. The air inside was heavy with the medicinal odor of illegal alcohol, the acrid smell of tobacco, and the sweet scent of wood oil. A murky light crept through the stained-glass windows facing the street. She blinked, unable to make out more than lumps and shadows. Lawrence crossed the room to switch on a single lamp. She exhaled, uncurling her fingers.

"Is it what you imagined?"

The brick walls were studded with iron lanterns, and the long wooden bar glowed in the lamplight. The lumps turned out to be nothing more sinister than tables and chairs spread across the room. Glasses were stacked on top of the bar and ashtrays sat on each table. A large painting of a juniper tree hung over the center of the mirrored wall behind the wooden bar. Bridget stepped forward. This tree wasn't like the carvings in the doors. The roots and branches were twisted and spread wide as though reaching—for what she didn't know. The ground around the tree was dry and barren. Angry clouds hovered over the lonely tree. She wanted to look away, but she couldn't. "Is it dying?" she asked.

"What?" Lawrence arched one eyebrow. "The tree?"

"Yes."

"I don't know. I've never thought about it."

"It seems so sad."

He laughed, not bothering to hide his amusement. "Dear Bridget. It's only a painting."

"Yes, of course." Her cheeks flamed.

"Still, if you like it so much, I could have one done for you."

Her gaze went back to the cheerless painting. Did she like it? She didn't think so, and yet, she was drawn to it, nonetheless. "That's very kind," she said. "But it's not necessary."

Lawrence shrugged. "Well, that may be for the best. I don't know why people believe in such things as luck and protection. It's mumbo jumbo, if you ask me. It's not as though it does anyone any good. A man, a real man, makes his own way. He doesn't rely on luck."

Bridget still wondered at the meaning. "But why are junipers supposed to be good luck at all?"

"Well, there are some who say it was a juniper that hid the baby Jesus and his parents from King Herod when they fled to Egypt." He shrugged again. "Who knows? And it's no secret that junipers are used in some medicines. Some drink too, which is at least a better reason for the name than the other nonsense." He paused. "Although there is another story, one quite different from the others."

"What story?"

"You've never heard the story 'The Juniper Tree'?"

"No. Should I?"

"Well, it's a fairy tale, a Grimm's tale." He angled his head toward her. "Would you like to hear it?"

She'd always loved stories. "Oh, yes."

He ducked behind the bar, picking up two glasses. Reaching underneath, he found an amber-colored bottle, uncorked it, and poured. Handing one to her, he raised his glass. "To the juniper tree."

She took the glass. Her nose wrinkled at the odor, and she held it away from her. As she watched, he tipped his glass back and swallowed the vile-smelling drink.

He tipped his chin toward the glass in her hand. "Drink up, Bridget. It's one of the few times I'll allow you to drink anything other than champagne."

She didn't want the drink but knew better than to disobey. The few drops that slid down her throat burned, and she coughed. He laughed again, and she took a second sip. It didn't taste any better, but it didn't taste any worse. By the third sip, she felt a warmth spread through her limbs, dulling the pain. The glass was still half full, but it was enough. Lawrence may have given her the drink, but he didn't fool her. She set the glass back on the bar and said, "I'm afraid I'm not much for liquor."

"Quite right."

She knew instantly she'd made the right decision. He came out from behind the bar, carrying her glass for himself, and directed her to sit down.

"Once upon a time," he said, "there was a young couple, unable to have children. The woman was particularly upset, and one day, she went outside to dream under her favorite tree." He lifted a finger in the direction of the painting. "A juniper tree. While there, she cut her finger peeling an apple. Her blood dripped onto the ground, staining the white snow. It was then she made a wish to have a baby boy as white as snow and as red as blood." He paused to sip from Bridget's glass. "Soon, she was with child, which gave the couple great happiness. But not long after, she ate too many juniper berries and fell ill. She then begged her husband to bury her under the juniper tree should she die. To her great joy, she gave birth to a baby boy, but she died soon after. True to his word, he buried her under the tree." He looked at Bridget. "What do you think so far?"

"It's incredibly sad. The poor woman."

"Bah! She made a wish to have a baby, and her wish was granted. There is no need to be sad for her." Although Bridget disagreed, she said nothing. "But the husband was in a bit of a pickle. For here he was with a baby boy and no mother for the child. So, after a time, he married again. His second wife bore him a little girl. Naturally, she favored her own child, and as the boy got older, she grew to despise him."

"I don't think I like this story much."

Lawrence's skin darkened. "You will not interrupt me, wife."

"I'm sorry." Bridget clasped her hands together and batted her lashes. "But the story has affected me so." Even as the conciliatory words slipped from her lips, she wondered at herself. Was she acting to keep his anger at bay? Or was it the truth? She decided it didn't matter when the hard lines around his mouth smoothed, and he returned to the story.

"When the husband wasn't home, the new wife abused the boy. It was no secret she wished her daughter to inherit the man's wealth and not the son. Then one day, an idea popped into her head. It nagged at her brain, growing and growing until she was consumed by it. When the boy came home from school, she instructed him to choose an apple from the chest. As he leaned in for the apple, she slammed it closed, lickety-split." Bridget raised a hand to her neck. "And what do you think happened, my young wife?"

"I—I don't know."

"The boy lost his head." Bridget covered her face with her hands. Lawrence chuckled but kept talking. "Upon seeing the dead boy, the stepmother became anxious to hide her deed. She set him up in a chair and using a scarf, bound his head to his neck. She set an apple in his lap. When the little girl came into the room, she asked the boy for the apple. As you can guess, he said nothing. The little girl turned to her mother, who told her to box the boy on the ears for his insolence. When the little girl hit the boy's ears, his head fell off and rolled right up to her toes. She began to scream and sob about what she'd done. The child was inconsolable, for in spite of her mother's best efforts, she was fond of her brother.

"To hide the dead boy, the stepmother dismembered him and cooked him up into a soup as red as blood. When the husband arrived home, she told him the boy had gone to visit with a relative. The man was unhappy but sat down to dinner the way he did every night. The wife served the soup to her husband. As he ate, he proclaimed the meal to be the most delicious he'd ever eaten. Neither the wife nor the girl ate the soup, but he didn't notice. After dinner, the woman took the bones and buried them beneath the juniper tree."

Bridget was suddenly glad she was sitting, sure her legs might give out on her otherwise. She reminded herself the tale wasn't real. It was a story, a fairy tale, although unlike any tale she'd heard before.

"Now this, dear Bridget, is when things really start to get interesting." Lawrence drained the glass and slammed it down on the table. "No sooner had she buried the bones than a great mist rose from the tree and out flew a beautiful bird. Do you know who that bird was?" Lawrence asked. Bridget shook her head. "It was the boy. He flew to town as fast as he could and began to sing a pretty song all about his murder at the hands of his stepmother. A goldsmith was so entranced he gave the bird a golden necklace. A cobbler gave him a pair of red shoes, and a miller gifted the bird with a large millstone. The bird returned home, where his stepmother was complaining of the burning blood in her heart. Upon seeing his father, the bird placed the necklace around the man's neck. The stepmother cried out as though in pain. The bird then gave the shoes to his sister. The girl danced in a happy circle, and the stepmother fell to the ground, rolling around as though on fire. Waving her arms, she ran outside for relief, and it was then that the bird dropped the millstone on her head, killing her instantly."

"Oh, dear."

"The land around the juniper erupted into smoke and flames and from the smoke, the son emerged, alive again, no longer a bird. The small family was reunited, but for the stepmother, and lived happily ever after." Lawrence sat back and lifted an arm toward the painting. "There you have it. The story of the juniper tree."

K. L. Murphy

"Th-that's horrible."

He shrugged. "I didn't write it, Bridget."

Repulsed, her thoughts swirled. "But how could anyone say the juniper is good luck then? I don't understand how anything in that story is good."

"Of course it was good luck. Without the tree, the boy wouldn't have been born, and without the tree, the stepmother wouldn't have been killed."

What he'd said was true, but the rest was too terrible to think about. What the stepmother had done could only be described as evil. "But the berries poisoned the mother."

"She ate too many. She was a stupid woman, Bridget."

The air in the room seemed to shift, and a chilly draft brushed the skin of her neck. She glanced behind her, but the heavy doors were shut tight.

Lawrence watched her, his lips twitching. "Did my story frighten you?"

"A little."

"No need to despair. Our child will not be the result of a desperate wish made by a weak woman, will it?" His tone slipped from amused to something else, something she wasn't sure she understood.

"No, Lawrence."

"Good." He stood up, his chair sliding back behind him. "For if my wife is unable to give me a child, it will not be to a tree that she will need to pray." The air grew colder, and she trembled with each word he spoke. "Do we understand each other, Bridget?"

She answered in a whisper. "Yes, Lawrence."

His face changed again, and one thin lip curved upward. "Why, who knows? Maybe there's a child already growing inside you, right this very minute." Her hand fell to her waist and the hollow below. His voice sounded far away as he talked. "Yes, a son, tall and strapping like his father. He'll be a man with rules and principles. A man to take over the business and the farm. A man who doesn't abide fools, who isn't made a fool of. A boy who will make his father proud."

Fear snaked through her belly. What if she couldn't bear children? What if it took too long? "We've been married one day," she said.

"You're right. Only one day. Perhaps I'm overly eager, but I am not a patient man, Bridget. By this time next year, there will be a child or one coming soon." The whites of his eyes glowed in the flickering light. "Or so help me, God, you'll wish you had a forest of juniper trees."

PRESENT DAY

CHAPTER
43

VAL
Wednesday, 9:21 a.m.

Terry's late. I've been waiting in the security room, seated at our desk, for twenty minutes. I shoot him a text asking where he is.

Taking another run at Wyatt. Have a few more questions.

My fingers fly over the screen.

Without me? I should be there.

I wait, but there are no dots indicating another text. Laughter from across the room makes me look up, and when my phone rings, I'm sure it's Terry, apologizing or explaining.

"Why didn't you wait for me?" I make a move toward my bag. "I can be there in ten."

"Is this Ms. Ritter?"

"Yes," I say, Terry forgotten.

"This is Detective Barnes."

"Oh. You got my messages."

"Messages? I was calling because I was wondering if you could come down to the station. I have some questions about your sister's case."

Case. Sylvia's death is a CASE. Finally. "What is it?"

"It would be best if we speak in person. Now, if you're available."

I spring to my feet, my skin tingling. "I'll be right there."

Detective Barnes is waiting for me in the same tiny conference room. He gestures at the empty chair across from him. I see the file folder on the table. It's thicker than the last time we spoke. Another positive. "Is Detective Newman coming?" I ask.

"He's running down a lead."

Maybe Newman is looking into Wyatt after their talk with him the day before. "You said you had some questions for me."

"I do." He clears his throat. "How would you characterize the relationship between your sister and her husband?"

"Haven't we been over this? I showed you the text she sent me."

"I'd like to go over it again. Before you got that text, did she hint at anything that might make you think that your brother-in-law had become violent or unstable?"

"Unstable?" Did throwing away your family count? Or following your ex-wife? Hitting your girlfriend? Or punching holes in walls? Sitting knee deep in empty beer bottles alone? I swallow. "It's hard to say."

"Was Mr. Spencer's behavior different in any way that you'd noticed?"

Falling back against the chair, I try to think. "Until Sylvia died, I hadn't seen him in about a month. Not since Merry's school play."

"And how was he then?"

"Fine, I guess. He sat in a different row during the show, but he came over to say hi to the kids after. He didn't stay long or go to the reception in the cafeteria. I thought it was kind of strange, but to be honest, I was glad to see him go."

"And how did he seem around your sister?"

I tip my head back, remembering.

"Sylvia didn't say much to him. That was normal. I mean, she kept things cordial and polite, especially in front of the kids, but it was mostly for show. They'd been separated for months. I don't think she was still mad at him, if that's what you were wondering."

"He had regular visitation?"

"Yes."

"How did that work?"

"Wyatt would have dinner with the kids on Wednesdays and Sundays. He'd wait in his car for her to bring them out most of the time. Every other weekend, he took them to his parents' house."

Barnes makes notes. "Was his girlfriend with him on these occasions?"

I almost laugh. "No. Sylvia wouldn't allow it, and I don't think Dani liked kids much. As far as I know, Wyatt never challenged Syl on it."

"Okay. So, friendly a month ago."

"I would say restrained."

He taps his pen against the notebook. "What would you say if I told you Mr. Spencer has painted us a very different picture?"

I hear the question in his voice and fold my arms across my chest. "No doubt he gave you some Disney version about how everyone was one big happy family."

"Something like that."

"Well, don't believe it. The man's a liar." In spite of his selective admissions the night before, he had a history that couldn't be dismissed. "My sister learned that the hard way."

His pen hits the notepad a few more times. "Okay. Let's move on. Did your sister say anything to you about Mr. Spencer in the last month—outside of the text?"

Again, I turn the memories over in my mind. There was the time Sylvia had been dressing for one of her dates with the new boyfriend when I popped by.

"I guess there's one good thing about Wyatt having visitation," I said. "At least you have every other weekend where you don't need a babysitter."

I expected Sylvia to have some sarcastic comment or maybe even laugh, but, instead, she picked up one of the dozens of pictures of the kids from her dresser. "You're wrong, Val. I'd rather have them here, where they belong."

That's when I saw the melancholy behind the makeup and the pretty dress. No matter how much she'd moved on with her life, she couldn't get used to her children being gone, even for one night.

"Wyatt goes out when they're at his parents' house. They don't know where or with whom, but it's not hard to figure out. It's got to be her," I said. Alarm flickered across Sylvia's face. "Don't worry. According to Miles, he doesn't bring Dani around. The kids never see her. And I'm sure they're fine with Wyatt's parents, but maybe you could talk to your lawyer and get his visitation reduced. Dani would be thrilled."

Her face changed. "Val . . ."

I held up my hands. "I know. Stop butting in. It's your life."

"You say that, Val." An edge crept into her voice. "I'm a grown woman. Let me handle it."

I told Barnes about that conversation now. His head bobbed as he wrote. "And did she handle it? Talk to her lawyer?"

"I don't know. I mentioned it a couple of weeks later, but she gave me the brush-off." In truth, she didn't just ignore the question. She asked me to let it go before turning the subject around. "She did say something," I say now. "She asked me if I thought Wyatt was really that bad, if I thought there was any goodness in him at all."

"Interesting. And what did you say?"

"I said I thought he was an idiot loser who messed up the best thing he was ever going to get. That he didn't deserve her or the kids."

"Sugarcoated it, huh?"

"She didn't disagree." But sitting in the police station now, I wonder if my response was the reason she didn't tell me about the fights. Once the words were out, she wouldn't be able to take them back. Had Sylvia been hoping to find some good left in Wyatt after all? I fight back tears. If I'd been a little less stubborn, she might have confided in me. It's true that Sylvia deserved better than Wyatt, but maybe she deserved better than me too.

"We brought him in yesterday."

I shake off my guilt and self-recrimination then, and fill him in on Wyatt's stalking, Dani's phone call, and the scene at the hotel.

"Right. We got a tip," he says.

"From whom?"

He evades the question with one of his own. "Is there anyone else she might have confided in? Your parents? Or a best friend?"

"Not that I know of. Her therapist maybe." I stop short of mentioning her new boyfriend. "Why does this matter? You know he was threatening her. And following her."

He waves the pen in the air. "We've verified the text you received was sent from your sister's phone, which would indicate things were not good between them. It's also possible he was stalking your sister."

"Possible?"

Before he can answer, the door opens behind me, and I spin around in my chair. Newman.

"Barnes. Can I see you for a minute?" Newman doesn't acknowledge me or look in my direction.

The short minutes the young detective is gone feel like hours, and my leg bounces up and down against the tabletop. When the door opens again, his expression is grim. He tosses a new file on the table. "Have you ever heard of a company called Medspharmco?" He doesn't wait for me to answer. "It's an illegal pharmacy. The kind where you don't need a doctor's prescription. Popped up on the FDA's list a few months ago."

My mouth goes dry. "I've never heard of it."

Barnes pulls a sheet of paper from the file and slides it across the table. He thumps it with his finger. "Your sister had."

I stare at the receipt in disbelief, still shaking my head when he lays a second page on the table, an order form dated two weeks before Sylvia's death. Her name is on it, along with a request for sleeping pills, the same medication she'd been prescribed nearly a year earlier. This time though, there's no doctor signature or evidence of a valid prescription.

"Where did you get this?" I manage to ask.

"Off her laptop. It wasn't easy to find. She deleted it, but forensics was able to pull it up."

He has no reason to lie, and yet, I don't believe it. "Is this what Detective Newman was doing? The lead?"

"Yes. Everything at the hotel points to your sister," he hesitates, "doing what she did, but the pills bothered me. How could she have overdosed on so many pills when her original prescription was half that amount? And then, when we got the tip about her ex showing up at the house late at night, stalking her, I thought it was possible you were right. Newman didn't agree, but he went along with it."

I push the piece of paper away from me. "This doesn't change anything."

"I think it does." There's a finality in his tone, and I feel the sting of tears. "You may be right about your sister's ex. Maybe he was stalking her, maybe even making her life hell, but all the evidence says she illegally sought out those pills in order to take her own life." He pauses. "I'm sorry."

It's all I can do to breathe in that moment. Could it be true? Wyatt's threats, his stalking, the loss of the marriage Sylvia once valued so much—did all of it make her feel so hopeless? Was she suffering from deep-seated depression? My own words come back to me. *If she did what they say she did, I'll accept it.* Theory three. I feel like I can't breathe.

The detective is still talking. "She hadn't told you about Mr. Spencer. Maybe that's why she didn't tell you about the pills. She was protecting you."

Barnes pushes a box of tissues across the table. "I'm sorry," he says again.

I stand up in a rush. I have to get out of there, away from the order and receipt, away from his pity.

Outside, the air is biting. It smells of exhaust and smoke and the promise of rain and sleet. I manage to get to my car before I scream. An ear-splitting, gut-wrenching scream. I pound the steering wheel with my fists until they're red and throbbing.

"Why?" I shout it out loud. "Why? Why? Why?" My voice fades to a whisper. "Why?"

My phone buzzes, and I look at the screen. Dani. I stare at it and feel a sense of rage bubbling up. How can this woman be alive, and my sister be gone? It's not fair. If I were a more generous person, I might feel sorry for Dani, but there's a little piece of me that thinks maybe she's getting what she deserves, karma even. My phone stops vibrating. A ping tells me she's left a message. I ignore it and dial another number, the one that matters most now.

"Hey, Mom," I say. "Can I talk to the kids?" She puts them on. "How would you guys like to go ice skating tonight? You would? That's great. I'll call you when I'm on my way."

I hang up and wipe away my tears. Sylvia is gone. Wyatt is . . . well, I don't know what he is, but he needs help. Merry and Miles need me now. More than ever. It doesn't matter why Sylvia is gone, only that she is. Maybe I'll never know the truth. Maybe I'll never know why. I hang my head and take long, deep breaths. A car door slams nearby, and I give myself a shake. In a few hours, I'll put on my best smile and slide across the ice with my niece and nephew. I'll take them for pizza and hug them tight. It's what Sylvia would want.

Billy lifts a hand when I return to the hotel's security office.

"Is Terry back?" I ask.

He shakes his head, and I plop myself down and throw my bag on the floor. I check my phone, but there's nothing from Terry. Sighing, I scoot toward the desk, my hand hovering over the keys. I push play and wait. When Sylvia walks across the lobby, I lean in, my face inches from the screen. Her golden hair is pulled up into a ponytail, and she wears a scarf around her neck. She doesn't hurry or dawdle. I see the bellman open the door, the same bellman Terry quizzed the day before. She breezes through, passing in front of the camera, and then she's gone. There's a tightness in my chest, and I hear a soft moan. It's a minute before I realize the cry came from me.

"You okay?" Billy asks in his cigarette-scratchy voice. "I don't mean to intrude, but you seem upset."

I surprise myself by telling the truth. "I am."

"Is there anything I can do?" The southern twang is back.

I blink hard, looking at him. His face is open and kind and matches his wide-set gaze. I decide he's probably softhearted—a marshmallow—a sucker for more jaded folks like me. I don't think I've misjudged his ability as a cop, but I realize I've let that cloud my vision of Billy as a person. "No, it's that—" I stop, stumbling over my words. Waving a hand at the screen, I try again. "Seeing my sister is hard, harder than I expected. But if I don't watch, I'm terrified I'll miss something even though I know there's nothing to see."

"Maybe there is, and maybe there isn't." He shrugs. "Once, when I was still on the job, I searched this apartment for a perp. I looked under the beds and checked the bathroom. I opened the closets. Nothing. He wasn't there. My partner looked too. The thing was, we knew he had to be inside. We'd been watching the apartment for two days. There was no way he left because nobody saw him. So, I looked again. Still nothing. And then I heard it."

I half listen, somehow managing to mumble at the right times.

"It was one of those notifications, you know, the dingy thing on your phone."

"Oh, right."

"Anyway, it was faint, but I could tell where it had to be coming from. There was this closet in the bedroom. I'd already checked it like three times. Pulled the clothes back, you know, but he wasn't there. So, I stand there a minute, staring at a damn wall. And then I remember. The closet runs along the same wall as the closet in the other bedroom. Same size doors you know. But one of them isn't the same on the inside. It's smaller. Like part of it is missing. And that's when I found him."

I'm paying attention now. "In the closet?"

"Yep. He'd cut a space big enough to stand inside, then drywalled it over. The door was flush with the wall so you couldn't see it unless you knew it was there. But I didn't let on how I'd figured it out. We made a bunch of noises about how pissed we were he'd gotten away and pretended to leave. He didn't come out right away, but when he did, he got a helluva surprise."

After Billy returns to his own desk, I think about his story and tell myself that one more time won't hurt. I fast-forward until Sylvia comes back into the hotel. Her cheeks are flushed pink, and her scarf has blown back over her shoulder. In one hand, she carries a paper bag. In the other, a paper tray with coffee.

"What the . . . ?"

I hit rewind, watch her come in again, and slow the recording for the best view. I'm still not sure. I enlarge the picture until it blurs. The image isn't precise, but there's no doubt in my mind. My sister is carrying a tray with coffee. Two coffees. Not one.

CHAPTER
44

TERRY

Wednesday, 9:24 a.m.

I knock on the door, my knuckles loud against the heavy wood. The hallway is quiet. Gleaming sconces shine down from cream-colored walls onto cream-colored carpet. The ten-foot ceilings are dotted with tiny recessed lights that shine like stars. Modern art—the kind that looks like black and gray splotches of paint on white canvas—hangs on the walls. I don't care much for magazine-style living, no matter the doorman or expansive views. I can't see the harbor from my living-room window, but Mrs. Hayes waves every morning and Mr. Johnson stops in most weekends for a cold beer. My house is old with a creaky porch and rooms that are drafty in the winter and stifling in the summer, but it's home. A building like this makes me feel like a five-year-old with ice-cream stained fingers, afraid to touch. I lift my hand to knock again. The elevator dings, and I swing around. Wyatt, coffee in one hand and a brown bag in the other, steps into the hall. He slows when he sees me.

"What do you want?" the man asks. There are dark smudges under his eyes. "Where's Val?"

"I came on my own." There's no point in beating around the bush, so I don't. "I thought you might want to talk about things. It's been rough on Val and—"

"It's been rough on everyone."

"Right. I got the feeling last night, you wanted to explain. I'm here to listen."

Wyatt scowls. "Why? What's in it for you?"

The man's question is valid. Again, I decide to be honest. "Nothing. Former cop in me, I guess." His mouth drops open. "Last night, we left before you got a chance to tell your side. Now's your chance."

Wyatt stares past me down the empty hall, chewing his lower lip. "My side, huh?"

"Yep."

"Fine," he says after another minute and gestures with the paper bag toward the elevator. "Not here. Let's take a walk."

We cross the street to the corner park. The wind whistles through the bare trees, but we keep walking until we reach an empty playground with a wooden bench. I sit down at the far end facing the swing set. Wyatt sits a few feet farther down, sips his coffee, and hunches his shoulders against the cold.

"What was your name again?" he asks.

"Terry Martin. Call me Terry."

"Are you a private detective now or something? You still kind of seem like a cop." He tips his cup toward me. "No offense."

"None taken. I'm in security now."

He takes that in and shifts his body in my direction. "I still don't understand why you're here."

"Like I said, I got the feeling you might have more to say."

"What difference does it make if I do?"

"Maybe none. Maybe some."

Wyatt seems to consider my answer, his gaze locked on the cup in his hand. When he looks up again, there's a kind of resignation on his face. "Where would you want me to start?"

"Wherever you'd like."

"Oh." He drinks from his cup and opens the bag. Frowning, he closes it again. "Look, I don't know how much you know about what happened with Sylvia, but . . ." His body sags. "It's not good."

"Val told me you cheated on Sylvia, got caught, and separated."

"Huh. Well, I guess that sums it up pretty well." He stares out at the empty playground. "I met Dani at a conference. I was there for estate law, and she was there for some kind of digital software something. Computer science stuff. I guess all the panels were boring because we both ended up in the bar. She was young. Beautiful. I could give you the same excuses I gave Sylvia, tell you the same lies I told myself, but I won't." He gets up to toss the paper bag and coffee into a metal trash can. "I didn't realize my mistake right away. Dani wanted us to get an apartment together. I guess I didn't want to make a second woman unhappy, so I said yes." He tips his head toward his apartment building. "She picked this place. It was okay at first. I was busy at work and trying to see the kids as much as I could. Dani didn't like that. I thought she was upset because Sylvia didn't want her around the kids, but that wasn't it. She was jealous of my time with them. I tried to be understanding. I told myself it would get better, but . . ." his voice fades.

"But it didn't."

"No, it didn't." He shoves his hands in his pockets and sits down again. "Dani went away for a weekend, ostensibly to be with her girlfriends, but I think it was actually to make me miss her. The thing is, I didn't. The joke was on me with that one, right? I didn't blame Dani though. It wasn't her fault. And I thought I loved her." With his every word, his breath is a mist, and he shivers. "I created a mess. I'd already hurt one person. I didn't want to hurt Dani too, but I didn't know how to get out of it." He rubs at the stubble on his chin. "So, I didn't do anything."

"You stayed."

"Yeah."

Dark clouds roll overhead. The wind shifts and the bare tree limbs rattle like empty cans.

"I don't think I was the nicest guy to be around," he says. "One night, Dani told me she wanted to get married. I don't know what got into me. We were living together. It was a reasonable request. But I snapped."

I sit silent, waiting.

"I'm not proud," he says. His eyes are squeezed shut and he pinches the creases above his nose. "We got in a fight. A terrible fight. We both said things we shouldn't have said. She screamed at me, pushed me, started scratching my face. I should have let her, but I didn't."

I speak up then, my voice quiet. "What did you do?"

Wyatt doesn't answer at first. "You're not going to like me very much."

"What makes you think I like you now?"

He stares back at me for a moment before he nods. With each word he utters, he wilts in front of me, growing smaller on the bench. "Dani told me something after that. Maybe she thought she was showing me how much she loved me, but when I heard what she had to say . . ." His shoulders roll forward and his body shudders as though whatever happened was happening again. "I couldn't even look at her."

My own heart beats faster in my chest. "And what was it that she told you?"

A minute passes before he answers.

"Everything I'd been holding back came out that night." I strain to hear the words. "All my anger and frustration. Dani knew I didn't want to be there anymore. She knew we were through. She wanted to hurt me." Another pause. He kicks at the ground and sighs. "I'd always wondered how Sylvia found out I was seeing Dani."

"Ah." I sit back.

"Dani dropped an envelope under the windshield wiper of Sylvia's car when she was at work. I didn't even know she knew where Sylvia worked, much less what car she drove. At the time though, there was so much fallout to deal with that I didn't think about it. Sylvia—she could barely look at me. And there were the kids."

"And Dani?"

"Dani was always so happy to be with me. At the beginning, there was never a problem. God help me, it reminded me of the early years with Syl. Just the two of us. It's funny, you know, but until Sylvia found out, it never entered my mind to leave her. I swear." I say nothing. "Maybe she would have found out on her own, even if Dani hadn't told her." He takes another ragged breath. "And maybe if I'd been less of a jerk, none of this would have happened."

Nothing about Wyatt's story surprises me, but it does fill in some of the gaps. "What did you do to Dani?"

"When she told me what she'd done, all I could think about was how much I'd hurt Sylvia and the kids. Don't get me wrong. It was my fault. Not Dani's. No one forced me to be with her." The muscles of his face tighten under my gaze. "But that night, I was past angry with her. I was livid." He forces himself to look at me then, squaring his shoulders, his hands twisting in his lap. "I shoved her into the wall. Hard."

"You hurt her."

"Yes," he says, the admission no more than a whisper. "I hurt her."

1 9 2 1

CHAPTER
45

BRIDGET

Lawrence locked the doors to the Juniper, and Bridget averted her gaze, no longer charmed by the detail and artistry of the carved wood. Shivering, she knew she would never think about a juniper tree the same way again. She hadn't liked Lawrence's story, or at least not his telling, but she was catching on to him now. That had been the point of their little tour. He'd delighted in her horror.

She'd caught the nasty gleam in his eye and the way his thin lips had curved upward as he spoke. And if she'd had any doubts about how eager he was to have a baby—a son—she didn't now.

Lawrence pocketed the key and gripped her elbow, steering her toward the elevator. "What did you think of the Juniper?"

Knowing there was no right answer, she said, "Very interesting. Thank you for taking me."

"Did you find it a learning experience?"

"Very much so. I will stay away from juniper trees from now on."

For one brief moment, she worried she'd said the wrong thing.

But then he threw his head back and laughed. "Quite right," he said through guffaws. "Quite right."

"Mr. Hartwood?"

Lawrence halted, swinging around. "Ah. Mr. Ryan." He leaned closer to Bridget, his voice low. "The assistant manager, my dear." He nodded at the man coming toward them. "I believe this is yours." He retrieved the key he'd pocketed and handed it over. "Thanks, my good man. My wife found our little tour most enlightening."

The assistant manager offered Bridget a polite smile. "Congratulations on your wedding, Mrs. Hartwood. I trust you found your suite satisfactory."

"Yes, thank you."

"And the service?" His mustache twitched when he spoke.

"Very good, sir."

The man bowed his head before addressing Lawrence again. "Mr. Hartwood, I was hoping I might have a word with you."

"A word?"

The assistant manager's polite smile turned upside down. He gestured with his hand. "In private."

Lawrence's lip curled as he regarded the hotel man. "What is this about, Ryan?"

"A brief matter I'd like to discuss."

"Surely it can wait." He tipped his head toward Bridget. "My new bride is eager to get to the farm, aren't you dear?"

"Y-yes. Eager," she stammered.

Lawrence started to pull her with him, but the man was not so easily brushed aside. "Actually, sir, it can't wait. It's about your account." There was something in the way the man spoke that made Bridget look up. Mr. Ryan's pale face turned pink, but he held his head high, his mouth set in a hard line. Something was wrong. Lawrence's fingers closed over her elbow. "Perhaps Mrs. Hartwood would prefer to wait for you in your room?"

A door opened behind them, but no one moved or spoke. Lawrence's anger rolled off him in waves.

Bridget did not envy Mr. Ryan, but to her amazement, he showed no sign of backing down.

Mr. Ryan raised a hand. "You there," he called out. "Joseph?"

"Sir?" The voice was tentative, but unmistakable. Bridget sucked in her breath, but she kept her head down.

"Would you escort Mrs. Hartwood back to her suite, please?"

"My wife is not in need of an escort, Mr. Ryan. She is perfectly capable of getting back to our room on her own."

"As you wish, Mr. Hartwood. That will be all, Joseph." Bridget heard the sound of retreating footsteps. "Shall we step into my office then?"

"Fine. But let's be quick about it, Ryan. I am on my honeymoon, or have you forgotten?"

"Of course not, sir. This won't take long."

Lawrence looked down at Bridget, his fingers still tight over her elbow. "I won't be long, Bridget." He handed her the suite key. "We will leave as soon as I return. I trust you will be ready."

Without another glance, her husband followed the hotel man down the hall and into an office. The door clicked shut behind them. She exhaled and rubbed her elbow. There would be finger-sized bruises in the morning, but she didn't care. Margaret would be at the farm. They would be together. Her step lighter, she walked back to the elevator and rang the bell.

"Bridget?"

She spun around, her hand at her throat. "Joseph."

"I need to talk to you."

Casting a wary eye back down the hall, she shook her head. "We can't. We shouldn't."

"Please."

The elevator clattered to a stop and the operator pulled the wrought-iron gate open. He straightened his uniform, nodded at Joseph, and tipped his hat at Bridget. "Going up?"

"Yes, thank you," Joseph said. "Going up."

CHAPTER
46

BRIDGET

The elevator operator slid the gate closed and rotated the lever. Not knowing where to look, Bridget's gaze settled on the gate. The operator sat down on his stool, his hand resting on the lever. Joseph moved to the corner, as far away from her as the small space allowed. They rode higher, the minutes slow and grinding. Her knees knocked, and her fingers clutched at the fabric of her skirt. Sweat trickled down her back. Why would Joseph want to talk to her now?

The car bucked and stopped. The elevator operator stood up and slid the gate open again. "Thirteenth floor," he said. She stood still, frozen. What if Lawrence found out about Joseph sharing her elevator? What if he was there now, waiting, right outside the door? She was shaking so hard, she wasn't sure she could walk. "Ma'am?"

Her head came around. "Yes." She stepped off the elevator. "Thank you," she mumbled.

"Carl," Joseph said. "I'm going to help Mrs. Hartwood with her luggage, but there's a couple on the fifth floor—the Lelands. Do you know them?"

"Yes, I know them."

"Good. They're in need of an elevator. They've requested you come down and wait for them."

"Happy to oblige." The man raised a hand to his hat. "Good day," he said to Bridget.

She watched as the elevator went down and his smiling face disappeared from her view. They were alone in the hall.

Voice shaking with dread, she whirled around. "You need to leave. You can't be here."

"I need to talk to you."

"I—I don't know what he'll do if he sees you here."

"Your husband will be a while, and Carl will be on the fifth floor. Mr. Hartwood will have to wait for Carl to finish helping the Lelands first."

In spite of her fear, her heart leaped at his words. This man wasn't the boy who'd kowtowed to Lawrence the previous night. Nor was he the boy she'd walked with in the park, the boy she'd kissed, the boy she'd imagined she loved. This boy was a man.

"When I saw you in the room last night, I couldn't believe it," he said. "I thought I was mistaken. He told me you were engaged, but I didn't see how that could be true."

Bridget wanted to tell him if she could turn back the clock and undo everything since she'd met Lawrence, she would, but the ache in her bones served as a reminder that there would be no going back. What if Joseph was wrong, and Lawrence was getting on the elevator that very minute? She knew she didn't have the strength to endure another punishment if she were caught now. "We were married yesterday."

The softness around his mouth hardened. "The girl I knew wouldn't marry a man like . . . a man like Mr. Hartwood. A man who would . . ." His lip curled up even as he left his sentence unfinished. "I thought maybe . . . but I can see I was wrong. I hope you will be very happy," he said, although there was nothing about his tone that suggested he wished such a thing.

Her mouth dropped open, and her reserve faltered. How dare he?

"You disappeared without a word, without even the courtesy of saying good-bye. What business is it of yours who I marry?"

He held himself erect. "None of my business, Mrs. Hartwood. I thought maybe . . . I don't know what I thought. It doesn't matter now." He bowed at the waist. "I'll leave you to your husband."

Joseph backed away. He walked past the elevator and headed toward the stairs.

"Wait." She started after him. "What did you mean when you said you didn't think I would marry a man like Lawrence? A man like what?"

Considering, Joseph cocked his head. "Did you think I wanted to disappear, Bridget? This job is fine, but I loved working at the store."

"Then why did you leave?"

He looked past her. "Your husband told me if I didn't quit, he would tell the manager he'd seen me stealing."

Bridget gasped. "What? Why?"

"Why do you think? He said you were to be married, and my behavior was intolerable. He insisted I leave my job and never speak to you again."

"Or he would accuse you of stealing?"

"Yes."

All the pieces clicked into place. "He saw us in the park. He'd been following me."

"Why didn't you tell me, Bridget?"

"I didn't know until last night. I wasn't engaged. Lawrence didn't propose until the fall. You'd been gone since summer."

He blinked. "You weren't engaged?"

"No. I thought you and I might . . ." Heat rose from her chest to her cheeks. "But you left, and after that, he began coming around more. He—" Her voice quavered. "He gave my father money."

Joseph shook his head as though he didn't know what to say. "When I brought your bags, I wanted to see you, but I hoped it wasn't true—that you hadn't married him—and the woman would be someone else. Not you." There was no mistaking his disappointment in her, but there was something else. "I'm ashamed. I was afraid. Afraid of your husband and what he might do."

She remembered the fear she'd seen when he'd brought the luggage. While she'd wondered about it then, she understood now. Joseph didn't have to say it for her to know. Lawrence's threats had gone beyond accusing him of stealing. Yes, she understood his fear. Even better than he realized. "Don't be. It's not your fault."

"I should have had more faith in you. In us."

His words filled her with joy. Joseph didn't leave her because he didn't love her.

He came toward her, and her pulse quickened. He reached out and took her hands in his. "Can you forgive me?"

Before she could answer, the clank of the elevator chain rattled, echoing in the distance. She jerked her hands away. "You need to go."

"But—"

She pushed him toward the stairs. "Now. He can't find you here." Without waiting for him to comment, she ran to her door and pulled the key from her pocket. Hand shaking, she dropped it. The key bounced on the carpet. The clatter of the elevator grew louder. Snatching it up again, she used both hands to hold the key steady and slide it into the lock. Breathless, she fell into the room and slammed the door, the grinding elevator chain echoing in her ears.

PRESENT DAY

CHAPTER
47

VAL
Wednesday, 10:47 a.m.

My mind jumps from one possibility to another. New thoughts bounce up and down and over each other, but I can't make sense of them. Two coffee cups. A bag of bagels. Food for two. Not one. Someone had been in the room with my sister. This is logic. But it was Sylvia who bought the sleeping pills and Sylvia who packed them in her suitcase. I'm struggling with these two seemingly inconsistent truths. I put on my reporter hat and push aside my heartache. Sylvia took those pills. Logic. It's the only explanation. And yet, someone else was there. Maybe.

I run one scenario after another through my mind, but it all comes down to only a few options. Theory two or three? A combination? If someone was in that room, they saw her take those pills and didn't do anything. They let her die. Or they were there and didn't know. But if that was true, they must have known when she didn't wake up. And they left her there to be found by a maid. Or they'd gone before she took the pills. Why? I tap my pen against the table, my gaze glued to the blown-up image of paper coffee cups. Who was the coffee for? Steven Morris? I consider calling Barnes, but

I'm not sure what good it would do. I see Billy leaning back in his chair, a stack of papers in his hand. I scramble to my feet.

"Billy, can I ask you a favor?"

He sets the papers aside. "Not sure I got any more favors to give."

"I promise it will be the last one."

"That's what Terry said."

"I know, and I'm sorry. It's about Steven Morris."

"Morris is off limits." His voice isn't hard, but it's not as friendly as it was earlier. "Front desk is tired of me asking about him."

"Please. I just need to know when his next reservation is."

He shakes his head. "Nope. I don't like the sound of that one bit."

"Please." I tell him about the cups.

Billy taps his fingers on his desk. "Thought you were interested in her ex-husband? The one that caused the ruckus in the lobby?"

"I am." I know I'm not making sense. I am furious with Wyatt, but I have to find out what Morris might know. It's those two cups. "Wyatt was harassing her, and I do think he had something to do with how she was feeling."

"Which was?"

"I'm not sure. Desperate maybe. Scared. He'd been making threats. But she'd been happy too. I need to know why that changed. Why the happy side of her life wasn't enough to stop her from taking those pills." I hear the neediness in my voice. We both know I'm grasping at straws. I'm pinging back and forth between Wyatt and Steven Morris, casting blame in both their directions, but I don't care if I don't make sense. "Or if there was something else wrong besides Wyatt."

He appraises me, and I wait, hoping I've said enough to make my case. He winds his feet around and pushes up from his chair.

"I'll be right back."

I hear his heavy footsteps before I see him. "What did you find out?"

"That's the last favor," he says. "You understand?"

"Absolutely."

"Good. You're in luck then. Steven Morris has a reservation for today. He's requested an early check-in and based on how often he stays here, that was approved."

My lips feel like rubber. "What time?"

"Couple of hours from now. Noon." I almost hug him, but I hold back. He brushes by me, then turns around. "I hope you find what you're looking for," he says. His voice is kind, like his face, and I think again about that hug. I understand better what Terry sees in him.

He leaves me to brood and wait. I pace the floor, scroll through video, check my phone more times than I can count. My coffee is cold, and I stare down at the cup like it's a foreign object, as though I'm not sure how it got there. My foot swings hard under the desk, and I check my watch. It's still early, but I'm not taking any chances. In the lobby, the chandeliers blink overhead, brightening the somber-colored ceiling and ornate trim. Outside, the street is dark, the sky threatening. I find a soft sofa facing the lobby doors and perch on the edge of a cushion. My fingers do a dance across the velvety arm.

I don't have to wait long. A few minutes before noon, he strolls in with his bag over his shoulder. His hair is mussed, and his jacket flies backward as he comes through the doors. He stops to talk to the bellman, who nods and chuckles, before he strides across the lobby floor to greet the desk clerk. She grins in recognition and cocks her head. Whatever he says makes her laugh. It's clear the staff knows him well. He's friendly and likeable. From a distance anyway. He tosses his coat over his arm. Sylvia's friend and the waitress were right. Steven Morris is a good-looking man. Very good-looking. He's tall, with the kind of build that can only come with regular exercise. Muscled but not muscular. He has a long, straight nose, a square chin, and dimples that make him appear younger than he is. I stand up. A quizzical expression crosses his face. The desk clerk says something, and he turns back. She hands him his key, perhaps holding it a bit longer than necessary. I move closer, intercepting him as he walks toward the elevators.

"Mr. Morris?"

He slows. "Yes."

"We haven't met, but I'm wondering if I could talk to you for a few minutes. I promise I won't take too much of your time."

His confusion is back. "Have we met? You look so familiar."

"No." I take a deep breath. "But you knew my sister."

He stares down at me. His handsome features shift into something less genial. "You're that woman on the phone." He doesn't wait for me to admit who I am. He hurries toward the elevator.

I rush after him and grab his arm. "Wait. Please."

"I'll call security."

"Please," I say again. "I'm begging you. My sister . . ." I pause, struggling to choke out the words. "I'm trying to find out what happened."

He scans the lobby, but we're alone near the elevators. The desk clerk is on the phone and the bellman's back is to us.

"Why don't you let me buy you a drink? We can go upstairs to the bar," I say. "Please." I've lost count of how many times I've said this already. "I have a few questions. About Sylvia. I promise it won't take long."

He ignores me and pushes the button.

"I'm not going to tell anyone. Whatever you say, it's between us. I promise." I don't even know if that's a lie or the truth, but I need him to talk to me. "But Sylvia was my sister. And she's gone now. So, I . . ." My voice falters a second time. "You understand, don't you? I need to know everything about her. Everyone she knew. Please."

The elevator bell rings, and the doors slide open. He doesn't move. A low hum of voices spills out from the dining room. A couple holding hands passes by. The doors slide closed.

"I knew your sister," he says, his voice quiet.

I take a step toward him and wonder if he can hear the thudding in my chest. "How about that drink?"

His head swivels toward me. He blinks. "You look a lot alike. She was taller and her hair was different, but same eyes, same face."

It's not the first time I've heard this. We both favor our mother, according to our father.

The corners of his mouth turn down and he looks past me. "Strange how things happen, isn't it?" he says. I have no idea what he's talking about, but I hang on his every word. "You think you know a person, but that's not who they are at all."

Which person? Him? Sylvia? I open my mouth to ask, but the faraway look is gone, making me wonder if it was there at all.

Coming back out of his fog, he waves a hand. "Sure. I could use a drink."

CHAPTER
48

TERRY

Wednesday, 11:16 a.m.

Wyatt talked for more than an hour. I understand why Val doesn't like him, given what he did to her sister, but likability isn't a determinant of guilt or innocence. Evidence is. He tells a good story. A compelling one even. It could be true. But I'm not convinced without proof.

The pictures on Wyatt's phone were something though. Still, they could be fake. I don't know much about how that stuff works, but I know it can be done. And the man couldn't explain the missing texts.

"I must have deleted them," he said. "I swear they were there, and now, they're not. But I've been having problems with my phone. My assistant was supposed to fix it for me, but I guess it didn't work."

I know what Val would say. "He deleted them because he didn't want anyone to see them. He was probably sending Sylvia threats and ultimatums. Of course, they're gone. What else would you expect?"

It's a sound argument, especially in light of the other things Wyatt admitted. And then there are the number of times he answered my questions with, "I don't know." Too many for my taste.

In spite of no real proof that he intended to hurt Sylvia, there are plenty of red flags around this guy.

His phone buzzed so many times during the conversation, I finally told him to answer it. His tone, though, was sharper than seemed warranted, and I wondered again what kind of man Wyatt Spencer was.

Hanging up, he said, "Angela—that's my assistant—wanted to know my order for lunch. I keep telling her I can get it myself." He angled his head, eyes lowered. "She's always trying to take care of me. Offering to work late. Doing things to help me . . ." He plucked at the fabric of his coat. "I should be grateful, right? But sometimes, she's more like my mother or my wife than my assistant."

I remembered Val's suspicions about the woman then. "Sounds nice though. To have an assistant who cares about you."

He shrugged. "I guess."

"She wants to protect you?"

He gave me an odd look before nodding. "Maybe. Sometimes."

I walk up the street now, my head low to block the wind, and consider what I've learned. What does it mean? It could be everything or it could be nothing. I keep walking, relishing the way it clears the mind. What if I decide to believe Wyatt? It wouldn't bring Val's sister back. This I know.

I slow, tipping my head back as I get closer to the Franklin. The roof line is high above me, but that's not what draws my attention. It's the tall, glittering windows in the south corner, thirteen stories up—on the floor now labeled the fourteenth. The suite. Sylvia's suite. The air swirls around me, and my coat tails snap backward. I shiver, but I can't be sure if it's the cold or something else.

It's not the same, I tell myself. This is now. It has nothing to do with then. The wind dies and my coat falls into place. *If it's not the same, why are you here?*

I drop my chin. I know Val is inside, probably watching video of the lobby and the elevators. I should join her, tell her about Wyatt, but I don't. Is it because I want to believe him? He's made mistakes. A lot of them. But in spite of everything, I understand better why Val says women like him. Why people are drawn to him.

"How'd you become a cop?" Wyatt asked.

I glanced over at him, but his curiosity seemed genuine. "Family business. My dad was a cop. My grandfather. I can't remember when I didn't want to be one."

"Why'd you stop?"

This was the hard question. I had a standard answer. The job is dangerous. Then there's the burnout. These were the things people expected to hear. And they were all true. But they weren't my reasons.

"I was on this case," I said to Wyatt. "A homicide." This was where I usually fell back on a tale of burnout. But the words I spoke in the park were different, truer. "A man had killed his wife, bludgeoned her to death with a hair dryer."

"A hair dryer?"

"Yeah. He held her by the hair, so she couldn't get away. There were clumps of it all over the bathroom." Wyatt's mouth opened and closed. "Forensics came. And the techs. It was a pretty clear-cut case. Whatever had gotten into the husband must have been gone because he cooperated. Told us what he did and why. After they took him out, I was standing there with my partner when I got this bad feeling. It started at the tips of my fingers and crawled up my arms and into my head. Whatever it was, it filled me up." I paused, shuddering.

"Oh, my God. That's horrible." Wyatt's skin went white.

"That's when I knew," I said, falling back on burnout. "Guess it was one crime scene too many. I put in my resignation the next day."

I spoke the truth, though not all of it. The feeling that day. The voice. So quiet at first. And then louder. It scared me to my core, and I had no choice but to quit. There've been some tough days since. I miss being a cop. A lot. I suspect Val recognizes that, even thinks it's the reason I've been helping her. She wouldn't be entirely wrong, but she wouldn't be entirely right either.

It all comes back to the Franklin. I know what people see when they look at the famous hotel. They see the detailed stonework and the architecture. They see a spacious lobby and luxurious couches and golden staircases. They see marble floors and fine dining and king-sized beds. But that's not what I see. I see a bathroom dripping in blood. I see the hole where a hair dryer was ripped from the wall. I see a shaken man being led away, face blank, hands stained red. I shiver again.

When the management of the Franklin came to me to head security, I passed the job to Billy. I had no intention of setting foot in the Franklin again. But then Val collapsed on the floor of the library. I saw the pain, heard the anguish in her sobs. Some part of me suspected it had happened again. I don't know if I'm right, but either way, she's counting on me now. I don't want to let her down. Still, I can't go inside. There's one more thing I need to do first. I tap out a text. Val will have to wait.

1 9 2 1

CHAPTER
49

BRIDGET

Bridget threw herself into action. She raced around the suite, picking up the last of her items and tossing them in her bag. She ran a brush through her hair and pinched her cheeks. She ran back to the door and heard the crank of the elevator gate. Scurrying back to the bed, she straightened the pillows and scanned the floor for anything she'd missed. It was then she remembered. The bang on the door made her jump. She plucked Margaret's letter from between the pages of the Bible and tucked it in the pocket of her dress.

"Bridget, open the door," Lawrence shouted, pounding on the heavy wood. She flew across the room. He pushed the door wide, and she fell backward. "What took you so long? Were you sleeping?"

She wanted to laugh then. After everything Joseph had said, she was far from tired. She'd been exhilarated when she'd realized Joseph did care for her after all.

But remembering, she was plunged into despair again. She was a married woman, and Lawrence would never let her go.

"Well?" he said, drawing out the word. "Have you been struck dumb?"

Bridget reddened. "I'm sorry, Lawrence. I'm afraid you did catch me dozing, but my bags are packed. I'm ready as you asked."

He stomped across the floor and threw himself on the bed. "There's been a delay. The manager can't locate that stupid porter." His mouth curved into an ugly sneer. "You should thank me for saving you from that doddering fool, Bridget."

"Thank you."

In the silence that followed, she crossed the room to the window. She looked out past the buildings to the harbor. The murky water churned in the winter wind. The boats and small ships rolled with the choppy waves, bobbing up and down. A large steamer crawled over the water before pulling into the harbor. She touched a hand to the window. Footsteps behind her made her spin around.

"If I had my wish, we'd be out of this infernal hotel this minute, but an accounting error and an idiot porter has meant that isn't possible." His gaze traveled the length of her body, stopping at her bosom. "But perhaps there is a way to pass the time after all."

Heat rushed to her face. Her legs trembled under her skirt, and her hand fell on the slip of paper stowed in her pocket. "Wh-what kind of accounting error?"

"A misunderstanding. Nothing for you to concern yourself about, my love." He reached out with one hand and caressed her cheek. His hand dropped lower. She willed herself not to move. "We are but newlyweds, and this is still our honeymoon." His mouth found hers, and he pulled her to him. Her arms hung at her sides, her body unyielding. She sensed the anger in him before he dropped his hold on her. His eyes, dark and hard, bore down on her. "At least pretend you are my wife, Bridget."

"I—I don't know what you mean."

"You forget. I saw you in the park. An idiot boy is worthy of your kisses and not your own husband?" His face came close to hers, his rank breath hot on her skin. Every time he mentioned Joseph, her heart fluttered. She feared he would see her betrayal in her every move and hear it in her every word. Would he find out she'd spoken to Joseph? "You're a married woman, Bridget. Act like it." Unlike Louella, Bridget had fallen from her pedestal almost as soon as she'd become a bride. Was it her, she wondered, or him? He bore down on her. "I will not have an iceberg for a wife. Do we understand each other?"

Memories of her wedding night flooded her brain. New bruises dotted her arms and legs, but she doubted he remembered. He'd drunk enough champagne not to notice her lack of participation. That was not to be the case in the light of day. "Yes, Lawrence," she whispered.

"Good girl. Shall we try again?" He didn't wait, crushing his lips to hers.

She moved her lips with his, let her arms encircle him. He held her tight, his mouth finding her neck. She shuddered at his touch but forced herself to respond, rubbing his back in a circular motion. His hands found the buttons of her day gown. He worked the tiny silk pearls from their eyelets until the dress lay in a heap on the floor. Her cheeks flamed but she dared not move. The next minutes passed in a hazy blur, her mind floating in and out. When it was over, she blinked back tears. The tender skin of her backside burned, chafed by the rug. Her lips were swollen and bruised. His teeth had left their impression in the flesh of her shoulder. She rolled her head to one side, a single tear sliding to the floor.

He stood over her, his legs spread wide, staring down at her. For one brief moment, his mouth went slack, and his body uncoiled, and she was reminded of the man who'd visited her in the shop, who'd pledged his love and devotion. The man she'd thought she might grow to love in time.

Her husband's face contorted. "Get up, Bridget. It's almost time to start your new life at the farm."

CHAPTER
50

BRIDGET

It hurt to move. Bridget rolled over and crawled to her knees.

"For God's sake, Bridget, don't be a baby. We don't have all day." He grabbed her by the arm and yanked her to her feet. She swallowed a cry and covered her breasts with her hands. His laugh hit her like a slap. "I could get used to seeing you like this. Don't be shy." He bent down and scooped up her gown. "I suppose you'd like this back."

Eyes like saucers, she couldn't speak, afraid.

"Ask me nicely."

Bridget stared at the man she'd married. It struck her then. He would always take delight in humiliation. There was cruelty in his heart and his soul. How could she have been so blind for so long? She thought about his first wife, Louella, hiding behind heavy curtains in a dark and dreary house, afraid of being seen. Louella hadn't escaped. She was still a prisoner, more dead than alive. Bridget considered her options. She could leave Lawrence, but where would she go? Home? Her father would be in ruins, Lawrence's money withdrawn. Her sister? Lawrence would track her down and bring her back. She was a possession now. She had nothing of her own, was nothing.

He pulled out his pocket watch to check the time. The corners of his mouth turned down, and she steeled herself for another onslaught. Instead, he said, "This has taken too long. Put your clothes on." He threw her dress at her. "And don't dawdle about it."

Catching the woolen gown in her hands, Bridget exhaled. She held the gown against her body and moved to hurry by him. His hand shot out and snapped around the bones of her wrist.

"What's this?" he said, snatching Margaret's message from the pocket with his free hand. Her pulse jackhammered under her skin. "A letter?"

Stammering, she hurried to explain. "F-From Margaret. Didn't I tell you?"

His fingers tightened, his grip punishing. "Tell me what?"

"Margaret decided to come and visit us at the farm before returning to Washington."

"On whose invitation?" He drew himself up. "Sister or no, I will not have your family showing up at my doorstep whenever they like. It's bad enough they've invited themselves to the farm for the holiday. We have been married but one day, and they are already foisting themselves upon us. I won't allow it."

Her knees buckled. "You're hurting me."

"I asked you a question. On whose invitation?"

"No one's. She misses me. She's my sister and . . ." her words died in a whimper as he twisted her wrist.

"Enough." He shook the note open. Every part of Bridget's being tensed. She saw the lock of his jaw as he skimmed the message. "How dare she suggest a wife should conspire behind her husband's back?" His voice grew louder, and his cheeks darkened with rage. "The day you became my wife, you forfeited your allegiance to your sister." He dragged her across the room to the secretary and pushed her down on the chair. "You will write your sister a letter and instruct her not to come. And you will do it immediately. Before we leave this hotel."

Letting go of her hand, he slammed the lid back and tossed the paper in front of her. She rubbed at her wrist, hot tears rolling down her face. The leather of the chair was cold against her skin and goose bumps erupted over her body. He dipped the quill in ink and handed it to her.

Hand shaking, she took the pen and put it to the paper.

My dearest Margaret,

He bent close to her ear. "You will write what I tell you to write. Are you ready?" Her mind numb, she managed to move her head up and down once. "I regret to inform you that I do not wish you to visit me at the farm." The pen stuttered over the paper and ink dropped in blotches. She picked up the pen, the sentence unfinished. His hand closed over her shoulder and squeezed until she cried out. "Finish writing."

When she was done, he spoke again. "My duty is to my husband now. Please do not contact me again before the holidays." He waited for her to catch up. "Very good. You may sign off now." He straightened and loosened his grip. "See? That wasn't so hard, was it?"

She dropped the pen on the page, the words in front of her a sea of blurry letters. He spun the chair around. "You disgust me," he said, sneering. "You've proven to be such a disappointment, Bridget." He cocked his head. "But you may serve a purpose yet." Taking his handkerchief from his pocket, he wiped a bead of sweat from his brow, then reached out toward her. Repulsed, she drew back. In the second that followed, she knew her mistake. He smacked her hard across the face. Her head snapped, and the room spun around her. She toppled sideways, slipping from the chair to the floor. He grabbed her by the hair and jerked her neck back. Rage seeped from his every pore. His pupils were as black as night, and the veins of his neck throbbed and bulged. She scrambled backward on her hands. He gave a short laugh and snorted, advancing on her. Unbuckling his belt, he pulled it from the loops. "What do you say, Bridget? Shall we finish the lesson we began last night?"

CHAPTER
51

VAL
Wednesday, 12:29 p.m.

"When your sister gave me her number, I was happy to have it." Steven Morris runs his fingers through his longish hair in a way that makes me think he does this often, an instinctive type of flirting. He has long lashes that fringe deep-set eyes as dark as the ocean on a moonlit night. I can see the initial appeal of the man. "I didn't call right away, but when I did, she didn't seem surprised. I have to admit, that was kind of a turn-on for me. I like a confident woman." I squirm in my seat. The man is good-looking but less so the more he speaks. "I asked her out for a drink."

"When was that?" I ask.

He shrugs. "I don't remember. She turned me down."

My mouth drops open. "She said no?"

"The first time, yeah. But I called her again the next day. I'm a persistent guy. I told her that Sherry and a few others were getting together at Havana Pier. I don't think she was sold at first, but I wore her down. I couldn't get Sherry to come after all, but a couple of other folks from my office were there, so I didn't lie exactly."

It's a small thing compared to lying about being married, but I bristle anyway.

If he notices, it's not apparent.

"I introduced her when she got there. It was okay for a while, but I could tell she wasn't really into me." He gives a shake of his head, his grin sheepish. "I'm not used to that. When she said she couldn't stay because of her kids, I believed her."

This sounds like Sylvia. Cautious. Taking it slow. I'm also getting a handle on Steven Morris. "You asked her out again."

"I did. Figured if I'm going down, I'm going down swinging."

The waitress pops by our table, and he brightens. After ordering drinks, he says, "I called Sherry. Once I knew your sister's favorite restaurant and wine, I figured that would do it. I gave her another call." His drink arrives and he takes a sip. "I barely got past hello before she shut me down."

"Huh." I wonder if he's lying, but I don't think so. "And then what?"

"Then nothing. That was the end of it." He picks up his glass. "I met someone else."

"Someone else who is not your wife."

He frowns. "You said this—"

"Don't worry," I say quickly. "I may think you're a jackass, but I'm not going to be the one to tell your wife."

"Jackass, huh?" He half smiles, and one dimple pops. "I've been called worse."

"I'm sure you have." I sip my wine, grateful for the moment to refocus. "You never went out with my sister again?"

"Nope. I told you. I met someone else. I'm seeing her tonight."

Again, I consider whether or not he's lying, but the truth is, I can't see my sister dating this man—married or not.

"Why did you think I was the guy she was dating? She sounded pretty into him, although she tried to be casual," he says.

My mouth drops open again. *The guy she was dating. She sounded pretty into him.* "What?"

"Did she say it was me or something?" Morris drains the last of his gin. "It'd be the first time I was the beard, but whatever."

I straighten against the hard-back chair. "She told you she was dating someone?"

"That's what she said when she turned me down. Yeah. She said she'd been seeing someone for a couple of weeks, and she wanted to see where it went. Normally, I wouldn't let that stop me, but I could tell she was serious. Dating two guys wasn't her thing."

My hands grip the edge of the table. "She didn't tell you who he was, did she?"

"No, but I didn't ask."

Then I remember the two cups of coffee. "You ran into her at the hotel though. Near the elevator."

"How do you know that?" he asks, lips pursed now.

"There's a camera near the lobby elevator. That's why I thought you might have been the guy she was dating," I say.

"You watched video? Why?"

"I thought maybe it would help me to understand."

Seconds tick by. "You thought I was her boyfriend based on the fact that I got in an elevator with her?"

"Partly. Plus, she hugged you when she saw you."

"I'm a friendly guy."

"And your initials are S. M."

He leans back. "Lots of guys have those initials. I still don't get it."

I explain Sylvia's fake business trip and the calendar. "So, instead of going away for work like she said, she came here—to the Franklin. I thought maybe she came here to be with him, her boyfriend, S. M. And you're here a lot. People know you." My voice fades. "Your initials are S. M."

He takes that in. "So, you put two and two together."

"Yes."

"You were wrong. Look, I don't want to drag my girlfriend into this, but if it comes to that, I will."

"It won't."

"Good." He pushes his empty glass away. "For what it's worth, she did seem happy."

It's a common refrain, meant to comfort, but it adds to my confusion over her actions.

"She was here Monday evening. In the Juniper. I don't know if that helps. She was meeting someone," he says.

The hair on the back of my neck stands up. According to the hotel, she called the front desk that Monday night and asked not to be disturbed. "She was?"

"Yeah. I came in for a drink before going out to meet my girlfriend." He points to a dark corner of the bar. "She was sitting over there, reading a book, so I didn't go over."

"If you didn't talk to her, how do you know she was waiting for someone?"

He shrugs. "Simple. There was a bottle of wine on the table. And two glasses."

I stand up. Two glasses. Two paper coffee cups. The boyfriend was here. He had to be. I sit down again. What does it mean? It doesn't change that my sister got a prescription for sleeping pills two weeks earlier. That while everyone thought she was so happy, she was hiding the truth from all of us.

My phone buzzes, vibrating across the table. I snatch it up. "Terry?"

"No. Dani. Who's Terry?"

I grit my teeth. "What do you want?"

"Where are you?"

"The Franklin."

I hear the sharp intake of her breath. "W-why?"

"That's none of your business."

"Oh, my God. Why would you want to be where your sister died? That's so morbid."

I hold the phone away from my ear. I don't care about Dani and her problems. I've got plenty of my own. "I need to call you back." I hit end. The phone buzzes again, and I shove it in my purse.

Morris is watching me, amused. "That bad, huh?"

"The worst." Dani may have gotten more than she bargained for with Wyatt, but that doesn't mean I have to put up with her. She's Wyatt's problem, not mine. And not Sylvia's anymore. I remember my shock the first time I saw her. Blond hair that brushed past her shoulders. Athletic build. Even Sylvia had noticed Dani was practically a carbon copy. Younger and tanner, sure, but the resemblance had been striking. Morris cocks his head at me now, and I can't help myself. "The woman who had an affair with my sister's husband. She won't go away."

He doesn't miss a beat. "Despite what you think of me, I have no intention of leaving my wife."

"Most cheaters don't. At least until they get caught."

"You don't like me, do you?" He doesn't wait for my answer. "It's okay. Clearly, my charm doesn't work on you any better than it did on your sister." Morris throws some cash on the table. "I am sorry about your sister. Maybe you could talk to the woman your sister met that night."

For the second time, Morris has taken me by surprise. "What woman?"

"When I was leaving, a woman came up to the hostess and said she was meeting someone. She looked around, saw your sister, and headed to the corner."

I'm leaning so far over the table, I can feel the wood digging into my ribs. "And then what?"

"That's all I know. I didn't stick around to watch girl talk."

His flippant manner makes me want to scream, but I manage to keep my voice level enough.

"What can you tell me about her? Anything?"

"She was hot." He flashes a sheepish smile. "Don't look at me like that. I'm a guy who notices a good-looking woman. Dark hair. Long legs. That's about all I remember."

I can't hide my irritation. He's no help. Until he is.

"Why don't you go check out your video? Maybe she was on there."

Jumping out of my seat, I practically run from the bar, then catch myself and turn back. "Wait. What time was my sister here?"

"Um, let me think." The sound of my foot tapping the floor matches the racing beat of my heart. This woman may have been the last person to see my sister alive. "I had a dinner reservation with Janie. Seven thirty is our usual time, so I probably left here at seven. Maybe a few minutes after."

"Thanks." I turn back a second time. "For everything."

I race down the hallway and burst through the security-room doors. Two heads swivel toward me. "Sorry," I mumble and flop down in front of the monitor. Billy is nowhere to be seen. With one eye on the time stamp in the corner, I fast forward to Monday evening. I stop at six thirty and push play. The minutes drag. I watch couples and families and singles stream through the lobby door. None match Morris's description. Then I see her.

She walks through the doors at five minutes before seven. I watch her cross the lobby toward the elevators. I pause the recording, rewind, and watch again, but it's no good. There's no clear shot of her face. I switch to the elevator view, fumbling with the time until I get it right. She comes into the frame and hits the up button. She slides out of her coat and drapes it over her arm. Long dark hair hangs down to the middle of her back. My eyes narrow. There's something familiar about the way she holds her right leg out as she's waiting. A man joins her. She glances over at him. The doors open and she steps in, the man right behind her. I back it up again. She looks at the man. I stare hard. I know her. I'm sure of it. I zoom in. The woman's face blurs, and I back it out. The picture isn't crisp, but it's good enough. Her dark hair is tucked behind her ear. A gold hoop with a single diamond winks in the light. My blood runs cold, and I can't breathe. It can't be. But I know it is.

CHAPTER
52

TERRY
Wednesday, 1:42 p.m.

My car comes to a stop in the circle, and the valet hurries toward me. I toss him the keys as Wyatt climbs out of the passenger seat.

"She's not going to believe me," he says, keeping his hand on the door. "Maybe this isn't a good time."

"There's never going to be a good time." I push him toward the waiting doorman. "It has to be today. Before this gets any worse. You can't keep pretending you're not a part of this."

He raises a hand to his forehead and squints up at the hotel. His hand drops again, and he nods once. "Okay. Let's go."

We walk through the doors, and the outside noises of wheels on pavement and squealing brakes fade away. Across the lobby, a young man sits at the piano. The tinkly sound of the keys is background to the buzz of conversation at the front desk. We scoot past the line. I keep my head down, the better not to see the sculptures and their hooded, watchful eyes. Wyatt lags behind, his footsteps trailing me up the stairs.

The glass doors slide open.

"What is this place?" he asks, looking around at the bank of monitors and screens.

"Security department."

"Where's Val?"

I shoot a glance at the small table outfitted with the single monitor. A paper cup has been left on the desk, but the chair is empty.

"She must have stepped out," I say. "We can wait for her."

"Sure." He shuffles his feet backward. "I need to use the restroom."

Before I can protest, he's out the door and down the hall. I watch as he passes the stairs and finds the restroom located outside the Juniper.

Billy is huddled with his men near the bank of screens along the wall.

"Have you seen Val?" I ask him.

"Yep. She was in and out most of the morning. Ran out of here about twenty minutes ago like a swarm of bees was on her butt."

My hand closes over my phone. "Thanks." I try Val's number. No answer. I dial a second time. A third. "Val. Call me back. It's important. There's something you should know." I hesitate before adding, "And something else I should have told you before. I'm at the Franklin. Call me."

I cross the room and sit down at the monitor. An enlarged image glows on the screen. It's a woman with dark hair, her face turned in profile toward a middle-aged man in an overcoat.

"Billy?" I call out. "Could you look at something?" I gesture at the image. "Do you recognize this woman?"

"Nope."

"What about the man?"

He says he doesn't.

"Are you sure?"

The security man gives a short laugh. "You know I can't know every guest here, right? We get hundreds of people every day. And then throw in the dinner crowd and the bar crowd." Billy studies the woman on the screen. "The man looks like every other guy who checks in this hotel. She's a looker though." He pauses, blinking at the screen. "The way she's dressed, it figures she's headed up to the Juniper. If she were a regular, I might recognize her, but this one . . . no."

Thanking him, I stare at the frozen image. The woman is wearing a pair of black slacks and a fitted black top. Over her arm, she holds a black coat. Billy's right. I don't know much about clothes, but they look expensive. The man is shorter than the woman, and the bald spot on the crown of his head glows under the lights. I study the woman's face as she looks at the man. There's nothing to indicate interest. She doesn't lean toward him. My gut tells me they're strangers. The woman is the focus. What I don't know is why.

I pull out my phone and scroll through Val's last texts for clues.

Barnes showed me evidence that Sylvia refilled her prescription. They found it on her laptop. One of those illegal mail order places. He says the case will be closed later today. Sorry I got you into this mess. I don't know what to think anymore.

Another text followed a couple of hours later.

Tying up some loose ends. Wish me luck.

And the last one.

I almost gave up. I'm such a fool. Where the hell are you?

I slam my hand against the table. I should have called her earlier. I should have trusted her with the truth. What was it Billy said? Val ran out of there like she had a swarm of bees on her butt? I look back at the woman with the dark hair. I read the time stamp in the corner of the screen. Monday night. The hair on my arms rises. "I have a bad feeling," I say out loud. It occurs to me that there's no one to hear, and I shudder. No one but the Franklin.

Wyatt appears at my side and takes Val's chair. "Is she coming? Did you tell her I'm here?" he asks.

"She stepped out." I start to tell him about Sylvia's prescription when he reaches into his pocket and pulls out a package.

"I brought this for Val. Maybe it will help."

I don't move. "What is it?"

"Sylvia's diary."

Val's been so sure the diary would give her the answers she's been looking for. I stop short of telling him that. "Where's it been?" I ask.

His gaze drifts to the monitor on the table, to the image of the man and woman outside the elevator. "What's that?"

"Wyatt, you didn't answer my question."

"And you didn't answer mine. Why do you have that picture?"

His eyes are wide as he stares at the screen. Forgetting the diary, I rewind the recording. He watches the woman enter the screen then press the button for the elevator. The man walks into the picture.

"This was Monday evening," I say. "The night Sylvia died. The time stamp is a few minutes before seven o'clock."

The blood drains from his face. "Seven?"

"Yes." I slide closer until there are mere inches between us. "What are you not telling me?"

He tears his eyes from the screen. "I got a call from Dani that night. Must have been six thirty or a little after. I was getting ready to leave my office. My assistant—Angela—was packing up to leave for the night. Dani was crying. And screaming. Not making any sense. I tried my best to calm her down."

Dani is not my concern. Val is. I consider steering the conversation back to the screen, but the words die on my tongue when I spot the way his hands are trembling. Whatever bad feeling I had minutes earlier is quickly turning to something worse. Wyatt is still talking.

"When I was finally able to understand her, she begged me to meet her at the apartment, said she needed to see me right away. I started to tell her I couldn't, and that's when she said I had to." His hands are wrapped around the arms of his chair, his knuckles white. The whine of his voice is now only a whisper. "That if I didn't come, she'd kill herself."

I lean in. "And then what?"

"Angela asked me if I wanted her to call the police, but I told her no. I'd take care of it."

"Is it normal for your assistant to be privy to what's going on in your personal life?"

He blinks. "It's not like that. I can trust Angela. She's very, uh, protective, that's all. Maybe a little more since Sylvia and I separated."

"I see," I say, although I'm not sure I do. "And did you? Take care of Dani?"

He stares at the wall behind me. "I got to the apartment as fast as I could. Ten minutes at the most. But she wasn't there. Everything in the apartment had been turned upside down. She'd trashed the place."

"She still had a key."

"Yeah, I guess. After seeing that, I was even more scared of what she would do. I tried to find her. I drove to her house and called a couple of her friends, but outside of that, I didn't know where else to look."

"Had she made threats like that before? To kill herself?"

"Once." His chin drops to his chest. "Before I knew her. When she was eighteen. There were scars on her wrists." He shakes his head. "She's more fragile than she seems. I tried to be strong for her, but it was never enough. After I couldn't find her at the house, I drove around to some of the places I know she likes. I couldn't live with myself if anything happened to her. I'd already hurt her once."

"Did you find her?"

"No. She called me again later. Still upset but calmer. She wasn't making threats anymore."

"What did you do then?"

He rubs his eyes with his fingers. "I tried to call Angela, but she didn't pick up. That was a little strange, since she's usually available, but I thought maybe she'd finally decided to have a life. I'm not sure she would have been as relieved as I was anyway. She doesn't like Dani much." His hand drops. "That's when I saw the text from Sylvia. The one I told you about."

"The one that miraculously disappeared."

"Yes," he breathes. He's drawn to the image on the screen again. "I don't understand why she's there."

I point at the woman. "You know her?"

His head dips again. "Yes," he whispers. "God help me, I do."

1 9 2 1

CHAPTER
53

BRIDGET

B ridget clutched her dress to her naked body and lurched to her feet, fresh tears flowing. She measured the distance to the door. She could make it. Maybe. But before she could gather her courage, he laughed again. "Will you run out into the hall like that? Show the world what a whore you are?"

She backed away, sidestepping the bed. He took his time coming after her, closing the gap with each stride. She took another step and another until she ran into the dining table. In an instant, she understood her error. She was trapped. He advanced on her, slapping the belt against his open palm. Panic bubbled up and a sob escaped.

"Please," she said.

He sneered. "You should have begged when you had the chance." He spun her around and pushed her over the table. "If you move, it will be worse."

Through her tears, she stared down at the polished wood. She heard the hiss before the sting.

Whack.

Her teeth closed down hard over her tongue, and she tasted blood. *Whack.*

She reached out, grabbing at empty air. *Whack.* Her hand closed over the brass candelabra. She forgot the stinging and the pain and slid the heavy brass ornament closer.

"I cannot tolerate your deceit, Bridget." The belt cut through the air as though punctuating the cold nature of his soul.

Whack.

Her body jerked and she nearly lost her grip. With the heavy fabric of her dress hiding her hands, she wrapped them around the base of the candelabra. The white candlesticks, thick with drippings, jiggled in their holders. The air behind her whistled, and the belt snapped hard again. She tried not to think about the pain. She had to stop him now, or he would kill her.

"You will never see your family again, Bridget." His breath was raspy now, heavy with the effort of the beating. "Not your precious Margaret or—"

Using both hands, she lifted the candelabra and twisted around in one motion. His eyes widened right before she brought the solid brass down on his head.

"*Oomph.*" He staggered sideways. The candelabra dropped to the floor. A small gash opened at his hairline, and blood dripped down over his nose. His shock turned to anger, and he drew himself up to his full height. He took an unsteady step forward and righted himself.

Terror gripped her. She'd only slowed him.

"You'll pay for that." He drew back his arm. Averting her face, she slid down the table. Lawrence missed and roared. Rearing up, he came at her again. This time, the belt caught her on the leg, tearing through the flesh of her upper thigh. Bridget's legs gave out and she slipped. The belt found her back and cut across her spine. She crawled back upright, her arms and legs like jelly. With both hands, she gripped the fallen candelabra, straining under the weight. Behind her, his breathing slowed. She caught the glint of his buckle rising high in the air. Bridget gripped the brass candlestick holder and swung with all her might. The sound of crunching bone and teeth made her gasp. The candelabra dropped to the floor with a bang. Lawrence fell to his knees, the belt slipping from his hand. His face, the parts she could see, were bathed in blood, shiny and slick. He blinked. His eyes rolled backward, and he swayed until he landed on his broken face with a thump. Bridget opened her mouth and screamed.

CHAPTER
54

BRIDGET

Voices rose and fell around her. Men's voices. Some were loud and angry. One was softer, quieter. Bridget lay still, listening.

"What do we do with her?"

"The police will take her." This voice was neither angry nor kind. It dripped with a kind of indifference that scared her more than the others. "Her fate is sealed now."

Bridget's eyelids fluttered open. Brown shoes shuffled past. Black boots and dark pant legs followed behind. They circled something she couldn't quite see.

"What do you think happened?"

"She killed her husband. What more do you need to know?"

"Maybe there was a reason."

Her pulse quickened. Joseph.

The cold man again. "What's he doing here?"

"He found them. Came up to get the luggage and heard screaming. He had to bust the door down."

The boots crossed the floor, and she could see Lawrence, his body folded in on itself. Dark blood stained his shirt and coat and formed pools on the floor.

"What did you see, boy?"

"Not much. Whatever happened was already over by then."

"Was the man dead?"

"Yes, sir."

"What did the woman say?"

"Nothing. I think she was passed out by then. She wasn't screaming anymore."

Heavy footsteps came near, and Bridget closed her eyes again. "Who put the blanket over her?"

"I did." Joseph again. "She was naked, sir."

She heard a murmur of voices.

"And you say this woman and man were married?"

"Yes, sir." Another voice, familiar. "Mr. and Mrs. Lawrence Hartwood. Newlyweds. Mr. Hartwood stayed here quite often. In fact, I spoke to him this morning."

"Oh? What about?"

"A small financial matter, sir. Mr. Hartwood was quite annoyed, but these things happen."

"I see." A silence hung over the room, and Bridget strained to hear. "Was Mr. Hartwood prone to being annoyed?"

"I wouldn't know, sir."

A fourth voice, still reedy and undeveloped, interrupted. "What do you think happened?"

The black boots marched back toward the lump that was once her husband. "See this?"

"Yes, sir."

"It appears Mr. Hartwood was hit with this candelabra. Do you see the blood and bits of flesh?"

"Yes, sir." The younger voice was less sure now.

"Based on the damage to Mr. Hartwood's face, I'd imagine whoever hit him took a mighty swing." There was a murmur among the men in the room. "Unlikely the man could do that to himself, which leaves his wife as the only other person who could have committed the crime."

"Sir?" Joseph again. "I don't know if this matters, but Mrs. Hartwood was in bad shape herself when I arrived."

"Bad shape?"

"It looks like she was beaten by that belt over there. Her legs were bleeding. She's covered in bruises."

A second silence settled over the room. Bridget did her best to process. She'd killed a man. Lawrence was dead. The day before, she'd been a bride. She didn't know what she was now.

The first man spoke again. "Beaten or not, this woman took a man's life in the eyes of the law. As egregious as her injuries may be, he is not alive to defend his actions, is he? She, however, will mend to stand trial for his murder."

Bridget's heart sank at the truth of the man's words.

"But, sir, she couldn't—"

"Young man, this is not your affair. I must ask you to step aside and allow me to handle this as I see fit."

The man's footsteps neared. Hot tears fell to the carpet. She would be punished for what she'd done. It didn't matter that Lawrence was evil. He'd won after all. With one swing, she'd freed herself of one prison—only to enter another.

CHAPTER
55

VAL
Wednesday, 1:45 p.m.

The house sits on a corner lot. Smallish and plain, the squat bungalow is painted a shade of brown that reminds me of mud. This bothers me. Everything about this house is the opposite of the woman on the recording. That woman is stylish, chic. I check my information and drive by again. It's the middle of the day, and the driveway is empty. She'll be at work now, her legs crossed under her desk, her thick hair shining, her plastic smile at the ready. I pull around the corner and park on the next block.

My hands rest on the steering wheel like claws. I keep seeing her image on the screen. The long dark hair. The straight nose and brightly colored lips. The earrings. I don't need to show Morris a picture to know she was the woman who joined my sister at the Juniper. I don't understand why she was meeting Sylvia, but I'm going to find out. In my bones, I know it was wrong. So wrong. I've run through multiple scenarios in my mind as to why, and every time, it comes back to Wyatt. The man is like a walking magnet for trouble.

Worse than I'd even imagined.

I glance around the unfamiliar neighborhood. The streets are quiet, the homeowners either at work or inside. Smoke rises from one or two chimneys. The windshield wipers on my car whip back and forth over the glass, squeaking every third or fourth swipe. I stare out the window at the box-shaped houses. They remind me of game pieces or those plastic building blocks the children like.

Climbing out of my car, I pull my coat tight around me. My list of questions is a mile long. For days, I've been searching for answers. I'm close now—I can feel it—and my heart ricochets against my chest. I tell myself this is research, although not the kind I do in the library. And maybe not entirely legal.

I glance at my phone when it vibrates. Dani.

We need to talk. I know I'm the last person you want to see, but I'm trying to help. If Wyatt finds out I'm talking to you, he'll never forgive me, but we're finished. Call me back. Please.

I shove the phone in my pocket.

Thick clouds rumble overhead. A light rain is falling, and I shiver in the chilly wind. I look up and down the empty street before jogging across lawns until I come up on the back of the house. A dog barks down the block. I jump and throw myself up against the siding. The dog's cries fade and I fall forward, my chest heaving.

When I can stand up straight again, I slide down toward the back door. Locked. I peek through the windows, but I can't see anything through the blinds. I walk around to the front of the house. The blinds are drawn on these windows too. I don't try the door. Instead, I lift the flowerpot on the front stoop. I look under the mat. Nothing. She lives alone. It makes sense she would hide a key. I scan every broken brick around the door for a convenient crevice. I step back off the porch. That's when I see it. A stone sculpture of a rabbit. It's chipped and covered in some kind of dark mold, half-buried and forgotten. I toggle it back and forth until it loosens from the mud. Dirt-coated worms slither out. I crouch down and dig until my fingers close over a hard metal key.

My hands shake as I slip the key in the lock and push open the door. The darkened living room smells of vanilla and cinnamon. Candles of assorted sizes sit on an oval coffee table. More candles top the mantel. But the scent of the candles can't mask the stale odor of the threadbare carpet and shabby drapes.

Again, I'm unsure. The woman on the recording drips couture and style. This house is a far cry from either of those things.

I stand still, listening to the wind whip against the windows. I cross the living room to the mantel. Behind the candles is a single photograph. It's the same house, still brown, but brighter somehow. A couple stands on the front stoop, their hands on the shoulders of a young girl. Ringlets frame her somber face. Her arms hang stiffly at her sides. The couple is already elderly, and I know the girl must be their granddaughter. The house makes a kind of sense now.

I make my way to the tiny kitchen. Another set of candles sits in the windowsill. I pull open a few drawers and cabinets, but I don't see anything out of the ordinary. In the hallway, I find three closed doors. The first is to a small bedroom. There's a twin bed and a matching white dresser. Faded pink stripes decorate the walls. The closet and drawers are empty, as though no one has ever slept there. I move on.

Behind the second door is a tiny bathroom with a pedestal sink and a ceramic tub. A single towel hangs from the rack, dry and unused. I shut the door and tiptoe to the end of the hall. My hand hovers over the handle. Outside, thunder booms, and sleet spits against the windows. I turn the handle and push the door open.

The rest of the house is stuck in the past. The yard. The furniture. The kitchen.

But this room is modern and sleek. It's muted and serene, with recessed lighting. Over the bed are a series of paintings. They remind me of Andy Warhol except in subtler colors, and they're all of the woman. Walking into this room is like a time warp, almost jarring. But my pulse races. This is what I've come for.

The gun surprises me. I find it in the top drawer of the nightstand on top of a pile of fashion magazines. I start to pick it up, then hesitate, pulling my hand back. There's a long desk that lines one wall. At one end are two laptops and three monitors. I move toward the other end and rifle through the cubbies, but I find nothing more interesting than catalogs and stamps. Inside the top drawer of the desk are bills, sorted alphabetically, and copies of the deed to the house. I pull open the bottom drawer, and the files inside shift backward, one falling open. I catch a glimpse of my sister's face. Stunned, I reach in and pull it out.

"What are you doing here?"

I whip around, my hand flying to my throat.

Dani stands in the doorway, her finger outstretched, pointing at me, her face flushed with anger. The rain from her hair drips over her cheeks. "How dare you come into my house? You have no right. No right." She lifts her hand toward the door. "Get out. Now."

I have no intention of leaving. Not without the answers I came for. "Why do you have a picture of my sister in your files?"

She crosses the room in two strides and slams the drawer shut. "What are you doing going through my files?"

My phone buzzes in my pocket. "You didn't answer the question."

Cocking her head to one shoulder, Dani ignores the picture I'm waving in the air and my question. "You broke into my house. You need to leave now."

"I didn't break in. I had a key."

The woman scowls. "I should call the police."

"Maybe you should," I say, but we both know she won't. It's her word against mine. We stare at each other. "You have a picture of my sister. Why?"

Dani snorts. "Sylvia was no saint, you know. She used the kids. Called all the time. Wyatt didn't think I knew, but I know my way around a computer and a phone."

None of what she's saying makes sense, but before I can ask, she reminds me of the reason I came in the first place.

"I thought things would be different after Sylvia was gone. It was supposed to be me. I'm the one who's there for him. But men are always disappointing you, aren't they?"

I don't know what to say to that. "You were the last person to see her alive."

A fresh round of thunder rumbles. Lightning crashes outside, closer than before. The woman steps toward me, any trace of civility gone, replaced instead by something less rational, something that makes me shiver. Hot anger boils inside me.

"It was you." I point at her, my hand shaking. "What did you do to my sister?"

Her jaw drops, then snaps shut again. "That's rich, you know. You're so desperate to believe your baby sister didn't shove a handful of pills down her throat that you'll accuse anyone—even me."

My phone vibrates in my pocket again. I slip my hand inside, fumbling with the buttons, but she catches me.

"Give me your cell."

I hesitate, desperate to distract her. "Hotels have cameras," I say, my voice softer now.

She lifts one brow, then shrugs. "Have it your way." With one quick motion, she grabs me by the arms and throws me hard against the desk. My side slams into the wood and my head hits the wall. I stumble and slip to the floor. I crawl to my hands and knees. My phone vibrates in my pocket again.

"Give me your cell." She's standing over me, the gun from the nightstand in her hand. "Now." I sit back down, my head fuzzy. "We can do this the easy way or the hard way. Are you going to give me your phone or not?"

The barrel of the gun is closer, in front of my nose. I hand the phone over.

"Password? And don't bother trying to give me a fake one. I can find out myself eventually."

I tell her. She scrolls through my messages. "Someone named Terry is trying like hell to get in touch with you. Too bad for him that's not going to happen." She turns the phone off and tosses it on the bed.

My head clearer, I get to my feet, my eyes never leaving the gun. "How'd you do it?"

She shakes her head. "You're wrong."

"I saw you on the hotel video. You went up to the bar to meet my sister. She was waiting at a table in the corner. She was reading a book." Her chin comes up, and her lips press together. I was right. She was there. Every part of me is trembling now. "You were the last person to see her alive."

I expect her to lie or say something to defend her actions, but she does neither of those.

"It's funny," she says. "Your sister—she laughed at me, didn't she? Called me Barbie? You both did." I draw back, her outrage sharp as a dagger. "Didn't think I heard you, did you?" Her lip curls, and she tilts her head to look down at me. "Look who's laughing now."

My legs buckle, and I have to catch myself on the desk. The air in the room seems to evaporate and for a moment, I can't breathe. I want to cry, but I can't let my warring emotions come to the surface. Straightening, I force myself to inhale and exhale as she talks.

"I saw the cameras, you know," she's saying. "I'm not stupid. But they should have been far enough away, and I made sure I didn't look directly into any of them." Her forehead wrinkles. "How'd you figure it out?"

The dark hair confused me at first until I remembered blond wasn't Dani's natural color. "Your earrings." I saw them only once, but they were distinctive and pretty—delicate gold hoops, each with a single drop diamond. She flipped her hair the day I noticed them, showing them off, making sure everyone admired her latest gift from Wyatt. "I recognized them."

Her empty hand rises to her ear, but she's not wearing hoops now.

"You think you're so smart."

She's wrong. If I were, I might understand. "Why?"

A crocodile-like smile spreads over Dani's face, slow and toothy. "It's her own fault, you know. Always so superior, like she was better than me. Even to the end. Acting like she cared."

I feel tears prick, but I blink them away. "You went to the Juniper," I say again.

"Your sister wasn't expecting that. It took a little convincing to get her up to her room, but I have my ways. I told her I needed to tell her something about the kids, something important, but I could only tell her in private. That's all she needed to hear. So predictable, your sister. That was the difference between her and me." She's bragging now, enjoying it. "What else do you want to know?"

I glance toward the open door, my hands slick with sweat. It's not far. Nine feet, maybe ten. But she's between me and the only way out. I don't know if I can make it past her. And she's got the gun. "Sylvia didn't refill her prescription, did she?"

Dani laughs now. "People don't realize how easy it is, you know. I found a picture of Merry's graduation on her school website. Then I sent it to your sister in an email, along with a bit of spyware. Of course, she clicked on it. As if she needed any more pictures of the kid. I started watching what she did, who she was doing it with." Her face hardens. "That's how I knew she was going to the Franklin. I saw the confirmation email."

My lips part, but I have no words.

"It was you who gave me the idea for the sleeping pills. Arguing about them. Sylvia saying she'd stopped taking them, and you telling her to throw them away. A couple of weeks ago, I found an online pharmacy—the kind that doesn't require a prescription—and placed an order. The same medication as the pills in her medicine cabinet. Or should I say, Sylvia placed an order with her credit card. The one I found on her computer. I had it shipped to a PO box I took out in her name."

"You were in her house?"

"Wyatt has a key. I made a copy months ago. He trusts me."

I'm putting the pieces together now. "And the pill bottle? When did you take it?"

"I waited until she left on her bogus business trip. I didn't want to take a chance she might notice it was gone." She shrugs again. "I told you it wasn't hard."

There's a sick kind of triumph in her eyes. I know now she planned it. All of it. For weeks. Maybe months. The woman in front of me is mad. The realization leaves me speechless, and I wonder why it's taken me so long to see it.

She grimaces then as though she's swallowed something foul. "But so typical, your sister steals the spotlight after all. It should have been fool-proof."

Tree limbs thump against the window. "Your plan to kill my sister?"

She laughs then, a screeching sound that makes my skin itch. "Is that what you think? That all of this was to kill your precious sister?" Her upper lip curls. "I didn't go to all that trouble to kill Sylvia. I went there to punish her. To make her watch."

I grip the desk behind me, my mind spinning. "Watch what?"

She tosses her hair back and stares at me. "God, you're dumb. I went there to kill myself. Not her. Me."

CHAPTER
56

TERRY

Wednesday, 2:23 p.m.

Sleet and wind batter the windshield as I pull the car up to the curb. "Are you sure this is the right place?"

Wyatt doesn't hesitate. "This is the address."

Scanning the street, I say, "I don't see Val's car."

"Do you want to try her cell again?"

"I'll call her again if we don't find her." I keep my voice low, doing my best to calm Wyatt's jumpy nerves. "Let's do this."

We climb out, our shoulders hunched against the wind and icy rain. Reaching the sidewalk, I spot jagged pieces of ceramic rock scattered near the front door. There's part of a face and one long rabbit ear. I motion toward the smashed ornament. Wyatt blinks and nods.

Raising my hand, I pound on the door, unsure anyone can hear me over the storm. No answer. I glance back at the road, at the darkened houses. "I'm going to take a quick look around," I say. "Wait here."

I circle around the side of the house to the back. The house is dark, like the others on the street. I trot around to the other side and glimpse the tiniest sliver of light through drawn blinds. I creep closer. There are two voices. Female, but I can't make out the words.

"Val's in there," I tell Wyatt when I reach the front again, my breath coming fast. "I think something's wrong."

Wyatt doesn't wait. He grabs the front doorknob. Surprising both of us, it swings open. He hurdles through the living room to the kitchen and the hall. I'm fast on his heels, catching him by the arm. I gesture at him to stay quiet. A light can be seen from a half-closed door at the end of the hallway. A voice I know must belong to Dani carries over the sound of the wind outside. We creep forward, careful to stay out of the light.

"She was supposed to watch me. I gave her five, maybe six pills. Enough to make her drowsy and knock her out after a while, but not enough to kill her. It's amazing what someone will do when you hold a gun to their head, don't you think?"

Whatever Val says is drowned out by thunder.

I pull Wyatt back, lean close, and whisper, "Go to the living room. Call 911 and wait." He disappears, and I slide down the wall, closer to the open door. Instinctively, I reach down to my waistband but come up empty. "Shit," I mutter under my breath. No gun. No badge. Pulling out my phone, I hit record.

Dani is still talking. "I had the pills in my hand. I had a letter to Wyatt on the nightstand. I stood by him for so long. But he never appreciated me. Not really." Her words take on a dreamy quality. "And then the voice came."

"What voice?" Val asks. "Who?"

"Nobody. I don't know. At first, I thought someone had come in the room, but there was no one there but your sister and me. That's when I knew. The voice whispered at first. It was all around me, in the room and then in my head, like a cool breath swirling inside me. So soft, so soothing. Like the walls were speaking to me. I think I stood there for a while, listening. But the voice got louder and meaner until it hurt inside my head. It hurt everywhere. It kept saying her name. Sylvia. Sylvia. Every time, pounding and pounding. I didn't know what it was telling me. I wanted it to stop. It hurt so bad."

A chill steals over me, and my mind burns with memories of my own.

"And then I knew," Dani says. "It was supposed to be me, and your sister was supposed to take the blame. But the voice had a different plan. It kept telling me she deserved to die for what she'd done. Don't get me wrong, I hated your precious sister, but more than that, I needed the voice to stop. The pain kept getting worse. So, I made up my mind, forced her to take the rest of the pills. It was hard by the end. She was more asleep than awake."

I inch forward. I can see Dani now. She's standing at the far end of the room, her back to the doorway, a gun in her outstretched hand.

"I watched her drift away, so peaceful. It wasn't supposed to be that way."

Backed up against the desk, Val's head hangs low. I feel Wyatt's presence behind me again, and I shift toward him. He nods once.

"I can't let you leave," Dani says.

Val stiffens and lifts her head. "You'd really kill me? And then what? How would you explain that one to the police?"

"Easy. You're deranged, obsessed with your sister's death, and desperate to blame someone. You broke into my house and attacked me. Self-defense." She pushes her hair off her forehead. "You shouldn't have come here."

I wait a beat before sliding up to the door. I raise a finger to my lips.

"You won't get away with it." The way Val says it, with confidence, I know she's seen me.

Dani snorts. "Please. I've been calling and leaving you messages for days, warning you, practically begging you to talk to me. How's it going to look when the police see the video of you breaking in? Or the nasty text you're going to send me? It's funny, isn't it? Texts are just a bunch of words strung together without context. They might mean one thing, but people believe what they want to believe. Same as you believed Sylvia was afraid of Wyatt."

I'm inside the room now, Wyatt behind me.

Val pales. "That was you?"

"You were so easy, always believing the worst about Wyatt. And Sylvia, idiot that she was, made it even easier." Caught up in her tale, Dani's hand

and the gun slip lower. "I called the front desk, pretending to be your sister. I put the sign on the door. I didn't know it would be so many days before they found her, but I guess the hotel was busy." The gun comes up again. "So now you know everything. Well, almost everything."

The distance to Dani grows smaller. Ten feet. Eight. Tree limbs whip against the window, but inside, the only sound is Dani's voice.

"It doesn't matter anymore," she's saying. "Wyatt doesn't want me. Even without Sylvia around." Her voice grows louder, harder. "This has to end now."

"Wait. You said I didn't know everything. Tell me now."

Wyatt's breath whistles in my ear. The tension coming from him vibrates in waves, but I don't dare look at him. Not while Dani is holding a gun on Val.

"I don't want to anymore."

He pushes past me before I can stop him. "Then I will."

The gun swings toward Wyatt, then toward me and then Val, and back again. The open barrel travels in an arc, back and forth between us, as though in slow motion. We all stand there, frozen. A picture of Sylvia has fallen to the floor along with a file folder. A drawer is open on the nightstand.

"You shouldn't have come," Dani says to Wyatt. Her voice is shaking as she looks at him.

"You don't have to do this." He starts to take a step toward her, but she jerks the gun higher, and he halts. "Please. Whatever I've done to make you do this, I'm sorry," he says. "I really am."

"You're sorry? Are you sorry you didn't appreciate me? That you didn't love me the way I loved you? I did everything for you. Everything." Spit flies from her mouth, and tears spill from her eyes. "When I asked you what was wrong with us, you told me to be myself. I didn't need to try so hard." She lifts a hand to her hair. "I went back to my natural color. I didn't plan nights

out. I didn't complain when you spent all your free time with those kids."
She swings the gun toward each of us. "It didn't matter. You wanted to leave
me. Like my parents. Like everyone." Her movements have a jerky quality
to them, as though she can't control her limbs. Dani wipes her eyes in one
angry motion, focus trained on Wyatt now. "It's all your fault."

"You don't have to do this," Wyatt says again, pleading.

I raise my hands to draw her attention, show her I'm unarmed. "Why
don't you put the gun down and let us help you? There's no reason for anyone to get hurt here."

"Back off." She points in my direction. Satisfied when I retreat a step,
she swings back toward Wyatt. "What did she have that I didn't?" she asks.
"Am I not beautiful enough? Not young enough? What?"

He gives a small shake of his head. "No. You are beautiful. And smart.
And most guys would say I'm crazy. I know that. It isn't you. I swear."

Her chin rises higher. "It was because of Sylvia, wasn't it? She wouldn't
let you go."

Val's eyes widen.

"She didn't do anything," Wyatt is saying. "You and I—it was me," he
says. "Not you or her. Me."

"Liar." Her red lips press into a hard line. "I followed you. I saw the texts
on your phone. The pictures. Do you think I'm stupid?"

"No, of course not. Things with us didn't work out. That's all."

"You'd been reading Wyatt's texts for weeks," I say. Her eyes land on me.
"You knew Sylvia was at the Franklin. Would be in the Juniper that night."

One corner of her mouth turns up in a half smile. "Score one for Wyatt's
friend."

"You've been spying on Wyatt's phone, monitoring everything on it."

She shrugs. "It's not hard, if you know how to do it." She looks at Wyatt
again. "And you asked me to look at your phone. More than once."

"Dani . . . can I call you that?" I ask, drawing her attention back to me.
She lifts her shoulders. "You knew Sylvia and Wyatt were meeting at the
Franklin."

The color drains from Val's face.

Her eyes fill with tears as she looks at Wyatt. "You're S. M.," she says, her voice a whisper.

"I'm sorry, Val," Wyatt says. "Syl wanted to keep it quiet, give us time to try things out first. And she thought you'd be mad at her." Val flinches. "I thought you knew." His words come faster. "At the police station, when we got the medical examiner's report, you said she texted you and told you everything. I . . ." His words trail away. "I thought you knew."

"Shut up," Dani shouted. "Sylvia. Sylvia. Sylvia. I'm sick of her. Calling you that stupid nickname. As if—"

I interrupt again, keeping my voice even. "And you knew Sylvia was expecting Wyatt after work, right? That's why you called him, threatening to kill yourself."

Her gaze swings back to Wyatt. "Scared you, didn't I?"

He shakes his head. "I shouldn't have believed you. I should have known better."

"And you sent the text to Wyatt, didn't you? From Sylvia's phone. Telling him she wasn't feeling well, and she would see him in the morning."

Dani nods. "I couldn't have him rushing over to save her, now could I? So, I sent a few texts from Sylvia's phone for her. It's not like she could have done it. She was pretty out of it by then."

"You deleted most of the texts between Sylvia and Wyatt," I say. "And the one where he told her he'd lost his room key, the one you took from his apartment when he went home to change."

"I had to. I knew after the police found her in the hotel, Wyatt would tell everyone how they were getting back together." Dani shoots Wyatt a look. "I knew all his passwords. I deleted what I needed to from his cloud account. One minute, it's there; the next, it isn't."

Tears roll down Val's cheeks now.

"It didn't seem fair. Sylvia had him in life. She couldn't have him in death too. I thought without her, it would be my turn. But he didn't want me."

She stiffens and her finger tightens against the trigger.

"But you said Wyatt hurt you," Val said, shaking her head, still trying to understand. "I believed you."

"He did hurt me. He deserved to be punished for that. Ask him if you don't believe me."

Val stares at Dani a moment, as though considering the accusation, before she looks at her brother-in-law, her brows arched.

"You should have punished me." Wyatt's fists are clenched at his side. "Not Sylvia."

A siren wails in the distance, and Dani's head jerks toward the window.

In that split second, Wyatt flies across the room and Dani's body rises in the air, landing with a thud. The gun, in her outstretched hand, skitters across the carpet, but not before the sound of a gun blast rocks the room. Val's scream fills the air, and I rush toward her.

"Are you hurt?"

"No, I don't think so." Her breathing is shallow though, and I can feel her heart racing.

Underneath Wyatt, Dani raises her knee, connecting with his jaw. The crack of bone on bone is almost as loud as the bullet, and he grunts in pain. I let go of Val. The gun is still on the floor, an arm's length behind Dani. She rolls toward it before I can get there, snatches it up, and points it at me. The barrel, inches from my face, is a black hole.

I raise my hands for the second time and take a step back. Wyatt, rubbing his jaw, scrambles to his feet.

Outside, the sirens whine, screaming over the booming thunder. The lights flicker. Dani smiles, but there is no warmth in it. I barely notice Wyatt at my side, Dani and the gun my only focus. Her long finger curls itself around the trigger. I no longer hear the storm or the sirens or see the blinking lights. I charge forward, my eyes never leaving the gun. The shots, when they come, stop me in my tracks. For a moment, there is no sound at all. And then there is only darkness.

CHAPTER
57

VAL
Wednesday, 3:13 p.m.

The paramedics wheel the gurney out to the emergency truck, slam the
back doors shut, and race to the front seats. The whirling lights grow
fuzzy as the ambulance speeds down the street. When they're gone, I let the
living-room curtain fall and hug my arms to my chest. There is blood spatter
on my shoes and my pants, and the sight sends a shudder up my spine. My
arms tighten. A uniformed officer stands in the foyer, his hands on his hips.
He doesn't look at me, but I'm not fooled. He has one job. To make sure I
don't leave.

The small house is crawling with police. Barnes and Newman are in the
bedroom with Dani. Terry's there too, explaining, giving me a moment to
myself. I'm grateful for that if nothing else. I was in the room when the gun
went off. I saw Terry rush toward Dani as the lights went out, and I heard
Wyatt fall to the floor—so close I could touch him—although I didn't know
it was him then. I draw in a breath.

They'll want a statement when they're done in the bedroom. My arms
fall and I square my shoulders. I'll be ready.

Footsteps sound from the direction of the hall. Dani appears, chin low, her hands locked behind her. Newman guides her out the door. He pushes her head down as he directs her into the backseat of the police cruiser, and they drive away, the sirens silent now. I exhale, but I can't stop shivering. I've been at crime scenes. I've witnessed testimony in murder trials and viewed horrible photos. According to my editor, I've got a nose for the worst kind of crimes, but this is different. I'm reminded that being on the outside, being the reporter, is not the same as being on the inside.

I feel his presence behind me before I turn around.

"Val?" Terry's skin is pale in the darkened living room, his eyes large and shadowed. "Are you okay?"

"Fine," I manage to say. He reaches out to me, but I back away. "You defended her."

"No."

"I heard you. You told them she heard voices. That the voices told her to kill Sylvia." Each word is louder than the one before. The uniformed officer steps into the room from the foyer.

Terry waves him away. "I recorded her," he says. My mouth falls open. "On my phone. When Wyatt and I were in the hall."

I'm not an expert on admissibility, but it could be evidence if she claims some kind of insanity defense. The idea only makes me madder.

He steps closer to me. "I wasn't defending her, Val. I told them what she said."

There is truth in what he's saying now, but there's another truth, one I witnessed in the haggard way he held his head, in the quietness of his voice. "You believed her. You bought the whole thing."

Terry's gaze slides away, and I know I'm right. My stomach sinks, and my chin drops to my chest.

"You don't understand," he says.

"What's there to understand, Terry? She killed my sister. She took the pills with her. She went to the hotel. She planned the whole thing." I've gotten everything wrong. I thought Wyatt was the stalker, but it was Dani. It's his ex-girlfriend who is guilty. I'm not wrong about this. "She murdered my sister."

"You're right. She did."

"So, what's with the voices then? Are you saying it's okay because she's crazy?"

"I don't know if she's crazy and neither do you. That's for the doctors to decide."

My head is swimming. We're going in circles. "I don't understand. What are you saying then?"

He draws himself up, his voice apologetic. "I should have told you about the hotel. About," he hesitates, "some other things."

The front door opens. More men come in carrying lights and forensic equipment. I look out the window again. A TV news truck has pulled onto the street, parking as close as possible to the scene. A camera emblazoned with the station logo is trained on the house. I pull back, stepping past Terry. "What kind of things?"

He jams his hands deep in his pockets. "About the people who've died at the Franklin. All of them. From the beginning."

I start to say something, but any retort dies on my tongue. He did tell me something about the hotel. In the library and at the grill. I think about how he reacted to learning that Sylvia had died at the Franklin. About how he could barely be in the suite where she'd been found. About how his steps slowed whenever we got close to the old hotel. He's uncomfortable there. Wary. Maybe even frightened.

A voice sounds behind me. "Ms. Ritter. Detective Barnes would like to have a word with you in the kitchen." The uniformed officer crooks his finger. "If you'll follow me."

I don't look at Terry as I walk out of the room, but I can picture him now, that day in the library. I can hear his words in my head. *The Franklin's got a history. A history of death.*

EPILOGUE

VAL
Two Weeks Later

I ask Terry to meet me at the hotel. He hedges, but I insist. I stand inside the lobby, waiting. When he comes in, I don't miss the dark circles or the stubble covering his strong jaw. He halts twenty feet before he reaches me, stopping as though a train is rushing toward him. I know he doesn't want to be here, but I won't give in.

He lets me take his arm and guide him to a sofa. He perches on the edge of the deep-seated couch as though if he sits back, it will swallow him whole.

"Are you still angry with me?"

"Depends," I say. This isn't entirely true. I am still mad, but not for the reasons he thinks.

And not at him.

"Why did you want to meet here?" he asks, his voice hoarse.

"Because you can't erase the past."

He plucks at the fabric of his slacks, his fingers twisting over the dark gray wool. "You know about it?"

In the days since Dani was arrested, I did what I always do.

I researched, digging through whatever I could find. "I know part of it," I say. "Do you want to fill me in on the rest?"

His head falls to his hands. Seconds pass. A minute. I force myself to be still, to wait.

He straightens, slides back an almost imperceptible distance. "My grandfather was raised by his aunt and uncle. They adopted him the day after he was born. He never lived with his mother. Never knew his father. The family lived in Washington for a while, but they came back to Baltimore when he was still a boy. He became a cop when he grew up. My dad did too."

"And you."

"Yes. My grandfather was conceived right here in this hotel. In a suite upstairs."

Terry wears the face of a man who knows more about darkness than he should. I hold my breath, waiting.

"The same suite where Sylvia was killed," he says.

I turn this over in my mind. In an odd way, I must have known. I remember how he stood frozen at the door of the suite, unwilling to enter. I know some of his story now. The case was famous in its day, although I would never have thought to connect Terry with any of it. Still, it's the rest I want to hear about. "Go on."

"My grandfather's mother killed her husband. She was convicted of murder and spent her life in an institution. Her name was Bridget Wallace. Hartwood, after she married." He sinks lower into the sofa, and I lean back with him. "She was raised on Calvert Street with her mother and father and her sister."

I let him tell me in his own way. He stops and starts. It's clear that everything about this story bothers him. I could remind him that things would be different now, that Bridget wouldn't have been convicted, that she had every reason to defend herself against the man who bought her hand in marriage and beat her.

But these are things he already knows, and so I don't say anything.

"Joseph attended every day of Bridget's trial. After she was taken away, he became a lawyer, vowing to do everything he could to get her out. He did his best, but it was harder then. He never gave up, according to my grandfather. It was Joseph who arranged the adoption. Bridget wanted her son to have a chance at a life. Margaret's married name was Martin."

"Lawrence Hartwood is your great-grandfather."

"Yes." He clasps his hands together, his knees bouncing up and down. "I should have told you about the voices."

This is the part I've been waiting for. If I'd been paying attention, I might have heard the things he didn't tell me. *A history of death.* I'm listening now.

"The things Dani said. The voices in her head. I've heard the same thing more than once. From other suspects." Terry looks over at me. "I told you about the man who almost killed his wife."

I nod.

"There were others. Worse."

"But if that's true, why doesn't anyone know?"

"There were multiple deaths in the twenties and thirties, but those were blamed on the market, the wars. Sometimes decades passed between deaths. Besides, in those days, claiming you heard voices was likely to get you thrown into an asylum for life."

"But times change."

"True, but there are always extenuating circumstances. A murder. A suicide. A whisper in your ear. It's the stuff of ghost stories and legends. No one would believe it."

My voice is quiet when I speak. "You do."

"Yes." He glances up at the painted ceiling, at the sparkling chandeliers. "There's evil in this place, seeping through the walls, whispering evil thoughts, distorting the mind. Whatever it is, it's real." He lets out a shaky breath. "I felt it once at a crime scene—or what was left of it." He shoots me a wary glance.

"Tell me."

He stands up then, as though even being there is haunting him somehow. "Can we get out of here?"

I touch his elbow. "You're here now. Tell me."

Terry looks around the lobby for a minute. Soft music plays in the background. Two couples are sitting near the oversized fireplace. Nothing out of the ordinary. He sits down again.

"The time I heard it, I was working a case with a woman who was new to the department. Chet—he was my partner—was out after having knee surgery. She was filling in. Melanie was her name. Melanie was a good cop, organized, dedicated. But she was green. When we first arrived, we were told that most of the blood was confined to the bathroom. Melanie had this idea that she needed to prove herself, show she was as tough as the more experienced guys." He licks his lips and hangs his head.

"She didn't wait for me. Went busting into the room and headed straight for the bathroom. Next thing I know, she's running for the hall, her lunch all over the carpet." His voice drops lower, and I lean forward to hear. "It was true that the blood was mostly confined to the bathroom. But we should have been warned. The walls were covered. And the floor and the shower. Every inch. And what wasn't covered in blood was covered in parts of the victim's head."

I let out a breath. "A woman."

"Yes."

Having already read about the case of the hair-dryer murder, I nod.

"No one wanted to be near that room. Not forensics. Not anyone. I was standing there by myself for no more than two minutes, three tops, when I first felt it."

He stops. I wait.

"My toes and fingers went cold. Then my legs and arms. It's sort of that feeling you get when they give you an IV and whatever they're injecting you with is like ice being put into your veins. Even my brain felt cold. Then I heard him."

His chest rises and falls, and I take his hand.

"I couldn't understand the words at first, but they got louder, banging against my skull. 'She needs to die.' Over and over. I think I asked out loud: 'Who?' 'Her,' was the answer. The sound of the voice was like an anvil, sharp and cutting. I wanted it to end. I would have pulled my own brain out of my head if I could have. I remember holding my hands against my ears, trying to drown out the noise. 'Now,' the voice said. 'Now.' I couldn't understand who until I looked around and saw her standing right behind me. Melanie."

He pulls away, unable to meet my gaze. "My hands curled up into fists. A part of me needed to hurt her the way the voice was hurting me. She stood there, not even seeing me. When she did, she flinched. Her eyes got big before she hit the floor."

My own breath is ragged. "You hit her?"

"No. She fainted. I never raised a hand." He runs his fingers through his hair. "The uniforms outside the room came rushing in and got her over to a chair. I ran out of the room, doubled over, sure I was going to be sick. And then it was over. The voice stopped. The pain. All of it. No one knew any of it. I resigned the next day." His eyes slide back to mine, fall away again. "Sounds like I'm crazy, right?"

I don't answer right away. *Crazy* is a strong word. For days, it was Terry who kept me from going over a cliff, kept me sane. He was steady and reliable and smart.

A young boy skips by us then, his knees high, swinging his big sister's hand. A man and a woman follow. They laugh at the boy and lean in close, their heads touching. A man in a business suit hurries past, his briefcase swinging from his right hand. From across the lobby, I hear the tinkling notes of the grand piano. It's only a hotel. That's what I want to say. And yet, I can't. I've read the stories. There were two families and one couple, the rest women. Suicide. Murder. Most of the deaths happened on the upper floors. Six in the same room. And I heard the way Dani spoke about the voices. Something happened in that suite, although I can't be sure what. "I don't think you're crazy."

"Ah. Well, I'm not sure I believe you, but thank you for saying it."

"You're welcome." A bellhop passes by with a rolling cart full of bags. "Do you suspect a ghost of some kind?"

He gives me a weak smile. "Are you asking me if I think Lawrence Hartwood is haunting this hotel?"

I'm not sure I would have thought to frame the question in quite that way, but it makes a kind of sense. "Yes, I guess I am."

"He's the odds-on favorite in my book."

His answer is not a surprise. He said it earlier. His great-grandfather died here. Like my sister. Sylvia is the last on a list of deaths that has spanned a century. Not a suicide as they originally thought. A murder. It makes me wonder, if Terry is right, how many deaths were the same?

"What stopped you from hitting her? Melanie?"

It's so long before he answers, I wonder if he heard me.

"I'm not sure," he says. "I think I yelled no, but it must have been in my head. I do remember the pain subsided then, for a minute. It was like there was a war in my brain. The cold and the voice and something else, something lighter trying to save me." He shrugs. "If Melanie hadn't fainted, I don't know what would have happened."

"Nothing would have happened." I can see he's not convinced, but I've got a new idea.

"Maybe there are ghosts at the Franklin, but they can't all be evil. Good people have died here too. Good people like Sylvia. Maybe those are the ones that gave you the strength to resist."

He's quiet a moment. "Good ghosts, huh?"

"Yes. Good ones."

A wide band of light creeps over the marble floor, bathing us in warmth, and some measure of the gloom seems to lift off of him, floating away. "I like that," he says.

I shift toward him. "Can I ask you a question?"

"Sure."

"Is that why you helped me? Because this hotel is where Sylvia died?"

"Partly. At least at first. As much as I didn't want to come here, I wanted to know if it had happened again. You don't know how much I wanted to be wrong. For you. And your sister."

His expression changes. It's less troubled, more hopeful. This is the face I like best.

"But if I hadn't been in the library that day," he adds, "I wouldn't have met you. I'm glad I did."

"Me too."

"I should have told you about the rest."

I shake my head. "It's better that you didn't. I was enough of a basket case without any scary stories."

He chuckles for the first time. "You were that."

I laugh with him. "Wyatt says to tell you hello."

"How's his shoulder?"

"Okay. Dani didn't hit any major arteries."

"And his leg?"

"Better. He's still on crutches, but he and the kids are moving back into the house next week." I lean back now. Wyatt has his faults. Lots of them. Our relationship since the shooting is still not great. Our conversations sometimes feel like every word is a grenade, loaded with the potential to maim. But we're trying. I'm trying. If for no other reason than my sister loved him. And she was right about one thing. Merry and Miles need him.

Sylvia gave Wyatt her diary on that Monday morning, never knowing it would be her last. She wanted him to read it, to know she believed in him again, to understand she was ready to start over too. Tucked inside was a letter addressed to him, to Sailor Man, the nickname she gave him in college. There was so much hope on those pages, so much love. He stored the diary and letter in his safe-deposit box when they found her, when he knew she was gone, hoarding it the way a homeless man clings to his shopping cart and tattered blanket. It's taken me some time, but I understand. He's no longer the man my sister fell in love with back in college, nor is he the man who broke her heart. Some days, I still hate him for what he did. And other days,

I wish I could take back my own words. I wish I would have listened more. But the past is gone and all we have is now.

"It's for the best," I say. "They're a family."

"That's good." His mouth turns down. "Dani will plead not guilty by reason of insanity. Considering the tape, her talking about the voices, it might work."

A lump forms in my throat. It's odd. I know she killed my sister. Sylvia won't see her kids grow up. She won't grow old with Wyatt or anyone. This is Dani's fault. She forced those pills down my sister's throat. I want her punished for what she did. And yet, I was there when she talked about what happened, about wanting to make the voices go away. Was she telling the truth when she said she went there to kill herself? I may never know for sure, but I do believe she's unstable at a minimum, maybe seriously ill. "Will you have to testify?"

"Maybe. I don't know yet."

"What will happen to her?"

"Most likely she'll be remanded to a mental institution for psychiatric treatment. I know Jensen, the D.A. She'll push for the maximum."

I glance over at the elevators. An image of my sister smiling and happy fills my mind. I'm glad of that now. "Maybe that's what she needs."

"Maybe." He rubs his hands over his thighs and slides a little farther back into the sofa, some of his tension melting away.

"You know, you're pretty good at this detective thing. Maybe you should try it again, put out your shingle."

"Maybe," he says again, shooting me a grin. "What about you, Val? What will you do?"

I could say I have my career and my friends, but I know that's not what he means. There's a hole in my life now. I can hear Sylvia's voice in my head.

"Val, you don't have to check on me all the time. Why don't you worry about yourself for a change? All you do is work and take care of me."

"Taking care of you is what I love," I said.

"Uh-huh," she responded with a snicker.

"I do."

"I know." She touched my arm, voice gentle. "But you can't take care of me forever, Val."

Tears slide down my cheeks. I'm never going to stop missing her, but I still have Merry and Miles. I'm grateful for that.

"I don't know really," I manage to say.

Terry reaches into his pocket, finds his handkerchief, and hands it to me. Steadying my breath, I wipe my face. My hand falls to my lap, my fingers wrapped around the damp handkerchief. Neither of us speaks. When he places his hand on my wrist, the warmth of his skin sends a tingle up my spine.

His deep brown eyes search mine before he nods. "I have a feeling you'll be fine, Val Ritter. Just fine."

THE END

If you have thoughts of suicide or self-harm,
or if you have been affected by suicide, contact:

National Suicide Prevention Hotline:
1-800-273-8255
or dial 988

Suicide Prevention Resource Center:
https://www.sprc.org/

American Foundation for Suicide Prevention:
https://afsp.org/

International Suicide Hotlines:
https://blog.opencounseling.co/suicide-hotlines/

If you or someone you know is or has been affected by domestic violence, contact:

National Domestic Violence Hotline:
1-800-799-SAFE (7233)
https://www.thehotline.org/

International Shelter Resources:
https://www.domesticshelters.org/resources/
national-global-organizations

ACKNOWLEDGMENTS

In 2019, I attended Malice Domestic, the convention that celebrates mysteries. After I finished speaking on my panel, I attended a session where Mikita Brottman was talking about her nominated nonfiction book, *An Unexplained Death: The True Story of a Body at the Belvedere.* I left that session with three thoughts. First, I needed to buy the book. Impressed by Ms. Brottman's research and persistence, I wanted to know more about the body found in the condo building/former hotel. Second, I wondered how I could use the idea of a suspected suicide in a historic hotel in a new way. And last, I questioned whether the popularity of ghost tours could play a role in that story. The seeds of *Her Sister's Death* were sown.

Taking those seeds and turning them into a completed manuscript takes time and lots of nurturing. I owe an enormous debt of gratitude to my Sisters in Crime critique group. Thank you to current and former members who read these pages: Heather Weidner, Frances Aylor, Amy Lilly, Sandie Warwick, Cat Brennan, Susan Campbell, and Margie Bagby. Their questions and comments helped me fine-tune the direction of this story.

More important, their support and encouragement are appreciated with every turn. This group makes writing the first draft a true pleasure.

I am also incredibly grateful to my beta readers. Their insight and feedback are both constructive and essential. Thank you to Mary Berry, a true mystery fan who never fails to tell it like it is and is always willing to read an unedited version on short notice. Additional thanks to Donna McGrath. Your well thought out notes make every book better. I'm also fortunate to have a daughter who is an excellent writer and reader in her own right. Thank you to Cameron for making my stories a priority. And a special thank-you to my husband, David. I know addressing each of your comments can only be a good thing and improve the flow of any story.

Although *Her Sister's Death* is a bit of a departure in style and genre from my previous works, I truly loved writing these characters and this story. It was great fun to swing between 1921 and the present and bring the two tales together at the end. I also loved creating the Franklin, a hotel with charm and style but a questionable history. While this book is different from my others, Rebecca Scherer still offered great insight and advice on an earlier version of the manuscript and for that, I thank her. Her opinion is always valued and appreciated.

I owe a huge debt of gratitude to the team at CamCat Publishing. Thank you to Sue Arroyo for loving this book and choosing to add it to the CamCat list. Thank you to Helga Schier for all your hard work and for helping make my manuscript shine. Thank you to Maryann Appel for a beautiful cover and to the rest of the team for all you do: Laura Wooffitt, Bill Lehto, Gabe Schier, Bridget McFadden, Meredith Lyons, Elana Gibson, Abigail Miles, Ellen Leach, and Jessica Homami.

Thank you also to my parents for their support through the years, to my extended family, and to my friends, who never fail to ask when my next book is coming out. Thank you to Cameron, Thomas, Luke, and Meredith. You are my heart always, and I am the luckiest mother ever. And finally, to David, the one who makes me laugh every day: thank you for everything.

ABOUT THE AUTHOR

The first thing K. L. Murphy wrote was a modified screenplay of a 1970s TV show. She and her siblings performed that show for their own built-in audience (mom and dad) to rave reviews (again, mom and dad!). Later, she moved on to high-school journalism before graduating from college and taking a detour into finance and banking. Once she began writing again and focusing on fiction, the process felt like coming home.

She is the author of the Detective Cancini mystery series: *A Guilty Mind, Stay of Execution,* and *The Last Sin.* Her short stories have been featured in the anthologies *Deadly Southern Charm* ("Burn") and *Murder by the Glass* ("EverUs").

In addition, K. L. (an avid fan of recording personal histories) is the author of *The Center: From Generation to Generation,* the seventy-year history of the Richmond Jewish Community Center. She's a member of Mystery Writers of America, International Thriller Writers, Sisters in Crime, James River Writers, and Historical Writers of America.

K. L. lives in Richmond, VA, with her husband, children, and amazing dogs. When she's not writing, she loves to read, entertain friends, catch up on everything she's ignored, and always—walk the amazing dogs.

If you enjoyed

K. L. Murphy's *Her Sister's Death,*

you will enjoy

Marcy McCreary's *The Murder of Madison García.*

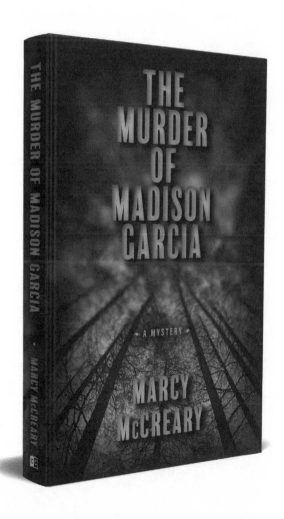

1

SUNDAY | JUNE 30, 2019

SLID UNDERNEATH THE BUBBLES. My knees poked out above the surface. One. Two. Three. Four. Five. When I came up for air I heard "Radiate"—my phone's annoying ringtone. *Need to change that.* I lifted my body slightly and my boobs collided with the edge of the tube. Damn, that hurt. I inched my fingers across the floor but the phone was unreachable, resting on the edge of the bathmat. I gave up and pulled my entire body back into the warmish water. *If it's important they'll leave a voice mail.*

I inspected the tips of my fingers. Wrinkly. I reached for the towel that laid crumpled on the toilet lid. With the towel secured around my midsection, I picked up my phone. A missed call from my daughter Natalie. I hit "Recents" to call her back and noticed an incoming call from the night before. A red phone number, indicating a person who was not in my contact list. Boston, Massachusetts, displayed below the number. Probably one of those spam calls—a request for my social security number or a plea from a political fundraiser. There seemed to be a lot of that lately with the presidential campaign heating up. The American people had taken sides—

lefties, centrists, wingers—and it wasn't pretty. *It never used to be this way.* Or maybe it was, but social media and cable news exaggerated and exacerbated the divisiveness. Made me think of that Stealers Wheel lyric: "Clowns to the left of me, jokers to the right, here I am stuck in the middle with you."

After applying a fair amount of goop to tame and defrizz my curls, I slipped into my black yoga pants and gray drawstring hoodie. I settled on my bed, opened my laptop, and Googled "reverse lookup." Curiosity is a strong motivator to get to the bottom of things—and as a detective, I found it hard to pass up the chance to solve this tiny mystery. I entered the phone number into the rectangular box at the top of the screen. The results page displayed the name Madison García, a resident of Brooklyn, New York, not Boston, Massachusetts. I opened my Facebook page and typed "Madison Garcia" in the search box. There was one Madison García living in Brooklyn. But the page was private. And her profile picture was a black cat. When I clicked on the name I was greeted with a handful of pictures she must have designated shareable and therefore accessible to the public. There were people—mostly millennials—in the photographs, but no one I recognized. All personal info was hidden.

"Susan, you up there?"

"Yeah!" I shouted, closing the lid. "I'll be right down!" I plucked a tissue from the box on the bedside table and blew my nose, then headed downstairs with the laptop tucked under my armpit and the box of tissues in my grip.

"Feeling any better?" Ray asked.

"Fucking summer cold. Just popped a DayQuil." I shook the tissue box. "And I got these bad boys."

"You look like shit." A beat later he added, "And I mean that in the nicest way."

"Yeah, well I feel like shit."

"I heard your phone ring last night just before ten o'clock. But you were out cold."

"The wonders of NyQuil. It was a wrong number. A Madison someone. Never left a message. Probably heard my voice-mail message and bagged out when she realized she misdialed." I blew my nose with more force than necessary. "What's your plan today?"

"I'm heading into the station soon." Ray put on his serious face and wagged his finger. "You are to stay put. I'll pick up dinner tonight."

"Yes sir," I said, military salute included.

My phone rang and we both glanced at it. I thought it might be the Boston/Brooklyn caller, but the caller ID displayed "Chief Eldridge."

I swiped to answer. "Chief?" I bobbed my head a few times as Ray shot me dirty looks. "Got it. On my way."

"Susan, is this your idea of staying put?"

"We got a dead body over at Sackett Lake." I blew my nose in my semi-used tissue. "Besides . . . it's just a little summer cold." I coughed up some phlegm and headed back upstairs to change into real clothes.

A **POLICE** vehicle and an ambulance were parked along Fireman's Camp Road. I spotted Officer Sally McIver and her partner, Ron Wallace, at the edge of the parking area. Two paramedics stood beside a black Lexus, the only car in the small Fireman's Camp parking lot.

Sally waved as I got out of my car. Ron held up a roll of police tape and shook it like a tambourine. I looked out toward the lake and took in the scene.

From this distance, the dead woman in the car simply looked like she was daydreaming, staring out at the placid water without a care in the world. I donned my white protective outerwear, then joined them.

"What can you tell me?" I asked Sally.

"You sound like shit," she replied.

"Top of the morning to you too."

"That guy over there tapped on the driver's side window," she said, pointing to the gray-haired gentleman with a German shepherd. "Thought she might be sleeping or something. When she didn't respond, he opened the door. Saw the blood. Then he called 9-1-1. Ron and I got here about five minutes ago."

One of the paramedics approached us. "Hey. Nothing we can do. All yours."

"Manner of death?" I inquired.

"Homicide. Multiple stab wounds to her torso. I noticed a bathing suit in the backseat. Perhaps here for a swim and robbed?" He shrugged, then walked back toward his partner.

There wasn't much we could do until Gloria and Mark showed up. Gloria Weinberg was our forensic photographer. Back in the Borscht Belt days, when the Catskills resort hotels were in full swing, she took pictures of the guests, who would then purchase their portraits encased in mini keychain viewers.

Now she photographed crime scenes . . . and the occasional wedding. And once, the crime scene of someone whose wedding she also photographed. Mark Sheffield was our crime-scene death investigator. He joined the Sullivan County ME's office last fall—wanted to get away from the grim murder scenes of the city. Wait until he gets a load of this blood-soaked tableau.

I turned to Ron. "Let's get a perimeter going. From this area here all the way around to the water," I said, sweeping my arm across the landscape to indicate the area I wanted cordoned off. I wiped my nose on my sleeve. "Sally, run the plates. I'm going to have a little chat with the man who found her."

I approached the gray-haired man and introduced myself.

"Benjamin Worsky," he said in response.

"Okay, Mr. Worsky. Just a few standard questions and you can be on your way."

"It's no trouble. None at all. In all my years, never thought I'd come across a . . . a dead body. Poor woman."

"When did you happen upon the car?"

"I left my house at seven o'clock on the dot. I'm a man of habit. Seven on the dot every morning to walk Elsa." He petted the top of Elsa's head.

"It takes me ten minutes to walk from my house to this spot, so I would say I spotted the car around seven ten. But I didn't think anything of it and continued my walk past the car. But when I came back this way—and I'm thinking that would be around seven thirty because I walked another ten minutes and then turned around—the car was still here."

"Why did you approach the car?"

"I'm not really sure. Perhaps a sense that something was wrong." He looked down at Elsa, who looked up at him. "Elsa was a bit agitated. Maybe it was that. So I peered in and she didn't look well." He frowned and shook his head. "I tapped on the window just to ask her if she was okay and when she didn't answer I opened the car door. That's when I saw the blood and called 9-1-1."

"Did you touch anything?"

"Just the car door handle."

"Did you see anyone else around, either when you came through or off further on your walk?"

"No. But you might want to visit with a woman who lives up the road a bit. She walks along the lake every morning at six o'clock. She might be able to tell you if the car was here at that time."

"Yeah, that would be great. Her name?"

"Eleanor Campbell."

"I know her. The woman with the birds, right?" I chuckled softly, recalling Eleanor Campbell's birds driving Dad crazy when we were working on the Trudy Solomon case last year. She was a character you didn't easily forget.

"Yeah, budgies, I believe," Mr. Worsky replied.

"Okay, great. If you can just give your address to that officer over there . . ." I said, pointing at Sally, ". . . then you're free to go."

"I don't mean to step out of line here, but . . . you sound awful." Mr. Worsky tugged at his whiskers. "You should really be in bed."

A BLUE Honda Accord pulled into the parking lot. The blaring rock music ended abruptly when the ignition cut out. Mark's lanky legs emerged first. When he fully stood, he maxed out at six foot six inches. His nickname was Pencil, and he seemed to have no qualms about that. He had a penchant for wearing khaki pants and tan shirts, and his hair was the color of graphite. He was such a good sport about his nickname that at last year's Halloween party he wore a tan T-shirt with "No. 2" emblazoned on the front. He opened the trunk of his car, pulled out a pair of overalls and suited up.

"Good morning, ladies! What brings you out on this fine, fine day?" Mark winked. He looked over at the black Lexus. "Ah. Has the scene been photographed yet?"

"No. Still waiting on Gloria," I said checking my watch. "Thought she would've been here by now. She lives just a little ways up the road." As if on cue, Gloria's Chevy pickup rumbled up the road. "The gang's all here."

"You sound like shit," Mark said. "Bad cold?"

"Yeah, I'm on the back end of it." He nodded and lifted an eyebrow in that way people do when they don't believe you. So I added, "No longer contagious."

We watched as Gloria pulled off the tarp and lifted her gear from the rear bed.

"Sorry for the delay, guys. I was over at Horizon Meadows." Gloria laid her camera bag on the ground and slipped into her protective wear. "My sister was in a bad state this morning. They're moving her to Level Six care." She knelt and removed two cameras. She hung one of the cameras around her neck and held the other. "There but for the grace of God go I."

We all nodded.

"I'll start with a few global photos," Gloria said, snapping photos to capture the entire scene from a distance.

Mark and I followed her as she headed toward the victim. As we neared the body, she asked, "Is this how you found everything?"

"Minor scene contamination. A passerby opened the driver-side door and the paramedics checked for life. But we haven't touched a thing," I replied. "Looks like someone stabbed her and walked, drove . . ." I looked up at the lake ". . . or swam away."

"You sound like shit," Gloria said.

"That seems to be the consensus today."

The humidity was setting in, further irritating my sinuses and making it harder to breathe. My hands were also a sweaty mess. On days like this it was hard to tell whether my palmar hyperhidrosis was the cause of my sweaty palms or the clammy air was simply making my hands wet. I used the front of my pants to sop up the moisture. Then I slipped on my bright blue latex gloves.

We stood bunched together at the open driver's-side door while Gloria laid her duffel bag on the pavement and unpacked her yellow number markers and photo scales.

"Do we have an ID on the woman?" Mark asked.

"Still working on that," Sally replied as she zipped up her Tyvek white jumper.

Mark crouched down next to the body. "What a fucking bloodbath."

"Paramedic said she was stabbed a few times." I peered over his shoulder to get a closer look. "Mid- to late twenties. Maybe early thirties?" I coughed into the crux of my elbow. "I suck at guessing ages."

"I'm getting a late-twenties vibe," Mark said.

"There doesn't appear to have been a struggle. Perhaps she knew her attacker. A date gone sideways?" I inferred.

"I don't see a purse," Sally said, cupping her hand like a visor over her eyes and gazing into the passenger-side window. "There's a duffel and a bathing suit on the backseat."

"Try the door," Mark said.

Sally opened the passenger door. "Not locked."

"How about the rear door?" I asked.

Sally opened the rear door. "Not locked."

Gloria moved around the rear of the car to take mid-range and close-up photographs of the objects on the backseat.

Sally's phone pinged. She glanced at it, then said, "Car is registered to a Dr. Samantha Fields, a doctor who lives in New York City. Should be easy enough to find someone who can provide a positive identification." She drummed her fingers on her cheek. "Unlocked doors. No handbag. No phone. I'm thinking robbery."

"Or someone trying to make our job harder by making us think it's a robbery," I suggested.

Mark leaned over the body to get a closer look at the stab wounds. "Three wounds . . . here, here, and here," he said, pointing to each incision. "What's this?" he muttered, mainly to himself. "Well, lookee here." Mark reached down into the well between her feet and pulled out an iPhone. He held the phone up to the woman's face and the device sprang to life. "Here you go," he said handing me the phone.

I hit the green-and-white phone icon on the lower left corner of the phone. "Holy shit. This is *not* Dr. Samantha Fields."

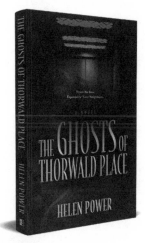
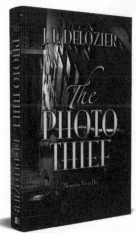